semi-charmed life

NORA ZELEVANSKY

semi-charmed life

ST. MARTIN'S GRIFFIN
NEW YORK

SEMI-CHARMED LIFE. Copyright © 2012 by Nora Zelevansky. All rights reserved. Printed in the United States of America. For information, address St. Martin's Press, 175 Fifth Avenue, New York, N.Y. 10010.

www.stmartins.com

ISBN 978-1-250-00118-4 (trade paperback)
ISBN 978-1-250-01272-2 (e-book)

First Edition: July 2012

10 9 8 7 6 5 4 3 2 1

For my own oddball parents.

I forgive you for the carob-covered rice cakes.

1

LITTLE DID NAÏVE BEATRICE BERNSTEIN KNOW—as she hacked and sniffled privately at her parents' rent-controlled Upper West Side apartment—that her bothersome cold was New York's "must-have" ailment of the season.

Everyone who was anyone caught the bronchial cough that just wouldn't heal and thoroughly enjoyed whining about it in cultivated Kathleen Turner voices at the chicest upscale dives. "Do I sound sexy?" was an oft-repeated phrase from Soho House to Pastis and, though the question was generally followed by a cough or sneeze, the answer was almost always affirmative. For just an instant, postnasal drip was the new black, and lymph nodes and swollen glands jutted out proudly like so many anorexic models' rib cages.

Meanwhile, Beatrice lamented her "bout of consumption" from a perch upon her childhood bedroom's antique radiator and interior window ledge. Five days into her illness, she was still sick and officially missing her first week of senior year in college. Her overprotective parents—who would never take no for an answer unless it was barked over lentil soup by Midtown's infamous Soup Nazi—embargoed her plans to make the thirty-five-block trek uptown to her waiting off-campus apartment. And they remained resolute even after she promised to mummify herself in itchy alpaca wool. At twenty-one years old, Beatrice still rarely

won a battle against her mother and father. In this instance, she
was too congested to try.

Instead, she choked back boredom like so much phlegm, opening the window wide and gazing twelve stories down with stir-
crazy longing. As a child, Beatrice spent many restless evenings
in this same spot, as shrill laughter echoed in fits and starts from
her parents' dinner parties. Tracing the radiator's geometric grate
with her fingers, she would pretend the cool winter breeze was
arctic and the honking car horns were fellow explorers' boats.

Now, in one hand she clutched a small Moleskine notebook,
in the other a salty licorice cough drop from a stash on a midcen-
tury moderne Lucite bedside table her parents had picked out. To
their chagrin, over the years she had covered the stark collectible with stickers, from childish Smurf puffies to Andre the Giant "Obey." The walls around her—once littered with pictures
of her high school friends in Sheep Meadow, Justin Timberlake
and Strokes posters, Degas prints and her own Magic Marker
drawings—were pockmarked from thumbtacks past.

Beatrice popped the lozenge in her mouth and shuddered, la-
menting her parents' love of all things unusual. Gary and Madeline Bernstein were forever infatuated with esoteric food, music,
and design from revolving cultures based on whatever contemporary art show Madeline was curating at "the Museum."

During a Brazilian projects exhibition, Havaiana flip-flops and
feijoada brunches were all the rage in their household. The apartment smelled of smoky sausage and black beans. But then—with
the introduction of an Asian group show—Korean spicy tofu
stew stole the focus. Kimchi, mixed with pungent Chinese oolong
tea, was the prevailing scent, and Japanese neo-punk blared from
the stereo.

Currently, Beatrice's mother was in discussions with a young
photographer from Holland. His new series featuring aging

red-light-district prostitutes in homey settings with their ador-able pets—"a strong juxtaposition," everyone said—had created quite a stir in Amsterdam. Thus, Beatrice was stuck with her father's new favorite salty licorice cough drops from the Nether-lands, as if black licorice wasn't bitter enough. Beatrice gagged as the putrid flavor spread across the back of her tongue.

She leaned against the window frame, whimpering martyred last words in the vein of Beth March from *Little Women*. "Be brave, dear family. I'm not afraid to die." Wait—did she say that out loud?

"I hardly think you're going to die," mocked her father, march-ing into the bedroom in his uniform Levi's and black T-shirt and setting her lunch down on a folding bedside table. "Unless you fall out the window. For the umpteenth time, *please* do not stick your head out that way. It's bad enough when the cat does it."

Beatrice rolled her eyes so wide that a witness—had there been one—might have sworn he heard a comical *boing!* as her irises popped back into place.

"A healthy dose of Daddy's Soup Surprise should do you wonders."

Gary could not cook. The one food in his arsenal was a "con-sommé" concocted from Campbell's Chicken Noodle Soup and hot sauce. His ownership over said recipe seemed tenuous at best, but he had always believed that, as life was art and art was life, what pervaded the zeitgeist was pretty much fair game. When-ever Beatrice poked fun, suggesting that heating something on a burner and adding Tabasco Sauce hardly seemed worthy of copyright, her father replied, "Tell it to Andy Warhol."

At present, she wasn't telling anything to anyone. Treating Beatrice like a child was part of a deep-rooted family dynamic that no one dared upset, least of all her. And staying put was the norm: Though the Bernsteins analyzed groundbreaking cultural phenomena from around the globe, they were the worst kind of provincial New Yorkers, believing that venturing outside the immediate vicinity was a waste of time.

Thus, Beatrice's parents' world—though immaculate and well designed (never a comfortable couch did abound)—was insular, revolving mostly around the not-so-mean streets of the Upper West Side and around friends and family who understood and cared about contemporary art. And that is a *very* small demographic.

As preschoolers at gallery openings, Beatrice and her older sister, Gertie, navigated a sea of black-clad legs, above which hovered asymmetrical earrings and angular haircuts. Pictures of frequent Bernstein home dinner guests in compromising naked positions with words like "Walk" or "String" painted across their foreheads lined the walls beside monochromatic paintings (all black, all blue, all white). Beatrice learned at an early age that staying within the confines of said world was tricky. There were many rules to being unorthodox, one of which involved almost never setting foot outside New York City.

"Why should we, when we have everything we could want around the corner?" Her parents would shrug.

Beatrice's mother, Madeline, first made a name for herself as an expert in American abstract expressionism from Jackson Pollock splatter paintings to Mark Rothko's color block works, so she rarely needed to travel. By the time she developed an interest in more contemporary artists from other countries, she was so established within the field that—most of the time—she could send enthusiastic underlings in her place, while she perused catalog images and JPEGs from behind her gigantic desk. The internationally renowned curator's resistance to leaving New York was written off by the art world as a fascinating philosophical idiosyncrasy shared by her quirky artist husband. Besides, the Big Apple *is* the center of the universe, art fans insisted.

But Beatrice couldn't leave well enough alone. "Aren't you

curious? Don't you imagine luxuriating in art nouveau chairs at Parisian cafés, while sipping hot café au lait, or buying organic carrots at outdoor markets in Aix-en-Provence?" she would suggest to her father. Her mother had tired of the debate long ago.

"Have you tasted the espresso from Fairway, around the corner?" replied Gary. "How could the cafés in France offer anything better?" Thus began an inevitable tirade about French anti-Semitism.

"But wouldn't you like to be temporarily blinded by Tokyo's fluorescent lights, while sorting through T-shirts with nonsensical English slogans like 'Eat Your Toe'? Imagine waking up in autumn in Kyoto inside a traditional ryokan hotel, back stiff from sleeping on a tatami!"

"Have you wandered Central Park in fall? Tasted the cucumber martini at Nobu? Let Hasaki's beef negimaki melt in your mouth, knowing you'd drink the sauce if no one was looking? Perused T-shirts and comic book stores on St. Mark's? Why leave?"

"What about cultures you've already learned to love from afar? Don't you want to sip fresh watermelon caipirinhas under the watchful eye of Sugarloaf in Brazil? Wonder at your own ability to loll on the beaches of Ipanema while *City of God* gang wars between eight-year-old children are playing out in the favelas above?"

"I hate the beach." Her father would smile.

Beatrice's sister Gertie (named for Gertrude Stein, of course) had wholeheartedly adopted her parents' philosophy. She rarely emerged from her small apartment down the hall, where she'd been examining the minute details of Marcel Proust's life's work for the past few eons thanks to the world's largest literary grant. Her readings, also held in-house, had become a sort of elite salon for posturing academics, who would later brag to friends and professional nemeses alike around the proverbial watercooler—which in this case was generally an instant hazelnut coffee machine—about the rare intimate experience with the doyenne of Proust studies.

Gertie also edited a lauded poetry journal called *In the Dark Room,* which she started at age eight in third grade, after famously penning a poem during the verbal section of a standardized test:

> *In the dark room,*
> *Where humans don't sleep*
> *Doll children are searching for something to eat*
> *Clown on a box,*
> *Tin soldier around,*
> *And doll child, of course, upon the bare ground.*
> *They search for an apple*
> *Or even a pea.*
> *They search for something that humans can't see.*
> *In the dark room.*

Gertie was the youngest person ever to win Canada's prestigious Winchester prize for poetry. "Apparently, the Canucks don't know a hoser when they see one," she'd joke modestly.

Her famed beauty didn't hurt. Long oil slick–colored hair (or so *The New Yorker* described it) and jet-black eyes were only further complimented by her signature fire-engine-red lips. Some claimed she tattooed the shade on. Others whispered that she had naturally dyed them, after years of subsisting on Twizzlers and cranberry juice—a sort of hunger strike for lip color. But Beatrice remembered the day when her sister first appeared at the dinner table with the color smeared across her wide lips: Gertie was fifteen years old.

"A new look?" the girls' father inquired.

"Very Algonquin," their mother chimed in. "And that's a fact."

"This is just what I look like now," said Gertie.

And she never went back on a proclamation. Eventually, Revlon created a gloss based on her famous mouth called Dark Room Red. Once, Beatrice snuck into her older sister's bedroom to try the stuff on. But the shade was all wrong: she looked like a thin-lipped transvestite.

At the Proust events, tickets were so scarce that sometimes even Beatrice couldn't gain access. Gertie's bouncer/administrative assistant—an enormous bald and tattooed artist named Oscar with a penchant for esoteric prose and collage—stood outside her mauve-colored door and selected guests. Failure to produce a ticket was of course grounds for refusal, but Oscar was also known to reject people—with just a shake of the head, as he rarely spoke—based on attire alone. Too many tweed coats with elbow patches made the place smell of mothballs and pipe tobacco for weeks, Gertie complained. Beatrice once pointed out that hardly any professors actually smoked pipes anymore.

"It's in their blood." Gertie shook her head sadly. "It's in the paint of their office walls, embedded in the plastic of their rollerball pens. It's even in the instant coffee machine, each time they press that Hazelnut button."

Oscar was not Beatrice's fan, as he once caught her with a stack of Sue Grafton alphabet mysteries at a bookstore café up the street and deemed her undiscriminating, lowbrow at best. She looked up from *J Is for Judgment* and found him glowering at her. For a while after that, she could hardly make it in to her sister's apartment, even during nonevents.

"But I just want to borrow a scarf!" she'd cry. "I need to ask relationship advice! I need to use her blow-dryer; mine is on the fritz!"

He'd just shake his head dismissively.

"*G is for Give Me a Goddamn Break,*" she finally snapped.

Gertie—who adored her little sister as only an older sister can—had a chat with Oscar and the conflict was resolved. But she had a talk with Beatrice too: "Sorry, Bea Bea Gun, but you might challenge yourself more. If you want a mystery, why not explore something worthwhile, like why Salinger stopped writing, or why cell phone charger packaging is so hard to open?"

When Beatrice complained to her sister about their parents' incessant worrying, Gertie would only quote Proust, "Everything great in the world comes from neurotics. They alone have founded our religions and composed our masterpieces. Never will the world know all it owes to them, nor all they have suffered to enrich us." Beatrice considered banging her head against the wall.

But then she often disappointed her family ("intentionally defied," they might say), as she was involved in a deep, sordid love affair with the pop mainstream: trashy reality TV shows or non-PBS TV at all, for that matter, pop music, Lucky Charms cereal, suburban high schools populated with vicious cheerleaders and beefy blond football players named Chad. And, as with any real love affair, guilt only fueled her desire.

"Where did you come from?" her mother sometimes wondered aloud with an appreciative smile, but also a furrowed brow.

Beatrice's preoccupation was natural, actually: She was in love with what she was not, just like all the Greenwich, Connecticut, Republican girls dating liberal Jews from Brooklyn or the thousands of corn-fed Middle American college boys devouring rogan gosh with their bohemian Indian girlfriends. Afterward, she mused, one either settles happily into that altered world or has his or her heart stomped to bits in the most unrecoverable way and returns home to the sheltered nest (or to white bread, mayonnaise, and bologna sandwiches, as the case may be for the corn-fed boys).

Beatrice studied obscure literature, as expected, and strove to be a journalist, which she viewed as a sort of compromise between the two worlds. She could act as voyeur, observing the "junk food of life" from a loving distance, while remaining on the right side of the law; if, that is, she could *ever* conceive of anything worthwhile to write. For now, her Moleskine notebook remained blank.

Meanwhile, she dreamed wildly of Hostess CupCakes and Sandra Bullock movies as she sat around the Bernstein family dinner table ignoring preach-to-the-choir debates about neo-postmodernism in a postmodern age or the revival of modernism in an antimodernist millennium or even Fairway belly lox versus Zabar's nova. When they weren't looking, she downloaded cute kitten videos from YouTube, flipped through tabloids and luxury travel magazines, and watched marathons of *The Biggest Loser* and *Jersey Shore*. One day, perhaps, she would immerse herself completely in the cotton candy–scented bubble bath of movie popcorn existence, learning to do keg stands at Daytona Beach spring break and becoming a contestant on *The Real World*. Then she'd luxuriate in the warm embrace of the contentedly clueless.

Her parents had insisted she stay close to the nest for school, of course. "Why would you go anywhere else?"

Still, Beatrice had thought college might open doors to adventures beyond books and intellectual discourse. Maybe she would meet boys, apart from the same indie types who marveled at her wit—or maybe it was just her famously artistic family—and tried to stimulate her with talk of literature and art, mostly their own. Though these guys believed that worshipping at the altar of "museum" or that their own prose was superior to, say, Kappa Delta Phi fraternity's, sloppy make-out sessions and fumbled groping on dorm cots showed there to be no real difference once you got down to brass tacks, at least as far as Beatrice could tell.

It was too late: The Bernstein playbook was ingrained. Nothing had changed, despite keg parties and long nights spent on ripped red leather bar banquettes, some drunken hookups, a single one-night stand (with an economics major!), and a short-lived boyfriend or two. Beatrice's pretty green eyes, quirky freckles, the emergence of a statuesque build, and even the introduction of low-cut shirts, short dresses, and dark eyeliner failed to ratchet up the excitement. Life remained the same. New York was still New York and she was still Beatrice. And now, as a senior, she accepted her fate: She would graduate and find a job, at best writing about exhibitions she never actually saw unless they traveled to New York. She would likely never eat roast suckling pig on a French Polynesian beach, drizzle honey on hot fried sopaipillas in Santa Fe's plaza, or even devour a grotesquely large order of Tex-Mex nachos at a Dallas fast-food chain.

As for her writing, that trusty Moleskine notebook—though always nearby—remained empty, save her own scrawled name. And even that was written at an unsatisfactory slant. As her father wandered out of the room in search of his favorite new Dutch electronica CD (a surefire lullaby for his ailing younger daughter), Beatrice leaned out the window and into September's fresh warm air. It wasn't even cold season yet, which is why catching those early flu germs was considered so fashion forward.

Despite her stuffed nose, Beatrice rightly imagined that the breeze smelled of onion bagels and fireplaces. Just up West End Avenue, she watched the first precocious loose leaves gliding past brownstones and proud prewar buildings. All were momentarily bare of scaffolding. Prep school boys from Saint Mary's in navy blue blazers, gray ties, jeans, and enormous backpacks, roughhoused across the street. A lone scrawny student shuffled past the adjoining church's gates, dragging a rolling school bag behind him. At that age, easy prey is unmistakable. An older boy approached, grabbed the cap off the kid's head, and knocked him down. Beatrice cringed.

Out of nowhere, a large pigeon—with a strange yellow faux-hawk and glossy oil-spill feathers—landed on the windowsill just inches from Beatrice's hand. It peered at her sideways, as if posing a question: *What is your purpose?*

Like most New Yorkers who didn't regularly feed birds stale bread in the park, Beatrice considered pigeons plague-carrying winged rodents, but she felt sympathetic toward this little guy. Like her, he was disenfranchised, trapped by circumstances of birth. She placed her Moleskine notebook slowly on the outer ledge, climbed inside to a standing position, and then leaned her body entirely out the window to face the pigeon, inching a bit farther into the open air.

"Oh, Mr. Pigeon. You have no idea how good you have it," she explained. He bent his neck the opposite way and stared at her, awaiting her wisdom (or so she felt). "People may not like you much, but at least you can fly around and see the world from above. I wish I had that kind of freedom."

I'm confiding my innermost thoughts to a pigeon, Beatrice thought. *I doubt if this is what my mother meant when she said I might "benefit from talking to an objective third party."*

Still, Beatrice continued: "I wish that I could go wherever I chose without the pressure of an unforeseen future. I wish I could observe things—while unobserved myself—that inspired me to write. I wish my life were more raucous and wild. I wish—"

But just as she began to wax poetic about the migrations to Florida she'd take and the "birds of a feather" she'd meet if she were lucky enough to be born vermin of the beaked world, a tiny tickle began wiggling at the very top of her sinuses. It tangoed its way down her nasal passage, growing with speed and momentum, until it erupted in an enormous *ta-da!* sneeze.

The pigeon froze, offended perhaps by this show of incivility. Then, squawking, it took off into the air, almost hitting Beatrice in the face with rapidly beating wings. She was so surprised that she lost her balance and fell forward, feet no longer grounded on the floor of her bedroom. The interior ledge hit her square in the stomach, as she braced herself with one arm and the other dangled perilously into open air. She landed with the right side of her face squished against the filthy ledge, facing her Moleskine notebook.

And just when she began to catch her breath and recover from the terror of almost falling to her death (and, worse, proving her father right), something white and gloppy dropped from the sky and landed splat on the black leather-bound notebook just inches from her face.

She peered slowly upward in disbelief, only to spot the pigeon looking down from the window ledge above. The ingrate! It almost seemed to cackle as it took off and flew away into the wild blue yonder. Faced with the big mess of bird crap on her notebook, Beatrice didn't know whether to barf or cry.

She reached for the hardwood floor with her feet and pulled herself back inside to catch her breath. She ran her fingers across her now dirty face and through her shoulder-length brown hair, only to discover a knotty rats' nest behind her head. "I should be quarantined."

The comment fell on deaf ears, though, as the only audience was her huge cat Waldo, who sat watching at her feet. "Where were you when the pigeon tried to kill me, huh?" she asked. He narrowed his eyes and considered attacking her in the absence of a Friskies chicken liver treat.

She hobbled into her bathroom, washed her hands and cheek with some weird Nicaraguan lava soap her father had ordered, and then flopped down onto her bed. Gary walked back in holding a Chinese soup spoon. "What's wrong? You look all flushed."

He put the back of his hand to her forehead to test for fever. She wasn't about to confess that she'd almost fallen out the window. "A bird shit on my Moleskine notebook."

"Is that a joke? How many pigeons does it take to shit on a Moleskine notebook?"

She felt like a moron. "I left it on the outer ledge."

"You know, they say it's good luck when a bird craps on you." Gary smiled as he crossed to the window. "But maybe only because it wasn't a bigger bird." He picked up the notebook. "Where's the bird shit, Monkey? There's not a spot of anything on it." He opened it up. "Or in it. Plan on ever writing in this thing? You carry it everywhere."

"Very funny," she said. "There's nothing on it? I just saw it with my own eyes." She studied the notebook in his hands. "It couldn't just magically disappear."

"You must have imagined it. Maybe I gave you too much cold medicine. Why don't you climb back under the covers?" He bonked her playfully on the head with the notebook and then handed it to her.

Beatrice examined the leather-bound thing and found it inexplicably clean. But when she glanced over her shoulder back toward the window, that damn pigeon sat watching from the outside ledge. He ruffled his odd yellow hairdo and flew away, leaving Beatrice—and her now alert cat Waldo—spellbound in his wake.

2

A FEW DAYS AND MANY TYLENOL PMS LATER, Beatrice headed in a packed taxicab—that smelled of lemon-fresh deodorizer and sleep—to her senior year in unfashionable good health. Most of her boxes had been sent ahead and would be waiting inside her much anticipated apartment in the Dorchester. Though university owned, the off-campus building was designated for seniors and graduate students only and was mercilessly free of dorm staples like whiteboards, flyers for ice cream socials, and self-righteous announcements from resident advisers: "Hello! Smearing peanut butter all over the 2nd floor common area is not funny, people! Whoever did that is disrespecting this whole community!" Beatrice was looking forward to living like an adult. Plus, her best friend Dolly had a place in the building too and was waiting there with Beatrice's keys. Aflutter to see her dear pal again, Dolly tracked Beatrice's progress uptown via text.

"Have u passed the space formerly known as h&h bagels? u above popovers? u spotted carmine's yet?"

The girls liked to eat. Food was one way to experience the world without traveling far and, for Beatrice, that was most often from the perspective of a hot dog cart. Luckily, her appetite had yet to catch up with her metabolism.

Despite the cab's stench, Beatrice enjoyed the ride. At least she was outside. The day was crisp, blue skied, and sunny, and she watched as preadolescent schoolkids overheated in warm, but sublimely new fall clothing. Each pretended that the oddball walking a few feet behind was not an embarrassing parent. As the cab zoomed up Broadway, the streets Beatrice knew best blew by in a blur. But, like pointillist landscapes viewed throughout her childhood, with some distance the whites, greens, reds, yellows, and blues came into focus: high school–age homeboys in old-school Air Jordans and Yankees caps hanging on paperbag–strewn stoops, leashed dogs lifting legs against graffiticovered streetlights, young boys pretending to avert their eyes while walking past candy- and porno-magazine–stocked newsstands, a middle-aged bottle blonde—on her way to the dry cleaner—stepping in a spot of sticky pink gum and cursing audibly. Beatrice wondered absently if people considered stepping in gum good luck like a pigeon crapping on your notebook.

"The far corner, please."

And, finally, with no help from the taxi driver, who claimed lower-back issues so severe that even his intuitive acupuncturist couldn't cure them, but who seemed capable of swiveling 180 degrees when a scantily clad girl sauntered by, Beatrice was surrounded by bags outside her gray stone apartment building. Before she could buzz the superintendent to gain entrance, three tall guys—wearing T-shirts and basketball shorts despite a sharp chill in the air—came barreling out. Two ran ahead, while one stopped, held the glass door for Beatrice, and, after yelling "Where's the fire?" to his friends, winked and ran on his merry way. Smiling, she readjusted her black cashmere scarf that smelled of faded Issey Miyaki perfume and winters past, propped the door with a rubber stop, and dragged her luggage into the lobby.

The Dorchester sounded grand. In reality, the dilapidated interiors begged for a paint job and old rusty fixtures were in danger of falling to the unswept cracked "marble" floor. But, like many of her predecessors, Beatrice thought the mess looked like freedom. And that was a beautiful thing. She texted her arrival to Dolly and received an instantaneous response: "Meet me in apartment 333 on the 3rd floor! Just wait til u see!"

Beatrice left her bags off to one side of the lobby with a silent prayer that they wouldn't be stolen and took the rickety elevator upstairs, wondering with each spastic jolt between floors if she was about to get stuck. She arrived safely, exited, and wandered down the hallway—atop carpet the color of butternut squash and dog excrement—toward apartment 333.

Incense wafted through cracks in various doors, behind which, after three years at this school, Beatrice could easily imagine the residents. At least those familiar types were now older incarnations of themselves: Freshman year's fearful plain-faced girls with tightly wound ponytails, who nested amid floral Laura Ashley sheets and played games like bridge sixty years too early, would now have trimmed their hair into neat bobs and begun internships in laboratories, libraries, and research centers.

"Bohemians," who once hid bongs under flaxseed-filled mattresses, shining black lights on Guatemalan tapestries and sympathizing—just loudly enough so everyone could hear—with Sudanese refugees, were knee-deep in law school application essays on civil rights (though most would eventually go corporate). Pretty suburbanites with tattoos of butterflies on their hips and Chinese symbols for "hope" and "truth" on their backs were already dreaming of leaving wild college days behind. After some requisite years in PR, they'd return as Pilates-bodied housewives to Westchester, New Jersey, or Long Island. Indie kids in Ramones T-shirts and black Converse uniforms, who bellied up to iPod docking stations, belting out Bob Dylan (whom they'd always hated before but in whom they could now see value, even if their parents *did* like him too), graduated to Joy Division, lesser-known indie art bands, and mustaches. Surely in their IKEA-adorned apartments, they were busy drafting business plans for sustainable design and branding companies. Perhaps their Brooklyn offices would have gentleman herb gardens out back. Even as Beatrice rolled her eyes in anticipation, she felt excited for this next phase of life.

The ordinary door to apartment 333—which she assumed belonged to Dolly—stood just slightly ajar, an oversight Beatrice planned to warn her trusting friend against; this was New York City, not Westport, Connecticut! She worried momentarily about her bags stashed downstairs. But before she could even knock, the door swung wide open to reveal a space transformed. In place of the claustrophobic uniform two hundred square feet with kitchenette (read: hot plate) that residents were allotted, she witnessed a display so magnificent that it seemed to inhabit several planes of existence at once, evoking a TriBeCa loft, a Parisian penthouse, a Bridgehampton estate, a Malibu mansion, Oprah's Santa Barbara compound, a London town house, an Upper West Side brownstone, an indoor ski slope in Dubai, a Tuscan villa, an Australian ecolodge, a thatched beach bungalow just a hop from Bangkok, a Sun Valley ranch, a Caribbean-based yacht called *The Golden Ticket,* a Tokyo presidential suite, and a flower-filled hacienda in the Ecuadoran highlands.

Stark white walls supported three-story ceilings, while gold-embroidered magenta, turquoise, and kelly green silk—bright enough to suit any Bollywood star—seemed to levitate in midair. Machines spewing black cotton candy circulated amid carts of decadent but exotic confections with acquired tastes like champagne and yuzu marshmallows, sesame jujubes, and fleur de sel caramel cream puffs. A man who alarmingly resembled the late Jerry Garcia spun records in the corner, while all manner of beautiful young hipsters mingled, debating the merits of New York versus LA, all the while orbiting their brilliant sun: the elusive Veruca Pfeffernoose.

Beatrice recognized the famous-for-nothing socialite from tabloid rags. But in person, Veruca made a resounding impression without seeming to make any impression at all: Her easily tousled fire-engine-red hair—of course wash and go—was at once punk and classic, shagging above a perfect ski-jump nose, mildly freckled, eternally sun-kissed cheeks, naturally coral-colored dewy lips, and one blue-gray and one almost yellow tiger eye. She was edgy like a young Courtney Love, but refined. Her body was beautifully fragile beneath layers upon layers of the world's most fabulously expensive clothing (carefully calculated to appear as if snagged from a deeply blessed $5 vintage bin).

Periodically, she cast a beneficent smile upon her sycophantic subjects, many of whom giggled uncontrollably thanks to nitrous oxide whippets from whipped cream cans. Her expression was all vulnerability, but she exhibited a frighteningly powerful pull that just dared people not to stare. She was ravishing and self-possessed. Of course, from the dish Beatrice had read about her habits, she was just as likely hopped up on horse tranquilizers.

Dolly's flushed face appeared inches from Beatrice's own, shocking her out of a hypnotized stare. How long had Beatrice been standing there, mouth gaping like a dead frog? "Can you believe it?" Dolly asked, pushing her overgrown bangs behind her ear and then excitedly twisting a strand of curly brown hair, a nervous habit that—if it persisted without constant brushing—Beatrice imagined might one day give her dreadlocks. "Veruca Pfeffernoose." Dolly yanked Beatrice inside by her wrist.

"Is this your apartment? How?" Beatrice asked. She had almost forgotten what led her to this remarkable display, but she suddenly remembered her keys, shot her best friend a warm smile, and embraced her. Dolly was skinny, strong, relatively tall for a dancer—about five seven—and looked a bit like a lollipop thanks to her crazy mop of curls. With her ceaseless energy, unconscious hair twirling, and general lightness, Dolly, Beatrice often thought, would have made a fabulous Muppet.

Dolly peered quizzically at her. "It's such a shame that you're better. I was sort of hoping I could catch that husky voice from you. It's all the rage."

"Did you just say 'all the rage'? What's going on here, Doll? You're sort of freaking me out."

Dolly laughed and led her friend—well, practically waltzed her friend, as dancing was her habit—over to a remote corner of the room, where a pretty ceramic tank filled with spring water, freshly cut cucumbers, mint sprigs, and oranges sat alongside rolled white washcloths in a tub of ice. "I'll explain everything. But first, would you like some spa water? A lavender-infused towelette, perhaps?"

"Dolly!"

"Okay, okay. Jeez. No, this is obviously not my apartment. Veruca Pfeffernoose just transferred here. This is *her* place."

"Transferred here from where? The Playboy Mansion? This is insanity." Beatrice motioned toward a recognizable young design duo, who were silk-screening rainbow tie-dye T-shirts in one corner. In the next, a former *Top Chef* contestant (who would have won had it not been for that panna cotta that never set up) experimented with molecular gastronomy. He was creating edible foams, gelées, and steaming potions out of bacon, sage, and hot pink dragon fruit, all the while muttering something about "Judges' Table."

Dolly shook her head and whispered, "No one is quite sure where she transferred from: The guy in the corner dressed like Al Capone says she transferred from the University of Chicago,

the brunette in the ripped stone-washed skinny jeans swears she
went to the Sorbonne and left because of a torrid affair with a
professor (a very famous writer), and that blonde over there with
the sunglasses claims she's actually in the CIA."

"Isn't that Kirsten Dunst?" Beatrice asked, squinting to see
across the room. The blonde shot her a dirty look and she quickly
averted her gaze. Beatrice was duly amazed by the scene, but this
was not how she'd envisioned moving into her first apartment.
She was looking for a little normalcy. She had planned to hang
shower caddies, hook up her iPod docking station, and drink a
glass of wine or six, while Dolly told her all about her summer
ballet fellowship in LA. Though Beatrice had almost as little
cooking experience as her father, she was looking forward to
stocking her kitchen with all the preservative-filled junk foods
she pleased. She would throw elaborate dinner parties, she imagined, at which she would serve takeout Chinese and Twinkies.

Dolly tucked her hair nervously behind that trusty ear and
teased, "I was worried you'd react this way. Don't be such a *Bernstein*." (That meant "judgmental.") "Veruca invited some choice
residents to hang out. She just loves creative people, you know?"

"She found out that you're a dancer?" Anyone who saw merit
in Dolly had to be worthwhile.

"Well, not exactly. I sneezed at the right moment," the Muppet admitted. "But she did bless me, which was very polite."

Beatrice shook her head and looked to the ceiling for guidance. "Now she's the pope."

Dolly giggled. "Look, I'm not saying that these people have
depth, but she seems like a nice person and she deserves open-
mindedness as much as you do, right? Plus, you've been complaining about being bored with keg parties and, look, not a keg
in sight!"

As if on cue, a waiter arrived with a tray of drinks. "Lychee and basil martini with antioxidant-rich pomegranate, açaí, and amla?"

The friends exchanged a look and burst into laughter. "I *could* use a drink." Beatrice sighed, accepting the champagne-colored concoction and a cocktail napkin. She experienced a first wave of relief. She was officially out of her parents' house. Before she could take a taste, the waiter dropped what looked like Pop Rocks into the glass, which began to bubble and foam. She took a sip. "Yum. This is delicious. It tastes like, I don't know—everything good: tropical beaches, hammocks, apple orchards, and . . . is that lemongrass?"

Dolly sipped her own and smiled. "Tastes like a great senior year. To us!" She clinked glasses with Beatrice, who shut her eyes for a hopefully imperceptible instant, while she wished—like a child blowing out birthday candles—for Dolly's pronouncement to be true. She needed something better than great; she needed the year to blow her mind.

Beatrice sat down on a large daybed to their left, dropping her purse to her side. "This is kind of cool, I guess. Sorry, Doll. I was just practically strangling at my parents' house. Ugh, and you should have smelled the inside of my cab over here. I'm pretty sure the driver was holding 105-degree Bikram yoga classes inside the taxi." She mimed covering her nose and lips with her scarf, so she looked like a bandit, and then lay back. "Is this thing a massage chair? I feel like it's vibrating. Or is that my body?"

"You must be exhausted. Wait here a sec and I'll go get your keys out of my purse." Dolly slipped out the front door and into the regular world, which smelled of curry, wet dog, and industrial-strength lemon Pledge.

Thank the Lord for Dolly. When the two girls met freshman year on the never-ending line for registration, they felt instantly kindred, probably because Dolly was too cheerful, Beatrice was too cynical, and they unconsciously recognized a need for some balance. Also, it was nice not to feel conspicuously alone. After Beatrice helped strong-arm an administrator into creating an extra spot for Dolly in a "filled" African dance class, the Muppet offered to share her pot stash, sent as a care package from her Vassar boyfriend. Many hours, packed bowls, and Liz Phair songs later, they found themselves in front of the dorm lounge's snack machine with a serious case of the munchies.

But disaster struck: Their Famous Amos cookies got stuck in the machine's metal grip and they were out of change, as cash, in general, is something college students are constantly without. As their stoned state trumped common sense, they left an absurd message on Post-it notes, asking that the next person who punched the code for Famous Amos cookies please return the extra package that would inevitably drop into the machine's plastic cubby. They included Dolly's room number. The girls parted ways, hungry but happy.

The next day, when Beatrice returned from class, she found a paper towel filled with cookies outside her room. A note read: "The vending machine man came to refill it today and actually returned the cookies! Here's your share. XO Dolly." Beatrice laughed until she cried, ate the cookies, and then used the paper towel to wipe away the tears. The friendship was cemented for life, through battles with teachers and parents, crushes and breakups (with Vassar boyfriends, for example), good hair days and bad.

Now Beatrice was left alone to ogle Veruca's main room, which was more like a carnival tent at an Oscar party than any living space she'd ever seen, even considering the museum-sized apartments she'd visited growing up in New York. Her family was known in their small circle and were what her father called "comfortable enough," but she had often marveled at her classmates' enormous homes, where important Lichtenstein, Picasso, and Warhol pieces hung above matching couches, as directed by interior designers.

Here, she felt contentedly invisible amid the frenzied activity. She couldn't eat another spoonful of Daddy's Soup Surprise if someone paid her. Though she could have used the extra cash. Beatrice set down her drink and crumpled up her cocktail napkin, only to realize that it was made from the most beautiful delicate fabric instead of disposable paper. She examined it and exclaimed aloud, "Is this Chantilly lace?"

"French Chantilly, actually," came a voice from above, sweet and soothing like chimes but with a dry edge of European sophistication, a slight Southern twang, and the smallest hint of a California valley girl lilt. And, of course, a bit of throatiness thanks to an au courant cold. Veruca Pfeffernoose herself hovered above Beatrice, peering down with what seemed to be genuine curiosity and . . . was that sympathy?

"Isn't it beautiful?" she continued. "I spotted it on an Orient Express train trip through Eastern Europe. The style is French, but the lace is actually handmade by a group of formerly oppressed women in a tiny Russian village. They've started a collective since I discovered them that's paid for heat, fur hats, and pierogis for their children. Now all the women in the village are self-sufficient and warm."

Beatrice was spellbound and a bit embarrassed. Maybe she had underestimated this strange creature. Fur hats sounded nice. She grabbed her purse and quickly stood at attention. "And here I was crumpling up all their beautiful handiwork."

"No, no. That's why I use them as cocktail napkins!" said the socialite. "See, the more I order, the more money they make to self-sustain. I'm Veruca, by the way."

"Oh, I'm Beatrice. Sorry to invade your place, which is amazing, by the way. I mean, literally *amazing*. I heard they had some bigger lofts in the building, but this is . . . Anyway, my friend Dolly was here and she has the keys to my apartment and the cab driver's acupuncture didn't work and she sneezed and so, here I am. And that probably didn't make a lot of sense, but thank you for the lychee martini." Where the hell was Dolly?

If possible, Veruca's smile grew warmer. If she didn't know better, Beatrice would have said it had its own halo. "The more the merrier!"

"Assuming the merrier are desirable, that is," chimed a woman to her left. Only then did Beatrice notice the three hangers-on who had traveled across the room with the hostess.

"Oh, Kendra's just kidding. Right, Kenny G.?" Veruca chided. Kendra did not look like she was kidding or as if she liked her nickname. Her piercing eyes surveyed Beatrice, who half expected them to light up neon yellow and shoot lasers. She was worked out to within an inch of her life, with toned arms and legs to rival Sarah Jessica Parker's, and the rest of her—clenched fist, stiff back, Zac Posen purse adorned with bullets—looked tightly wound too. Her style was a bit more tailored than the rest; she probably would have called it "classic." In a navy blue jumpsuit thickly belted at the waist and Louboutin heels, wielding her BlackBerry like a light saber, she had "type A" written all over her. She stood beside Veruca, part bodyguard, part publicist, part best friend (or stalker, depending on whom you asked).

Veruca introduced the other two members of her constellation: Dreyfus wore nerd glasses and a carefully calculated sweater vest, bow tie, and saddle shoes. He was small and slight, almost delicate, with chocolate brown hair and a cultivated smirk befitting any self-respecting bitchy gay man. He came off prickly. If he loved you like he loved Veruca, then he'd probably be your security blanket wherever you traveled, Beatrice surmised. If he hated you, beware. "Charmed," he managed.

The third sycophant was a stunning girl of ambiguous ethnicity named Imelda with speckled violet eyes, dark skin, full
lips, enviable cheekbones, and the shiniest black curly hair. She
was so tall that her face seemed almost blurry as Beatrice peered
upward, crooking her neck as if in a planetarium. Imelda was as
skinny as one could possibly be without floating away, perhaps to
an emergency room for IV nourishment. In any old oversized
tank top and ripped jeans, she looked just off a runway. She nodded tersely, as if she could barely be bothered.

"Imelda is a woman of few words," quipped Dreyfus. "Right,
sweetie?" He shot a toothy smile at Imelda, who glanced away
and examined her nails, bored. Suddenly, Beatrice had the impression that she was being shaken down instead of welcomed.
Cornered, she scanned desperately for any sign of Dolly.

"I may be wrong, but are you by any chance related to Gertie
Bernstein? Aren't you her sister?" Veruca asked. And just like that
the purpose behind this special visit became clear. People often
crossed rooms to get the inside scoop on Beatrice's sister.

"She doesn't look like Gertie," said Kendra. "Where are your
red lips?"

"I am, actually." Beatrice ignored the jab and directed her
next question to Veruca alone: "Do you know my sister?"

"I've met her, yes, and she is just lovely and fascinating. I've always wanted to attend one of her readings. I've heard they're extraordinary, just beyond, but I've never been in town at the right
time. I'm studying literature here, you know."

"I didn't know," said Beatrice. "So am I. Well, literature and
journalism. Oh, there, I see Dolly." And, yes, thank goodness,
her friend had finally emerged from behind the door to Normal
Land. The Muppet froze at the sight of her best friend surrounded
by Veruca and her cohorts.

"Well, it was nice to meet you." The socialite smiled. "I'm

sure you're dying to get to your place, change, and settle in." She took in Beatrice's baggy jeans, T-shirt, cardigan, and favorite camel-colored leather bag, worn in, out, and all around. Veruca gasped, "Oh, this bag is perfect. Just perfect! Who did you have wear it in for you? I need to hire them!"

"Pardon?"

"Veruca doesn't wear in her own leather bags, jeans, or Converse," Dreyfus explained with impatience. "She hires experts to wear her clothing until the pieces are perfectly distressed."

"People need work right now," Veruca chimed. Then she lowered her voice and leaned in: "There's a recession."

"I did it myself. I've just had it for like five years," Beatrice choked. She really needed to get out of there. Her cashmere scarf felt itchy and tight—like a noose.

"Five years." Veruca pondered the concept. "The same bag for five years. Fascinating."

Dolly was motioning with spastic shrugs, thumbs up and down, and demi-pliés. "I should go," said Beatrice, ducking only slightly under Imelda's arm to escape the corner. "But thank you so much for having me over."

"Anytime." Veruca smiled. "Hope you get comfy quick. Creating a welcoming atmosphere is just about telling the right fragrance story with a red currant–scented candle or wild blackberry diffuser." Beatrice nodded, though her brain was processing very different messages, and headed for the door.

"LOVE your sister," Dreyfus raved, as he strutted away, close behind Veruca.

"If she really *is* your sister." Kendra sniffed and marched back toward home base on the room's center ottoman.

3

BEATRICE YANKED DOLLY OUT THE DOOR. In the hallway, she took an enormous deep breath and felt oddly fond of the hideous carpet and water-stained wallpaper. Dolly opened her mouth to fire a barrage of questions, but Beatrice stopped her. "Doll, I beg you. Not now. Later, okay? It's not interesting. They just wanted to hear about Gertie. Thank you for the keys." She was too tired to dish.

Dolly shut her mouth and nodded, knowing that sometimes— for Beatrice—being known as "Gertie's sister" or "a Bernstein" felt like being nobody at all. Key in hand, Beatrice trudged toward her own apartment, thrilled at the prospect of alone time to shake off the last few minutes. Who was she kidding? The last few years required some digestion. She would find her place and then go grab her luggage—assuming it was still there.

Veruca was prettier in person, and her gravitational pull was undeniable. No wonder people wanted to be near her. Apparently, even Beatrice's own brilliant sister was susceptible. But if the socialite wasn't vapid, then why did she surround herself with those three hipster goons?

More importantly, why did Beatrice care? She shook her head to dispel the preoccupation and instead envisioned her own little sanctuary, far away from the Bernsteins and even starstruck Dolly, who seemed to have lost a marble or two over the summer. Maybe they rolled out of her head during a pas de bourrée lunge at some hip-hop ballet class in Los Angeles. (When it came to dance, Dolly was primarily interested in hybrids.)

Deciding against the questionable elevator, Beatrice hopped down the institutional cement stairs, sliding a hand along the painted orange banisters and past large plastic signs offering instructions for EXIT IN CASE OF EMERGENCY. (Of course, during any real emergency, people would be too panicked to remember how to read.)

Reaching the first and bottom floor, she exited into the corridor in search of her apartment, number 33. As she passed each door, she cheerfully read the numbers out loud, oblivious to eye rolls from already jaded residents, particularly a Goth girl in black lipstick, who made sure to scoff at any earnest enthusiasm.

Beatrice was confused: The numbers weren't adding up. The rooms on the first floor were three digits long and started with the number 1: 103, 105, 107. She checked over and over again, pacing the halls back to the lobby, where a bulletin board bore a notice of plumbing maintenance from two days prior. Her bags were still there. She asked other students, but they all seemed clueless or were running late for free food at a performance by the "edgy" a cappella group Hells Bells. Finally, an athletic, sandy blond–haired guy in cleats and a dirty sports uniform (who might as well have been the football-playing Chad of Beatrice's suburban high school fantasies) stopped on his way to "hit the shower" and offered the first viable explanation.

"Have you tried the basement?" He motioned toward a nearby gray door, which stood slightly ajar. "I've heard rumors that sometimes overlooked seniors get stuck down there. They almost always commit suicide. Seriously, the ghosts of the dead people chill down there and like freak people out." He figured he'd try to make her laugh, always good for points with hot chicks. Distractedly, he eyed a nearby janitorial closet, as if considering how quickly he could coax her inside for a quickie before never speaking to her again. She'd probably make a good story to tell the guys over beers and Atomic Wings.

Beatrice had a sinking feeling, and not just about the panting guy in front of her whom she'd already secretly dubbed "Hormone Guy." She turned on her heel and headed—as if the thought didn't bother her at all—toward the basement. She pulled the door open with a squeak and crept down a dark set of stairs. No colorful emergency warning signs here. They would have seemed like decoration in this dank setting. She tried to ignore the goose bumps rising on her forearms against her cardigan sleeves.

Before the lights ever went on, Beatrice heard the unmistakable sound of dripping water. Drops fell like slow tears from neglected air conditioners and leaky faucets. They cried for lost owners, for the days when they were shiny and full of promise in their original boxes back at the factories. She could sense unsavory, clouded pools of loss collecting on the cement floor below. *Plunk, plunk, plunk.*

"Hey, I was kidding," Hormone Guy shouted after her, but then he followed her down the stairs. Maybe this was some lurid sex game? Worth a shot. At the bottom, Beatrice felt around for a switch and then flipped on a light, which revealed a storage area and laundry room, littered with broken plastic hampers, misshapen cardboard boxes, and old fencing swords, bicycles, and rusty wrenches.

"Dude, this can't possibly be your apartment." Beatrice's brain screamed an echoed sentiment. But just as he said it, they both spotted a decrepit doorway amid the clutter with a brand-new sign posted near the top: #33. Beatrice willed the absurd situation to be a trick as she inserted the key into the lock. Unfortunately, it fit.

Though the door's paint was peeling and possible bullet holes

peppered the outside, she irrationally hoped that the studio itself would be wonderful with plush pillows and an enormous
window—somehow built into the basement wall—and a very
clean, waxed wooden floor.

No such luck. Inside, the room—and that's all it was, with
nary a kitchenette—looked even worse than the outside: more
tiny prison cell than Sandals resort suite. The only window was
the narrowest sliver almost at the ceiling. The source of that sad
and spooky dripping sound was in fact *inside* the room, as murky
water leaked from high up in one corner and created a lopsided
beige stain that spread like a rash across the ceiling. This was one
Rorschach test that no one wanted to take.

Instead of a cot, which is hardly dreamy in its normal incarnation, Beatrice was confronted with an ancient bunk bed, which
took up three-quarters of the room. A bunk bed? Was she eight
years old? The striped mattresses—with mysterious stains and
gray stuffing–filled rips—looked as if they had been plucked
from a street corner. She never thought she could miss the dorm,
but suddenly she longed for those dorky ice cream socials and
whiteboards. The worst part was the smell: A rancid sulfur odor
emanated from God knows where and flooded Beatrice's newly
decongested nose so completely that she wished for her cold
back. If there was any doubt left about whether this condemned
closet was meant to be her apartment, Beatrice spotted her pre-
shipped, carefully labeled boxes stacked neatly to one side.

She and Hormone Guy stood frozen, his gaping mouth and
wide eyes confirming the irregularity of her situation. "Dude,
this can't be your room," he repeated. His own fabricated story
about suicidal students weighed heavily on his limited mind. He
scratched his sandy blond crew cut like a cartoon character, willing a thought to break through the dense fog.

"Thanks for coming down here with me." She sighed, peering around. "I think otherwise I might actually be a little scared. I guess that's silly?" She was looking for a little comfort. He wasn't the most ideal companion, maybe, but he was large. At least, his head was big.

Even in the midst of the grime and stench, Hormone Guy seemed to think he might get some action. He stepped toward Beatrice, so she could better see the steroid-associated acne creeping from beneath his crewnecked collar, and placed a sausagelike finger lightly under her chin. "No problem. I'm not going to let a sweet little thing like you walk down somewhere like this by herself." Beatrice loved being referred to as a "thing." At a rustle from the room's far corner, they both whipped around in time to see a piece of newspaper—presumably with something good sized and furry underneath—scurry across the floor.

"Is that a rat?!" Hormone Guy yelped. "That's it. No ass is worth this. I don't do rodents." And, with that, her knight in dirty uniform ran up the stairs and out of sight, leaving her alone in her own personal dungeon. She hugged her trusty brown leather purse. The newspaper moved again. Had she bothered to check out the story moving up and down with the creature's every twitch, she would have read an informative article about the city's best Vietnamese sandwich shops according to Veruca Pfeffernoose, artist pal Maldrake Maldrake Capri, and art dealer "to the stars" Mr. Patrick Stone. Instead, up the stairs Beatrice ran, though not in pursuit of the sweaty jock.

4

AT THE REGISTRAR's/HOUSING OFFICE in an administration building a few blocks away, Beatrice waited patiently on a line that snaked out the door. A few hours before, she might have resented time wasted in this overly air-conditioned office that smelled of Xerox machines and what she could only imagine was Jessica Simpson perfume. Now she was just grateful to be out of the basement.

At a simple tap on the shoulder, she jumped about a foot and a half and her heart started thumping like a stereo bass. Next stop, the cardiology wing at Beth Israel hospital. Beatrice's body could take only so much. That same Goth girl from the Dorchester was standing behind Beatrice in line. "You have a cobweb attached to your head." She pointed. Goth Girl pulled it off, examined it, and licked her fingers.

Beatrice shuddered and combed her own fingers through her now contaminated hair. Maybe a heart attack wasn't such a bad idea, after all. At least a hospital room would be sterile.

Finally, at the front of the line, an older woman in either a wig or a very impressive *naturally* pinkish mane greeted Beatrice with a frown. Apparently, that hair was her lone endearing quality. Her name tag read Estelle Ogvlogovich. No wonder she was grouchy.

"Hi, I'm Beatrice Bernstein. I'm a senior here. I was promised—"

"NO." When Ms. Ogvlogovich spoke, Beatrice could see that impressive amounts of amber lipstick had been transferred from her lips to her gold-capped teeth.

"Excuse me? I haven't asked you for anything ye—"

"The answer is NO."

"I don't understand. You don't even know what I need. The thing is, I'm sure if you saw my apartment, if you could even call it that, you'd understand. It's just not even livable because—"

"Yeah, yeah. I know all about it," spat the administrator. "The space is too small. Your dorm is coed; you asked for single-sex. Your roommate is a psycho. She doesn't shave her armpits. She slept with your boyfriend. She likes gangster rap and you like Britney Spears and other blights on society who flash their hoo-has to cameras. Her favorite food is peanuts and you're deathly allergic. There's botulism in your sink. None of it matters, prom queen, because we don't have a single room left. So, no. The answer is NO."

"But I'm not in the dorm. I'm in off-campus housing and I—"

"NO."

Beatrice stood stunned for a moment and then murmured, "I think there really is botulism in my sink." But Estelle had returned to her computer to play online poker and shop for discount porn. How could this be happening? When had Beatrice's life turned into a practical joke?

Off to the side, Beatrice stood dumbly for a moment, rotating a gold stud in her right ear. She pulled out her BlackBerry and considered calling her parents or even her sister. Suddenly, the PDA heated up in her hand until it was so scorching that she was forced to drop it back into her bag. What the hell?

That must have been a sign from the Sprint gods. Calling her parents was a bad idea. They would just rant and rave about the plight of the middle class and then insist that she stay at their place until another solution emerged, maybe when she turned forty. No way that was happening. Beatrice would not consume another spoonful of Daddy's Soup Surprise. She would buck up. Also, when she was out from under this mess, she'd take her cell phone to the store to get it checked out. It almost burned her hand!

Making the best of a bad situation, Beatrice decided to scrub, clean, and pretty up her apartment à la an "Eye of the Tiger" montage. As for the moving newspaper, she would adopt him as her pet and name him Roger. Or, conversely, maybe she'd buy some rat poison and murder Roger. Newly resolved, Beatrice set off to collect her bags from the Dorchester lobby.

5

ANY *ROCKY* FANTASIES WERE WIPED AWAY Etch A Sketch–
style and replaced with bleak reality an hour later, as Beatrice
and Dolly stood at the center of the basement pied-à-terre. Beatrice's suitcases, green plastic stacking shelves still wearing Target price tags, and boxes of books remained unpacked for fear of
contamination or, worse, infestation. Dolly crossed her arms
over her own shoulders, as if to shield herself from the surrounding griminess.

Beatrice's dear friend sighed. "Maybe we can still spruce it up?"
She eyed the room suspiciously, shifting her weight from toe to
calf in relevé, rocking like a mental patient. Her elbow briefly
grazed one filthy wall and she jumped (elegantly executing a
changement de pied) as if she'd made contact with radioactive
materials. She snatched her arm back, then searched through her
gym duffel until she found a small bottle of Purell. She rubbed
it first on that section of her arm and then feverishly over any
exposed skin. "Okay, Bea, I can't pretend anymore, even to comfort you. This is horrible. This literally can't be real. I've held
your hair while you puked Jägermeister. I've watched other dancers clean oozing foot sores with rubbing alcohol. I've helped
really smelly homeless people across the street, but this . . . I don't
know if I can do this. Just move into my place!"

"No, no. What about your roommate's enochlophobia?"

"Her what?"

"Fear of crowds."

"Of course, you know that." She shook her head. "What does that have to do with anything?"

"Three's a crowd! Plus, I couldn't bear to steal space from two dancers. Where will you twirl? What am I going to do, sleep on your bathroom floor all year?"

Dolly had sent her housing forms in late and was awarded a slightly larger studio apartment—euphemistically dubbed a "loft"—shared with a fellow dancer roommate. The space was tiny even for two, but at least it didn't smell like rotten eggs. She performed another relevé in frustration and almost tottered over, gasping at the thought of physical contact with the floor. "Bea, I can't leave you here! At least call your parents and tell them the situation. I'm sure the college would respond to them, even if that housing office hag ignored you."

But Beatrice refused to call. That would mean admitting defeat, proving once and for all that the big bad world was too much for their flighty younger child. Also, she was a little afraid of her burning-hot phone. This was an *experience*. At least, she would keep telling herself that. She examined the chipping red polish on her nails and then—as if remembering she had fingers—rubbed her sore temples. She had a headache. Maybe from the toxic fumes?

Dolly sighed. As the daughter of a suburban tax accountant and a businessman, she could never quite understand Beatrice's resentment of what appeared to be an enviable upbringing. The Bernsteins counted the young dancer as their third daughter, attending her recitals and expressing deep interest in her performance studies. Though Dolly did witness Beatrice's suffocation at the hands of their rigid doctrine, she sometimes felt that her friend overreacted. What could be cooler than parents who encourage artistic pursuits?

Dolly peeked at her cell phone. "I'm so sorry, but I have to go to Modern Mexican Jazz class. Call me if you need anything." As Dolly reluctantly ventured upstairs, she looked back pleadingly at her friend. "Come to my room, at least for one night, while we figure this mess out."

Beatrice resolutely shook her head. She wasn't shying away from a little adversity. "I'll get cleaning supplies and maybe you could help me tomorrow, though?"

Dolly nodded, her curls bouncing. "Of course. So stubborn," she mumbled, sprinting up the stairs.

"I'm lucky to have you!" Beatrice called after her.

"Yeah, yeah. Bring carnations to the hospital when I get a fungal infection from scrubbing this place." The basement door shut softly with a click.

Alone save vermin, Beatrice pulled a fitted yellow sheet out of one suitcase, stepped up on the frame of the bottom bunk, and pulled the linen around the dilapidated upper mattress. Better to sleep as far up as possible, so fewer creatures—especially the kind that snack on human flesh—could join her in bed. She pulled out a large towel to use as a blanket, so as not to destroy her new comforter. It was hard not to compare the bedroom she'd imagined for her first apartment, adorned with cozy blankets and a cheerful striped rug.

As satisfied as possible with the evening's bed setup, she went in search of a particular cardboard box. In a short time, Beatrice found the one marked WALL HANGINGS/POSTERS and opened it with a box cutter, which she briefly considered sleeping with for protection. She sorted through papers, pulling out a single laminated picture: a primitive map.

Beatrice collected maps, but not just of the world, the country, or even her city. Her maps were of outlet malls, directing shoppers to the nearest J. Crew or Theory stores, obsolete subway

systems, amusement parks and zoo loops from rides to conces-
sions. (Those were often stained with remnants of corn dogs and
cotton candy.) She traced the route of Jack Kerouac's road, Hollywood stars' homes hidden behind enormous hedges and metal
gates, the inner workings of the human body from the intestinal
tract to the nervous system. She kept an illustrated path of a
single cell's life cycle. And she loved maps of mazes, which could
be viewed with omniscience from above. She especially appreciated the keys at the bottom, illuminating distance via the length
of a dotted blue line per mile, the route to the nearest restroom
or fast-food joint, the fastest way to find Waldo in his red-and-
white-striped shirt. Maps laid out paths before the viewer, offering up myriad options, including the option to turn around and
travel home. Maps made Beatrice melancholy, hopeful, and also
sometimes frustrated. Her favorites by far were intimate hand-
drawn ones, created in haste with smeared pen on menus, napkins, and scraps of receipt for a friend or a stranger. These led
the way to the corner store or across town to a barbershop, a
cemetery unveiling, or a wedding reception.

Now she unpacked her most treasured item. Her sister Gertie
conceived the hand-drawn masterpiece when they were quite
small. An elaborate map of their childhood home took Beatrice
in wild loops to the back of coat closets that smelled of mildew
and her mother's Paris perfume with only rolls of forgotten holi-
day wrapping paper for company, under beds where treasures
like No. 2 pencils gathered dust, and to pantry cabinet nooks
where only cats might dream of squeezing.

As an adult, Beatrice understood that the map was created in
hopes of keeping a younger sibling occupied and out of her sister's hair while Gertie read *Marjorie Morningstar,* wrote poetry,
or gossiped on the phone with friends. Beatrice's parents had
adopted the map too, directing her to hidden spots in their office

bathroom's tiny square tub or behind a big wooden dollhouse. During such quiet times, her mother could finish a catalog essay for the latest exhibition and her father could look out over the Hudson River from a stool in his vast art studio and resolve ideas for his next conceptual piece.

Now, in this desolate basement, Beatrice climbed up onto the top bunk, ripped off a strip of masking tape from its spool, and mounted the map on the nasty wall as best she could. What might the map to her current situation be: a dull gray one that led in circles, no doubt, perhaps on that moving piece of newspaper? She laughed despite herself and settled under the towel to sleep, fully clothed lest someone or some*thing* surprise her. At every minor sensation—from the terry cloth brushing against her skin to her shirt tag irking her upper back—she flinched. She knew a long night loomed ahead, so she stared across the ceiling at that morphing stain and considered what she thought it resembled more: the state of Mississippi or that girl Kendra's face?

As she closed her eyes, she heard a rustling behind her and peered up toward the window slit. For an instant, Beatrice swore she saw that pigeon with the yellow tuft perched just outside.

6

HOURS—THAT LIMPED LIKE YEARS—LATER, after Beatrice finally fell into a twilight state between rest and alarm, she awakened with unease. Huddled under her brown seventies hand-me-down towel, which barely covered her shins let alone her feet, she shivered despite layers of clothing. A warning tingle crept down her spine.

She could have sworn she saw that taunting ceiling stain move. She sat upright and backed quickly away. It moved again and again and then, suddenly, as her eyes adjusted to the dark of the room, she distinguished a sizable creature scurrying across its face. Like any sane person, she shrieked and flipped on the light—she was so high up in the tiny room that the switch was actually below the top bunk—and found herself staring in horror at the largest cockroach she'd ever seen.

Nobody—or at least not most citizens of New York City—particularly likes cockroaches. Ever since a rumor circulated that they alone would survive a nuclear holocaust, even bleeding hearts turned against them. But this was no average roach: This was one of those monstrous creatures that city dwellers euphemistically refer to as water bugs. These insects couldn't be killed without a horrible resounding crunch as their exoskeletons cracked—usually underfoot—and green gunk oozed from within their enormous bellies.

Beatrice's fear of these creatures far surpassed the average person's rational distaste, dating back to—at least in her mytho-logized memory—the day her paternal grandfather died. While walking down the street with her mother, the granddaddy of all cockroaches scurried across her exposed flip-flop-clad foot, forcing her to drop her Creamsicle. Just moments later, they arrived home to the sad news that Papa had passed away. Ever since, Beatrice had hated the bugs more than any other earthly creature and she considered a sighting the worst kind of omen. She wasn't such a big fan of Creamsicles either. Still, she would have eaten a whole warehouse full of them now if it meant getting out of this basement hole. How could the situation get worse?

As if in answer to that challenge, the cockroach sprinted across the cracked plaster ceiling above Beatrice's paralyzed body. It stopped just as abruptly and Beatrice allowed herself a tiny breath of relief, right before the nasty thing dropped directly from the ceiling onto her bed with a *plunk*.

Beatrice shrieked. She shrieked like no one has ever shrieked before. Her cries carried across the Manhattan Bridge and were mistaken for music by Williamsburg hipsters. And then she leaped off the bed and ran for the exit, where she struggled with the loose metal knob, opened the door, slammed it behind her, and raced blindly—like a maniac—into the pitch-dark basement area. And that's when something—no, some*one* in a hood that she could barely make out—grabbed her forcefully. A strong hand closed around her upper arm, as thoughts pinged off her now frantic brain: Was this hooded being Death incarnate? A garden-variety rapist? Hormone Guy here to stake his claim? The cockroach's alien leader, come to take her back to the mother ship? Would she be found in this stupid towel? And, if this was in fact the end of her days, why wasn't her life flashing before her eyes? Why was she only seeing a montage from *The Bachelor*?

She struggled against the being, whatever it was. "Get off me!"

"Calm down, calm down," It repeated. "You're okay. You're okay!"

She stopped fighting It, as the creature seemed to be human and, for a rapist, quite concerned for her well-being. She took a deep breath, as Its hand relaxed against her arm.

It asked, "Now, what the hell are you doing down here in that closet?"

So she had scared It too. It sounded male. Its question grounded her in reality, so she took a second deep breath to calm her nerves and stepped away. Judging by the sound of fading footsteps, It seemed to be walking away somewhere. She heard rummaging and then the light switch flipped and there It stood. Only It wasn't an It. It was the most beautiful boy—just the right combination of scruffy and quirky and lean and tall. Even in her state of sleep deprivation and terror, she paused to fix her pony-tail. He flipped his hood off to reveal a dark brown mess of hair. She figured he hadn't brushed it since he got out of bed . . . in only boxers. She shook her head clear. What was her problem? He was probably some psychopath who snuck into the building. They really should implement a better security system.

"What are you doing here?" he asked again. "Are you okay?"

He actually seemed spooked. He probably thought she was a homeless meth head mole person.

"I live down here." Ah, yes, that explanation made her seem much more appealing.

"You're squatting here?"

"No, I'm not squatting!" Beatrice gathered herself, cranky from lack of sleep as the adrenaline subsided. "I'm a student. The housing office placed me down here. That's not a closet. That's"— she cleared her throat so her voice wouldn't waver and betray imminent tears—"my studio apartment."

He stared at her for a moment, as if waiting for a punch line, and then smirked in disbelief. "So you actually live down here. Okay, then. And you were shrieking because?"

"Because"—and she straightened herself up to deliver this information—"a giant cockroach tried to kill me."

He laughed. He actually laughed. And why shouldn't he, really, because Beatrice had sort of been kidding? Still, while she knew intellectually that the circumstances were ridiculous, maybe even funny in retrospect in a decade or two, she didn't appreciate his cavalier attitude.

"Show me the cockroach. I'll dispose of the alleged murderer. If you really live down here." He glanced around the space and grimaced. "Why don't you tell the housing people to move you to a real apartment?"

"Good advice," she snapped. "I should have thought of that."

He grabbed a random newspaper off the floor and she flinched, considering what might be hiding below it. He also snagged an old plastic Starbucks iced Grande cup from the floor and strolled over to her room. He swung the door open and found the cockroach sitting companionably on the bed. It might as well have been taking a nap.

"There he is," he said mildly, approaching the insect like a lost puppy. He stopped and surveyed the sealed boxes, until his eyes rested on the map taped to the wall. "What's that?"

She shot him a look that read, *Now? Really? You want an explanation about my wall art?* Why did he have to be so cute? Why was she being so irritable? Why did she keep thinking about *The Bachelor?*

He turned back to the roach. "You don't look so scary for a vicious killer." He tossed the edges of his hair out of his eyes and easily scooped the thing up between the newspaper and transparent cup. In the doorway, she winced.

"In fact, you're kind of cute, little guy." He turned toward

Beatrice, holding up the cockroach trapped inside the plastic cup. "Are you sure you don't want me to make a formal introduction? By the looks of this place, you may be meeting more of his family: cousins, siblings, ex-girlfriends, homeboys. You may want to have an in with someone. You know, affiliate. And this big guy looks like he'd have some pull with the family."

Beatrice knew she should laugh, but she was cold, tired, upset, and a millisecond away from bursting into bellowing sobs. And this guy was sticking a bug in her face. She narrowed her eyes at him. "You know, you never said what *you* were doing down here. Are *you* squatting?"

"What?"

"You asked what I was doing down here, but what were *you* doing? Stealing?"

"Stealing? Are you serious? Have you seen it down here? I think you mean, 'Thank you for saving me from the bug that doesn't pose even a minor threat.'"

"Um, don't you mean, 'Thank you for scaring the shit out of me'? Who goes skulking through dark basements that way? I mean, except maybe attackers or Peeping Toms." She crossed her arms.

"You think I was spying on you?" He looked her up and down. Beatrice was suddenly quite conscious of being clothed in far too many layers with an old towel wrapped around her shoulders. She looked like a kid playing a game of superhero, about to take imaginary flight.

"I was grabbing my bike." He gestured toward a worn-out Trek bicycle, a little rusted along the body with band stickers adorning the limbs. It looked loved. She irrationally wanted him to leave it behind as a comfort to her.

Apparently, her mouth and her mind disagreed, as she continued her tirade. "All I'm saying is, who needs a bike in the middle of the night? What, do you have like a paper route or some-thing?"

He peered incredulously at her. "I know you don't have many windows down here with the pod people, Princess, but it's actu-ally almost noon." Noon! She'd completely forgotten to set her alarm. Lovely. She'd missed her first class. "Anyway, I'm gonna go rejoin the land of the living. You're welcome. I think." He turned to leave.

"For what? You said the roach didn't pose a threat yourself."

He walked back over to her and held the plastic cup just inches from her face. She screamed at the sight of the enormous brown creature and jumped back. He smiled and shook his head. And, with that, still clutching the cockroach in the plastic cup in one hand, he grabbed his bicycle by the center bar with the other and headed upstairs. Beatrice stood at the bottom amid the clutter, alone again.

7

WITH MYSTERIOUS HAIRS CAUGHT in clogged drains, soap scum infestation, and squatting urinators with bad aim, public restrooms are often disgusting. Which is why—after years of enduring other people's filth—Beatrice saw a private bathroom as one of her apartment's big perks. (A few of the Dorchester's less desirable studios shared hallway showers like an old-world boardinghouse.) She got her privacy, but the basement's "water closet" was unspeakable, down to its pungent aroma. Somehow Beatrice managed to get herself clean(ish) enough to emerge from the dank depths, though she felt like some kind of vampire super-villain. She masked her true dark identity during the day, only to descend back beneath the depths and wreak havoc as a supporting character from *The Metamorphosis* each night.

Now she plopped down next to Dolly on one side of a large, round communal table to wait for their Latin American literature class to begin. Beatrice's chair made a horrible screeching sound against the floor, pulling unwanted focus. Meanwhile, Dolly eyed Beatrice's feet.

"What? Is the transformation finally complete? Are my toes actually webbed?" the basement dweller snapped. She checked just to be sure.

"You're wearing two different ballet flats."

"Oh, please." Beatrice sighed. "The fact that I'm wearing shoes at all is a miracle of epic proportions." She was relieved to be in

Dolly's company, but nothing could compel her to feel anything other than repulsive.

"Somebody's grumpy."

"*Somebody* almost died last night."

"Oh, I see. Are we still referring to the killer cockroach and the 'rapist'?" Beatrice had called Dolly and filled her in earlier.

"Well, whatever, somebody *thought* she might die. Besides, I'll probably keel over eventually, when I develop flesh-eating gangrene from the black mold spores down there."

"Gangrene actually doesn't come from outside pollutants. It—" Beatrice shot Dolly a withering look. Her friend took a deep breath. "Bea, this is getting ridiculous. You have to come stay with me. You wouldn't even have to sleep on the floor. You could share my bed! And we're getting a couch one of these days, if we can figure out how to fit it through the door."

"Doll, that's really sweet. I'm sorry I'm being such a nightmare. I haven't really slept." Beatrice let her head fall heavily into her waiting hands, fingers interwoven like a straw basket. "What about your roommate and her whole 'crowding' issue? It sounded like she was serious about that whole 'no guests' thing."

Dolly rolled her eyes. "I'm pretty sure she was just being melodramatic. I mean, if you really had a phobia, you wouldn't stay in a tiny apartment with some stranger, right?"

"Where would you stay?"

"I don't know, maybe in a mental institution? All I'm saying is that she doesn't freak out when we're in a tiny dance studio with a 'crowd' of dancers. The other day, the teacher walked us through a choreographed set called 'Tsunami' from last year's fall recital. We had to link arms and be the wave, you know?" Dolly mimed a swaying ocean current, linking arms with an imaginary accompanying dancer. "She didn't freak out during that. I almost did. It was so lame."

Beatrice sifted her hair through her fingers, finding a now familiar gnarled knot at the nape of her neck. She hadn't been able to uncover a brush in all the bedlam. Plus, she'd rushed because she didn't want to be late for a second class of the day. Only twenty-four hours had passed since Beatrice arrived at school, but she could hardly remember a time when she lived above-ground with the "normal" folks. She felt like a dead and buried character from *Our Town,* studying the modern world with new eyes, stunned by open windows, sunlight, and the companionship that regular people seemed to take for granted. Thornton Wilder probably hadn't envisioned his characters in mismatched shoes.

Her mind adrift, she saw herself wrapped in a pretty purple blanket and resting on her parents' velvet chaise longue with a book, looking every so often out the twelfth-story window at the Hudson River. She opened her eyes to dispel the tempting picture. "Doll, you're sweet. But I can't. What am I going to do: sleep in your room for the entire year? That's just not a solution, as nice as it is of you to offer."

"If you have to, you can!" said Dolly.

"Thanks. But can we talk about something else? Anything else? What's up with Stephen?"

Dolly and Beatrice had befriended Stephen, Mina, and Cynthia freshman year, when they all lived in the same dorm and discovered a shared love of twisted documentaries. Somehow, a tradition developed of meeting in the common room on Tuesday nights. They'd wear funny hats, drink bad scotch, and watch movies about serial killers, sexual deviants, and conjoined twins. Soon Tuesday nights gave way to parties, bars, and other hat-free activities. And by the end of their junior year, Dolly and Stephen's friendship had evolved into a little bit more, though they both claimed that it was just casual fun.

"Oh, Stephen? He's being annoying. He sent me some texts babbling about commitment. I think he romanticized things over the summer. Or maybe he was just drunk. Something tells me that the real Prince Charming doesn't communicate his love via text."

"Yeah, he sends telegrams by courier, but by the time they arrive, you've died of scarlet fever." Dolly stared at her hard. "Sorry. What I meant was: But seriously, would you want a relationship with Stephen?"

"What I *want* is to hear more about your killer from last night." Dolly twirled her hair with mock seductiveness. "He sounds sexy."

"The cockroach?"

"The guy!"

"I'd rather hear about the cockroach," deadpanned a nearby eavesdropper. The twosome turned to discover Goth Girl staring at them from three seats away. "I love cockroaches." She promptly went back to doodling an execution.

"Do you know that girl?" whispered Dolly.

"Don't worry about it. She's just the arsenic icing on my crap cake."

"So about that basement guy? I know you said he was kind of a douche, but from the story, it sounds like he got rid of that disgusting bug. That's nice."

"I suppose." Beatrice didn't want to admit it, but she hadn't stopped thinking about him all morning. What had prompted her to be so defensive, when all he'd tried to do was help? Oh, yeah: total and utter humiliation. She rotated the stud in her ear again, a new habit forming without her consent.

"Well, maybe he's a dick, but he sounds hot."

"I didn't even describe him!"

"Well, in my imagination he's hot. For one thing, if he was gross, you wouldn't be bright red right now. What was his name?"

Beatrice willed her hot cheeks to simmer down, as she peered self-consciously around the table. "I actually have no idea."

"Ooh! Good. Let's give him one. How 'bout 'the Cockroach Slayer'?"

"Technically, he didn't slay anything."

"I think he kinda slayed you." Dolly grinned. Goth Girl hissed.

At that moment the door swung almost off its hinges, and in marched Veruca Pfeffernoose in all her sparkling glory. A spotlight emanating from some unseen source followed the girl as she walked. A trail of golden confetti—like dust glittering in a stream of sunlight—swelled and then disappeared in her wake. Today, her outfit riffed on a Catholic schoolgirl uniform: Her hair was pulled up in a Gwen Stefani–inspired ponytail with an exaggerated rockabilly rise at the front, and her plaid miniskirt screamed punk. Her nails were painted tangerine and her lips were again the color of dew-touched coral. Had her cheekbones actually lifted overnight? All the girls and gay boys in class rustled in their bags for pens, pencils, and iPhones to scrawl "orange nail polish" on grocery lists. An emotional few even shed single tears. The straight guys just stared, mouths agape, and dreamed of tousling that perfect pony.

Before Beatrice could stop her, Dolly yelped, "Veruca, Veruca, over here!" and motioned to a free seat by them, sounding more like a crazed fan than a friend. Veruca lifted her oversized sunglasses and peered at Dolly without recognition. But then those same odd orbs fixed on Beatrice and a smile that charmed even the basement grouch spread across Veruca's beautiful, quirky face. The socialite headed toward them.

"Mind if I sit here?" she cooed, pulling a chair out from the table. She levitated into the ugly metal thing as gracefully as any ballerina. The seat floated back into place. Her catlike charm was

magnified by the unkempt mess now sitting next to her: Beatrice. Veruca even smelled like something otherworldly: gardenias, persimmons, Thanksgiving pumpkin pie, and cocoa butter.
What exactly was that scent? Beatrice, on the other hand, smelled
like mildew, old moldy pipes, and a burrito from two days ago.
And she sort of looked like the burrito too.

Veruca took a closer peek at Beatrice and gasped. "What's
wrong, Beany Baby? You look just beyond dreadful! Is everything okay?"

Beatrice and Dolly both took a moment to digest this new
nickname. Dolly silently pronounced it ingenious. Beatrice wasn't
totally convinced. And before she could offer an evasive answer,
citing lack of sleep, loud music, stuck elevators, and other normal
apartment building issues, Dolly jumped in.

"Oh, Veruca," she lamented. "It's awful. Just awful! The housing
crazies put Bea—Beany Baby—in this absolutely revolting apartment in the Dorchester's basement, of all places. The basement! It's
totally nast. And, on top of all that, she was almost attacked by an
enormous rabies-infested creature—heinous. Seriously."

Veruca's eyes widened. "That's horrible! I mean, just beyond.
I can't even imagine." Then she turned to Beatrice. "You should
move out! Find a different apartment in the neighborhood! There
must be some available?"

"I wish I could," Beatrice admitted. "But that's not really an
option for me." Convincing her parents to pay for her place at
the Dorchester had been difficult enough, considering their close
proximity. She'd argued that the apartment kept her near study
groups, classes, and friends like Dolly, so she didn't have to risk
late-night subway rides and walks alone down dark side streets.
But there was no way they would cosign and pay for another studio. They would insist she live at home. "I wish I could just pay
for it myself, but that's not in the cards."

"Maybe you should play with a different deck?" Veruca suggested.

"I don't really have another . . . deck." *What the hell were they talking about?*

The socialite continued. "Jeez, that really blows. And look what the creatures did to your sweater too!" She motioned toward a stain on Beatrice's gray knit sleeve. "You must not have realized until you got to class." She shook her head in pity.

"Oh, right." Beatrice tucked the stain at the edge of her sleeve under and decided not to mention that she'd created the spot herself a few months back during an enthusiastic run-in with a pile of mozzarella sticks and marinara sauce. Ah, to meet those old friends now.

Veruca crinkled her perfectly smooth brow, but then her face brightened. Beatrice swore she saw an actual lightbulb appear in the air above. "I know! Come to my place after class. My aesthetician Lili is coming over and she can transform any hot mess into . . . well, I mean. She's cool, not all woo-woo world music. We hang out all the time. She'll give you an oxygen facial and relax all that stress right out of your skin."

"Oh, I couldn't," Beatrice began, always suspicious of people who counted salaried employees as their "close friends." But Dolly took over. "We'd be delighted. Thrilled. Thrilled and delighted."

Beatrice made a face. Who talked like that? "Don't you have dance rehearsal?" she asked Dolly pointedly.

"Dance rehearsal? Oh, no worries about that," promised Veruca. "I'll just ask Mark to come over and give you pointers instead."

"Mark?"

"Mark Morris."

Dolly was floored. "The choreographer? You're kidding, right?"

That perplexed look appeared on Veruca's face again. "Why would I be kidding?"

"Oh, damn. I can't believe this, but actually, we can't tonight," said Dolly.

Thank God, thought Beatrice, *Dolly finally came to her senses.* "Right, we can't."

"Because it's Thursday."

"Right, because—" Midsentence, Beatrice realized what Dolly was saying. Her friend hadn't come to her senses. Thursday nights were mandatory Bernstein family dinners, which, even while in college, Beatrice couldn't possibly skip. She'd forgotten. "Oh, Lord. I can't deal." Beatrice laid her cheek on the table and closed her eyes, willing death to take her.

"Oh, don't worry," said Veruca. "I'll just have Lili come tomorrow instead. I'll see you then! Anyway, I'm off."

Beatrice readied to explain that her concerns extended beyond a missed facial, but the professor—who had been staring even more blatantly than the students at Veruca—finally regained enough composure to begin teaching class. She cleared her throat and shuffled loose papers to signal the start. God forbid she interrupt the mysterious heiress.

"Wait, *off*?" a naïve Dolly asked. "But class hasn't started yet."

"Oh, I just remembered I have other things to do." Veruca beamed. "See you later, Beany Baby!" And with that, she threw a beautiful leather bag—perfectly worn by who knows whom—over her shoulder and inserted her iPod earbuds in one smooth movement. Floating out of the classroom, she winked at a staring guy, then slipped her sunglasses back over her eyes. Behind her wafted the scent of . . . what was that? Orange blossoms?

8

BEATRICE WOULD HAVE GOTTEN DOWN on hands and knees to plead with Dolly to play buffer at Thursday night dinner, but no coercion was required. Her friend hadn't seen the Bernsteins all summer and she'd missed them, unfathomable though that seemed.

In her parents' building, awaiting the elevator in the familiar terra-cotta-tiled lobby, Beatrice bit her bottom lip. She planned to avoid all conversation about her senior year thus far, which she realized would be challenging since she was an inept liar. "Maybe I should pretend to have laryngitis?" she suggested to Dolly.

"So they'll think you've relapsed and tuck you back into bed?"

The elevator arrived with a thump and a few small wheezes, as the operator brought it to level. There was a clang as the metal gate shot back into its slot and then the outer door opened, revealing Beatrice's favorite elevator man, Oswaldo. Stepping inside the wood-paneled box with Dolly at her heels, she and Ozzy began the recitation of their regular exchange, as they rose toward the twelfth floor.

"Beatrice! Beeeeatreeese. You're home to stay?"

"No, just visiting. How are you, Ozzy?"

"Good, good. But the asthma's no good."

"You should rest!"

"Oh, no. I'm too young. I'm too young."

He threw his free hand above his head, snapped his fingers—most of which sported chunky gold rings—and feigned flamenco dancing. Beatrice adored Oswaldo, but after all these years, she still wasn't sure she got the joke.

The positive thing about Thursday night dinners was that, instead of some strange foreign concoction or (worse!) Daddy's Soup Surprise, Chinese delivery was the chosen cuisine: steamed dumplings, beef and broccoli, sesame chicken, cold sesame noodles, and pork and shrimp lo mein, aka "the traif special." Thanks to this tradition, though uncharacteristic of the Bernsteins' well-organized household, the fridge was cluttered—like some middle school science experiment—with boxes of dried-up white rice, so hard it could crack the most expensive caps.

The prodigal daughter and her friend made a right down the short wallpapered hallway and rang the doorbell.

"After you." Beatrice smiled.

"Oh, you're too kind."

They heard footsteps and the muffled hum of music. Gertie opened the door and exclaimed, "Dolly! Hey, you guys, Dolly came too!" She hugged both girls, first Dolly, then Beatrice. "Come in, come in. Welcome to Crazy Town." She raised her brows and widened her eyes. Apparently, the Bernsteins were at their most insane.

"What's up?" asked Beatrice.

"Oh, the usual. Dad is on some tear about 'the fucking conservatives.' Mom is having a problem with a painting at the museum. I'm horribly behind in my research. All is right with the world."

"Dolly is here?" Beatrice's father shouted from his studio.

"Hi, Gary!"

"Welcome, Doll!" he called. "That means no broccoli in the beef and! Our Dolly hates broccoli!"

"It's true. I do!"

Gary arrived shortly after his voice, and—as the crow's-feet on either side of his eyes wrinkled warmly—gave Dolly a quick hug and Beatrice a kiss on the cheek. "Well, if it isn't my favorite younger daughter and her lovable appendage." Beatrice half hid behind her friend.

"I'll order the food right now," Gary announced and then shouted toward his wife's home office: "Madeline, get off the phone. Dolly and your younger daughter are here!"

Madeline arrived in the entryway, firing staccato orders into her cell phone. "Call conservation immediately, just in case! Hang on!" Covering the mouthpiece with her palm, she kissed Dolly, and mouthed, "Welcome home, sweetie!" to Beatrice. "I'll be right off," she whispered. "Some child came right up to a Jackson Pollock with Magic Markers. Now we're trying to figure out if he actually drew anything. Does no one discipline his or her children these days?" Not surprisingly, Madeline and Gary felt their particular brand of tough love parenting far surpassed the rest.

Shooting questions about Mark Taper Forum, Disney Concert Hall, and other LA dance venues, Gertie led Dolly into the living room, where the furniture was stark and modern but placed atop a woven Turkish rug for contrast. Beatrice followed shortly after. Talking Heads played on the stereo: *You may tell yourself, this is not my beautiful house! You may tell yourself, this is not my beautiful wife!* There was a comforting chaotic rhythm to the Bernstein household.

Beatrice stripped off her jacket and threw it on the arm of the couch. Having forgiven him for disappearing during the pigeon incident, she bent down to pet Waldo. He had emerged from a secret corner, where presumably he'd shed white fur on some precious black garment. The cat sniffed Beatrice's hand, rubbed his head against her leg, then stopped, gagged, and vomited at her feet. Afterward, he stalked casually away.

Just then, Madeline walked into the living room sans phone, plopped down on the couch next to Gertie, and pronounced, "Everything is okay with the Pollock."

"Thank the Lord!" called Gary from the other room. "Order is restored! Hallelujah!"

She rolled her eyes and then looked with distaste toward Beatrice and the fresh pile of cat bile, as if her younger daughter was perhaps responsible. "Can you clean that up, Sweet Bea?"

Sighing, Beatrice trudged to the exposed-brick kitchen and grabbed some Whole Foods–approved Method spray cleaner and recycled paper towels, the kind that are too thin to effectively sop anything up. She could hear her father concluding the Chinese food order on the phone: "Beef and broccoli, hold the broccoli. No broccoli. That's correct. I suppose that, yes, it is a strange order, but we'd like it that way just the same. And cold sesame noodles. That should do it. Thanks."

He hung up, returning the phone to its cradle with a clatter. What felt like fifteen seconds later, as Beatrice was still wiping up salmon-and-liver-scented puke, the buzzer rang. "That should be our food!" Gary charged toward the call box to let the delivery-man in. "I swear the delivery guys cook on their bikes. It's extraordinary."

Minutes later, the family plus one was inhaling massive quantities of lo mein. They sat in designated seats clustered around the kitchen table, a vintage 1950s diner set with padded seats and chrome appendages, under a solemn black-and-white portrait of James Joyce with wire-rimmed glasses and cane.

Beatrice was focused intently on capturing a dumpling with

her wooden chopsticks when she noticed her mother studying her from across the wonton soup. "You look pale. Have you been sleeping?"

Beatrice shot Dolly a panicked look. A slipup here could prove catastrophic for her independence. Her friend nodded her curl-covered head almost imperceptibly, very 007-like, and answered in Beatrice's stead. "Who can sleep with all the excitement of our final school year starting? So, Gertie, we talked all about my summer. What's up with you?" Thank goodness for the Muppet.

Gertie used a napkin to dab at her lips—which somehow remained red—and knotted her black hair into the perfect sloppy ponytail. "I'm good. I have a reading coming up next month, so I'm just skimming *Swann's Way* for the fiftieth time. Oscar is away and I could use his help with organizing, so that's kind of a drag."

"I still don't understand why you won't date Oscar," complained their father. Beatrice felt the pressure slide off her slouching shoulders and onto her sister's well-postured ones. She nodded a subtle thank-you and well done at Dolly.

"Oh, Dad. For the love of God, don't start this again!" complained Gertie. The Bernstein banter was, like the language of many families, repetitive and composed mostly of mock irritation over beloved quirks, old stories, and unsolicited advice.

"What?" he continued against protests. "What's wrong with Oscar?"

"He's just—"

"Bald," finished Beatrice.

"My assistant," corrected Gertie.

"Gary, let it go," chimed Madeline. She pointed her finger across the table, as if the next words out of her mouth might be *"J'accuse!"* Instead she said, "Maybe Dolly would like Oscar?"

Dolly looked up with surprise from her plate of beef and beef.

Beatrice groaned. "Leave my poor friend alone."

Madeline took a large sip from her glass of Syrah, spilling a tiny drop on the Formica table. "What? He's a great catch. Just because your sister isn't attracted to him, even though he obviously loves her—"

"If he loves Gertie, why would you try to set him up with *Dolly*?"

"It was just an idea. Not every single one can be Nobel Prize–worthy."

"Maybe you should set him up with Bea," suggested Dolly with a mischievous snicker.

"Well, everyone knows that Oscar can't stand *her*," answered Madeline.

Gertie snorted.

"Thanks, Mom," said Beatrice.

For a moment, the table fell into relative quiet, as the clink of cutlery and the slurping of noodles tapped out its own dialogue. Waldo brushed his belly against Beatrice's legs again, begging as adorably as possible for a piece of, well, anything. She pulled a nugget of sesame chicken off her plate, ripped off a chunk, and, as inconspicuously as possible, threw it to him, careful not to glance after it. He scurried over and began chomping away happily. Madeline threw her daughter a look that read, *I saw that. That's why he throws up.*

After wiping his mouth with an ecofriendly paper napkin, Gary broke the companionable silence. "Gertie, we'd just like to see you dating more."

Gertie's mouth fell open. "Are you kidding me? Are we still talking about this? Stay out of my sex life! Who are you people?"

"Maybe you should go on *Millionaire Matchmaker*," suggested Beatrice.

"What's *Millionaire Matchmaker*?" Madeline asked.

"Something Picasso didn't paint," said Beatrice.

"Something that's decaying our society at its foundation, dumbing us down until we're as insipid as goldfish or Rush Limbaugh," said Gary.

Beatrice pointed a chopstick at her father, who shooed it away with his hand. "And yet you stood in my doorway when I was sick last week glued to an episode I was watching."

"Know thine enemy! I don't want to be a book burner, condemning something I've never seen. Anyway, that was research. If I'm ever single again—" Madeline punched her husband in the arm.

"What? If I'm ever single again because your mother leaves me for a much better-looking, younger man, now I'll know who to call. Meanwhile, speaking of knowing thine enemy, did anyone read that *New Yorker* piece about the history of censorship, starting in ancient Greece? That section on Heinrich Heine was fascinating."

"Who's Heinrich Heine?" asked Beatrice.

"Oh, Bea! Less reality TV, more reading, okay?" said Gertie. "Don't they teach you anything at that college?"

"Why would she learn about censorship?" Gary winked. "She's only studying journalism."

After that, an all-consuming argument started about the First Amendment (about which everyone was actually on the same side), so no one asked Beatrice any more questions about school. But as she gave her mother a parting hug at the front door, Madeline stared at her daughter's feet. "Sweet Bea, why are you wearing two different shoes?"

Ozzy's elevator arrived just in time. Beatrice made apologies and climbed inside.

9

THE NEXT DAY, BEATRICE RESISTED the "spa" afternoon planned at Veruca's place. She needed to buy a supermarket's worth of cleaning supplies for her dungeon. But Dolly coerced her with a promise of scrubbing and mopping help afterward. Plus, there was a certain allure to a sterile bed, even if only for a few hours.

Trailing pretty particles of evaporating glitter, Veruca led them to her very own spa dressing area, where vanity mirrors were illuminated by old-fashioned Hollywood bulbs. Yellow, pink, and gold Moroccan silk–cushioned mini-ottomans were available for lounging. How many rooms could this "loft" have?

It soon became hard to care: Neroli- and sage-scented mists fell like pins and needles on bare arms. An almost imperceptible pervasive humming spread good vibrations, healing and calming with every *om* like sonic Xanax. Already wildly relaxed and drinking immune-boosting smoothies that tasted to each like her own favorite childhood memory, Beatrice and Dolly slipped on robes spun from bamboo and blessed by Trappist monks. The fabric was said to moisturize the skin and clear the mind. Cushy slippers hugged the specific contours of the friends' feet. In search of a sauna or steam, Beatrice wandered into an adjoining room, which was bare save for dramatically varied doors (short, tall, frosted glass, polished wood). Each was labeled with a bronze placard: EUCALYPTUS & ROSEMARY STEAM, CEDAR SAUNA, SNOW & ICE IGLOO, HYDROTHERAPY ROSE PETAL BATH, WATSU

RETURN-TO-THE-WOMB POOL, BUBBLES & ECSTASY, GANBAN-YOKU-
HEATED BEDROCK, TURKISH HAMMAM, CALISTOGA MUD SLIDE,
LOMI LOMI LUAU, ACUPRESSURE, L.E.D. LASER TAG, and ANTIGRAVITY
CHAMBER. A transparent exit door on the left led out into a ram-
bling garden, somehow contained inside the Dorchester. Its cor-
responding sign read THREE-MILE REFLEXOLOGY PATHWAY.

Before Beatrice could call Dolly over to marvel, a portly young
woman with a bun appeared from nowhere. She gestured for
them to follow. And though they seemed to retrace their steps to
the main entry, the room they entered was most certainly not the
same. The air was balmy and pineapple scented. A quiet drumbeat
set a tropical vibe.

They were either being massaged or sacrificed, Beatrice
thought. Either option was fine.

Two impeccable massage tables stood side by side, separated
by a rice-paper screen, under jungle palms and amid impossibly
sprawling jasmine and lilac groves. Hummingbirds zoomed by
in search of nectar and howler monkeys roared like lions from
overhead. The sky was clear blue with sporadic perfect puffy
clouds. Was that a helmeted tourist zip-lining past? Beatrice
knew that she couldn't possibly be outdoors, and yet there she
stood, both inside and out, upside and down, right side and up.

As instructed, Beatrice and Dolly stripped off their robes and
slipped under the covers of their heated massage tables, limbs
already weak with contented exhaustion. At first, images of Brillo
pads, lemon-scented wood cleaners, pine-scented sprays, Swiffers,
mops, and vacuums (pushed by giant cockroaches) danced in
Beatrice's anxiety-filled head. But then, a warm organic lavender–
stuffed pillow was placed over her eyes and hot essential oil–
doused stones were strategically placed under her spine. The scents
of ylang-ylang, vanilla, bergamot, and Veruca's favorite orange
blossom wafted from the world's most emollient body butters

and creams, replacing Beatrice's worries with pictures of perfect honeysuckle and lobster-filled summers on the Cape, though she'd never been.

Lighting, temperature, and breezes shifted with time of day, as if the sun was getting higher in the sky. First, an energy healer touched Beatrice's feet, knees, arms, belly, and head, moving intuitively to areas of tension. The man could sense where negativity stalled energetic movement, which for Beatrice he said was all over. "Less hot dogs!" he commanded. And when he held his palm inches from where Beatrice's cell phone had almost burned her, she swore she saw a toxic green cloud lifting from her own hand. As for Dolly, the man's hands hovered inches above the strained arches of her dancer's feet, coaxing the pain from them, softening stubborn calluses, and healing open blisters.

Beatrice's and Dolly's faces were cleansed with warm towels soaked in water sourced from a natural hot spring just feet away. There were Egyptian cotton sheets, French face creams, Russian waxers, nontoxic Brazilian hair treatments, Chinese acupuncture needles, and, finally, a menthol reflexology foot massage administered by a Thai masseuse flown all the way from Bangkok's Wat Pho Temple of the Reclining Buddha.

In Beatrice's twilight state she had a dream, which she would later call a vision. She lay in a purple-and-white-striped bikini on a shaded hammock above a Costa Rican kelp-strewn beach with papaya juice in one hand, a great book in the other, and a person—blurry in the distance—plodding through the sand toward her.

Suddenly, Dolly shrieked. Beatrice sat bolt upright and readied to protect her friend with ... what? A scented loofah? Was the ritual sacrifice about to begin? Apologizing to Lili, the aesthetician who was readying her oxygen facial, Beatrice threw on her robe and peeked around the screen. Dolly was standing—in a terry cloth wrap—staring from Veruca to a beautiful, svelte woman at her side. It took only a moment for Beatrice to realize that Dolly's shrill cry was a happy one. Her hair bounced like its own entity, as she shifted spastically from toe to toe, a jack-in-the-box on broken springs.

"That's . . . I mean you're . . . is this really happening? I'm sorry. It's just you look so much like . . . but of course that's not possible." The older woman, wearing a leotard and a scarf, smiled mildly, as if she possessed the most amusing secret.

"I'm sorry," apologized Veruca, "but Mark was detained. Apparently, the dance he'd choreographed for a Lincoln Center performance next month was derailed when the whole cast developed a sudden interest in Justin Bieber. But I found you a wonderful replacement."

Even Beatrice could see the teacher's remarkable resemblance to famous dancer Isadora Duncan. She even wore a dramatic scarf, which was Ms. Duncan's signature. (It was also the nail in her coffin when it caught in the wheels of her convertible car.) Beatrice was reminded of a quotation from Gertie's namesake, Gertrude Stein, soon after Duncan's death: "Affectations can be dangerous." That was a lesson, Beatrice thought, to which her parents would no doubt subscribe. But she was too lulled by heavenly scents and Dolly's apparent bliss to sort out the notion.

Beatrice's best friend looked ridiculous, beaming through a neon green sea algae masque, as she cried, "Let me just wash this off my face and I'm ready! This is uncanny! Seriously. Isn't this uncanny, Bea? Do you mind if I leave to train with this . . . this woman?" As her facialist struggled to catch her midbounce and wipe off her face with a hot towel, Dolly dropped her voice to a stage whisper. "Who couldn't possibly be who I think she is because that person is dead, right?"

Beatrice stifled laughter for fear of cracking her own seaweed-and-apple–stem cell masque and gestured for Dolly to go ahead. Off the Muppet ran to a palatial marble restroom to change. The Isadora doppelgänger followed close behind in that ducklike way that serious dancers walk, feet splayed dramatically out to each side in eternal first position and back ramrod straight.

The rest of Beatrice's treatment was a blur of rubbed and kneaded happiness. She drifted in and out of an almost meditative half sleep, aware at some point that a cold gel serum—"hyaluronic acid" the aesthetician said—was applied to her face and that its contours were traced with a pen-shaped instrument that shot cold oxygen. Beatrice probably would have let them apply cat puke to her face, just as long as she could lie in that temperate cocoon.

When it was all regrettably over, she was handed a cup of vanilla-bourbon-rooibos tea made from legumes and led to a vibrating daybed, which she recognized from her first foray into the apartment. Had Veruca somehow converted the common area into a jungle spa retreat? But how?

As if in answer, the socialite appeared and sat on one of the enormous cushions beside a subdued Beatrice. "Holy shite. Beany Baby! You look amazing. Seriously." Her eyes sparkled with self-congratulation. She'd pulled off a feat with this one!

"Really?"

"Just beyond!"

Beatrice walked over to a large wall-mounted art deco mirror, framed in mosaic glass, and peered at herself. It was true. Her skin flushed pretty and glowed. She appeared unperturbed, dark circles from the past days' trials erased. Staring at her reflection, with her hair samurai-twisted atop her head and her body dwarfed by the enormous royal robe, she felt a bit like the witch from *Snow White* demanding, "Who is the fairest of them all?" For a fleeting moment she wondered if this was the kind of magic mirror that lied.

In fact, recalling her actual living situation, she felt and looked suddenly deflated. Real life awaited outside. She shuffled back to her companion. "Thank you so much, Veruca. It was so sweet of you to do this for me. I feel like I escaped to some amazing lavender-scented paradise. But now I should probably go deal with my own less fragrant situation."

Veruca's eyes bulged and she scooted closer to Beatrice. "Oh, I see. Your 'situation.' My people do prenatal massage too."

"Veruca, no! I just meant that my apartment isn't ideal." Beatrice almost started laughing.

"Oh, good. 'Cause that would be much more troublesome. You can call me V, by the way. That's what my *friends* call me." Veruca emphasized the word, almost as if she, a media princess and consummate cool kid, was asking for confirmation of the fact. Were those butterflies circling around her head, or was Beatrice dehydrated? She took a sip of tea. Veruca continued, "I'm not going to leave Gertie's sister in a bind, am I? Which is why I have a proposition for you. Just give me one minute before you leave."

So there was a reason behind the solicitousness. But what could this girl—this perfectly dressed, perfect-looking, perfectly poised vision with whom even sane people like Dolly and seasoned professors seemed obsessed—possibly want from marinara-stained Beatrice? Did she want her to wear out leather bags or boots? Did she want Beatrice to play guinea pig, testing danger-ous medications to treat a rare health condition unknown to the rest of the world? Did she want her to join a drug ring, delivering Special K and Ecstasy-laced candy canes to unsuspecting school-children? Beatrice almost ran for the door. But her curiosity, the residual effects of her heavenly spa treatments, and a sudden lethargy that descended when Veruca placed a hand on her shoulder made her unable to stand. She pulled the pink band out of her high ponytail, shook out her hair, and tried to appear serious, despite terry cloth attire.

"You may know that I have an interest in art," Veruca began. And in a flash Beatrice recalled a story, the details synapsing—hot and electric—between her neurons like breaking news on the wire. A year or so ago, Veruca had been at the inaugural New York show of hot young French artist Guillard Croissant at a new Chelsea gallery. The evening was going well. Attendees drank box white wine (not because they couldn't afford the good stuff but because that's what real artists do—they suffer). While a DJ mixed noise on an electronic board, club kids in black—posing as educated art world types—perused the work. Well practiced, they raised eyebrows when confronted with particularly simple abstract pieces and carefully feigned no reaction at the sight of shocking barbarity or nudity. Meanwhile, truly knowledgeable members of the art world, including Beatrice and Gertie's parents, Gary and Madeline Bernstein, kibitzed among themselves. They made the proper addresses to young Guillard and his dealer—"Great show!"—and then left early to drown their reasonable cynicism in burgers and craft brew beer at a nearby gastropub.

Guillard was having a gay old time, when his dealer brought Veruca and a group of the socialite's friends—the article referred to them as the "H.O.S. crew"—over to meet the master. Veruca was dressed for the part in black Comme des Garçons and was, by all accounts, legitimately looking forward to meeting the man who created her favorite piece ever, *Tout le Monde Sucks*. But as she approached him, she was suddenly consumed with an overwhelming nausea and, just before he reached out his hand to grasp her well-manicured own, she opened her mouth and projectile-vomited all over his shoes.

The truth was, in an effort to show her low-maintenance side (a rare mistake), Veruca had eaten some bad tacos from a stand in Mexico City earlier that day before flying back to the States. Now the carnitas came back to haunt her. But Guillard, being the egoist he was, assumed that she emptied her stomach because of extreme nerves at meeting such an extraordinary artist. He slipped off his shoes and—at someone's suggestion—had the entire mess enclosed in a clear Plexiglas box and titled *Le Gag*. Veruca funded the project, of course, and within moments an extremely embarrassing situation for anyone less charmed made her the newest toast of the celebrity art scene.

Now Beatrice snapped back to attention and nodded to Veruca, who continued, "After a bit of time, I've realized that the art world is my calling. I fit in there. I love it. And, actually, that's why I transferred here. I feel like I need to develop some New York legitimacy, you know? I need people like your sister and parents—real artists and historians—to take me seriously."

Beatrice doubted *that* would ever happen and, for a moment, she almost felt bad for the girl. Was this perfect specimen wandering around feeling less than immortal?

"The point is that, well, you know a lot about art, right?"

Beatrice shrugged and nodded simultaneously, the universal humble bob.

"And you obviously can write. I mean, you're a journalism and literature major?"

"Well, you know. I guess some people say I can sort of—"

"And we're around the same age, so you know something about my world and what it's like to be in your twenties? About music and fashion and beauty? You know about that stuff, right? I've heard that you used to go out a lot."

"You heard from who?"

"Just around."

Beatrice shared a love of clothing with her mother. They stared longingly through Barneys windows on a regular basis. Her father was music obsessed, so some of that information penetrated. Gertie—with her signature crimson lips—had taught her a thing or two about beauty. Dolly kept her abreast of gossip and, of course, any dance trends. And Beatrice had, at one time in late high school, frequented "listy" art bars, until inevitable boredom set in with the same crowd that clustered every night. Finally, one day she went to retrieve her forgotten credit card from a club. What she saw was a glimpse behind the Emerald City's curtain: Empty and brightly lit, the space was just an elaborate set with gum spots and sticky floors. Without carefully considered lighting and the snaking line to bypass outside, the illusion of exclusive possibility was gone. Right then, she gave up on that scene and instead resolved to prove to her parents and herself that she could be a serious student.

Veruca cleared her throat, recapturing Beatrice's attention. "I'd like to start a blog is the thing because, well, you're no one without one these days." Veruca studied Beatrice carefully as she spoke, those strange gray and yellow eyes searching for the right route inside. "But I'm not much for writing, so I thought . . . well, I wondered . . . if you might consider writing the blog for me."

Beatrice was flattered, but the idea also made her panic. She rifled through potential pitfalls: What about school? What about figuring out what to do after graduation? What about her toxic dump of an apartment?

Ever the mind reader, Veruca continued, "Of course, I would compensate you well, very well. And that way, by next year, maybe you could afford to move into your own apartment instead of moving back home? It's . . . what do they call it?" Veruca narrowed her eyes, perplexed for a moment, and then brightened: " 'Mutually beneficial!' What do you think? Don't say no!"

Beatrice was stunned. It was like a job, right? That was all. And it was a writing job, which was supposedly what she wanted. Even as her brain rationalized the plan, her willful lips parted and out shot the words "I'm not sure."

"You could stay here too instead of in that horrid basement closet you mentioned. I have an extra room, which is just beautiful! Kelly Wearstler designed it! It's a no-brainer, right?"

"Oh, Veruca, I couldn't. I mean, that's too much."

"You don't understand," said Veruca, an immobilizing hand still resting on Beatrice's robed shoulder. "I wouldn't be doing you a favor. I'd actually need to keep you close. How else would you learn the ins and outs of my daily life to blog about my—well, *our*—exploits?"

Beatrice didn't know what to say. Then she remembered the others. How would she bear hanging around Veruca's friends? They were quite the catty clique and she had no interest in re-living seventh grade. Beatrice was proud of having grown beyond the desire to blend and conform. She was an adult now with—albeit largely inherited—good values. She worked hard to avoid being impressed by status, which seemed to be this crew's lifeblood. Beatrice ran a thumb over a chipped red fingernail and considered peeling the polish off in lieu of making a decision, yet another habit she needed to break. "Where are Kendra and your friends, the model and the sweater vest guy?" she asked.

"They're not always here, silly." Veruca grimaced. "Honestly, between you and me, the three of them have been annoying me. Sometimes you need a little space, right?" More relevant words had never been spoken to Beatrice. The media princess continued her spin: "Anyway, you think on this. I don't want to push you. I just thought that it might solve both our problems, you know? And this way you could have all the spa treatments you need!"

Beatrice managed a smile at the word "need." In Veruca's world, people had certain inalienable rights: air, food, equality, and oxygen facials.

10

SKIN AGLOW AND BACK IN HER REGULAR—and now somehow too shabby for her face—clothing, Beatrice walked downtown on Broadway until she hit 79th Street and turned left toward
Central Park. She'd left the Dorchester with the express intent of
buying cleaning supplies, but instead she'd wandered past the
market. There was probably no 409 cleaner powerful enough to
combat her mess anyway, unless they made a Prozac-infused version that she could sniff. She considered hiring one of those
companies that clean up after murder scenes. Someone surely
expired in her apartment at *some* point.

The youngest Bernstein weighed her options. She could either hope that the housing department decided to be more reasonable—or that a broom closet opened up on a higher floor—or
she could take Veruca up on her offer: a lovely vermin-free room
and the promise of enough money for Beatrice's own place after
graduation.

But neither path seemed conducive to actually finishing
school. There was barely enough light downstairs to read a book,
even if she could get past the whole creepy-crawly factor. And, at
Veruca's, did anyone actually take courses? The socialite had
walked in and out of the Latin American Literature classroom
the day before as if she made appearances at her leisure. The professor was so impressed by her sheer presence that Beatrice wondered if Veruca and her crew got away with creating their own

"correspondence courses." What was tall, silent Imelda studying anyway: sign language? Her participation grades couldn't be good. Maybe there was a modeling major that Beatrice didn't know about.

She reached 79th and Columbus and took a deep breath. The sky was a faded denim blue. The air was crisp and slightly biting, a whisper of coolness to remind the citizens of New York that fall was officially on its way. Leaves creaked and shuddered in the breeze, their discolored edges hinting at future yellow, red, and purple incarnations. Soon, beautiful autumn days like this would give way to slushy sidewalks and yellow dog urine–sprayed snow, freezing-cold air blowing in off the Hudson River, the festive lights and jingling bells of the holidays from Thanksgiving to Hanukkah—and the Christmas music that made her father grumble.

As children, Beatrice and her friends were escorted by their parents to this spot by the Museum of Natural History each year on the night before "Turkey Day" to watch men scurry to inflate enormous Snoopy and Big Bird balloons for the Macy's Thanksgiving Day Parade. As she got older, Beatrice loved going on her own too, as she was sure to run into neighborhood friends—and perhaps even her latest crush—clustering on the surrounding sidewalk. They'd sit on cold curbs and stoops and feign less investment than they felt in the cute boys with toothy grins and floppy hair, who skateboarded around in circles and affectionately pegged them with rolled-up balls of aluminum foil from recently devoured street pretzels.

The next morning on Thanksgiving Day, the Bernstein sisters woke up and drank cinnamon-flavored Mexican hot chocolate (of course, not run-of-the-mill powder stuff) and watched the parade on TV. After seeing those men working all night, the sisters, in the manner of possessed sports fans, would root for the balloons to stay afloat.

Today, Beatrice trudged into Central Park on her way to Fifth Avenue and, like a rat in a maze, twice took a bike path loop that spit her out where she started, back on the Upper West Side. Finally, she made it to her far-flung destination on the Upper East: the Metropolitan Museum of Art.

Each time Beatrice walked up the Met's steps and—a little winded—waltzed through the front doors past bag check, she felt like she was returning home. Despite frantic museumgoers all around her colliding like ants as they struggled to decipher gallery maps, she usually experienced a wave of calm as she peered upward at the domed ceiling. But, for some reason, on this trip, she couldn't shake an ominous feeling.

Beatrice didn't need directions, but she couldn't help snagging a map. She walked over to the admission desk, made a student-sized donation, and received a green metal button bearing the letter "M," which she secured to her scooped collar. She turned left and, nodding to security, began her walk through the Egyptian corridors, feeling eerily alone. The galleries seemed unusually dim and narrow, crowded with mummified bodies. She shuddered and sped up.

"Why go to Egypt?" she heard her father exclaim, deep in the recesses of her brain.

Veering left into the Temple of Dendur, darkness gave way to blinding light. Three stories of slanted windows like an enormous skylight illuminated the large rectangular space. A shallow pool and wishing well, all sharp lines and stone, comprised one side. A bit raised, one edge of the water feature doubled as a long bench and people sat perched, sketching, eyeing the relics, or waiting for friends. A huge expanse of empty stone real estate unfolded before them, leading up to the main event: ruins of an actual ancient temple and shrine.

Usually, Beatrice felt comforted by this favorite contemplative spot, but today the artifact's protective statues—ones she hardly remembered seeing before—leered at her. Two side by side looked particularly threatening and she read their descriptive wall text in an effort to squelch a mounting irrational fear. The goddess Sakhmet had the head of a lioness and a feline mane and "represented violence, illness, and unexpected disaster." Beatrice swallowed hard, a shock of heat spreading across the back of her neck. Why did she feel like she was Sakhmet's next sacrifice? She could almost feel the presence of something unearthly close to her, creeping up until it grabbed her. In actuality, someone did grab her for the second time that week and she jumped straight up, releasing a high-pitched Chihuahua yelp.

She whirled around. Yet again, the culprit was hardly mysterious. A security guard—broad and imposing in an official navy blue uniform—stood impatiently behind her. He was unfazed by her scream, but a nearby nanny hurried her two-year-old towheaded charge away in the opposite direction. "You can't touch the artwork," the guard commanded. "Step away from the statues."

Beatrice hadn't realized she was standing so close. Of course, she knew better than to touch the art. "Sorry," she muttered, but he was already walking away, stuffing a headphone bud into his ear. Was he listening to instructions from some hidden boss or— from the beat she heard faintly—to Kanye West?

Beatrice took a deep breath, considered her own emotional instability, and walked up to the ledge above the dark pool in the far left-hand corner. She felt like she'd taken some kind of hallucinogenic drug. Maybe she needed water. Veruca's aesthetician had strongly urged her to hydrate, as she'd released unwanted toxins. So how come she couldn't exorcise these bad vibes?

As Beatrice sat waiting for an epiphany, she peeled off the rest of her nail polish, scraps of bloodred lacquer fluttering to the floor. She never would have guessed just days before, flu-ridden and bored in her childhood bedroom, that she could feel so unhinged. Veruca's solution was the only viable alternative. The sun slid behind a cloud, shrouding the space in shadow. The room grew colder by degrees. The "Axis of Evil," as she'd dubbed Dreyfus, Kendra, and Imelda, seemed to be on the outs and Veruca had proved to be nothing but lovely. Still, independence was the one thing Beatrice craved most. Would she be giving that up to be part of some entourage?

Since she couldn't decide, she made a wish in the fountain instead. She pulled a penny from her overstuffed wallet and held it tightly in her fist. She closed her eyes, feeling the metal against her skin, and murmured quietly, "I wish that . . . I could find the best possible solution to my living situation." And, with that, she tossed the coin in the pool. It made a gratifying splash as it hit the water and sank to the bottom like a sonic sedative.

The act was so cathartic that Beatrice began searching her bag for more coins and throwing them frantically into the fountain with sometimes contradictory wishes (always recited out loud): "I wish I knew what to do with my life. I wish that I saw my world in Technicolor instead of beige. I wish that I was content instead of bored. I wish that Gertie would try another lipstick color. I wish that Wolf Blitzer was on TV less often. I wish that Dolly would dance her way to whatever stage she pleases. I wish I lived in the Met in the Temple of Dendur. I wish that I could package melancholy, nostalgia, and crushes and pull them out whenever I needed them. I wish that I didn't live in a roach motel. I wish that my last boyfriend hadn't been exactly like the boyfriend before him but with worse hair. I wish that murderer guy from the other night wasn't such an ass. I wish I wasn't such an ass. I wish that fall days like this one lasted longer. I wish that my hair was a warmer hue. I wish that I will one day win a Pulitzer Prize, if I ever actually write anything. I wish for world peace like all the pageant queens. I wish that world peace had been my first wish. I wish that the Hudson River was clean and we could spend summer days wading in it. I wish that root beer and french fries were health foods. I wish that the walls of this building never crumble. I wish that my world always smelled like gardenias and roasted chestnuts. I wish that dressing in all fleece wasn't a sign of depression. I wish I was more like my family. I wish I was less like my family. I wish that that silly-looking five-year-old over there with the huge ears and the soulful blue eyes would get his wish. I wish that the color green would—"

"Bea? Bea Bernstein?" a voice above her called. She was about to snap, "I'm busy" because she truly felt that she was otherwise engaged, but then she realized how crazy she looked. She was sitting on the floor by the fountain and had emptied her sizable brown leather hobo purse of all its contents. And she did not clean out her bags regularly. Once she had gone through the pennies, she'd thrown in quarters, dimes, nickels, and even any Canadian coins that inexplicably appeared in her wallet. At this moment, pre-interruption, she was feverishly searching for any change she could find. She even briefly considered throwing in a dust-covered strawberry Mento.

She looked up hesitantly, fearful of who might have witnessed this display. Her worst concerns realized, she found herself peering up at a perplexed Mabel Palmer. Mabel had been a very close friend in elementary school, after which they'd gone to separate schools. They'd always lived in the same neighborhood, though, and their parents remained best buds. She and Mabel had some friends in common and bumped into each other socially throughout the years, smoking in Riverside Park or at debauched house

parties on the Upper East Side. Mabel's parents made Beatrice's
family look mainstream. They had turned their brownstone's
backyard into a vegetable garden and compost area in which they
grew all their own produce. They didn't believe in designer jeans,
gluten, or cable. They did, however, believe in peaceful protests
and boatloads of kale, which Beatrice once regularly ate for Mabel, when her parents weren't looking.

Mabel wore baggy boyfriend jeans, an oversized Che T-shirt,
and not a stitch of makeup and still looked unbelievably beautiful, her black bob—offsetting porcelain skin—so shiny it reflected light. Beatrice began to throw items haphazardly back
into her purse. She liked Mabel a lot, but she always seemed so
impossibly together.

"I . . . I couldn't find . . . my ChapStick. I was just searching."
She scurried to her feet, praying that Mabel wouldn't report this
odd meeting to her parents.

"Oh, were you going to throw the ChapStick in too?" Apparently Mabel had been watching for a while, as had that same security guard. He was eyeing Beatrice like she was about to chisel
a chunk off the temple or pull out a can of spray paint and tag. "I
thought maybe this was a performance art piece, but then I
didn't see any video cameras or anything." Mabel was joking, but
Beatrice couldn't bring herself to muster a smile.

"Sorry—ha—yeah, I'm a little . . . out of sorts." The girls exchanged a kiss on the cheek in belated greeting.

"Yeah, your mother told my mother you'd been sick. Are you
back at school yet?"

"I am, yeah." Beatrice sighed, flung her bag over her shoulder, and toyed with the strap.

"So, senior year, huh? It's crazy, right? I can't even believe it's
already here. Like, what now?"

Beatrice relaxed a little. "Tell me about it. I feel like I complained for years about homework, cruel professors, and classes and now I'm like, um, can I please stay for longer?"

"You like it that much?"

"No. I just don't know what to do next. I'll probably just move back in with my parents and get my substitute-teaching credentials. What about you?"

"Honestly, I wish I was content to stick around school for longer—it would make my parents less worried, I bet. But I'm so itchy to get going and actually do something in the world that I'm graduating a semester early and joining the revolution in Chiapas. Well, technically, first I'm heading down to Panama to build houses for Habitat for Humanity with my boyfriend, Raul. I met him at a Darfur protest last May. He's hot, I'm not gonna lie." She giggled. "We're contemplating the Peace Corps, but, you know, that takes a while to process. But, wow, that is so great that you have such a practical plan, substitute teaching and all. I'm sure your parents will be thrilled to have you back. I know how much they like to keep you close!"

Beatrice slumped a little lower with each passing word, but she nodded. Inwardly, she berated herself for feeling envious, but there was something about that sleek black hair and do-gooder dedication that just made her feel clumsy and inept. Well, *more* inept than usual.

How could someone look that good and be that well-intentioned at the same time? Was there some Change the World Workout that she'd somehow missed? She imagined Mabel leading a class littered with hand-woven macramé mats: "Lift that starving child over your head for twenty repetitions. That's it! Keep your core tight and your helping hand strong. Okay, now place the child carefully down on the mat and feed him *your* lunch. Now breathe through the starvation."

As Mabel left—presumably to save the world with some Javier

Bardem look-alike—and Beatrice slowly made her way toward the exit, the security guard tapped her on the shoulder again. "Excuse me, miss."

Beatrice froze.

"You left this on the floor over there." He handed over her Moleskine notebook with a disapproving look. She must have pulled it out when she was emptying her bag of coins. She hardly needed a reminder that she still hadn't gotten around to writing in it.

"Oh, thank you."

He left to return to his post by a white plaster column but, on second thought, turned around and said, "You really shouldn't throw Certs into the fountain."

"It was actually a Mento."

He glared.

"Noted."

As she moved to return the book to her purse, it seemed almost to jump from her hands. It hit the floor with a loud smack, narrowly missing the pool. The guard shook his head and stalked away. She shrugged apologetically. Embarrassment was becoming her default state.

As she knelt down to grab the blank notebook, she noticed some unfamiliar scribbling inside. It was open to a page right in the middle, where the binding was sewn. Words in thick blue ink read:

PAY ATTENTION: I figure whenever you're down and out, the only way is UP.

Weren't those lyrics from some musical? Why had the security guard defiled her immaculate notebook? Her father's chiding popped into her head: "Plan on over writing in this thing?" At least someone had. Was this stranger trying to encourage her? She glanced toward him and smiled, but he only rolled his eyes.

When Beatrice turned back to the notebook, she found herself face-to-face with a statue. It sat, previously unnoticed, at floor level inside the water itself. It was a crocodile, which, for the Egyptians, the description explained, "embodied the essence of evil."

11

AS SHE WALKED HOME, all the hot dog vendors in New York seemed to call Beatrice's name in harmonized singsong voices like modern-day nymphs and seductive sirens. After drowning her sorrows in four soft pretzels with mustard and a hot dog (how could she reject those beautiful voices?), Beatrice was once again back in her crypt, deep below ground and the rest of humankind, nursing blisters from her Converse sneakers. She lay in her bed in a bra and cotton heart underwear, the first ones she could reach in her suitcase. As much as she didn't like the idea of exposing her skin to the room's elements, it was insanely hot during the day down in the depths of hell. It occurred to her that singing bartenders bearing cold alcoholic drinks might have more successfully numbed the pain.

The oddest thing, though. She grabbed her Moleskine notebook from her bag and opened it again to the page with the security guard's message (or maybe Dolly had written the note earlier to cheer her up?). But no matter how many times she flipped through the pages, she couldn't find any writing except her own scribbled name at the front, which made her think about the bird crap that had also mysteriously disappeared. Maybe the ultrathin pages were simply stuck together. For now, she put it aside.

For once, her surroundings seemed fitting. She felt lower than low, so why not live that way? She had almost—*almost*—managed to romanticize the studio: It helped if she pretended that she was living through an apocalypse. Then she could reason, "I'm just lucky to be alive amid all these organisms that can reproduce and repopulate the earth. I'm like Noah and this basement is my ark." But the thought of there being two of every animal (two giant roaches, two newspaper creatures, two whatever she saw flying around the shower this morning) was actually pretty horrifying.

Maybe if she pretended it was the Blitz. She was just hiding down here through the bombing, which was easily simulated by the sounds of clomping feet above. But that rationale didn't work either: Beatrice did a terrible British accent.

At least she had made a decision: She would turn Veruca down and spend all her free time finding something meaningful to do with her life. The idea of substitute teaching and living with her parents wouldn't cut it. Plus, her metabolism wouldn't remain so speedy forever and she was starting to emotionally eat. The only thing worse than living as an adult with her parents would be living at home as a morbidly obese adult, lapping up Daddy's Soup Surprise from a trough.

As she stared at the cracked ceiling, she could hear her mother's voice: "Look, Sweet Bea. If you want to be a writer, you need to teach. It's like waitressing and acting, but hopefully more fulfilling. Unless they're quite famous, almost everyone who claims to be a writer is supporting him- or herself as a teacher, ideally a tenured college professor. So you might as well start early, because you can always write later. And that's a fact."

In high school, Beatrice's social life had definitely taken precedence. As the younger child with a literary genius for a sibling, she could never quite catch up at home. She was always the least informed and, though they may not have meant it unkindly, her parents and Gertie tended to laugh at her gaps in knowledge. She felt like the weak link in the Bernsteins' evolutionary chain. With her peers, though, she was comparatively precocious and in many ways among the most advanced. Naturally, she preferred to spend time with friends, vacuuming up as much positive attention—and tallboys of beer in Riverside Park—as possible.

And yet she'd spent the last few years trying to convince her family that she could hold her own among them, hanging mostly with Dolly and a few intelligent others and pushing through college in a comparatively tame, single-minded fashion. All to get where? She pulled out a cheek gloss compact from her makeup bag and checked herself out. Apparently, her "image" was developing a blemish at the bridge of her small, straight nose. Maybe she would join the Peace Corps with Mabel.

Exhausted from carbo loading, her eyelids drooped and she drifted to sleep thinking about her unplanned future, World War II, and hot dog vendors. How much was a hot dog cart anyway? She would run numbers in the morning.

That night, Beatrice dreamed she was hanging out in a living room with friends, when she realized that she needed to retrieve something from her brown leather purse. She found it perched upon an enormous metal bed in an adjoining, otherwise empty bedroom. The duvet's pattern looked Egyptian. She instinctively knew that this was her space. A few panels of sunlight fell across the bed, but when she looked up, the windows were only very narrow prison slits. She was opening her bag to search for a Mento when, abruptly, an enormous cockroach the size of a Mounds bar poked its head out the top. And, when she shrieked and threw the purse back on the bed, more dirty brown insects began to follow, until streams of thousands piled out, scurrying desperately on top of each other and all over her, tentacles interlocking and sticking.

Beatrice started awake in a cold sweat with no sense of time and a need to escape. She jumped down from the top bunk, turning her ankle and squealing in pain. She threw on the closest pair of shoes and a jacket and ran across the room, startling even the creepy-crawlies—who were just trying to get some sleep—out of restful slumbers. Then she sprinted upstairs toward Dolly's apartment, slamming the door behind her. Everything in the basement shifted imperceptibly and then settled down again.

Opening the door onto the first floor was like coming up for air while drowning. Beatrice took a gasping breath before steadying herself and heading to find her friend. The lights were dim, so it was probably still the middle of the night. She didn't dare take the elevator.

At Dolly's, Beatrice knocked quietly and then a bit more insistently until she heard someone stir. Her friend came to the door and, after turning numerous locks, opened it, curly hair pulled back and white pimple cream dotting her face.

"Bea, oh my God," she whispered. "Is everything okay? What time is it?"

"I have no idea and, hell no, it's not okay. There are thousands of cockroaches crawling out of my purse and then I turned my ankle and it sounded like the Blitz and I just can't go on pretending that it's the apocalypse, you know?"

Dolly couldn't even pretend to understand, but she took her friend's hand and led her inside. "Okay, okay. Calm down, Bea. Everything is going to be fine. You can sleep here."

Dolly led Beatrice into the small loft with a finger to her lips to urge quiet. Her roommate was down for the count, a freckle-faced being in a Hello Kitty nightgown, twisted from sleep. (Beware of twenty-year-old women who wear cartoon pajamas.) The space between the two single beds was just big enough for Beatrice, so Dolly threw down a few blankets and one of her pillows and climbed back into bed. "Nice shoes, by the way," she noted.

Beatrice looked down. She'd slipped on a pair of glittery high heels from last year's New Year's Eve, certainly an odd match with her bra and underwear and navy blue toggle peacoat. She'd unpacked them earlier that day while searching in her boxes for sneakers. No wonder running up the steps was such a struggle. "At least they're a pair."

She shed her coat and shoes and collapsed on the floor, likely red wine–, beer-, and ramen-soaked from twenty-something dwellers past. A week ago that might have seemed like a mildly disgusting prospect, but not now. Beatrice noticed a Xeroxed invitation to some dance performance on Dolly's bedside table. She'd written a to-do list down the left side in blue ink. Was that the same blue ink from the Moleskine notebook?

In the dark, Beatrice whispered, "Hey, Doll?"

"Yeah, Bea?"

"Did you write me a note in blue pen in my Moleskine?"

"What?"

"A note—something about 'the only way is up'?"

"In your notebook? No. I wouldn't dare touch that sacred thing." She paused for a beat. "But it does seem like good advice."

"I guess it does." Beatrice fell asleep.

No sooner had she drifted off, however, than she felt an odd pressure on her back, followed by a crushing pain and a scream—from someone else. She sat up disoriented, pushing off whatever weight rested on her back. She was about to scream herself, when she noticed that the other shrieks hadn't stopped. She was going to have to stop waking up this way.

"Calm down. Calm down!" she heard Dolly beg, as she flipped on the light. Beatrice clutched her lower back in pain, as the pale roommate, Marcy, huddled in a corner, shaking. Dolly tangoed over to Marcy. "It's okay. This is my best friend, Beatrice. She just needed a place to stay for the night. Sorry, I didn't want to wake you, so I didn't tell you. It was *unexpected*."

There was that word again.

Marcy continued to shiver. "It's so crowded in here," she whispered almost inaudibly, tears gathering in her eyes. "It's too much. It's too much." The crumpled Hello Kitty nightgown folded into frowns, the character's mouthless head quivering with Marcy's every breath.

Dolly and Beatrice locked eyes. "Sorry," mouthed Dolly, and a moment later Beatrice was back out in the building's hallway in her underwear, jacket, and party shoes, only this time she wasn't alone. Hearing a commotion, other residents had gathered and figured it was a buildingwide party. One bearded guy—who was up anyway thanks to insomnia—was already preparing "magic" weed-filled brownies in the kitchen. In Goth Girl's apartment, a few of the self-dubbed "Black-Lipstick Ladies" were researching ghost stories from tattered Wiccan texts.

Just Beatrice's incredible luck, among the hall's awakened hordes stood her attacker, the Cockroach Slayer, smug in all his perfectly scruffy five-o'clock-shadowed glory. Tempted out of his studio by the ruckus, he was shirtless in only a pair of beat-up jeans, clearly thrown on in a hurry. She suddenly recalled her open jacket and, pulling it protectively shut, restrained herself from checking him out, willing her focus downward toward the ugly carpet. Jesus. He even had nice feet! He looked her up and down and grinned. "Pretty impressive scream. Spotted another Peeping Tom?"

Beatrice looked to the stucco ceiling, cursed her fate, and returned his gaze. "Actually, the scream belonged to a different lunatic, thank you."

"Oh. See, I figured since you're wearing another one of your signature sexy outfits, someone probably couldn't resist spying on you. Unique. Really."

Her already blushing cheeks flushed redder, but she managed to stand up tall and announce to him and the other seemingly bodiless hovering faces still looking on in curiosity, "I apologize if I've woken you up. It was all a big misunderstanding. I just needed somewhere to sleep and I guess I made Marcy scream, but—"

"Wait," said a blond woman in a turtlenecked, long-sleeved, plaid flannel nightgown like something out of *Little House on the Prairie*. "You snuck into someone else's room and just went to sleep there?"

The bearded guy next to her nodded. "I heard that she climbed into bed with Marcy on accident, thinking this was her apartment, because of all the crack she does. I heard she was packing heat."

"I think I read that in *Us Weekly*!" chimed another.

The hallway was suddenly abuzz with rumors and speculation. People immediately ran to their laptops and searched the situation on Perez Hilton and TMZ. Of course, there was already coverage absent substantive information:

> *A nameless faceless girl snuck into another nameless faceless girl's room, reportedly thanks to crack use. All this, just a few floors away from the apartment of our favorite charmed socialite, Veruca Pfeffernoose! Lock your doors, V-Pfeff! Little Miss Drug Addict Psycho is on the loose, ready to pull yet another Robert Downey Jr., if you're not careful.*

"No, no!" scrambled Beatrice. "I didn't sneak in. I was invited. I'm not on crack."

"That's what addicts always say, right? It's just sad," lamented the blond girl, huddling with arms crossed over her nightgown. "Did you ever watch *Intervention*?"

Beatrice hung her head and promptly gave up. She limped toward the basement door, high heels rubbing her feet rawer.

"Hey, you can sneak into my bed anytime," said a voice to her left. Hormone Guy was leaning against the wall, thrusting suggestively with his pelvis, though—truth be told—there wasn't much to brag about.

Beatrice hugged her jacket around her. The Cockroach Slayer looked after her and called, "Are you okay, Basement Lady?" But, after all the teasing and crack accusations, she mistook his concern for sarcasm. She needed to get downstairs before he and the others saw tears start plummeting down her face in mass suicide. She kept her back to him. "I'm great, actually. Thank you for asking."

"One thing, Basement Lady."

She turned tentatively to face him. "What?"

"I'm pretty sure your sparkly shoes are on the wrong feet."

She looked down and sure enough she'd put the heels on wrong. No wonder they hurt so much. But there was no way she'd let any of these people see her discomfort. She turned around and continued hobbling down the corridor, which of course grew longer with every step, past a room from which strange chants emanated. As the apartment door was ajar, she heard Goth Girl begin a story: "It was a dark and stormy night, when a woman went to live in the basement—" Beatrice caught a glimpse of a ceremonial circle inside. For a moment, she almost stopped, as she could have sworn she spotted Imelda. But then she shook her head. On top of everything, she was obviously delusional. Imelda and the rest of the Axis of Evil wouldn't be caught dead here in an average apartment with a bunch of plebeian weirdos chanting spells. Beatrice limped her way to the basement door, which for once she was glad to see.

12

BEATRICE WOKE UP WITH EYES SO SWOLLEN from crying that she could hardly open them. She'd burst into tears as soon as the basement door closed behind her, the dripping of the broken air conditioner almost comforting. She cried about Mabel and about Hormone Guy and Goth Girl (who she thought would make a lovely couple), her unfinished homework, missed classes, uncertain future, ruined oxygen facial (because no amount of oxygen could refresh these new and improved cavernous dark circles), Dolly's comfy room just out of reach, unreturned phone calls from her parents, wasted years of schooling, blisters on her heels, nightmares about bugs, clothing she was afraid to unpack, her own self-pity, the fact that the hateful Cockroach Slayer didn't want to be her Peeping Tom (not that she *cared*), and that she hadn't been wearing a cute matching bra and underwear set when she accidentally flashed him. Maybe he hadn't seen her ridiculous heart-covered cotton undies. She cried for the cockroach's family, who might be wondering where he went, for other lonely people, and for dilapidated basements everywhere, storing seldom-used rusty bikes and broken washing machines that frowned from sad neglect.

Beatrice was reminded of her favorite childhood book, *Owl at Home,* where the owl turned his tears into tea. If her basement existed in a world like that, she could cry and cry until her tears cleaned the floors and washed away the dust and decay. She'd cry away broken pieces of forgotten objects, the newspaper creature and his newspaper shield. She'd cry so hard that the walls would begin to crack, just at the very top, so sunlight could slip in. She'd cry until the stain on the ceiling and cruddy areas on the bunk-bed mattresses washed away. Of course, her precious boxes would float safely above the fray, until the saltwater cleaning service left them unperturbed and her in her own immaculate paradise. And even though she cried so hard, her eyeliner would remain perfectly applied. That's what would happen in *Owl at Home*. That's probably what would happen in Veruca's world too. And everything would smell like orange blossoms.

Beatrice's cell phone began to ring. The word MOM blinked on the screen. She grabbed the PDA gingerly to make sure it wasn't hot, looked to the laminated map for courage, and steeled herself for the conversation. Even the toughest cookie is unhinged by the sound of her mother's voice.

"Hi, Mom."

"Hi, Sweet Bea! How are you?"

"I'm fine. Just"—she looked around the room—"lying in bed."

"In bed? Really? Shouldn't you be out and about? So how's everything going?"

Beatrice opened her mouth to mutter "Fine" or even "Great," but the words caught and she felt that, if she spoke, she might cry another pot of tea.

"Bea? Are you there? The thing is that I saw Diane yesterday. She said that Mabel ran into you at the Met and that you seemed distracted, so I was wondering if maybe you're overworked?"

Damn Mabel.

"Anyway, Sweet Bea, I just wanted to touch base. You know,

your father and I are really proud of you, so don't stress. And if you're in the neighborhood, come say hi. You don't have to limit yourself to Thursday night dinners. Of course, I'm at the museum during the week, but your father would love to see you and help you think through any creative quandaries. He's working on this new series and it's really fascinating. I know he'd love to show it to you. Are you still there?"

"Yes, Mom. Still here," said Beatrice. She was ready to confess it all, to ask for help, to cry "Mercy!" "The thing is, Mom, things have been—"

"What? Are you kidding me? I didn't approve this essay for the catalog. This show never sat well with me. This is a disaster. And that's a fact. Get the head of the board on the phone immediately! Then get me the Netherlands' minister of culture!"

It took Beatrice a few moments to realize that her mother's admonishment was not directed at her, but the outburst was enough to dampen her emotional meltdown. Asking her parents for help was not the answer.

"Look, Beatrice, I need to go. I'll call you later though, okay? The point is that, if you're really overwhelmed at school, your father and I think you should just move back in with us. Stay close to home. Have some Daddy's Soup Surprise. We all know that you're easily thrown off course and we're wondering if maybe you can't quite handle the pressure. And that's fine because we're not all cut out to be students, but—"

"I'm fine, Mom," snapped Beatrice. Despite all her hard work, their perception of her hadn't changed an iota. "When I saw Mabel, I'd just forgotten to eat lunch."

"Oh. Well, I'll have your father send you some tamari rice cakes from the Japanese grocery because you need to eat healthfully. Brain food! And that's a fact. Love you madly!"

Beatrice pressed the red button on her BlackBerry to end the call and then sat up resolutely. She was on a mission to uncover a map to her future and, while the destination remained fuzzy, she now understood exactly where her path began. It was marked with a hot pink X in her mind. Sometimes when you're down and out, the only way is UP.

13

"DOES THIS MEAN YOU'RE IN? Tell me this means that you're in!"

An attempted shower, hair brushing, and blind dressing later, Beatrice stood—in matching shoes on the correct feet—upstairs in Veruca's great room. The socialite appeared in her usual immaculate garb (jeans lacquered on, an oversized cotton T-shirt softer than a baby's cheek, and leather shoes, possibly made from one). Spotting Beatrice, she squealed mildly, a contradiction executable only by her.

Beatrice nodded. "I'm in, if the offer still stands."

"It stands! I think this is *absolutely* the right thing. Honestly? I was just beyond worried about you." Veruca linked her arm through Beatrice's and guided her new houseguest/employee in repetitive circles about the room like they were a pair of restless nineteenth-century parlor women. Odd as it was to be strolling around someone's living room, any residual doubts were swept from Beatrice's sooty sleep-deprived mind.

"I want you to know, you'll have plenty of alone time to do whatever you academic types do. The ground rules are simple: Never be dull and never listen to Miley Cyrus. She and I do *not* get along." Just as Beatrice began to wonder if Mr. Darcy was going to appear, Veruca flopped onto the ottoman and pulled Beatrice down beside her. "I'm just so relieved you're out of that rat-infested janitor's closet. I mean, what is that about? I can't even believe it was legal for them to place you below the stairs."

Something itched at the back of Beatrice's brain. For an instant, she wondered if Veruca—with her seemingly endless power—could have simply cajoled the Housing Office or landlord into moving Beatrice to a different apartment. That *would* be a lot to ask from a virtual stranger, though. If Veruca chose to come to Beatrice's aid by hiring her as a writer because the situation benefited her too, it was fair. "So, I guess I should go get my stuff?"

"Oh, don't be silly, Beany Baby." Veruca giggled, her laugh so like a spoon tapped against crystal that Beatrice looked for a groom to smooch. "Your stuff—whatever you want to keep of it—is already here."

"Whatever I want to keep of it? Don't you at least need my keys?" Beatrice had gotten dressed in her room just fifteen minutes before. How could everything have made it here in that time? Veruca must have been mistaken.

Veruca waved her questions off. "Well, don't look so shocked. I had a feeling you'd come around! Let Penelope show you to your new abode."

The portly young woman from the spa with thick black hair pulled back in a bun appeared before them in full maid's uniform—with beautiful avant-garde detailing designed by the Rodarte sisters—and waited to escort her. Beatrice rose to follow, clutching her trusty brown leather purse. She felt she was standing on a precipice. One false step and she'd fall down the rabbit hole. Suddenly, she was struck with a paranoid thought. "Hey, Veruca, how'd you know that my room was a janitor's closet? I don't remember telling you that."

"Oh, you didn't! But Dolly told me all about it. Don't you dare get mad at her. She was just concerned. And, for the bazillionth time, call me V."

That made sense. And so few things did these days.

"Spa water?" offered Penelope. Beatrice smiled—no, grinned—for the first time in what seemed like forever. Maybe living at Veruca's would in fact be "just beyond" to use the socialite's own words. Beatrice just couldn't decline.

14

AS IT HAPPENED, "awesome" was the most appropriate word to describe Beatrice's new room, which was more like a loft apartment than the Dorchester's actual "lofts." A large open floor plan was flanked on one end by a kitchen with a floating granite island. (When it comes to kitchens, granite is a precious stone.) The living area was sparsely decorated with Beatrice's favorite Eames leather lounge chairs and a simple comfy couch—the kind into which one could happily sink for entire lethargic Sundays—with a chenille throw or two and some mod patterned pillows in Beatrice's favorite coral and green tea shades. On the glass-topped Noguchi coffee table, magazines—like *Teen Vogue, Elle, Allure, Nylon, Paper, The New Yorker,* and *Us Weekly*—were fanned out.

Beatrice threw herself down on the plush memory-foam bed and was instantly swallowed whole by pillows, blankets, and a comforter stuffed with down from a golden goose. Her parents subscribed to principles of rigid minimalism, so this Hollywood movie bed with enough pillows to render sleep impractical was novel. On the wall behind her head and beside a bronze pharmacy desk lamp was a lighting design system with labeled buttons and a remote for various states of rest or unrest: Reading in Bed, Entertaining in Bed (with body-flattering lights to disguise any imperfections depending on time of day), Thinking in Bed, Sleeping in Bed, Bad Back in Bed, Postnightmare in Bed,

Nauseous in Bed from Hangover or Stomach Flu, Tossing & Turning in Bed, and, finally, Snoozing Postalarm in Bed. (A junior designer at the firm created the labels just after a Chinese food lunch and, having thoroughly enjoyed adding "in bed" to the end of each diner's fortune, had unconsciously continued the game.) There was even a button tagged Pondering the Universe in Bed. Intrigued, Beatrice pressed it. The ceiling parted to reveal a skylight for stargazing. A booming planetarium voice could be turned on or off, depending on whether the viewer wanted instruction on the solar system.

Beatrice leaped up to explore the rest. A work area—with a Lucite desk, a red Jieldé Signal lamp, ergonomic office chair, and birch shelves filled with thesauruses and resource books from art catalogs to self-help "classics" like *What Color Is Your Parachute?* and *He's Just Not That Into You*—was sleek and offered every dreamy Apple accessory. A fireplace stocked with maple and cedar logs had a remote control. Wild blackberry candles and, yes, red currant–scented diffuser bottles with long wooden reeds poking out created a not-too-intense tangy fragrance. This, combined with a pervasive scent of roasting sugar-covered peanuts, smelled like Thanksgiving at home. The palatial bathroom contained a "chromotherapy-mood" bathtub that changed colors depending on the user's current mind state: blue for calm, red for hot and bothered or angry, as the case may be, and purple for a sense of superiority. Beatrice discovered that she need only mutter the name of a song quietly into the air and music would begin to play.

But it was the view that blew Beatrice's mind most of all: Floor-to-ceiling windows comprised one wall and, though the natural landscape was none too shabby, with grand buildings stretching toward the sky, Riverside Park, and the Hudson River, the room seemed to hover on a plane high above its actual third-floor roost. Of course, that wasn't possible, Beatrice told herself, but she could have sworn she was looking down from a height not unlike her childhood twelfth-floor perch. Next to the window, more switches were labeled with sound machine options: Rain, Ocean, Babbling Brook, Frogs, Slide Show. But when Beatrice flipped each one, it created not only the sound track of a given weather phenomenon, creature, or environment, but also— through some fabulous projection trick, she assumed—changed the landscape outside too. Rain sent water running down the windowpanes and turned the sky a dark, threatening gray. The Ocean setting's view was of sand and sea, and the ground seemed much closer, as if the entire building had transformed into a Nantucket beach house. A brackish saltwater smell emanated from hidden vents. The Slide Show option featured the world's most boring professor, delivering the driest lecture in a monotone accompanied by the dullest slides of the most uninspiring images and almost put Beatrice to sleep on her feet. It was perfect for insomniacs.

Beatrice felt like the orphaned girl in *A Little Princess,* who awakens one morning to find that crumpets, muffins, pastries, handmade tablecloths, and woven blankets have filled her drab attic room while she slept. In the story, she imagines that she's conjured it all via a dream. This too seemed unreal enough, especially when Beatrice noticed framed pictures of not just her entire family but also her deceased beloved calico cat, Olive. She was pretty sure that she hadn't packed the photo in her boxes for school, so how had Veruca found the image? She wandered into her kitchen and discovered a full bar and some favorite snacks waiting: warm Zabar's potato and spinach knishes, sticky buns, and warm salt and raisin bagels. "Eh," she reasoned, "who cares how Veruca knows?"

With that, she inhaled a sticky bun.

She also ate one of each bagel and a spinach knish, then began catching up on schoolwork. This was a huge relief, as she'd been feeling stress on a par with naked anxiety dreams about high school gym. By midafternoon, she was soaking happily in the rose-and-citrus-scented tub—which had turned a lovely shade of periwinkle to reflect her mellow state—and reading Gabriel García Márquez. Beatrice climbed out, slid one of those plush bamboo robes around her shoulders, and luxuriated in the beauty of feeling clean.

That was when she opened the wardrobe door and discovered a walk-in closet the size of her entire room at home, stocked with her clothing and also an entirely new wardrobe with myriad Christian Louboutin higher-than-high heels, edgy party frocks, jeans in every color, wash, thickness, and cut, and buttery soft tanks and T-shirts, already paired with appropriate belts and bags. Little white satin-lined drawers scented with orange blossom held an entire fall collection of new lingerie too—who knew it was seasonal?—and a rainbow assortment of Hanky Panky underwear, certainly a step up from her cotton hearts pair.

Beatrice was floored. She knew she had to return it all, but, for a moment, she allowed herself to shop her own clothing, wandering up and down the racks, pulling down knit, silk, and nylon pieces to pet and purr over. In the end, she grudgingly threw on some old stuff, which now felt like rubbish, and ventured out to thank Veruca.

Closing her bedroom door behind her, Beatrice wandered through passages she knew shouldn't exist in this small apartment space. As she understood it, this was a building full of studios and Dolly-sized "lofts." And yet these corridors appeared never-ending.

Through an accident of fate, and not a sense of direction, she finally happened upon the main room. But, jogging around the corner, she slammed hard into something and was knocked to the floor, banging her head against the wall's molding. With a hand on her head, she peered upward, realizing that she'd knocked into not something but someone. This was turning into a bad habit. Through the flash of bright light that obscured her vision appeared a hand to help her to stand. She took it, stood, and absently kept holding it as if it were an extension of her own.

Cloudy from her fall, she stared into her helper's eyes and—with a jolt—found the Cockroach Slayer staring back. "You okay?" he asked, still clutching her hand.

"Yeah, I'm . . . thanks. I'm . . . what are *you* doing here?"

"I was about to ask you the same thing. Odd place to train for a marathon, if you ask me."

"Are you guys going to just stand there holding hands or what?" Kendra's gruff complaint brought Beatrice back to reality. "I'm pretty sure she can walk again."

They dropped hands, embarrassed. At least, Beatrice was embarrassed. Her male candy striper seemed completely unfazed: "All right, Kendra. Down, girl." Then to Beatrice, "She's all bark and, well, all bite too."

Beatrice glanced at her surroundings. The infrared beam that had temporarily obscured her vision was actually a spotlight. Still anchored by the vibrating daybed, the space was being converted into what looked like a fashion show runway, as clusters of people dressed in black and wearing headsets set up chairs around a white landing strip. Imelda and Dreyfus lounged on the floor against the central ottoman, as he futzed around on a laptop and she stared into space. Kendra paced back and forth, barking degrading comments at the scurrying workers. Veruca sat smiling calmly in the midst of it all. She was curled up on the ottoman, her knees pulled up to her chest, toying with the fringe of her lightly distressed jeans and occasionally twirling a red ringlet. Today her hair was curly.

"Hi, Beany Baby! Do you like your room?" she chirped.

"Oh! So you're 'Beany Baby'?" asked her attacker/helper.

"That's the newbie," answered Dreyfus without glancing up.

Beatrice opened her mouth to protest but changed her mind and focused her attention on her hostess instead. "I love it, Veruca . . . um, V. It's just amazing. I mean, everything in it is my favorite. It's like I would have imagined it in a dream, but better. I don't know how you knew!"

"She has an uncanny knack for that kind of thing." The Cockroach Slayer shot a lopsided grin at the socialite, who winked back.

"You can ignore him. Ben's just my . . . what am I calling you these days?" Beatrice found herself secretly rooting for words like "pal" or "brother" or "first cousin."

"I'm your boy toy."

"That's right. He's my long-term boy toy. Ben, this is Beatrice. Beatrice, Ben. But I guess you've already met?"

Beatrice experienced an unsettling jolt, which was quickly washed away by fear. Had he told them all the *hilarious* story about the rabid basement dweller? Please, she prayed to some unknown entity, don't let him have mentioned the cotton underwear. "Already met?"

"Yeah. When you slammed into each other just now." Veruca tilted her head and crinkled her nose in that adorably curious way. "Is your head okay?"

"Right," confirmed Ben. "Nice to officially meet you." He offered his hand. Beatrice shook it sideways and limply without making eye contact.

"Nice to meet you," she muttered.

"Anyway, I'm so glad you love the room. I totally took color wheel cues from your wardrobe. And I hope the clothing fits because you're going to need it, like pronto. Like tonight."

As Beatrice inched closer to Veruca and lowered her voice, Kendra took a step nearer too and tilted her head in their direction. Was that a Bluetooth earpiece she was wearing or some kind of supersonic amplifier for eavesdropping? "Actually, I wanted to talk to you about that. My room is more amazing than I could ever have even wished for, but I feel like you shouldn't have to buy me clothing, you know? I really can make do. It's just . . . too much."

Veruca sighed. "Beany Baby, you silly girl, you just don't get it. I bought you that clothing because I need you to hang with me—"

"Shadow you," Kendra interrupted. "She's an employee."

Veruca shot her a menacing look that worked like an electronic dog collar: Kendra growled but retreated, attacking her BlackBerry. Apparently, Veruca ruled her roost with something more than a passive threat of lesser inclusion, exile into the world of regular folks and tap water. Beatrice was impressed. Duly noted.

"I need you to come with me to openings and parties and you're going to have to look the part. If you don't want to keep the stuff in the end, you don't have to, but then I'll just donate it anyway. Poor people need Bottega Veneta too, I guess. I mean once it's used, what else would I do with it?" Veruca's voice was firm. The subject was closed. "So, about tonight—"

"Are we going somewhere?" Beatrice had two days to complete the Latin American Literature paper that everyone else had been researching and writing for the last two weeks.

"Maldrake Maldrake Capri's opening at Argolian Gallery. Fabulous," chimed Dreyfus, straightening his bow tie. Then he squinted at his computer screen and exclaimed, "OMG! There's a crazed drug addict stalker in our apartment building!"

"Pray tell!" Veruca commanded, eyes widening in excitement. She sat up on her heels. This chick wasn't afraid of much.

"Apparently, last night some crazy girl climbed into bed with an unsuspecting dance major and was found wandering the halls afterward in some totally insane get-up, mumbling about bugs or something? Who can blame her? Those dancer guys are hot."

"It was a male dancer?"

"No. A female one. I'm just saying."

Beatrice could feel Ben's eyes boring into the side of her head. Surely someone would guess that she was involved? Her paranoia would have done Edgar Allan Poe proud. She didn't dare look in Ben's direction.

"A dance major? I hope your friend Dolly is okay," said Veruca, who at least did an impressive performance of concern.

"Oh, she's fine. Really. Actually, do you think she could join tonight? We were supposed to grab dinner."

"Oh." Veruca frowned. "Actually, I have another session scheduled for her here. It seems like such a good opportunity for her to get a leg up for that senior showcase in front of dance companies that she keeps mentioning."

"Oh! That's much more important and really sweet of you . . . V."

As Dreyfus read on about the dorm psychopath, Ben kept his head down, although Beatrice detected a smirk. As usual, Imelda was completely disinterested. She fiddled with her necklace and lit a somehow smokeless, odorless cigarette, while sitting cross-legged on the floor.

"People are so bizarre." Dreyfus laughed. Beatrice had to agree. She excused herself and headed back to her room, since it could potentially take two hours to find it. "Beware of stalker crack addicts in sparkly heels!" Dreyfus called after her.

"I'm a big girl!" Beatrice forced a laugh.

Kendra rolled her eyes and puffed out her cheeks, impersonating a fat person. "You can say that again."

Dreyfus shook his head. "Oh no, you didn't. Girl, you should talk. Rumors aren't the only things spreading lately."

Beatrice aimed to get some work done on her paper before the big night, but—faced with the maze of corridors—felt that development was unlikely. Then she noticed a small white call box camouflaged against the many-textured white-on-white Parisian wallpaper. She opened it, tentatively pressed a red button, and was surprised by an instant blaring response: "How can I help you?"

"I'm, well, it's just that I, these hallways are very—" Beatrice stuttered.

"Understood."

And within an incredibly short stretch of time, almost as inexplicable as Chinese food delivery, Penelope appeared to escort her back to her room. Beatrice thanked her profusely, but the housekeeper seemed happy to oblige, turning her back to Beatrice and leading the way. Beatrice followed, pausing surreptitiously every ten feet or so to make a tiny mark below the moldings with Stila eyeliner from her bag. She felt a bit guilty about defacing the walls, but she couldn't expect Penelope to hold her hand every time she went to her room. From now on, like Hansel and Gretel's breadcrumbs, the dark Purple Tang marks would map the way home.

15

FOR A TWENTY-SOMETHING WOMAN, making the responsible choice—between reading for work or perusing a closet full of new clothing—is next to impossible. It's a scientific fact. The brain simply won't allow it. Ultimately, Beatrice surrendered *One Hundred Years of Solitude* and slipped on everything from Prada zippered spandex leggings to cozy cashmere Vince sweaters and ethereal chiffon Narciso Rodriguez gowns. Sure, she shot guilty glances over at her book lying abandoned on the bedside table, but, while the force was strong in young Bernstein, the lure of leather accessories won out. She chose a Betsey Johnson Archive floral frock already paired with a wide black patent leather belt, black Wolford tights with a pattern so intricate that it might as well have been spun by elves, Chloé ankle boots, and her brown leather bag. Though she was starting to get the loud and clear message, Beatrice still registered surprise when a hair stylist—who bore a striking resemblance to Paul Mitchell—knocked at the door, ready to give her the perfect bed head and snip a few inches off her "drab mop."

Beatrice didn't bother to resist. Instead, she picked a different battle, coercing the hair person into canceling the makeup artist, so she could apply her own. Even cosmetic geniuses were moved to darken her eyebrows, so she evoked Groucho Marx. She brushed some light pink NARS Orgasm shadow onto her lids, lined the top with purple to make her green eyes pop, and the insides with black to enhance their catlike shape, and then threw some coral gloss on her high cheekbones and heart-shaped lips. Paul bristled at the two-minute process ("No primer? No powder? No cellular renewal serum underneath? You can never start anti-aging too early!") but ultimately admitted that, yes, she looked "darling."

The usual suspects were already in attendance in the parlor when Beatrice entered. And they all turned to look. Ben raised his eyebrows and Veruca brought a hand to her mouth. "OMG! You look adorable! I knew it. I knew it. I knew there was a beauty under there!"

"Well, look what a little TLC can do for Beany Baby's T and A," quipped Dreyfus. Even Imelda paused while inserting a marijuana breath strip—all the rage with the legalization advocates in California, never mind that she was in New York—and nodded in approval.

All was well, until Kendra's snake eyes fixed on Beatrice's brown purse, a last bastion of her old life. "What the *hell* is that *thing*?"

"Oh, just my bag. I needed to bring a pad and pencil and . . . what? It's vintage."

"So is garbage, Sweet Bea." Dreyfus smiled, unknowingly adopting her mother's nickname for her. "But that doesn't mean you should wear it."

"Unless you're Billy Lee at last year's performance art show, 'Gang-Green: Our Wasteful Society,'" corrected Veruca.

"And even then avoid trash compactors—remember?" They all winced.

"I actually bought you a digital recorder, so you don't need that pad and pencil, though I appreciate the whole old-school thang," said Veruca. "Did you see it on your desk? And I do love that bag, but did you see the other bags in your closet? The over-sized ones fit your recorder and even your new iPad."

"I did, but . . ."

How could Beatrice explain that this brown leather bag was like a security blanket, something to hold tight to as she cliff-dived into unknown waters? Something to use as a parachute, in case she belly flopped? She knew she was a traitor to her generation, a dinosaur before her twenty-second birthday, but she preferred a No. 2 pencil and a pad, heavy books over digital readers, smudgy newspapers to online editions.

Ben came to her rescue. "I like the old school too. Want to know what I don't like? Standing here waiting to leave while you all blather on about crap. Can we get out of here, since Beany Baby finally deigned to show up?" Well, he almost came to her rescue.

Veruca rose slowly and sauntered over to him like a cat ready to strike. Was she about to snap? How much dissent would she endure? "Jeez, you're so temperamental and demanding!" She winked and grabbed his arm. "I like it." The tension broke. As they led the way out of the apartment, the others gathered their coats and followed.

"Someone's on the rag," sniped Kendra. "Did he just say 'blather'?"

To her surprise, Dreyfus linked his arm through Beatrice's and retorted, "Girl, I don't care what he said. I just like to look at him. That's some serious eye candy." Then he turned to Beatrice. "Am I right, newbie?"

She smiled back. "You're right." Much as she hated to admit it, Ben was undoubtedly good to look at. At least she and Drey-fus agreed on something. As they walked out the door arm in arm, Beatrice's cell phone began to ring. Had she bothered to look, she would have seen the screen flash MOM and sent the call straight to voice mail anyway.

16

SILLY BEATRICE ASSUMED they'd be jumping in cabs or even (gasp!) on the subway to get downtown, but—while they'd never admit the fact, as it would tarnish their street cred—this crowd never set foot on public transportation. A block-long shiny black Maybach waited downstairs, at least a little less humiliating than a stretch Hummer limo. A driver in uniform came to open the door with a cap tipped so low that Beatrice wondered how he could possibly see. She stared for a moment and then looked at Dreyfus, who shrugged and—behind the driver's back—mimed obscuring his face with his hand and walking into the car door. Beatrice laughed a little guiltily and climbed in. As the last one in, she sat facing Ben the entire way downtown. (He had volunteered to take everyone's least favorite seat and ride backward.) She kept her eyes purposefully focused out the tinted windows.

Their car dropped the group amply far from the event, so that no one might suspect that they'd arrived via chauffeured vehicle instead of the number 2 train. But a line of limos and town cars had formed at this same safe distance, all surreptitiously delivering A-list red carpet attendees right near the corresponding Chelsea subway stop.

Outside the event was an actual red carpet, which amused Beatrice, who had never witnessed such a spectacle in all her childhood evenings spent at downtown gallery openings. As they moved through the crowd toward the entrance, she recognized a few celebrity art world figures. Mostly, Beatrice knew these particular "artists" to be more like savvy businessmen, who harnessed the publicity machine, marketing themselves via semi-ironic denim collections, purses, and hair care lines without being dubbed "sellouts."

An indie band (or two) and an indie actress (or six) stood in line for their red carpet moments ahead of Veruca. She blew meaningful air kisses to all as they allowed her to pass in front. Even her fellow *Us Weekly* starlets seemed captivated by her presence. She grabbed Beatrice's hand.

Beatrice planned to stand in the immediate background and observe, but Veruca had other intentions. She dragged Beatrice onto the carpet itself, and as flashbulbs exploded in their eyes, paparazzi called out for attention: "V-Pfeff, over here! You know we love you! Where's the H.O.S. tonight? Is this the newest member? Does the carpet match the drapes?" (That last guy was thrown out.) Meanwhile, Dreyfus dropped instructions for Beatrice from a foot or two away: "Turn a three-quarter angle toward the camera, step back with your right foot, put all your weight on that same foot, put your hand on your hip and pull your arm back so you don't get 'fat arm,' lift your chin and one eyebrow, if you can, and smile mostly with your eyes, Tyra Banks style. Good job, newbie." Beatrice could only imagine the contorted expression on her face. Kendra was already onsite, spelling names for the reporters and photographers. "That's 'B' like boy, 'e,' 'a,' . . ."

With huge blue orbs still obscuring her vision, Beatrice moved blindly off the carpet and felt her way through the gallery's open glass doors, almost smashing into them.

"Why did I just do that?"

Dreyfus answered, "Because you need to be her to write as

her. You need to truly experience what it is to walk in her Rag &
Bone shoes. And to do that, you need to be accepted by this
crowd. Otherwise, you'll never quite get it. Got it? Good."

Beatrice nodded. "I think I do. But where did Veruca . . . V
go? I need to follow her, no?"

"Just keep an eye on her, honey, and get a basic sense of the
event. You're being hired to make her sound fantastic and smart
about the art but not to document her every move. Try to have an
interesting conversation or two of your own, if you can manage.
Kendra will stand by her side, keep track of the important names
to drop, and get back to you every evening. You'll get the hang
of it. Now, go look at the art. I need to mingle. Shoo. Shoo!"

And with that Dreyfus disappeared and, though Beatrice
could spot Imelda's beautiful head bobbing every once in a while
above the fray, she was on her own. She shrugged and moved to
the first piece, which was difficult to see through the posing
hordes. The artist, Maldrake Maldrake Capri, had photographed
celebrities in gender-bending scenarios: women smoking cigars
or peeing at urinals or, in the most racy version, simulating sex
with other women using strap-ons. The artist had then worked
over the images with fluorescent puffy paint, very retro '80s. Judging by the surrounding coos of approval about "the genius,"
people were impressed. People other than Beatrice, that is, who
was hard-pressed to find anything positive to say.

The event was, well, uneventful. Beatrice soon grew bored
and distracted. Mostly she was thinking about her paper and
wondering if there might be a corner into which she could duck
and read her book.

"So, whaddya think, *Beany Baby*?"

She snapped to attention and discovered Ben standing beside
her, double-fisting cups of white wine. She was glad to see the
alcohol.

"If you could stop calling me that, I'd really appreciate it."

"Okay, done." He smiled. "*Newbie*."

"Just Bea would be perfect. Thanks."

"Yeah, see, that's confusing to me. I mean, technically, I'm a B too—Ben. How will I know which one of us I'm talking to?"

"You talk to yourself often?"

"Only when I have to." He shrugged.

She raised her eyebrows. "When the voices in your head command it?"

"When I'm stuck in a room alone with Imelda."

Beatrice smiled despite herself and nervously rotated the stud in her ear. Why did he make her so jittery? She swallowed, hard.

Now he looked her up and down, as he had during their first two meetings. She was reminded of dental X-ray experiences, sitting as still as possible, mouth too gauzy for protest, heavy protective lead bib weighing her down. She was powerless to call him out and that was unfamiliar. "So you decided to wear actual clothing tonight, huh? Bold choice. A little disappointing compared with the heart underwear, but you seem to be pulling it off."

Beatrice squeezed her eyes shut. So he *had* spotted her heart underwear in the hall the other night. She cursed her idiotic choice. Why did she care? She needed to get a handle on herself. This was Veruca's boyfriend and he was just teasing her. Ben held out one of the wine-filled plastic cups. She put away her pad and pencil and accepted it gratefully, taking a large sip—more like a swig.

"Wow." He nodded in approval. "That's the first time I've seen someone drink that stuff in large quantities without gagging. Hard-core."

"I'm used to it. This battery acid meets saccharine flavor is the taste of my childhood. It's like art world baby formula. The first time I ever got drunk was on this same terrible wine with my sister, Gertie, at a SoHo performance art event. I've been drinking it my whole life." She lifted the plastic cup and peered at the inexplicable pulp settling at the bottom. "Actually, I'm a little surprised that they wouldn't raise the bar a bit at a swanky situation like this."

"And destroy the authenticity? Don't be ridiculous. Nothing says downtown like box wine." Was that a bit of cynicism? Ben gestured toward the painting. "So, Scoop, what do you *really* think?"

"I think it's nice."

He looked at her doubtfully. "You think it's 'nice'?"

"Yeah."

"No, you don't."

"Honestly, I think it's nice." Before she could stop herself, she blurted out, "For a derivative student art show. But people seem to be eating it up. Anything that features celebrities *and* dildos sells, I guess." Even as the words escaped her lips, panic and wine rose up in Beatrice's throat. Veruca loved this artist. What if Ben repeated what she said?

"If only he'd incorporated heart panties."

She breathed a sigh of relief. He wasn't going to let her off the hook, but he likely wouldn't tattle either. "Okay, enough with the underwear. And, for your own good, please don't say 'panties.' It really skeeves women out."

"But 'derivative' is not what's getting written on *The Pfeffer-noose Chronicles,* right?"

"What's *The Pfeffernoose Chronicles*?'"

Ben tilted his head sideways, as if to examine a foreign specimen more closely. "That's the name of your blog. You seriously didn't know?" She shook her head. "Wow, Scoop, you are totally in over your head."

"Hey, shut up, dude," she snapped.

But he wasn't listening, just shaking his head and snickering. "Amazing. You don't even know the name. That's so typical of Veruca and Kendra."

"Does *everything* amuse you? Or just my humiliating foibles?"

What Beatrice couldn't know was that Ben was a champion of the underdog. After years of being the shortest kid by far in his high school class, he finally grew about eight inches between his senior year and the beginning of college. Suddenly, he was tall. But *Rudy* remained among his favorite movies. And he never forgot what it meant to feel small. His teasing was good-natured.

At that moment, a Russian blonde in Swarovski crystal–laden "fashion" glasses, hooker heels, and a lower-than-low-cut fringed black dress wandered by wearing enough perfume for an army of aging strippers. She was actually from Staten Island and had to fake the European accent, but she thought the Russian persona was much more Bond Girl. Some partygoers managed to cover their noses in time. Others, like Ben, were tall enough to escape the storm's eye. But Beatrice was not so fortunate. The woman almost butted her in the face with her protruding fragrance-slathered fake bosoms. For the second time in recent memory, Beatrice felt a sudden tickle in her nasal passage that erupted into a gigantic sneeze.

The revolted woman pronounced in a villainous accent, "That cold, it iz zo last week."

The sneeze had created an alcoholic tsunami in Beatrice's cup, and wine that stank of turpentine was now spilling down her arm. She ignored the impulse to empty the rest of its contents over Ben, who was stifling hysterical laughter. He grabbed some napkins from a passing server and managed a "Bless you!" as he steered Beatrice toward a less crowded corner. She commenced drying her sticky forearm. He moved to help her but put his hands up in mock surrender when she shot him her best evil glare. "There doesn't seem to be a shortage of your 'foibles.'"

"Thank you so much for pointing that out. Speaking of you going elsewhere—"

"Were we?"

"Don't you need to be mingling with Veruca's people? The perma–boy toy and all?" Beatrice hoped she didn't sound bitter. She stopped another server, exchanging her old cup, now stuffed with wet napkins, for a new glass of wine. The server pursed his lips in disgust and considered abandoning acting for a more solitary career like crab fishing.

Ben leaned against the wall, brushed his hair off his forehead, and absently scratched his stubbled chin. Beatrice was starting to detect that as a habit. "Nah, I know nothing about art, and Kendra definitely prefers when I stay out of their way at these things. Plus, standing around and being introduced as 'Veruca Pfeffernoose's boyfriend' is not quite as novel as it might at first appear."

Beatrice nodded, not a little bit distracted by his full lips and tanned forearms.

"So, if you're not used to all this, how did you meet Veruca? I mean, if you don't mind me asking—as a journalist, of course?" She cleared her throat. The party was crowded now and she kept getting shoved closer to him. They were bellied up to each other as if on a rush-hour train. Her arm grazed his and she quickly pulled away. Had she felt a static shock? It wasn't even cold out.

He smiled that adorable crooked smile, revealing where laugh lines would one day form and only improve his face. "I'm from Austin, actually." That explained the slight twang. "I came here for college because I wanted to be a music writer and this is where the publications are based. I met Veruca accidentally like six months ago at this really remote hole in Red Hook, where this esoteric band I love from Beirut was playing."

"I didn't know she was into music."

"Veruca's into anything that's new. She never gets sick of it all. Although, come to think of it, she hasn't been back to Brooklyn since then, even for parties at Michelle Williams's or Keri Russell's town houses. When we met, I didn't even know who she was, though I guess that glow is pretty obvious from the beginning."

"Yeah, she's charismatic." Beatrice nodded thoughtfully. "People just follow her like the Pied Piper, and I get it, actually, because she has this almost planetary magnetism."

"I just meant that she was really hot. But that was definitely more poetic."

Beatrice laughed. She was beginning to feel more comfortable. Girls probably threw themselves at Ben. He was charming in a dry sort of way. But he was Veruca's boyfriend and also not her type at all. She gravitated toward guys who were serious and pale.

Wait, why was that her type again?

The wine was going to her head. That was one thing you could say for art-opening vino: The sugar and alcohol content was sky high. Beatrice was babbling: "I actually didn't even get it at first. I couldn't understand why Dolly, my best friend Dolly, was so fascinated. But Veruca is like a force. I'm mean, don't tell her I said that." *Shut up. Shut up!* She sounded like a stalker.

But Ben didn't seem to mind. "Yeah, most of the time there's no point in fighting it, when she wants something. Like, earlier today, I overheard you trying to return the clothing she gave you. I did that too. But the thing about Veruca is, like she said, she's giving you that stuff because it's important to her that you have it." He paused and looked himself over, smirking. "Or maybe

I've just rationalized it because I really do like these sneakers and jeans. Seriously, they're limited edition. Like three collector nerds in Tokyo have them and that's it."

"But you don't live with her?"

"Nope. I live in a regular old studio apartment on the floor where you tried to kill that dance major."

"I didn't!" But he was joking. "Anyway. So what happened to the writing?"

"The writing?"

"The reason why you came to New York?"

He frowned and swatted at an imaginary fly. "Veruca hooked me up with editors at the major music publications and they pretty much all agreed that I didn't have a lot of talent. Sometimes you're not good at what you like, you know?"

"I guess," Beatrice said. Sometimes you couldn't even get yourself to try. Her Moleskine notebook sat heavily in her purse. "And that was it? You just stopped?"

"I'd really rather not talk about this." For the first time that night, there was an awkward silence between them. Beatrice shifted uncomfortably in her mile-high heels. Ben stared at the ceiling fan.

She suddenly felt like fleeing. Why was she having a heart-to-heart with this guy when she should be writing a paper? "You know, I think I got a pretty good sense of the show. Maybe I should get going." Beatrice looked longingly toward the door, ready to bolt.

That mischievous smile surfaced again. "Oh, I don't think so, Beatrice. You're in it for the long haul tonight." He nodded toward Veruca, who was standing in front of a portrait of herself as a strong man, signing people's exhibit catalogs. The artist himself walked up and handed her some sort of envelope, one of the thank-you notes Kendra mentioned on the way over, no doubt.

Apparently, formal handwritten cards on organic stationery were the only way to properly say thank you these days. Veruca collected a ton from artists, whom Beatrice was instructed to mention in her blog posts to reward their correct protocol. Perhaps sealing with candle wax might come back as a trend too. A lot of the girls at the party were wearing corset tops. Maybe Victorian style—sans that pesky propriety—was in vogue.

"You're into food, right? I think you might actually like this next part," said Ben. Kendra was making a beeline for the two of them.

Within minutes, they were standing outside with Veruca and the Axis of Evil, who didn't seem quite so dastardly after a bit of wine. Dreyfus was recapping a conversation with an impossibly dumb young hipster band member who had never heard of Pink Floyd, when—out of the corner of her eye—Beatrice noticed Gertie standing not thirty feet away. Before Beatrice could greet her sister, Veruca was seized with the desire to leave. And as she was hurried away, Beatrice glanced back with guilt. For just an instant, she thought Veruca peered nervously back in the same direction.

Gertie seemed to spot her little sister too, as she looked out over the crowd, her red lips parted quizzically. But Beatrice rushed away, not wanting to hold the group up. Truthfully, she was happy to avoid concocting an explanation. Her motley Axis of Evil companions would likely garner disapproval and raise suspicions about how she was spending—no, *wasting*—her time.

17

BEN'S PREDICTION PROVED CORRECT: Beatrice "ate up" the
rest of the night. A feast at the nearby Meatpacking District restaurant Ipocrita—thrown and sponsored by Veruca—included
eighteen courses, which miraculously never made the diners
overly full. Each was prepared by a different celebrity chef
from a Michelin-starred restaurant and inspired by his native
country. Black truffles and white asparagus were a recurring
theme, as Veruca insisted that the meal be seasonal and farm to
table with zero carbon footprint (never mind the fuel required
for the international chefs' long airplane hauls, their particular
ingredients, and, of course, lucky pots, pans, and alchemistic
gizmos). The socialite also insisted that white asparagus *must* be
in season, as it looked so good on the plate; memo to Mother
Nature.

Veruca was not always a vegetarian per se, but this month—in
short-lived solidarity with Zooey Deschanel—she was going
without wheat, glucose, meat, dairy, and Cheez Whiz. Still, in
each incarnation the ingredients were uniquely and immaculately
emulsified; evaporated; sous vide; pickled; strained; smoked; dried;
salted; cured; drenched; doused; rubbed; frozen; coddled; chopped;
cured; grilled; fried; spiced; poached; caramelized; curried;
stewed; flambéed; diced; baked; basted; beaten; boiled; broiled;
braised; brined; tempura battered; panko crusted; Meyer lemon-,
yuzu-, lavender-, ginger-, or sriracha-infused; cooked down and

heated up into gelées, foams, confits, gratins, casseroles, bisques, compotes, consommés, ganaches, coulis, frittatas, and fricassees that tasted some sour, some sweet, some salty, some spicy, and some, of course, umami (the fifth and rarest flavor profile, which no one could describe but everyone claimed to be able to distinguish).

At the end of the night, Beatrice returned home to Veruca's place, tipsy from biodynamic wine and ready to collapse into her cushy new bed. Despite her objections, they took the elevator upstairs. It rose as smoothly as *Charlie and the Chocolate Factory*'s glass version, as if it too glided through open air. Maybe the decrepit old thing had gotten fixed? The doors opened and there they stood at the threshold of Veruca's apartment. The socialite grabbed Ben's hand and led him toward her bedroom with a giggle, while Imelda and Dreyfus staggered off in the opposite direction down another hallway. Kendra stopped Beatrice as she started toward her own room, passing her a handbook on how to post and tweet the blog in the correct tone and instructing her to start tonight.

"One last thing," Kendra commanded. "You are not a critic. You're Veruca Pfeffernoose. So don't even think about panning the show or criticizing anything. Just highlight the things you and Veruca liked and ignore the things you didn't. And talk up the artist, okay? 'Cause Veruca really likes him and he gave her a thoughtful card. Got it?"

Beatrice was too tired to argue. She practically sleepwalked back toward her room. It had, after all, been quite a few days since she'd slept through the night. Sliding into her desk chair, she opened her e-mail. She had in fact received the list of attending celebrities and pictures to post alongside the write-up, including one of herself in the car, which she had to admit was better than average. Oddly, she hadn't even noticed a photographer following from event to event. How was that possible? She lingered for a moment on Ben, smirking in the background. He and Veruca were certainly an odd match.

Though it hurt to Beatrice's very core in the vein of appendicitis, she betrayed her base instincts and constructed the blog post as the handbook stated: "Write as if Veruca is confiding in a friend. Make it funny and a bit self-deprecating. We want her to be accessible but also aspirational." And so it began:

September 24

Hello, adorable friends! Now seems like as good a time as any to begin exploiting my exploits for the benefit of you lovely dears. Don't ask what that means. I'm just a little buzzed after an above par evening in this enchanting city. Tonight, my BFFs (K-dog, Immy, D, and our crew's newest addition, BB, for "Beany Baby") and I took the train downtown to the latest fabulous Argolian Gallery opening, where artist Maldrake Maldrake Capri (MMC from here on out) unveiled his newest, Cindy Sherman–inspired works of staggering genius, including a gender-bending portrait of little ole me. I'm still all girl, though, promise. Just ask my love bunny, Benji Boy. He may have the name of a dog, but he's got the face and disposition of a prince. Oh, and I guess his personality is okay too (as if that matters). Just kidding, cutie! Sort of. Anyway . . . back to the art. Oh, and the food. Just wait until you hear about the white asparagus!

Beatrice felt dirty, but she'd been hired to do a job and, presumably if she made Veruca happy, she was doing it well. She tried not to think about her parents' response should they find out. She reminded herself that their opinions shouldn't matter. It wasn't like her father listened to *his* mother's guidance, Beatrice reasoned. Otherwise, Nana would have had Gary wrapping himself in scarves on hot summer nights, eating enough for a small village (perhaps an Eastern European shtetl before the war), and shopping the 99-cent store. As the sun rose behind the enchanted forest Frog setting Beatrice had chosen for her view, she was finally asleep amid coral-trimmed pillows.

The next morning—and eleven thirty a.m. was still considered morning in Veruca's world—Beatrice emerged and received a bizarre contorted look from Kendra, which she surmised was an attempted half smile. The PR machine admitted to liking the post, Veruca promised to "read it later," and Ben shook his head, amused at Beatrice's expense per usual. "I didn't know if you had it in you, Scoop. But, for better or worse, I guess you do."

"Have what in me?" Beatrice asked. The compliment sounded a lot like an insult.

But before Ben could respond, his girlfriend was kissing him good-bye and coaxing Beatrice out the front door to visit a bunch of designer showrooms. They were off to pick out Veruca's clothing for the following week's events. "Ready!" Veruca stated rather than asked.

Shaking off Ben's comment, Beatrice followed the mystical trail of orange blossom fragrance to the door like a cartoon bear hypnotized by the aroma of freshly baked pie. Once again, her cell phone rang on the way out. This time the identifier read DOLLY. Beatrice, already in the midst of being coached on plans, was forced to press Ignore.

18

BEATRICE PIECED TOGETHER HER PAPER on *One Hundred Years of Solitude* on time, but she'd had to read, research, and draft it in the middle of the night. At least the constant writing was making her fluid. Every evening afforded another Maybach journey to some wild event. With each night's corresponding blog post, Beatrice uploaded pictures of the socialite with her signature red hair pinned up or flattened down or just crazy, as she alternately winked either her yellow or her gray eye. Maybe it was just exhaustion, but Beatrice began to imagine that she could tell whether Veruca actually liked the person with whom she posed by which eye she narrowed. Yellow for Dreyfus and Kendra, but gray for that annoying Barbie Doll look-alike from the reality show about talented dog-and-owner teams, and for Miley, of course. Meanwhile, Beatrice got used to late-night writing.

September 30
I've been out every night this week, but—tired as I am—I'm never too exhausted to pull on Helmut Lang leggings and Louboutins. It's true. Sad as it sounds, new clothing literally wakes me up. Plus, I barely even look tired, since my aesthetician Lili introduced me to La Mer's Le Baume pour les Yeux Intense, or Eye Balm Intense. I mean, are you kidding me? Who needs sleep when you've got La Mer's cold applicator (and Lili, of course)? I'm so lucky! Plus, the

lighting was ideal at the opening of new club EMBER, where we danced until dawn amid orange banquettes and rustic reclaimed wood tables and sipped quinoa martinis with evaporated olive foam. The club is entirely solar and environmentally conscious (literally, when celebrities drink too much they use the puke as compost for the organic vodka garden). The VIP room displayed MMC and Billy Lee's newest capsule collection artworks for H&M. Who knew art could be so inexpensive? And you'd never know it wasn't the high-end paintings, except they're printed on seed paper. If you plant the artworks, sunflowers grow!

October 5

At the premier of artist (cum director) Inspektor Corsica's new indie flick, *The Inhaler,* everyone attended. And by "everyone" I mean that Miley Cyrus didn't show up (thank the Lord). D chatted up newly uncloseted R&B sensation Syrup, and even K-dog had a laugh over communication strategies with some big-name agents. Was it more effective to throw your Blackberry or your water bottle at your assistant? There were pluses and minuses to both. Even tough critics BB and Benji loved the film. The gift bags at the intimate soiree I sponsored afterward included my new favorite pink shade-changing Plump lip gloss. I offered Benji a gift bag, of course, but he says pink isn't his color. Next time, I'll make sure to go red to keep him hot and bothered. Or at least hot. Bothered is sort of a constant for him.

October 10

Tonight, as a favor to boy toy Ben for enduring a preview of the Whitney biennial earlier this week (he doesn't know

a Picasso from a Rembrandt, poor thing), we went to a
LES club to see his new favorite band, the Knobits. He just
went crazy for them and, you know, Benji bunny knows
every little thing about music. And I got compliments on
my new Alexander Wang T-shirt, so everyone was happy.

Ben had actually hated the band with a passion, calling them
"garbage, but not in a good way." But Beatrice derived pleasure
from making him sound cheesy via the blog. Considering the
plethora of opportunities that presented to make fun of her, this
was one chance to strike back. She tried to ignore the gnawing
sense that their interactions could be considered flirting, reasoning that witty banter went down between friends too. It turned
out the Cockroach Slayer was a bit of a brainiac, so he was helpful at times. As proof of platonic friendship, she went out of her
way to avoid touching him. Adopting a special brand of willful
denial, Beatrice told herself that the need for mandated physical
distance didn't mean a thing.

Mostly, she was beyond tired. She'd never really caught up
after the basement days. Penny, as Beatrice now called the
housekeeper, had become a friend. Beatrice often asked her outfit advice, begged her to join her for snacks of bagels and knishes,
or gave her beauty products to sample and report back on. Penny's late-night mugs of special antioxidant-rich green tea helped.
Oddly, Beatrice's appetite was starting to decline, maybe due to
the constricting nature of the clothing, her lack of free time, or
the fact that she was singlehandedly depleting New York's dirty
martini supply in place of food. So she sat drinking that odd-
smelling tea that everyone who was anyone *insisted* tasted good
but actually tasted like kelp, while she listened to the projected
frogs *ribbit*. Once, really late at night, she saw what looked like an
actual frog hopping across her soft rug, past her feet. She felt its

little slimy froggy toes on her own, decided she must be halluci-
nating, and promptly put herself to bed. In the morning, she found
tiny tracks across the floor but reasoned they must have been
droplets from spilled tea.

The runway setup in the main room that first day was, in fact,
intended for a loft fashion show, the first of many such events.
The biggest of the shows featured plays on the sarong by design-
ers like Tom Ford, Karl Lagerfeld, Phillip Lim, Derek Lam, and
Zac Posen all in one extraordinary display to benefit a new Bono-
endorsed charity along the lines of Save the Developing Nations'
Children's Depleting Water Supply in the Face of Natural Disas-
ter, Which Could Prove Carcinogenic, in Which Case Help Fight
Cancer and Facial Abnormalities Especially as They Relate to
Women's Health and Unneutered Dogs and Cats, Fur Coats, and
Gay Marriage (aka STDNCDWSITFONDWCPCIWCHFCFA-
EATRTWHUDCFCGM). Before that event, Beatrice sipped
champagne in Veruca's dressing area alone with the socialite and
a seamstress who looked remarkably like American flag creator
Betsy Ross, based on what Beatrice vaguely remembered from a
fourth-grade textbook.

Afterward followed a lavish cocktail party aboard a jet. Though
it never left the tarmac, the experience was still Beatrice's first on
a plane, as her parents had never taken her outside a day's driving
distance. Each night seemed to trump the evening before: yacht
parties, club openings, gallery exhibits, ribbon-cutting ceremo-
nies, personal concerts, birthday parties, hotel galas, wild circus
acts. And all the events culminated in another Veruca-sponsored
after-party. Within no time, people started to recognize Beatrice,
opening velvet ropes and doors for her like a person of note.
And if she was honest with herself, which luckily she rarely had
time to be these days, she was starting to like and, worse, getting
accustomed to the attention. It was like she was famous for

nothing too. She was, after all, Veruca's voice, even if no one knew that. And, according to Kendra, the blog was growing by leaps and bounds with more than nine thousand unique users a day.

Still, it bugged Beatrice that the central character in this whole Mad Hatter world never seemed to read the blog she'd begged Beatrice to write. Sometimes Beatrice tested Veruca, adding dated references to events that never occurred: *Vanna White wore grommet-studded Versace* or *The Bob Ross paintings of deconstructed nudes in graffiti-covered tunnels stunned*. But all that garnered her was reprimands from Kendra.

As Beatrice grew more exhausted, Veruca seemed to grow in stature like a creature from *Ghostbusters,* sucking superpowers from each new display of attention, interview, portrait, dedication, dinner, or diet Red Bull and vodka. It probably helped that, unlike Beatrice, she and her crew lounged and slept all day.

Occasionally, Ben opted out of parties, but usually he tagged along and hung at the sidelines with Beatrice until Veruca finished circulating. That fact had not escaped Kendra's notice, who sent extra scowls their way, but they couldn't help marveling together at what they witnessed: young indie starlets, who inhaled unfiltered cigarettes in VIP rooms while promoting veganism despite wearing leather shoes, band members who had never heard of Talking Heads or Patti Smith, magazine editors who freaked out despite heavy doses of Xanax, bloggers who couldn't string together a coherent sentence, androgynous boys in jeans so skinny and cuffed they could only be considered footless tights, and hip-hop heads reared in mansions on Great Neck, Long Island, who posed like ghetto-born mafiosi.

Veruca was grateful for Beatrice's Ben-sitting. "Thank you so much, Beany Baby," she whispered late one night on the way home to the Dorchester, as he slept peacefully, his head in the socialite's lap. "He was so sulky before and now he's so much more manageable." Beatrice nodded, unable to actually utter the words "You're welcome." One couldn't rely on antioxidants alone. Ben was key to her survival in this strange sphere and vice versa. It had never occurred to Beatrice that keeping him distracted was part of her job.

As usual, the town car didn't hit traffic or a single red light on the way uptown. They just glided above the street all the way home.

19

BY THE END OF WEEK FOUR, Beatrice was fading like a pair of overwashed jeans. She stayed out until three a.m. each night. Then she wrote that day's blog post, the coherence of which was a miracle of human endurance. One night, she wrote an entire post without including a single period, an accidental nod to James Joyce's *Ulysses,* but no one seemed to notice or care.

She'd been making it, half asleep and in her old clothing, to weekly Bernstein dinners, but her mother had caught her nodding off more than once. "Are you working too hard at school?" asked Madeline. Beatrice shook her head. She was generally a terrible liar, but it was true. She wasn't getting work done at all. Plus, her mother couldn't deny how fantastic she looked. Even her nails were perfect, sealed weekly with an LED light to keep her from peeling the polish. Her father's group art show with a crew of his most beloved artist peers was coming up in a matter of weeks and he was too excited about "some authenticity, for once!" to notice much. And Gertie had actually also missed a dinner or two while preparing for her latest reading. (Oscar was back in town to help, thank goodness.)

Otherwise, each morning, Beatrice awoke early for classes. Her eyes stung from too many hours stuck open, her word retrieval was limited to monosyllables, and her left eyelid twitched every three seconds. In fact, some guy who sat across from her in

Media + Culture class began taking donations to start a foundation for whatever awful illness afflicted her.

In the evenings at about five p.m., Beatrice returned home from classes, errands, and the chaos of the sunlit world to find Veruca lying leisurely on a pink chaise, cuddled up with Dreyfus. He read aloud from the latest *Wallpaper, Elle,* or *New York* magazine and, like a spokesmodel, occasionally displayed particularly scintillating pictures or text for the socialite to peruse.

When Beatrice arrived, Veruca would smile lazily. "Beany Baby, you're home. I suppose that means it must be time to get ready, no? When BB gets home?" At these moments, her voice was deliberate and relaxed like thick honey luxuriating on a spoon before finally dripping slowly off the edge. It was like she lived life at a different speed from the rest of the universe. Time existed in soft focus.

"It's time, Queenie," Dreyfus would confirm.

And, as Veruca rose with dramatic effort from the cushy chair like some kind of old Hollywood screen siren in cozy Gap Body instead of faded negligees, she'd sigh, "Going out is so tiresome. Maybe tonight—just this once—we should stay home?"

The first time Beatrice witnessed this exchange, she was naïve enough to believe that staying home was a real possibility and she was thrilled, as visions of flannel pajamas and trashy TV viewing (reality TV! Lifetime Original Movies! Oh my!) danced in her silly little head. In fact, Veruca's entourage *never* stayed home. The socialite would quickly realize—or be reminded by Kendra—that the night's celebrity birthday party or charity tribute concert was an unmissable obligation. Even the "best" night of the week at some swanky "dive" bar with cultivated idiosyncrasies like wildly expensive bad drinks or prevalent taxidermy and an impenetrable list even when it was empty inside was *must* attend.

"Next time," Veruca would chirp with a shrug. And off she'd

head down that long white corridor to be primped for the evening by some impossibly strange and emaciated stylist.

Beatrice limped in on a random Tuesday night, holding a hand to her cheek to stop her spreading twitch. (Maybe she would need that foundation money, after all?) She wasn't surprised to find Veruca draped across the center ottoman, though Dreyfus, she noted, was wearing an honest to goodness smoking jacket.

"Beany! Oh, thank goodness you're finally home. I have some bad news. Come here!" Veruca commanded affectionately, patting a space—only big enough for half Beatrice's butt, but two of Imelda's—next to her on the ottoman. Beatrice threw down her bag and perched as well as she could on the edge of the leather piece.

"I hope you won't be too bummed," continued Veruca.

Beatrice braced herself: Would she have to go back to living in the basement? Was the blog a flop, despite evidence to the contrary? Was twitching unsuitable for Veruca's friends? Was she going to have to give back the new clothing? Because she'd sort of gotten attached to a pair of Isabel Marant wedges.

"We're staying in tonight."

Beatrice was speechless. This was the big bad news? Veruca misinterpreted her incredulous silence as upset.

"Oh, see, Drey? You were wrong! I knew she'd be upset. I totally understand, BB. I wanted to go to the opening of RUFFIE as much as you did—I mean, I promised basically the whole cast of *Gossip Girl* and Blake already thinks I'm such a flake. But I just need a night in and that's it. It's rainy and cold outside and I'm putting my foot down."

In Beatrice's brain, angels were singing, but she told herself not to trust Veruca's proclamation. She'd heard it all before. Momentarily, the crew would get antsy or horny and off they'd go to drink vats of Moët and old-fashioned cocktails.

"That's totally fine, V. I'd love to stay in. Whatever you need me to do."

Veruca actually seemed relieved, as if Beatrice was the force propelling them out every night. "Great! I'll go get the den ready!" Veruca stood and scurried off toward the back rooms.

As soon as she was gone, Beatrice shifted her entire bum onto the ottoman, leaned back, and craned her head in Dreyfus's direction. "So. Where are we going tonight?"

Dreyfus looked up from his *Out* magazine and returned her stare. "Are you deaf, Marlee Matlin? We're staying in."

"Sure. Then what?"

Dreyfus put his magazine down impatiently, "Did you not hear the girl, newbie? We're staying in tonight."

"For the whole night? Like, for *real*?"

He nodded slowly, as if she might not otherwise understand.

"Like *all* night?"

"Maybe you're blind too, Miss Keller. Can you not see that I'm wearing my Hef jacket? We're staying in. All night. The H.O.S. crew needs some R and R, if you know what I'm saying." He pushed his nerd glasses up on his nose for emphasis.

Beatrice felt her twitch subside. "So I'm free? I can hang out alone and do work?"

"I mean, you can, Queen Bean, but you'll miss all the fun."

"You can skip, if you want to get fired," barked Kendra, who appeared as if from nowhere, always an unpleasant surprise. "Your loungewear is laid out on your bed. See you in the den in twenty minutes."

Beatrice stood up and grabbed her bag, confused but too tired to fight the power. In a perfect brainwashed state, she moved toward the hallway. Suddenly, she stopped and spun around. "Wait, where's the den?"

"Penelope will show you the way." Thank goodness for Penny.

20

"WE HAVE A DEN?" Beatrice asked Penny, who shot her a knowing smile. "Who knew?"

Penny sighed. "Who indeed."

Beatrice was led down an as-yet-unmarked-by-eyeliner section of the hallway in cotton pajamas softer than kittens, cashmere socks, and new Ugg slippers. Penny stopped at an imposing ceiling-height door and gestured for Beatrice to open it. She grabbed the enormous round knob and, at her touch, the door swung open on its own. Doors did that in this fun house.

The spread revealed was elaborate, including an impossibly tall leaning tower of John Hughes movies as a centerpiece. Five separate beds on raised platforms each featured a flaxseed-stuffed pillow, hand stitched with the person's name: *Kendra, Dreyfus, Veruca, Imelda, Beatrice.* The beds were covered with cumulus white comforters. Since Ben was nowhere in sight, tonight seemed to be all about "the girls."

On a long table, atop elaborate hand-sewn silk runners from Bangladesh and served inside Japanese pottery designed in collaboration with self-named Japanese artist Futomaki, sat dips from French onion to piping-hot spinach and artichoke, which automatically refilled themselves. Pizzas covered a three-yard stretch of table: the highest-end buffalo mozzarella and fresh basil straight from Italy, deep-dish Chicago, and the best of New York and New Haven's by-the-slice (which required a temporary truce in the cities' pizza battle). Desserts included an assortment of chocolate-covered, raspberry-filled, and almond-encrusted buttery Italian and Jewish cookies from every great bakery on the Upper West Side, like Fairway, Zabar's, and Lichtman's (though it closed twenty-five years before). In the corner, a man—who looked a bit like Dreyfus but even more like Orville Redenbacher in horn-rimmed glasses and a bow tie—flavored popcorn batches with seasonings from jalapeño to dill pickle and toppings like salted caramel.

A movie theater–sized plasma flat-screen TV monopolized an entire wall, beside manicure/pedicure stations with vibrating leather chairs and robotic reflexology water bowls for soaking and massaging feet. A vested bartender stood off to one side, blending various ingredients (bitters, egg whites, herbal supplements) for cocktails. They looked good, but Beatrice decided her liver could use a night off.

Unsure of how to relax amid such opulent vegging materials, she took cues from the others, offering air kisses to each and then settling onto her own cushy bed. As *Sixteen Candles* began, each member of the Axis made his or her way to Veruca's bed and grabbed a choice spot, leaving awkward Beatrice to sit with her knees to her chest on the floor at the foot like the family dog. A server came around with strange-looking sweets, which she explained in hushed tones were s'mores with green tea–flavored marshmallows. Beatrice wasn't one to turn down a new culinary experience. She devoured three quickly, pronouncing them tasty, before Dreyfus silently handed her a throw and she tucked herself underneath to watch the movie.

Toward the end, as Molly Ringwald's sister collapsed on her wedding day thanks to muscle relaxer overload, Beatrice found herself laughing a bit too raucously. And she couldn't stop. She sniffed her hot chocolate for traces of whiskey. She'd never felt so light and goofy. She lifted an arm and watched it float back down to the carpeted floor.

Dreyfus noticed and leaned over the side of the bed, whispering in her ear, "The s'mores, Sweet Bea. They're magic."

Magic? Beatrice envisioned men in top hats with rabbits and sequin-clad assistants roasting marshmallows. The word "magic" reminded her of something else too: the disappearing ink in her Moleskine notebook, which made her think of blue pens, of blueberries, of blue skies, and then of how weird it is that the sky is a color. She was about to share that seemingly profound thought when she finally realized what Dreyfus meant. A warning about the "magic ingredient" (aka pot) would have been nice.

"Don't worry," he hissed, sensing her concern. "They only use a Rainbow Puppy's worth."

"Rainbow Puppy?"

Dreyfus rolled his eyes. How could Beatrice be so dumb? "Oh, Beany. That's what they call a baby-sized joint. Anyway, if you didn't eat so damn much, you wouldn't be so stoned, you cow." At that, Beatrice had to giggle.

At the movie's conclusive famous over-the-cake kiss, Beatrice smiled, thinking that in Molly Ringwald's place, she probably would have leaned into the cake, set fire to her dress, and licked the icing off her fingers, while rolling around extinguishing the flames. She was a good multitasker.

"What's so funny, BB?" Veruca asked from high above on her bed. "Hey, get up here! You shouldn't be stuck on the floor!" Better late than never, a loosened-up Beatrice climbed up next to Dreyfus and sat cross-legged.

"Do you think that's supposed to be her first kiss?" asked Dreyfus.

"First kiss ever? No way," Kendra snarled, though a little less ferociously than usual. "She's already sixteen years old. She's not even supposed to be a virgin. Plus, first kisses are awful."

Veruca crinkled her nose, her red hair falling in her face. "I guess they can be awkward."

"My first kiss was a doozy," said Dreyfus, staring off into the distance in mock despair. "It was after a seven minutes in heaven game."

"What's with that game, BTW?" chimed Beatrice. "Like, it's not a game. It's just sitting in a closet uncomfortably with some other uncomfortable person."

"Shush, I'm telling a story," Dreyfus chided, bringing a finger to his lips like a surly librarian. "Incidentally, you're totally right." Beatrice nodded, as he continued, "But anyway, it was *after* a seven minutes in heaven game. We'd been locked in the closet together for ages, but nothing went down. I was more timid in those days. So then afterward, she came up to me as I was leaving the party, pushed me into a corner, and kissed me like she was out for revenge. I think she was on some kind of mission."

"Wait, *she*?" Beatrice laughed.

Dreyfus paused for a moment and glanced from Kendra to Imelda. Kendra rolled her eyes. Then he turned to Beatrice a bit sheepishly. "Yes, *she,* Beany. You uncovered my dirty little secret. There was a moment before I realized—or acknowledged—that I preferred boys. Anyway, it involved braces and watermelon Bubblicious and, well, it was a bit of a scene." Beatrice pictured a young Dreyfus, mouth full of metal and pink gum, pinned up against the wall by some eventual lesbian named Chris. In her experience, gay girls and boys had a way of finding each other and pairing off in high school, as a means of survival.

"What about you, Im?" asked Veruca. Beatrice was riveted. She'd only ever heard Imelda addressed with yes or no questions, easily answered with a nod or shake of the head. Would she actually speak? *Could* she actually speak?

In a surprising show of enthusiasm, Imelda leaped off the bed and stalked over to her purse on a chair in the corner. She rifled inside, found her iPhone, and loaded a Facebook page. Smiling, she brought it over to the bed and displayed a posted old photograph to the group. The image was of a somewhat unfortunate young boy, with a long skinny face, slightly crossed eyes, and serious acne.

"He's adorable, Imelda," Beatrice managed. Imelda beamed.

"Adorable?" said Dreyfus. "He looks like the scrawny kid from *Who's the Boss?* but ugly. I bet he's boning guys now too." Imelda snatched her iPhone back and glared.

"All right, all right, settle down, chickadees." Veruca smiled. "Are we ready to pick out nail colors for our gel manicures?" Always the diplomat, she urged Imelda and Dreyfus off the bed, leaving Kendra and Beatrice momentarily alone.

"What about your first kiss, Beatrice?" Kendra was the only one who called her by her full first name. Little did she know that Beatrice liked it. "You didn't dish. Still waiting for it to happen, good girl?"

For the record, if anyone happened to be keeping tabs, they would have noticed that Kendra hadn't told a story either. But that was per usual. She never revealed anything personal. Beatrice sometimes wondered if she was a robot programmed to do dirty work that ran solely on fuel made from lemon juice with maple syrup and cayenne pepper. That Master Cleanse diet concoction was all she ever drank. Maybe that's why she was so grouchy?

At parties, she never chatted casually and she didn't seem to have a sex life. Beatrice could only assume that she had zero internal world, returning to her room each night to plug in and charge via her Yves Saint Laurent belt. When the sun rose, she would crank her dark brown hair back into the world's tightest French twist, work out for hours at the gym (even her face was muscular), and then crack figurative skulls for Veruca all over New York City.

Maybe it was Kendra who didn't have a first kiss story, considered Beatrice. Perhaps she was one of those morbidly overweight children who drank soda from baby bottles and then grew obsessed with maintaining their weight as an adult. Regardless, Beatrice gladly shared her own story. "I had a cute first kiss. It was with Bobby Sentineli in seventh grade. We snuck away and kissed behind his father's Italian restaurant in Carroll Gardens on one of those first days of spring, you know, when you can finally wear a T-shirt with no sweater? I think of him every time I smell lasagna. I had such a huge crush on him. He actually wore a gold chain." She laughed.

"Of course."

"Of course, a gold chain? Maybe in mafia movies, but most Italian guys don't actually wear—"

"No! Of course, you had the world's only good first kiss, even if it was in Brooklyn back when it was gauche. He's probably a Nobel Prize winner now."

"He's an arts administration major at Yale. He wants to run the NEA."

Kendra groaned. "I can't even deal. This whole sleepover thing is so childish. And you shouldn't even be here. You're an employee."

Beatrice was sick of Kendra's attitude. She hardly needed someone else to make her feel out of place; she had that covered. "What is your problem?"

If possible, Kendra's updo pulled even tighter and her jaw grew more square. Her face looked whiplashed like a plastic surgery addict. "Honestly? Pollyanna types like you, who experience the world as rosy and perfect, stuffing food in your face and staying skinny and hopping along like moronic little bunnies." She gestured belligerently.

"What does that even mean? You are so off base. I can't believe I'm hearing this from you of all people. You're like the most immaculate person ever and, while you're also a total psychopath, you always have it together. What are you freaking out about?"

Apparently, Kendra didn't mind being called a psychopath as long as it was followed by the word "together." She sat still for a moment and then her face nearly creaked into a grotesque smile. "I am together, I suppose." The glimpse of a kinder Kendra faded as she remembered herself and sprung off the bed. "Anyway, I'm watching you, BB."

"Aw. You called me BB," cooed Beatrice.

"Oh, shut up and come pick out a polish." They joined the rest of the group by the nail display. As Beatrice tested the colors, she noticed that the polish didn't smell rancid as usual or at all. Was it unscented? Dior did just launch some rose-scented ones. "OMG!" exclaimed Dreyfus. "Remember when Imelda wouldn't wear anything but that horrible hot pink? What was that about?"

"When was that?" Beatrice asked absently, kneeling in front of the bottles of lacquer. Should she choose Berry Hard or Better Luck Next Time? Why did nail polishes have such stupid names? "You know, I've never asked how you guys know each other. How did the H.O.S. crew form? And what does it stand for, anyway?"

Veruca was busy studying options too and Imelda looked studiously at the ceiling, so Kendra began to answer, "Well, it was—"

"A very boring story then and it's still one now." Dreyfus grabbed Beatrice by the hand, stood her up, and twirled her around. She giggled. "Who knows where we actually met for the first time? The Hamptons, the Cape, the Vineyard, Vail, the Meadow in Central Park? I went to Saint Mary's, naturally. These girls went to Spence and Nightingale, although Mel almost had to finish at Dwight after an incident with a randy professor. I have a better idea than manicures and rehashing the days of schoolgirl skirts and those damn Saint Mary's required navy jackets, khakis, and red neckties."

He pointed upward toward the ceiling. Veruca raised her eyebrows. "Good plan. I'm in!"

And, though as usual Beatrice was clueless about their destination, she allowed herself to be led out of the room. How funny that Dreyfus had gone to school just across the street from her apartment and she'd never known him. She was getting used to abdicating control and living minute to minute, an unfamiliar phenomenon for the average New Yorker. The group ran up the stairs to the very top, opened an emergency door (the kind that would lock behind them on a sitcom), and rushed out onto the building's roof.

Beatrice was accustomed to the unfathomable rules of Veruca's world, so when she saw simply an industrial tar rooftop with the occasional satellite dish, she was surprised. She'd half expected a full-throttle party with hundreds of people and chandeliers that hung from the sky itself. The 360-degree cityscape view—the real, natural view—was fantastic and they were quiet as they absorbed the sparkling lights, New York's answer to constellations. Dreyfus broke the silence, grabbing Beatrice's hand and spinning her around again. She went flying across the black tar, turning and turning, her hair falling out of its ponytail holder.

Veruca did have one trick up her sleeve: A surround-sound

system mysteriously appeared and pretty soon they were danc-
ing, jumping, and singing to classics from the Rolling Stones,
Madonna, Journey, old school hip-hop by De La Soul and A
Tribe Called Quest, and more current Lady Gaga and Beyoncé.
They danced with abandon as if at a wedding, where there's a
presumption of kitsch.

Tired, Beatrice took a break on the sidelines, sitting with her
back against the roof's ledge. She smiled, watching Imelda and
Dreyfus dancing together in the moonlight: wiry, beautiful, and
young. Veruca slid down next to her and tipped her head onto
Beatrice's shoulder, captivated too and smelling—as usual—of
orange blossoms. Maybe the s'mores were working their "magic,"
but as Beatrice watched she felt genuine affection for all four of
her new friends, even Kendra. She felt like one of them.

Using her BlackBerry, Beatrice blogged her short post for
the day:

October 21
Tonight, we danced at the edge of the world, as the city
glistened from the tar rooftops to the cement sidewalks
far, far below.

When the rest of the party grew sleepy and chilly, everyone
trudged downstairs, laughter echoing as Dreyfus imitated their
dance moves. The group settled into their beds, awash in well-
earned exhaustion. That night, they all had the same dream: A
man shot a pellet into the moon to make it dissolve and then it
was daylight.

21

THE NEXT DAY, IN LATIN AMERICAN LITERATURE, Dolly was sullen at best. Beatrice fumbled past other students to reach her dear old friend as soon as the professor finished her lecture on applying magical realism and the fluidity of time to real life (right on schedule for next period).

Beatrice whispered, "Just one minute. I am so sorry. I really want to talk to you, but I have to ask the professor one question. Please, wait! I'm begging you!" Dolly frowned and crossed her arms but did indeed rest her bag back on the pen-marked table and begin playing a passive-aggressive iPhone game of Angry Birds.

As Beatrice approached the teacher, wearing her most earnest doe-eyed expression, Professor Bobadilla broke off a conversation with another student. "Señorita Bernstein, how can I help you?"

The professor absently fingered a diamond tennis bracelet, tightly encircling—and almost squeezing—her rather stout wrist, as she waited for a response.

"I'm so sorry to bother you, Professor Bobadilla. About the fluidity of time . . . I know our second paper on assimilation is due in two days, but I've fallen really behind in the reading. I haven't finished *How the García Girls Lost Their Accents* and I was wondering—"

Before Beatrice could even unfurl her intricately woven ex-

cuse, written and revised repeatedly in her head, Professor Bobadilla interrupted, "Whenever you can get it in, señorita. *No te
preocupes!*"

Beatrice peered blankly back at the professor, who rolled her
eyes. "It means, 'Don't worry!' *Ay, Dios mio.* Didn't you have to
take Spanish 2 in order to enroll in this class? I know you were
sick. Feel better."

Beatrice murmured an apology and thank you and then inched
away. She was pleased but also surprised. Hadn't this same teacher
preached perfect attendance, demonstrating an intolerance of
lateness just weeks before?

Dolly had overheard the whole exchange. "Sick?"

"Just in the head!"

Dolly didn't crack a smile. "You were sick like a month ago."

"I guess she only acts tough at first?" Beatrice shrugged.

Dolly pursed her lips and stared hard at the floor. She didn't
generally do a good impression of angry, but this was convincing.

Beatrice began her profuse apology. "Doll, I'm so sorry I
haven't returned your calls. It's not that I don't love you. I want
to hang out more than anything. You know I do. It's just that . . .
this job that Veruca gave me . . . the blogging itself is not a lot of
work, but the 'research' is killing me. I'm *so* sorry—how can I
make it up to you?"

Dolly inserted a finger through one of her curls and twirled it
tight like she was screwing it in. "Yeah, I read all about your
'hard work' in *In Touch.* That P. Diddy yacht party looked rough.
How *do* you do it? They should feature you on Oprah's network
for that impressive demonstration of martyrdom."

"It's just a balancing act that I haven't mastered yet." That
sounded hollow, even to Beatrice. In the picture accompanying
the article Dolly referenced, she'd raised flutes of Prosecco with
Lady Gaga.

Dolly grunted. If she was a Muppet right now, it was definitely Oscar the Grouch. Was he even a Muppet? He was more of a *Sesame Street* character. Beatrice pulled her focus back to Dolly. Sleep deprivation was making her ADD. "It's just . . . don't you think it's odd that every time we plan to hang out, Veruca offers me a dance session with Isadora? And you literally haven't seen any of our friends since you got to school. Trust me, they've noticed! Stephen, Mina, and Cynthia are like wondering if you even exist. I told them you're going through a rough patch, but it's hard to keep them convinced when you keep popping up on TMZ."

"The ballet teacher's name is actually Isadora?" Beatrice was stunned. Had that woman adopted Isadora Duncan's name because the resemblance was so strong?

"It's not that I don't appreciate it, but, I mean, I'm starting to feel like Veruca doesn't want us to see each other. And the training is amazing, but I've missed a lot of rehearsals too."

Looking at Dolly, her mop of curls falling more heavily than usual around her face, Beatrice felt awful. How could she be such a flake with the one person in her life who was always present and supportive? "Oh, Doll," Beatrice said, "all Veruca wants is what serves Veruca. She couldn't care less if we spend time together. She just wants me where she wants me at any given time and, unfortunately, lately that's *all* of the time."

Dolly's shoulders, which had been tensed to her ears, relaxed as her anger melted away. Even as a child, Dolly had never been able to hold a grudge. She'd once told Beatrice that when another kid stole her blocks and pushed her down in preschool, she'd cried for an instant and then moved onto doing somersaults across the floor. That's how she found dance. "I guess so. I just miss you. We *all* do. Well, maybe not Stephen. He's been working a lot too."

"I miss you too! Just beyond miss you. And I want to see everyone, but those guys moved downtown, so it's not only my life that's changed. Plus, Cynthia has been acting weird ever since she started sleeping with that Beat poet guy last year."

"Yeah, she's sort of on her alternative high horse," Dolly agreed, a big lipless Muppet smile returning to her happy felt face. "She got rid of her TV."

"Of course she did. Give me a break! You know she waits until he goes to bed and then watches *America's Next Top Model* on her laptop in the dark."

Dolly stepped back and looked at Beatrice from afar. Her friend wore perfectly tattered jeans—worn out by someone else, no doubt—tucked into stark white Converse high-tops and a Yohji sweater, designed to look as if no one designed it at all. Perhaps the piece organically grew out of the earth. Who could rightly say? Despite her lack of sleep, her hair had never looked so shiny and her skin had never glowed so clean. Her makeup was immaculate and her hairstylist Paul—who had chopped her locks into a shaggy bob—had taught her some tricks. Plus, she'd dropped five pounds or so. Who had time to eat? "You know what? You look amazing. Seriously. What *is* that lip gloss?"

Beatrice dipped into her trusty leather bag and pulled out a lip color that was neither red nor pink nor peach but an amalgamation of all three. "Because I'm writing Veruca's blog, people constantly send free products for her to try—which really means for *us* to try because I have to write about the ones we like—and this was another freebie. But I'm kind of obsessed. They created this technology just for Veruca. It supposedly intuits your skin tone and the shade changes depending on whether your complexion is olive, ruddy, porcelain, or whatever."

"People just send this stuff?"

"It's crazy. They just send us in for treatments or send stylists over with samples from new clothing lines, food from new restaurants. I had a cellulite treatment this week, where they attached electrodes to my thighs and shocked me with currents. And I don't even have cellulite yet! I think it cured my eye twitch, though." Dolly was wide-eyed. "Doll, take this!"

Beatrice pushed the lip gloss into her friend's hand, glad to have a peace offering. Dolly twisted the top off and lovingly eyed the sticky goop. "How does it know your skin color?"

"It measures your melanin, I think? Dude, I don't know. It's definitely not the strangest thing to exist in Veruca Land, though. Just take it!"

Dolly shook her head. "I couldn't."

"Um, yes, you could. Don't worry. I have like four of these in my room. In fact, why don't you come by in a couple hours? We *finally* have a night off without even TV room plans tonight— Veruca promised 'cause I'm so behind in homework—and I would love to spend a few hours hanging with you. I can get work done after you leave. We'll order room service."

"Room service?"

"At Veruca's, there's kind of a celebrity chef. Mario something." Beatrice felt a little embarrassed but then threw an arm around Dolly and gave her a squeeze. "I think you're going to like it—a lot."

"What about the Axis of Evil?"

"Oh, don't worry about them. They sort of grow on you. Like toxic flesh-eating fungus."

"Don't tell me you like them after all that grief you gave me for consorting with the, what did you call them? Oh, yeah: 'superficial nouveau trash.'"

"Let's just say that I despise them *less*."

Dolly raised an eyebrow as skeptically as she could. "This is a long way from your roach motel."

"Sure is, D. Thank goodness."

"I need to find Stephen at their apartment and have a talk tonight." Dolly bit her lip, her eyebrows meeting in a crinkled point above her nose. "I feel like he's been avoiding me because of all that commitment mumbo jumbo he was spewing after the summer and I have no idea how to let him down easy, you know? No one buys that whole let's-just-be-friends thing, even when you really mean it."

"It's going to be fine. It's Stephen. You guys are so tight. He'll totally understand. Who can blame him for loving you, anyway? And now it's even more important that you come over afterward, so we can dissect the incident and eat away the pain with molten lava cake and a hot toddy."

"I guess you're right." Dolly bent her knees in plié and then hopped, a hopeful sign. "Ugh. I hope Cynthia doesn't try to get me into a ménage à trois with her weird boyfriend again."

"Wait, *again*?"

"You don't want to know. See? You leave me alone and look what happens!"

22

BEATRICE WAS WALKING IN IAMBIC PENTAMETER toward her Romantic poetry class when Kendra tracked her down on campus. No sooner had the youngest Bernstein uttered the words "free night" to her Muppet friend than—unbeknownst to her, eight blocks away in a palatial loft—her evening at home became a celebrity spa party in South Beach, Miami.

"What? You're kidding me! I thought I had the night off?"

"You could have every night off and get the hell out of our lives, if it were up to me. But Veruca feels some bizarre attachment. I'll see you back at the apartment in fifteen. Don't be late." And Kendra was gone before Beatrice could construct so much as a "fuck you" haiku.

While misery and broken hearts propel poetic inspiration, anxiety is less fluid and Beatrice was spiraling into full-blown panic mode. She ran back to the Dorchester and—in her near advanced state of hyperventilation—took the elevator. It was inexplicably broken again. After the lift jolted back and forth and lingered between the second and third floors, deciding whether to finish the job or lie down and die, the doors opened.

She burst into the loft and spotted the socialite lounging stress-free on the ottoman in a silk kimono, while an army of others hurried to get her packed. Ever unperturbed, Veruca braided a chunk of her hair in boredom.

"Hey, V," Beatrice started breathlessly. "Um, can we talk?"

Veruca looked up, spotting Beatrice for the first time since her entrance. "Of course, Beany! What's up? You look awful! Is that . . . sweat?" She took her voice down to a whisper. "Did you take too many Vicodin?"

"No, no Vicodin. I'm just so exhausted, V. I have so much work and I haven't seen Dolly in ages. I was wondering if maybe I could skip the Miami trip. Just this once? I could write the blog from home, as long as Kendra sends me the tip sheets every night."

Veruca scrunched her nose like an adorable bunny, playing innocent per usual. "Skip it? But Beany, it's the biggest event yet. I know you're tired. We all are, really. But you can sleep on the plane. I already called all your teachers and got you extensions. And by that I mean Kenny G. called, of course." She giggled.

"Kendra called my professors without asking me? And you think that's okay?" Beatrice knew her voice was building to a shrill pitch, but she couldn't believe they'd interfered with her academic career without even consulting her. Her high-tops felt tight around her ankles.

Veruca blinked her eyes, surprised. "Well, don't be pissy, Beans. I just didn't want you to have to worry, since the trip is so last minute. Besides, don't you think you need a vacation? I mean, you've been so stressed that I think it's bumming all of us out. I mean, you're sweating *profusely*." "Profusely" was the word of the day on Veruca's vocabulary app.

On the other side of the ottoman, a half-hidden Imelda nodded in agreement. Beatrice unleashed an unhinged cackle. She was bumming *them* out? She was going to have to confess to her parents that she'd flunked out of college in exchange for a Yohji sweater!

"You could really use time away: pools, palm trees, tan Cuban men. You've been an absolute nun too. Strip off that chastity belt and let loose before a convent comes to collect! Plus, who else is going to keep Ben from slitting his wrists while I'm mingling with the elite?" Veruca laughed, but even that sound like meditation chimes couldn't calm the blogger-for-hire.

Beatrice was clearly in a delicate state. Veruca stood, padded noiselessly to her, kimono flowing behind in an invisible breeze, and placed a hand lightly on her back, steering her toward the passages to her room. "Relax, Beany. Breathe," Veruca repeated, her palm radiating heat, as it might during a Reiki energy treatment. Beatrice felt the majority of her angst seep out in one deep exhale. Her heart rate slowed to normal. And suddenly she was warming to the idea of a trip. She knew that going away was a horrible plan and might only sink her deeper into a backlogged hole. But dipping her body into chlorinated pool waters sounded like poetry in itself.

Veruca dropped her voice to a whisper. "Besides, isn't it true that you've never left the city? Wouldn't you like to see more of the world, while you can? I mean, you only live once and so far, if you don't mind my saying so, you've been living pretty sedately. And that's a fact." She giggled. "'And that's a fact.' Isn't that what your mother always says?"

"You've met my mother? Then you know she would kill me if I went on this trip."

"Really, Beany? I'm surprised at your reticence!" "Reticence" was yesterday's vocabulary word. "You're more mature than most of us and yet you allow your mother to dictate your decisions? You're not a teenager anymore, Beans. You're out on your own. This is *your* life."

It was a persuasive argument. Beatrice inflated her cheeks, then slowly released the air. "Of course I want to travel," she admitted sheepishly, shifting in her Converse and eyeing her tangled laces. "Please don't be offended, but is Miami really like 'the world'? Not to be ungrateful, but I'm not sure I need to fly to a different state to watch men with waxed chests and bad spray tans pop-lock to Latin rhythm techno."

"Wait, Kendra didn't explain? We're flying to Miami for some R and R, but then we're off directly to London for the Frieze Art Fair and then to art fairs in Paris and Rio. Then maybe we'll stop in at the Camino Real in Mexico City on the way home, just for fun. Or Cuba! Kendra says we have the budget to pay you double for your trouble!"

Dreyfus looked up from a *W* magazine and chimed in, "It's going to be fabulous. If you're lucky, I'll take you for a dance floor spin again."

However torn Beatrice felt about leaving school for at least two entire weeks, she could hardly turn down the chance to travel the world looking at art. According to Veruca, her teachers were being oddly reasonable. Maybe she could even talk them into independent studies about— "Wait! I don't have a passport!"

"Oh, silly Beany! Let us worry about that." And with that, she was dismissed. Veruca removed her hand from Beatrice's back and, though her blood pressure rebounded a bit as the socialite tiptoed away, the youngest Bernstein was now committed to the trip. Double the pay was a lot of money. Beatrice followed the eyeliner trail back to her room. Though Veruca had eyes everywhere, no one had seemed to notice the cosmetic breadcrumbs.

In her bedroom, the packing process was not only under way but practically finished. So much for free will in Veruca's world. Several enormous bags—new Louis Vuitton luggage, Beatrice surmised—sat zipped in the center of the room, while Penny and her assistants bustled around.

"We're finished, Miss Bernstein." Penny smiled, a small beauty mark on her cheek dancing with each word. "Bea."

Beatrice was relieved to see the housekeeper. "Penny, please tell me you're coming with us. You're my one foothold in reality." Beatrice flopped down on the bed on her back, sending a pillow or four flying to the floor.

"Sorry, Bea. We have to keep things under control from a distance, I'm afraid."

Beatrice sighed and sat up to grab a pillow and place it back on the bed. "I wish you were going to be there." She meant it.

At first Beatrice had taken Penny for a young woman, though she was short and plump in a motherly way; and then, an older one, though she was without gray hair or wrinkles. But Penny's age was amorphous: somewhere between twenty-eight and sixty-two and perhaps every number in between. Like a female Morgan Freeman, she had a slow, measured way of imparting wisdom that just seemed to make it true. For Beatrice, Penny's voice was like a spoonful of sugar. With only a sigh, the housekeeper could have convinced Beatrice to buy a bridge or two.

Beatrice eyed Penny from across the room. "Did you use that new shampoo that I gave you? The olive oil and cocoa bean one?"

Penny had the world's most beautiful thick brown hair. And, though she generally kept it knotted behind her neck, when she let it tumble out, she was like a squat brunette Rapunzel. Maybe that was why Beatrice saw her as a life raft. Her hair was their last-ditch escape route.

"I did! You know my husband goes crazy for my hair anyway, but now he's gone bananas."

"Who can blame him, Pen? I wish I had that hair too. I'll cover the product this week on the blog." Penny was always referencing her husband, but she never called him by name. And though Beatrice hadn't the guts to ask, she often wondered when Penny possibly found the time to see him, which was sad. The housekeeper was always available via the hallway's call box and she sat with Beatrice and the frogs during late-night blogging sessions, even when Beatrice begged her to abandon her post and go rest. Thus, Beatrice liked to imagine that there were many versions of Penny, who could simultaneously live life at home with a doting husband and work inside apartment 333.

"Don't worry about the trip, Bea. You'll have a wonderful time. Think of this as your very own study-abroad program"—Penny smiled—"but condensed and with fewer obnoxious American college students."

Beatrice smiled. Penny was probably right. And, in truth, so was Veruca: Beatrice had been supercelibate lately. Not that she'd had much past success with casual relationships, but a fling with a mysterious foreign man might raise her spirits. Her current identity seemed to have so little to do with her former one anyway. She could play dress-up as anyone she chose.

Penny—who could sense Beatrice's angst about taking a hiatus from classes—assured and reassured Beatrice that all necessary schoolbooks were packed and introduced her to her new MacBook Helium laptop (not yet released in stores), compliments of Veruca for the trip. Beatrice's old files had been transferred and, sure, it was crazy lightweight as if made of pure air, but she couldn't help thinking that her privacy was compromised.

As it was too late to correct any "security breach" anyway, she readied to vacate. That was when her phone rang. The shrill sound forecasted the caller's animosity in advance. It was Gertie. Penny waved a silent adieu and Beatrice, experiencing a sinking sensation so intense that she might have been free falling on a roller coaster, reluctantly picked up the phone.

"Gert? I really can't talk right now."

Beatrice had skipped last Thursday's dinner, citing an imaginary esoteric harmonica quartet performance. Plus, she hadn't exactly been on top of returning her family's calls lately. Damn. Thursday night dinners. How was she going to explain missing two more to her parents?

"Oh, really? You can't talk? What the hell else is new, Little Bea?" said Gertie. "I've been trying to reach you for weeks! Mom and Dad are practically about to send out a search party."

"Right. As long as the search party doesn't have to leave New York."

"What?"

"Nothing. Look, I'm sorry, Gert. I love you. But I'm running out and I'll be traveling abroad for a couple weeks starting today, so just tell Mom and Dad I'll be in touch. I think my BlackBerry may be working some of the time, but I have no idea."

There was a long, dead pause on the other end of the line. "Excuse me?"

"I said—"

"I know what you said, Beatrice. I'm not a moron. You're telling me that you're just leaving the country on a whim? You do know you're a college senior, right? With classes and responsibilities?"

"Gertie, I'm an adult. You're so—" Beatrice glanced impatiently at her wrist, as if she ever wore a watch, and stomped a foot though no one was there to witness her frustration.

"Look, I know who you've been hanging out with, Sis, and you're way out of your league. There are some seriously worrisome stories circulating about that Veruca girl. You've no idea who these people are. You can't know, because if you did, you wouldn't be hanging out with them. I love you, okay? I want what's best for you, and what's best for you is to get out of there and come home for a few days."

Beatrice was enraged. Why did everyone assume she didn't know her own needs? "What's best for me? Since when do any of you care what's best for me, unless it matches your own rigid doctrine? I want to do things my way and, for once, my opinions and skills are being valued. So why am I running off so 'irresponsibly' in the middle of my senior year? To have some real-life experiences, make some money, and maybe even to get away from you. And you can tell Mom and Dad that too."

Silence crackled, running electric suicides back and forth across the tangled telephone lines. Beatrice was about to hang up, but she hesitated. As always, Gertie remained calm. The younger sister could almost hear the elder parting those famous red lips. "Proust says, 'We do not succeed in changing things according to our desire, but gradually our desire changes.'"

"What the hell does that mean, Gertie?"

"It means be careful, Bea. You can't change the entire palette of your life overnight without losing something in the process. The kaleidoscope may be captivating, but it can also spin out of control."

"What does that even *mean*? Can you speak English for a change? I guess I'm too dense to understand." Apparently Gertie didn't have Penny's gift for soothing Beatrice.

"I know you saw me at that art opening a few weeks ago and ducked away. If you need to strike out on your own and rebel, then do your thing, but you know in your gut that this world isn't for you. Otherwise you wouldn't have left that night without saying hello. You can't change who you are at core. Love you, little sister. Be safe."

Beatrice heard the phone click off on the other end. She sighed loudly, unaware that her big sister was exhaling the same exact

tone downtown. She picked up her trusty brown bag. But then—
without hesitation—she put it back down. If she was going to
dive into this new experience, she needed to leave everything old
behind. She stalked into the closet and picked up a slate gray
Balenciaga motorcycle number, which looked angry enough to
match her mood, then transferred her wallet, new makeup,
condoms (clearly included at Veruca's instruction), blank Moleskine notebook, and iPad. She slung the new bag over her shoulder, leaving the former one slumped sadly, deflated, on her desk.

As she walked out the door, she finally composed her haiku:

Hold your attitude
I'm going to see palm trees
Just try to stop me

23

IT TOOK EFFORT TO STAY ALERT during the ride to the airport. Beatrice was the last person to exit the car and might have been forgotten altogether had the driver not popped that ever-hidden head into the Maybach and poked her awake. She and Dreyfus played an ongoing guessing game involving their strange chauffeur, who they theorized had some deep, dark reason for hiding his face: a disfiguring scar, a fugitive past, a glass eye.

The group flew private. Their plane looked modest from the exterior as private planes go but somehow managed to be disproportionately gargantuan inside. Each cushy seat fully reclined, expanding sideways like a card table, and, at the touch of a button, the leather chair was remade as a bed, complete with a metallic-wrapped chocolate pillow mint. Instead of the usual oval airplane windows, entire sections of the walls and floor were transparent, so travelers could look down and feel as if they were floating above the heavens. In fact, small billowing vapors sporadically appeared inside the space itself, so that one's feet might occasionally disappear into a fluffy fog.

Much of this unique experience was lost on Beatrice, who had never flown before and thus didn't note all the oddities. Novice Bernstein might even have believed that cars always drove up onto the tarmac and let travelers out inches from the flying machines had she not seen *Airplane*. She was blessed with a silent row mate in Imelda and gifted a pair of new custom Ugg Fairy Dust slippers designed with a top-secret material called Valium to lull wearers into even deeper lethargy than a normal pair. Thus, once she experienced her first ascent up, up, and away into the sky with a sharp intake of breath, she fell fast asleep before even having "made" her bed.

Beatrice might have remained in a blissful dream state had she not suddenly remembered—unconsciously in a dream about having left something amorphous behind—that she'd made an egregious error. She awoke with a start, her sleep-swollen face creased. In all the chaos, she'd forgotten to cancel plans with Dolly! She was supposed to have arrived before they left, but may be she'd gotten held up at Stephen's. And now she was thirty thousand feet in the air and unable to rectify the situation. She groaned, throwing her head into her hands and rubbing her temples.

"What's wrong, Igor?" asked Ben, poking his head around the side of the seat. The noise she made had sounded a bit monstrous.

"I forgot about Dolly."

"You forgot your dolly?" Kendra snarled from up front. "Aw. Poor little BB. You wanna go home?"

"No, I . . . just forget it. I need to get in touch with Dolly."

"Just e-mail her." Ben shrugged. He sat in front of her but next to Veruca. Beatrice tried not to stare at the couple's hands tangled together on their shared center armrest. She really needed to find some male distraction.

"I can e-mail from the plane?"

Veruca giggled. "Oh, Beany. We have WiFi."

Of course, they did. How foolish of her to imagine that they'd ever be out of contact with the outside world. "I'm not sure where they put my computer bag. Do you guys know?" Beatrice looked frantically up and down the aisle for a stewardess, having no experience with airplane call buttons.

"Don't freak out. I'll get Dolly a message right now saying you were called away," Kendra snapped.

"You would do that?"

"Yes, Princess Beatrice. I'll take care of everything, as usual. Go back to sleep. We can't have you looking like a damn raccoon at your first Miami event with V. You'll make her look bad. Well, worse than you usually do."

Everyone returned to their business, except Ben, whose eyes lingered on Beatrice's face.

"What?" she asked, feeling her cheeks for imperfections.

"You snore," he replied.

Great. A slightly appeased Beatrice eased back into sleep, but not before noticing a small yellow-tufted bird perched on the plane's wing. When she later awoke, she assumed she had dreamed it. And, once they landed, she descended the plane's steps into Miami's balmy air and forgot the sighting altogether.

Meanwhile, at home, Dolly knocked repeatedly at Veruca's apartment door and then gracefully sank to the floor against the wall like a dying swan (or like a dancer auditioning for *Swan Lake*). She waited for her friend to show up. Every now and then, she called Beatrice's cell phone, but it kept going straight to voice mail.

A day later, Beatrice sent Dolly an apologetic e-mail, explaining the details of the last-minute trip, but, by that late date, the dancer was far from happy, having been stood up and fallen asleep on the building hallway's nasty carpet. Hours later, she had been shaken awake and detained by a security officer named Frank, specifically commissioned to protect Veruca from stalkers. (The school felt they couldn't be too careful ever since that unnamed crack addict climbed into Marcy's bed.) Dolly was not amused.

24

AS SOON AS FLORIDA'S HUMID TROPICAL BREEZE hit Beatrice's face, she was seduced. Visiting an alien land is always a thrill, but especially when one's inaugural trip away from home is at twenty-one years old. Like adult chicken pox, the experience grows more intense with age. Beatrice had read about "white sand beaches" and "healing sea air," always good for constitutions in Jane Austen novels, but she'd never aptly imagined the sensation of standing under swaying palm trees, cloaked in warm cocoa butter–scented winds.

She breathed. "What is that smell?"

"Jet fuel," grunted a groggy Dreyfus, who had just awoken from a heavy Ambien-induced slumber. He clipped sunglass attachments over his horn-rimmed glasses to protect his light-sensitive eyes. But even his cynicism couldn't penetrate Beatrice's peachy aura. It bounced right off and hit him back in the face with a force that made him bare his teeth. She wasn't even embarrassed to find Ben eyeing her in amusement. After all, what else was new?

Kendra released a deep groan of irritation. "Can we get moving, people?"

As they drove from the airport on an unspectacular stretch of highway, Beatrice soaked up every detail: tropical flora, strange Floridian fast-food chains she'd previously seen only in commercials, Cuban sandwich stands, and eventually 1950s-style Technicolor hotels rising from South Beach's shores. She wished she could stop and sample every supersized, char-grilled, cheese-stuffed, tortilla-wrapped, and M&M-topped concoction. She wanted to sip mojitos and eat plantains dipped in sour cream at local hole-in-the-wall dives. She wanted to find Betty White. Didn't the Golden Girls live in Florida?

Beatrice would in fact drink mojitos, but not at authentic spots where there was no one to see or by whom to be seen. Instead, the group pulled up to the swanky Viceroy hotel. They dropped off their suitcases with a group of bellmen, actually moonlighting members of the University of Florida's archery team. Always craving a target, each had trained himself to hit the appropriate floor buttons with ballpoint pens from the far corner of the elevator. Sadly, Veruca's crew would never witness this feat, as they were whisked off to a lavish suite to be spray-tanned, lasered, sugared, waxed, threaded, plucked, steamed, brushed, combed, and accessorized assembly line–style to Miami perfection in time for Los Spa Event hosted by Latin royalty (though nobody could say from what country). Ben was dismissed to wander the neighborhood at his own aimless pace until the party began. Apparently, he'd arrived amply groomed.

The spa's white chaises and shallow geometric pools set the stage for langorous sunbathing, though the afternoon's bright light, beating through three-story windows, rendered the white marble "relaxation area" almost blinding. The décor—from yellow chandeliers to white leather banquettes—was in the style of Marie Antoinette's hedonistic court, but on futuristic steroids in outer space. An implanted, tanned, and tucked set already lounged in barely there bikinis and silky caftans, sipping champagne and dipping hot-pink-painted toes into steaming thermal pools.

Beatrice was not a good candidate for spray tanning. Being

naturally pale and freckled, she emerged from the booth looking more dirty than golden. And she arrived at the party in a skimpy purple bathing suit cover-up, glitter powder, and frosted pink lipstick that only accentuated the grimy orange glow. (This time, she hadn't been able to keep the makeup artist away.) It was not her most glamorous moment. Afraid the orange dye would wipe off, Beatrice avoided touching any pure white furniture.

She reached into her new Balenciaga bag to find a pencil and interview pad and discovered only a digital recorder. A switch must have taken place as she slept on the plane. No wonder Kendra encouraged her to rest. Normally, Beatrice would have been mad, but the lure of this new adventure was too strong to sour. She had agreed to play Veruca's game for opportunities just like this one. This was the real world—sort of. It was part of her job to buck up.

Still, a couple of hours and several plastic surgery consultations later, she found herself gazing with impatience at the street down below, wishing she could leave all the fancy people and pineapple and spiced rum cocktails behind to explore the city. As waves crashed and then foamed up on the shore, the ocean water seemed to stretch up toward Beatrice. Wasn't she feeling similar longing at her parents' home just a month or so before? Apparently, the old adage was true: No matter where you go, there you are.

"I was thinking about jumping too." Ben slouched on a nearby stark white love seat in a clingy gray T-shirt, flowered surf shorts, and flip-flops. "These people are awful, sure. But no need to end it that way, I decided. Messy."

It took her an uncharacteristic moment to react. "Not jumping, just eyeing the outside world. Have you been to Miami before? It feels pretty exotic, considering what I pictured." What she had imagined was informed by MTV and involved wet

T-shirt contests, grown man-boys drinking beer around kegs in diapers, and a mysterious spike in date rapes. She glanced over her shoulder at Veruca in a fringed beach cover-up and red-bottomed Louboutins, as she shook hands with Gloria Estefan.

"By 'exotic' do you mean stripperlike?" Beatrice didn't crack a smile. Ben tried again: "Why so blue? I'd ask why so orange, but I don't want to upset you."

Beatrice put a hand on her overly tanned hip and stared him down. Then, laughing despite all attempts to fight it, she sauntered over to him, recorder in hand. His eyes looked particularly blue in the unrelenting sunlight. "You really know how to ruin a good pout, you know that? They replaced my pad and pencil with a digital recorder."

"Say it ain't so. You know, I have a feeling they sell rollerball pens in Miami. Get another and then use that Moleskine thing you're always carrying around."

Beatrice's hand went protectively to her purse. "No, that's for my own writing. I mean, if I ever have an idea worthy of it. Anyway, it's not just that. I just . . . I'd love to be out exploring." Even as she heard the complaint, she knew she sounded ridiculous. She was lucky to be there.

"But instead you're here with the tanorexic hordes." He gestured toward a cluster of gold lamé–clad models, pop stars, and older men wearing large gold rings. For a fleeting moment, Beatrice missed Ozzy the doorman. "And listening to this!" Ben referenced the speakers from which electronica was blasting with heavy bass. "Welcome to my world. So, what can we do? Maybe a therapy session would help? Here. We'll record it, so you remember all the important breakthroughs." He took the device from her hand and pressed Record. He cleared his throat and then spoke into the microphone: "That totally sucks, Sweet Bea

Beans Beany Baby BB Bernstein. How do you feel about that?"
He angled the recorder up toward her mouth.

She stood above him. "If you feel that way too, then why do
you come on these trips?"

"Well, sometimes the company isn't so bad." Ben shrugged.
She punched him playfully, as he turned off the recorder and
examined it. Her loose fist lingered near his shoulder. She felt
like resting it a little to the left, where his thin T-shirt draped over
his muscular shoulder, not bulky but lean. What was that muscle
called? No, wait, forget that question. What was *wrong* with her?
In search of a turnoff, she checked the top of his head for signs
of balding. No such luck.

Unaware, he looked up at her. "Is it true that you had never
left NYC before this trip?"

She cast a guilty glance around the room. Could he tell that
moments before she'd been imagining running a fingertip down
the side of his neck?

He tilted his face to the left and raised an eyebrow. "Is this an
awkward question? 'Cause, even if it is, I think there's probably
a better solution than ignoring me."

She exhaled, pulling herself together. "No, totally fine. It's
true. I've never left the tristate area." It *was* a source of embarrassment, but she was used to feeling both comfortable and
idiotic in front of him. The truth was that they were becoming
friends. And friends don't think about friends' muscles. Not that
he would think about *her* muscles, should she ever develop any.

"Well, if you think this is exotic, you should see Austin."

"Really?"

He grinned. "No, not *really*. But it's home."

That snapped her out of her panicked state. Ben was a private
person who didn't share much about his past. If he was bringing
up Austin, he probably needed to talk. She could be a "pal." Why

not? Beatrice sat down next to him on the small couch and used her hip to push him over, ignoring the residual vibration down her leg. "Move down! I want to hear about Austin. You sound homesick. And you're wearing that pathetic Houston Astros T-shirt, so you must be in really bad shape."

"Oh, okay, Yankee girl. You want to talk about the richest sports team in the—"

"Ugh, no, let's not."

Ben threw an arm around her neck, playfully feigning a choke hold. She tried not to enjoy the proximity. Like every (even casual) Yankee fan, Beatrice had endured hours of sports trash talking. As with many great debates of our time, the accusations were always the same, refuted with the same points. And, right now, she just needed him to remove his arm from around her shoulders.

"So are you? Homesick? What's it like there?"

Mercifully, he dropped his hands to his lap and studied them. "Yeah, I guess maybe I am a little. Not much to tell. It's really a small quirky town. There's tons of good music. It's nothing like Miami or New York. Mostly, the city has small businesses and that's what the community wants, so they fight to keep chain stores out."

"Wow, that's not the impression I got of Texas."

"Austin's not really like the rest of the state."

"What about your family?"

"My family? You really want to hear about this?"

She nodded. She really did. He was, after all, one of her journalistic subjects. Also, she was starting to become overly conscious of where his thigh—warm from the sun—was grazing her own and she needed a distraction. He smelled like soap and peppermint gum.

"Well, my father, brother, and I are supertight. My dad is an urban planner and my older brother owns bars there. And my mother"—he paused to scratch his burgeoning beard as always when he revealed something serious—"died a couple years ago."

"Oh, Ben. I'm so sorry." She really was.

"That's okay. Don't get all emo on me now." He flicked her on the shoulder. His nail left a white mark through the spray tan's topcoat. "I was lucky, really. She was funny and tough. I miss her, but the way I see it I had an amazing childhood 'cause of her. And she was a terrible cook. At least now I'll never have to eat her roast chicken again. It was awful."

Beatrice thought back to the only story that Ben had told her about when he was little. Apparently, he'd loved magic. His parents were having a July Fourth BBQ one year in the backyard and he decided to gather a group of their friends for a magic show. It wasn't until they all sat staring at him from lawn chairs that he realized he didn't know a single trick. He tried to fake one badly with a deck of regular playing cards, which sent his mother and father into hysterics. They laughed so hard they cried, his mother burying her face in his father's shoulder and leaving tracks of joyful tears on his light blue polo. And so, what started as a magic show became a comedy routine. It was a pivotal moment for Ben, when he realized being funny might get him farther than a top hat. Beatrice could see him as a child now, shuffling his feet, embarrassed below a blonder fringe of hair. She hadn't realized his mother was gone.

She sensed his need for a change of subject. He toyed with a corner of the paperback in his lap, which Beatrice saw was *One Hundred Years of Solitude*. "You bought the book! Do you like it?"

He exhaled, cool peppermint. "I do. I've actually read it before."

"No! You let me babble about it for hours the other night! Why didn't you tell me?"

"I figured I'd indulge you. You seemed so pathetic."

She bumped him playfully with her shoulder. "But now you're rereading it, so I guess my ramblings had some effect on you."

"Yeah, I guess they did." He smiled a little sadly and they sat looking at each other in companionable silence for a moment. "I must be losing my edge."

Dreyfus's commanding—though high-pitched—voice interrupted the moment. "Sweet Bea! It's time for your Latin Rhythms Raindrop spa treatment. Run along, newbie. The blog won't research and write itself." He pulled Beatrice to standing, some tanner rubbing off on his hand.

Beatrice turned back to Ben, leaned in, and said quietly, "I think Austin sounds like an amazing place." Dreyfus smacked her on the bum and she scurried off toward the treatment rooms. Then he took her spot beside Ben. "They're going to drip warm, fragrant essential oils down her spine and then massage them into her naked body. Jealous? And I don't mean of the treatment."

Ben opened his mouth to protest, but Dreyfus just shook his head. "Don't bother, honey. I know, I know. You're just friends."

Late that night at her hotel room desk, Beatrice sat typing on her new Mac Helium, waxing poetic—in Veruca's voice, of course—about basil, grapefruit, and ylang-ylang oils, "the cathartic nature of this healing treatment," "one of music's most legendary singers," and "the city's sultry vibe." The Miami Beatrice described, which existed outside the Viceroy spa, came mostly from her imagination or research about an annual Floridian art world event, Art Basel.

Despite her reticence, she had to admit that the Raindrop treatment—and a few mojitos—had turned her muscles into happy oozing puddles and that, for at least a few moments, she'd hovered unconcerned, high above the massage table, not unlike that pigeon that shit on her Moleskine. The basement, school, and that empty notebook in all its mocking blankness had created tension. But when the masseuse dripped lavender oil down her back, she'd felt a release; the muscles eased and her spine stood straighter.

Back to work. Sorting through her recorded interviews from the day—between Gloria Estefan and the spa director—she came across her "therapy session" with Ben:

> *That totally sucks, Sweet Bea Beans Beany Baby BB Bernstein.*
> *How do you feel about that?*
> *If you feel that way too, then why do you come on these trips?*
> *Well, sometimes the company isn't so bad.*

He was half right. Despite the rooftop bonding night, Kendra still seemed to hate Beatrice. One could get only so close to mute Imelda. And Veruca was spread thin. Even Dreyfus, entertaining as he could be, constantly peered over her shoulder for someone or something more important. She felt affection for them all, minus Kendra, but they still seemed elusive in some fundamental way. What would she do without her good friend the Cockroach Slayer and minimagician? All the more reason to squelch those fuzzy feelings immediately. As Veruca pointed out, it had been eons since Beatrice even went on a date, probably the root of these stray thoughts. And, with snippets of their conversation percolating, she gave up on writing, climbed into her crisp eight-hundred-thread-count hotel sheets, and promptly started snoring. In a few days they'd leave for England, and for that chapter, she needed her sleep.

25

VERUCA'S BIG LONDON PARTY FELL on the third day of the crew's British foray and started off *literally* on the wrong note. The musical act, DJ Bangers & Mash, tended to work late and sleep even later and had been preemptively jolted awake by his wife, shouting about his housekeeping ineptitude. Particularly, she sniped, she was on strike from washing his dirty Marmite-crusted dishes, folding his knickers, and walking his "bloody" schnauzer. Thus, he arrived at the party location in a terrible mood, which managed to infect not only the technicians and party planners he abused but also the music itself once the festivities began. Each song ended with a nasty edge, which put the partygo-ers in argumentative, irritable, and shaky states, as if they'd forgot-ten to eat all day and were experiencing a collective blood sugar drop.

Beatrice was not immune to this contagious grumbling. Though she hadn't gotten the free time she craved in Miami, Florida was still proving to be the "relaxing" portion of the trip, as their schedule got progressively more harried. She'd already been dragged from teas and luncheons at Harvey Nichols and Marylebone's Patisserie Valerie (when all she wanted was curry!) to East End studio visits and Soho gallery parties. They wouldn't let her stop at a Boots pharmacy for beauty products, a Lion candy bar, or even blackcurrant TUMS when she feigned a stomachache. It was as if she'd never left New York, accents notwithstanding.

For Beatrice, the trip was a blur of cobblestone streets viewed from plane, Maybach, swanky penthouse, and hotel windows. Was she damned to spend the rest of her life nose pressed against windows like a poodle? Tonight, it took every ounce of self-control not to storm outside onto Jack the Ripper's gritty streets just to get some space.

Rumor had it that Veruca was distantly related to the royal family, though she probably knew Harry from the party circuit. Either way, she was offered a special room at Kensington Palace for her art fair fête, which—along with an event space at the Tate—she politely declined. A dark after-hours speakeasy-reminiscent Soho club was much more exclusive, she assured a doubtful Kendra. The building was centuries old and formerly housed an overflow of prisoners from the Tower of London. But tonight the only thing behind bars would be cage dancers. "Quite clever, really," noted the British society pages, well in advance.

Opting for this location meant hiring a curator from the British Museum to display work by Veruca's favorite artists, which was "just beyond" tricky thanks to steep dungeon staircases leading down to a narrow, chilly space below that allowed for only limited movement.

For once, it seemed, Veruca had made an ill-fated decision: The artwork, though somehow levitating above podiums, left little room for party guests, now forced to close-talk with bitter black and tans on their breath and literally rub shoulders with one another (not a Londoner's most favorite activity). There was nothing to do but drink heavily to numb the discomfort. Plus, in the dim light, starry-eyed attendees kept approaching Madame Tussaud statues of Madonna, Gwyneth Paltrow, Keira Knightley, Colin Firth, and Winston Churchill to gush and then feeling angry and foolish when they realized they were complimenting wax. What a waste of time!

All the usual suspects were there, plus a slew of grinning dentists hell-bent on disproving stereotypes about British teeth. After all, for the younger set, white Jude Law smiles are to London as substantial cleavage is to LA. You really can't leave home without it. Beatrice clocked some other notable guests for the blog: *Actress Sienna Miller (who could not be coaxed into ranting about Pittsburgh), Elton John sans baby, and then the usual artists like Guillard Croissant and Maldrake Maldrake Capri.* The latter, Capri, arrived draped in a stunning Swedish supermodel. Even before their first drinks were drained, his tongue was planted deeply down her throat, his hand was up her skirt, and, as far as Beatrice could tell, they remained in that position for the duration.

Kendra's mood was by far the darkest. Her hair was extra severe, cranked into a topknot so tight that her eyebrows appeared in a constant state of surprise. In the midst of handling this party debacle, she'd forgotten to eat her daily two ounces of salmon and steamed vegetables. Thus, an uncharacteristic two cocktails in, she was two sheets to the wind. Ben and Beatrice watched her stumble around on her mile-high spikes, glaring at people she should have been placating and barking at one bartender until he cried. (It turned out that he was actually a partygoer, a cast member from *Harry Potter.*) As Beatrice struggled to maintain straight-faced conversations with strangers, Ben tried to distract her with absurd lines from *Fawlty Towers* and *Monty Python,* his whispered breath on her ear sending inappropriate shivers up and down her body.

But that all stopped when Veruca pulled Ben away to talk music to some British band called the Beetles, who swore the name was unique. "See, the spelling is different, isn't it?" Ben glanced back apologetically but didn't protest as the socialite sat him down at a VIP table and positioned herself on his lap. Apparently he made quite the comfy chair. Beatrice had no choice but to watch them, as the bar was the size of a hamster cage. Veruca held Ben's hand on her waist and pushed aside his floppy mop to gab in his ear. *What did they talk about?*

Usually, Beatrice did her best to ignore any romantic feelings that had developed on her end, but at present she felt a little pouty and a lot hurt. And that was absurd! Ben was Veruca's boyfriend, she reminded herself. (Maybe the four hundredth time was the charm.) His friendship was way too important for Beatrice to risk jeopardizing it. And so she decided in that instant, as a delusional person on the outside of a love triangle often does, to simply change. She would spend less time with Ben. She would treat him like a buddy, tell him dirty jokes, punch him in the arm, and call him "man." She would restrict her thoughts to the friend zone.

A large bang startled Beatrice out of her decisive reverie. She whipped around in time to spot Kendra fully sprawled on the sticky dungeon floor. "Mistress Together" had fallen apart. As far as Beatrice could piece together, Kendra had been trying to lock that poor *Harry Potter* kid in one of the cages when she swayed dramatically and almost tumbled into the wax Madonna statue. Instead, she overcorrected, slipped on a spilled Pimm's Cup, and grabbed the nearest object for support: a bedazzled strap-on sculpture by Maldrake Maldrake Capri. Instead of steadying herself, Kendra broke the dildo off its pedestal and fell to the floor with the rubber thing still in her clutches.

Capri temporarily pulled his hand out from under his date's Herve Leger dress and stormed over. "What is *wrong* with you, you idiot?" he yelled at a speechless—or maybe just incoherently drunk—Kendra. The artist yanked the sex toy from her hand and stomped off.

A nearby cage dancer looked down her leather-masked nose at Kendra and pronounced loudly, "How naff!"

Beatrice wasn't sure what that meant, but it didn't sound kind. She kneeled down to help Kendra up, waving away a group of dentists who wanted to check her teeth. "You okay?"

"Blathmaaaachram," she answered. She smelled like a sour vat of Long Island iced tea.

"Sorry?"

"Blacghk calb."

With considerable trouble, Beatrice helped a wobbly Kendra to her feet. The chick needed fresh air and a toothbrush STAT. She sat Kendra on a barstool and propped her up, using her own back to hold her in place, wondering how in the world they'd get her up those stone stairs.

"She said, 'black cab,' newbie," Dreyfus said, standing to her right with whiskey-thick breath. "And Her Drunkness is correct. You need to get her out of here and into a taxi before people start talking."

"Me?" said Beatrice. "But she hates me!" Kendra was leaning facedown on the bar muttering something about caged bartenders, her cheek squished against a pile of ash.

"Sweet Bea," said Dreyfus, "we can hardly leave Veruca alone to host the party, can we? With Kendra down, I'm obviously the next line of defense." He straightened his glasses for effect. His eyes seemed particularly magnified and Beatrice suddenly found them creepy. "Unless you want to let her lie on the bar." They both looked over at Kendra, who was open-mouthed and inches from a wad of old gum.

"Fine. But you owe me. And I need help getting her out of here."

"You rang?" Ben appeared heroically. "I'll help you get her out. But can I draw on her face first?" Pretending not to strain, he grabbed Kendra off her barstool and threw her over his shoulder. Before mounting the steps, he turned back to Beatrice. "For the love of God, warn me if she looks like she might puke."

"I'll try, but you never do know."

Just as DJ Bangers & Mash began a set dedicated to his wife starting with Guns N' Roses' "I Used to Love Her (But I Had to Kill Her)," Ben did in fact get Kendra safely to the top of the stairs, though she kicked, screamed, ripped his favorite Clash T-shirt, and then promptly nodded off. Outside, he propped her against the side of the stone building, where many a drunk partygoer had slept off a buzz before.

"Thanks," said Beatrice. "Sorry."

"Why? You're not the one who passed out with a dildo in your hand."

"But I needed to get her out of there somehow."

"They did," he corrected. "*They* needed to get her out of there."

"I guess." Beatrice wasn't interested in arguing the point.

"So, where are we taking her now?" Ben asked. "I guess I should get us a taxi? Or is the car around here somewhere?" He peered up and down the crowded street. Hordes of Londoners en route to clubs wove in and around them, stepping over a disheveled Kendra. Others stood on a mile-long line, hoping to gain admission to the dungeon.

Beatrice would have loved to take Ben up on his offer to help, but she had established new rules about their relationship. And rules were meant to be followed. Or that was the rumor. "*We* are not going anywhere." She smiled and gestured toward the club's door. "You go back inside and hang out with your girlfriend and I'll take Kendra home. Now that I have her at street level, I should be all good."

"You don't want me to come?" Ben sounded almost injured. He ran a hand through his floppy hair. "Veruca would understand."

Beatrice was warming up to this new "friend" vibe. "No, I'm all good. Have fun! I'm going to flag down a cab, throw Kendra on her bed facedown, and then watch reruns of the original *Office*. But thanks, *man*." Beatrice punched Ben in the biceps.

He looked down at where she hit him and frowned. "Did you just call me 'man'?" He muttered something incoherent and then ducked back inside without saying good-bye. He disappeared almost instantly, as the pitch-darkness of the club swallowed him whole.

Twenty minutes later, Kendra and Beatrice sat across from each other in an orange corner booth under fluorescent lights. Beatrice tapped her fork to the beat of Middle Eastern drum and cymbal music playing from a crackly old ghetto blaster behind a greasy counter.

Try as she might to take Kendra home, her drunken sidekick insisted that she would expire without carbohydrates. That seemed like such a rare and reasonable request on Kendra's part that Beatrice felt inclined to comply. Plus, she was hungry too. After all, she was awake.

Kendra drooled on the cab's cracked leather seat as they drove in the hotel's general direction and Beatrice called the front desk to ask for nearby restaurant recommendations.

"A place round here at this time of night?" repeated the concierge. The neighborhood was residential and quite upscale. Only riffraff and Spaniards craved food this late at night. Beatrice could hear typing on a computer keyboard. "Our chef's gone home, but there is an all-night sushi restaurant, I believe?"

"Great! What's it called?"

"Iko Lai."

"What?"

"Iko Lai."

"Did you just say E. Coli?"

"That's right, miss."

That seemed like a bad sign on par with Creamsicles and cock-roaches. "Do you have any other suggestions?"

"No, miss." Apparently, they let the helpful concierge staff off duty at midnight.

Before Beatrice could snap something about supplying dry crackers, the cabdriver interjected: "You'll have trouble finding anyplace open at this time of night, love. But nearby that hotel is one local chippy and Middle Eastern spot, I know. Nothing too fancy, mind you. Shall I take you and your friend there?"

And so, there Kendra and Beatrice sat, sharing fried cod, falafel, and chips showered with salt and malt vinegar and served in a crumbled newspaper sports page. This was clearly a cabbie spot, as a bunch of drivers in woolen caps gathered outside and ranted about corrupt politicians, though no one knew to what country each referred. Drunken company aside, Beatrice couldn't have been happier. Kendra seemed pretty content too, although she was still sloshed. Beatrice had to stop her twice from swigging out of the catsup bottle.

The PR monster became somewhat coherent halfway through the french fries. She was eyeing the sports page—a list of cricket scores. "I never eat like this 'cause I'm an athlete."

Beatrice raised her eyebrows. Might as well humor the drunk lady. "An athlete, huh?"

"Yeah," said Kendra. "People think I'm obsessed with looking good, but really I'm just accushhhtomed to being in shape. I was almost in the Olympics, you know."

The slur was slowly waning. Beatrice shook her head vigorously, mouth full of pickled turnips. She wasn't sure how much of what Kendra was saying was right-minded, but it was interesting enough. She threw her hair up in a bun and got down and dirty with her pita, while Kendra continued to talk. Who says romance is dead? She and the falafel had found love.

"I was a championship ribbon dancer."

Beatrice almost spit out her food. "A what?"

"A gifted ribbon acrobat. My mother even moved us to a different trailer park to be closer to the gym. All the money from her Wig Emporium job went into my training." Kendra was staring off into the distance, toward the deep fryer, as if it reminded her of something, perhaps double-wides past.

"Wow. That's . . . surprising." Beatrice tried to picture a young Kendra hopping around on blue mats in tattered leotards, dragging a colorful strand of cloth behind her, perhaps made from an old bedsheet. Try as she might, she just couldn't imagine anything in Kendra's hand besides a BlackBerry or a leather whip. Still, she was intrigued by Kendra disarmed. "So you competed?"

"I did. I won at Nationals, in fact. But then, I didn't. I met a boy. A man, actually. He was a little older. I decided to follow him instead." Kendra contemplated a single droopy french fry and then snatched it up in one frightening bite.

"What happened?"

"What do you think? It's an age-old story. My mother begged me to stay, but I didn't listen. The guy got tired of me, but by that time it was too late for my career." She shrugged. Now Beatrice realized that Kendra's ramrod straight posture and tight bun were less affect and more habit. Was she truly this tortured soul? Did she actually dance with ribbons? Did she once wear (*gasp!*) color?

For the first time that evening, Kendra's jet-black orbs met Beatrice's own eyes. Behind the intensity was either sadness or astigmatism. "The ridiculous part is that I still love him. I'd do anything to please him. It's pathetic." She went back to attacking her fries. "Don't ever give up anything for a man, Beatrice, 'cause he won't do the same for you."

Beatrice sat with that for a moment, licking salt from her lips.

Apparently Kendra wasn't a robot, after all. Instead, she was regular old vulnerable flesh and bones, entangled in some unrequited love affair from which she couldn't break free. Finally, Beatrice whispered, "Where is he now?"

Kendra's head snapped up and the sharing spell was broken. "Why? You want to have a talk with him?" Kendra rolled her eyes. "I don't even know why I told you. I must be really fucking drunk."

"I won't tell anyone."

"No. You won't. Ever," warned Kendra. "Or you'll be sorry."

The two women were silent for the rest of their time at Ralphie's Fish, Chips & Falafel shop. Full and a bit nauseous, they returned to the hotel and exited the elevator on the eighth floor. As they turned their backs to each other and walked to their respective rooms, Beatrice barely heard Kendra mutter, "Thanks for helping me tonight. There's nothing uglier than a drunk publicist."

26

VERUCA'S DUNGEON PARTY may have been a mess, but no one was neat enough to notice. It got rave reviews from London's elite. Most could barely remember attending, which had to be a good sign, right?

The next morning, Beatrice was last down for breakfast, as she generally skipped the meal. Kendra sat decked out in matching black workout gear, having already exercised, and she barely looked up from her egg whites when Beatrice arrived. The message was clear: There would be no more incidents of public drunkenness, no more true confessions.

The events and parties continued throughout London and then Paris. On the upside, Beatrice intuited rules of unspoken etiquette. At art fair parties, no one actually looked at the art (until the next day, when one could roam without social constraint). At restaurant openings, no one ate. At club openings, no one danced. At birthday parties, no one discussed age. And, in foreign countries, where she'd hoped for that disorienting Tower of Babel experience, everyone spoke English. No one even called her a "stupid American!" At a random café in Paris, where she'd convinced the group—under the guise of a blog photo op—to stop for a quick cappuccino, she attempted to use her French. But the waiter lapsed into English, with a Southern accent, no less, and announced proudly that he was on his semester abroad from the University of Oklahoma. "Go Sooners!"

A grumpy Beatrice entered her Parisian suite that evening and, in the kitchen, found warm New York soft pretzels and mustard from her favorite street vendor, along with a few éclairs, *mais oui*. Veruca had a way of intuiting each travel companion's breaking point in advance, swooping in to produce some magical antidote just before he or she collapsed or went ballistic. She materialized the impossible. When Ben was on the verge of revolt, he arrived at a party to discover one of his favorite old bands playing, though he had mentioned his love for them only two hours before and they'd broken up years back. Even more bizarre, Beatrice and Ben both remembered that the drummer had died of a heroin overdose in 1998. But apparently their *Behind the Music* recall was flawed because there he was, banging away in front of them.

It was as she drifted off to sleep that Beatrice grew most lonely for her friends and family. While Dolly wouldn't return her barrage of e-mails, Beatrice's parents wrote incessantly, especially her father: "When can we get an espresso, Monkey? I want to show you the new series!" Beatrice's return e-mails were cursory with excuses about homework and exams. She hated lying to them.

And they were starting to get suspicious, at least judging by her mother's most recent e-mail: "You haven't been to Thursday night dinner in ages. And that's a fact. Are you cheating with some other lo mein? Waldo is starving to death without your illicit table scraps. And that's a fact too. That's right. I know about those."

Clearly, Gertie hadn't tattled about the international jaunt.

Things weren't copacetic with her sister either, so Beatrice could hardly expect a note inquiring about the rain in London or even describing some stinky professor's lascivious come-on at Gertie's latest Proust reading. She did buy her older sister a striking hot-pink lipstick that was "all the rage" in London, but then belatedly realized that Gertie would probably never deign to try it. It was silly to try to change someone against her will.

On the last evening in Paris, at yet another cocktail fête at a palatial chateau, Beatrice sat on a silk-upholstered sofa and watched partygoers mingle. She caught herself trying to peel off her nail polish again. Old habits die hard. To her left, on a table, petit fours as delicate as jewels—and covered with as much gold leaf—were there for ogling. (Actually eating them was considered gauche, though this was the now chic Left Bank.) Orchids, as tall and skinny as Imelda, lined the walls. And models dressed in actual gowns from la Belle Epoque–era film *Gigi* floated around as moving mannequins. Inexplicably, when a guest leaned in to examine delicate stitching or a rouched hip, music from the film would begin to play softly in his or her head. A few hours in, most attendees were humming "The Night They Invented Champagne," though Beatrice unconsciously hummed "It's a Bore." Outside, horses and buggies were parked with top-hatted drivers to escort everyone home.

For the moment, Beatrice was taking a much-needed conversational break. Across the room, Ben chatted with Veruca and a partygoer dressed like a "gentleman" with a cravat and cane. Perhaps he'd known the party's theme in advance. Or maybe he'd recently escaped a mental institution.

Ben caught Beatrice's eye, winked, and then excused himself, straightening his own imaginary cravat behind their backs. Beatrice couldn't help giggling as he strolled toward her, hands resting comfortably in his pockets. He looked as if he'd just rolled off the pages of the world's sloppiest J. Crew catalog. Over the last week, Beatrice had exercised her new "friend" tactics and was successfully weaning herself. She could now sit next to her pal without so much as a butterfly in her stomach. He paused to grab some canapés from a waiter's tray and then plopped down next to her. "Tuna tartare?"

"You know, I never thought I'd say this, but I think I'm officially off finger food. Like maybe forever. Tuna tartare be damned."

"Zut alors!" Ben smiled. "Say it ain't so." He popped the tartare cones in his mouth, one after the other.

"Good?"

"Ooh la la!" He shrugged. "Actually, yeah."

"Who's your friend with the cravat?"

"The count of somewhere."

"Chocula, maybe?"

"Yeah, that was it." Ben raised an eyebrow. "I could introduce you. I hear he has a whole wing of his Aix-en-Provence *maison* just filled with antique canes. Wooden canes, ivory canes, Michael Caine."

"Oh, my God. That's a terrible joke." The count did seem to be showing Veruca the intricately engraved top of his cane. The socialite feigned interest, endlessly tolerant. "Thank you for the offer of introduction, but no, *merci*. I was sort of hoping to find the object of my international fling here in gay Paris, but so far no such luck."

"What now? I didn't know you were looking to be flung." He cracked his knuckles.

"Isn't every girl?"

Ben's smile looked a little forced. "If I'd known, I would have helped you find someone, maybe without a cravat, but with a bolo tie instead."

"You know, I think a bolo might be easier to find in your native Texas." There wasn't even a French word for the cowboy-beloved leather strands connected by a silver pendant, except maybe *"répugnant."*

"No, I'm afraid I'm sadly out of luck. Aside from Johnny Depp over there"—she gestured toward the celebrity, who wore his sig-nature beret, as if people still didn't get that he preferred France—"I haven't seen anyone quite to my liking." But then her eyes lingered on a new addition to the party, a cute blond guy in a black concert T-shirt and jeans. "Although," she said, "who's that guy?"

"Wait. You're serious?" Ben was clearly put off. He tapped his toe rapidly against the marble floor, making a knock-knock-knocking sound.

"Why? What's wrong with him?" Beatrice readied herself for some funny anecdote.

"Nothing's wrong with him. He's a nice guy. I'll hook you up, if you want." When Ben turned to face her, his usually relaxed expression was contorted into what could only be described as judgment. He looked mad. Maybe she'd spent too much time in France, but Beatrice suddenly pictured him with an executioner's axe poised to chop off her head like Anne Boleyn (or some other Boleyn girl). "It's you I'm confused about," he grunted.

"Ben, what are you talking about?" Beatrice was taken aback by his visible anger. Just moments before she sat alone, minding her own business. She felt a pang of solidarity with Little Bo Peep.

"You talk all the time about finding some higher purpose or satisfaction in your life. You really think a fling is gonna solve your problems?"

"Who said I have problems?"

"You do, all the time. All you do is complain."

And here she thought they'd been complaining in jest to-gether. "I guess I got confused when you commiserated with me over and over again."

Ben opened his mouth to retort and then closed it. He rubbed his eyes with his palms and sighed, resting his elbows on his thighs. With his face still covered, he said, "I'm sorry, Bea. I'm just jet-lagged and a little, I dunno, I guess confused. Things have been different lately."

"Confused about what?" He didn't answer. Beatrice spotted Veruca across the room, tapping out clear distress signals against her thigh with her Vuitton clutch. She was trapped in the corner by a close-talking art dealer Beatrice recognized from past events. She gestured toward the socialite. "I better go save her." From basement dweller to social life raft in just two months.

"No, let me." Ben grabbed Beatrice's arm as she stood. Nervy sensations like alarms shot down through her fingers, numbing the tips. She wanted to shake off his hand or, conversely, bury her head in his shoulder and cry. Instead, she froze. "Better yet, we'll both save her and afterward I'll introduce you to that guy you liked. He's in a British band. They always get famous. You can say you knew him when, if you know what I mean."

Ben was trying to smooth things over, but Beatrice hadn't yet recovered from the preceding onslaught. Too many mixed signals left her feeling like an overloaded traffic control worker. She wasn't sure she could hold it together. She needed to escape. "No, it's okay. I think I'm going to find *les toilettes*." See? She used French. That would keep things light.

"Sorry, Bea. I really didn't mean to snap." Ben looked up at her, his blue eyes pleading. And that was no easy feat, as light eyes never seem to project quite as much meaning. His palm slipped down from her forearm to her hand. He squeezed her dangling fingertips, then let his own hand collapse onto his leg.

"It's cool, *man*," she said.

Awkward Beatrice stumbled away to nowhere in particular, leaving Ben—who had never even seen *Gigi*—humming "She Is Not Thinking of Me" and staring at his lap. She found herself in a far corner, up close and personal with a particularly disturbing Picasso. Dark faces were contorted into displaced geometric shapes, features floating disembodied off center. She dragged her cold fingers across her own face, as if to make sure it was still intact: chin, lips, nose, cheekbones, eyes, lids, lashes. Check.

Beatrice watched as Ben rose to interrupt the art dealer's conversation with Veruca. His girlfriend gazed up gratefully at him, but then moved onto the next conversation. Meanwhile, Beatrice reached into her bag for her recorder, pressed Record, and repeated the words "tuna tartare canapé" into the microphone, along with "Johnny Depp" and "beret," so she could refer back when she wrote her blog post later that night. She threw it a little angrily back into her bag.

Just then, out of the corner of her eye, Beatrice spotted a tall man waving at her from across the room. Wire-rimmed glasses, a purple ink stain on one trouser pocket, and a tweed blazer with ironic elbow patches identified him as an academic. At first, she glanced over her shoulder, but only Picasso's muse stood in oils behind her. And this man was not deformed enough for that woman's scene. In an instant, Beatrice placed the face: One of Gertie's most beloved friends, *In the Dark Room* editor and NYU professor Conroy Fletcher, was striding across the room, arms outstretched in cheerful greeting.

Beatrice panicked. Though recognition had been delayed out of context, she'd known Conroy for almost a decade. She couldn't face him. Not right now, when her relationship with Gertie was unstable and her sense of self hung above her head like a Cathy cartoon's question mark. But he was seconds away and she could hardly hide behind a willowy orchid plant.

Fortunately, academics are notoriously clumsy. Not ten feet from Beatrice, Conroy attempted to bypass a particularly aggressive moving mannequin and wound up catching her gown's taffeta train between the cracked rubber soles and worn leather of his dilapidated oxford shoes. He offered genuine apologies, while fumbling with the fabric, until an awful ripping sound echoed throughout the party. In this case, the music really did stop and, for an instant, everyone stood staring at this bumbling man, whose glasses were also now askew. Thank goodness he was charming (code for "good-looking"). Grateful for the distraction, Beatrice ran out the great room's entrance, leaving Conroy standing foolishly in the center without even his target as an excuse. In her rush, she didn't notice as Ben and that cute British musician both turned with disappointment to watch her exit down a long corridor.

So far, Beatrice had successfully avoided Gertie's literati pals and her parents' art world friends. However, a few random insiders had confirmed that she was in fact "one of *those* Bernsteins," which was important to Veruca for authenticity's sake. Beatrice willed her heart to stop pounding, as she reached the hallway's end, finding another right turn. She peeked around the corner in search of a restroom and instead spotted Kendra and Dreyfus in a heated discussion with the same art dealer from whom Ben had extracted Veruca.

"You need to move faster," barked the dealer, Mr. Stone, who was sweating so much that his shoes would likely slosh when he walked. "My sources tell me that he's close to finishing. The opening is in less than a week. My client cannot have that, so you better earn your—"

"Don't you dare tell us we 'better' anything, unless you want your client to lose all notoriety," Kendra retorted, her nostrils flaring as she kicked a foot back. She was a bull about to charge and the unfortunate Mr. Stone was sporting a red handkerchief in his breast pocket.

Dreyfus sighed, placing a hand on each of their shoulders. "Okay, everyone calm down. Stone, you have to trust us. It's under control."

Beatrice didn't want to interrupt the argument, but she couldn't just stand there. "Excuse me, guys?"

All three members of the conversation turned so sharply, she imagined their heads popping off and dropping bloodless to the ground, spilling sand. "Do you know where I can find the bathroom?"

Dreyfus pushed the glasses up on his nose—a cultivated idiosyncrasy turned nervous twitch—and gestured to the door behind them. She excused herself and slid by, mind reeling. Resting on the closed cold porcelain seat, she strained to hear the rest of the argument. But they'd taken their voices down to whispers. Beatrice glanced around the marble bathroom, noticing a small jade statue on a table beside the bidet. She would have recognized the subject anywhere: It was Sakhmet from the Temple of Dendur, the goddess of unexpected disaster. Beatrice shuddered.

Now *Gigi*'s "Say a Prayer for Me Tonight" was playing in her head. *And while you're praying, keep on saying, she's much too young to die.* By the time she washed her hands, reapplied lip gloss, and slathered on lavender hand lotion, only Dreyfus waited outside.

"Are you tired, Bea?" He linked his arm in her own. "'Cause I'm just exhausted. Let's call it an early night and get back to the hotel."

Thank the Lord. She eyed him suspiciously. "Not bedding some French house *garçon* tonight?"

"Not tonight."

"What was that all about with that art dealer?"

"Who? Stone?" Dreyfus waved the question off. "He wants Veruca to buy this artwork by his client, but she's not ready to commit. He's just got his panties in a bunch. And I do mean panties. I hear he prefers women's lace G-strings—Agent Provocateur."

"How very French!" Beatrice laughed. But she detected strain on Dreyfus's ferret face.

27

BACK AT HER PALATIAL "LOUIS XIV" HOTEL SUITE, Beatrice quickly wrote a blog post (*Johnny Depp, canapés, important Picassos hanging in the great room, blah blah blah*), then changed into her favorite bamboo eco-nightgown and washed the makeup from her face. However tiring it was to travel, she loved hotels: fresh white linens on king-sized beds, hazelnut truffles at turndown.

She nestled in bed with *Love in the Time of Cholera*—still trying to keep up with her Latin American Literature class—but there was an irritating tickle at the back of her brain. Was she uneasy about Dreyfus's nervous vibe? Was she annoyed that Ben had snapped at her? Was she losing her grasp on reality from lack of male sexual contact? Why had he snapped at her, anyway? Did it mean anything and, if it did, did it matter? Everything felt a little off-kilter. Intellectually, she understood that the shadows flickering across the incredibly tall French pleated drapes with golden roped tassels were a reflection of her book's pages turning, but they still made her uneasy.

With self-preservation in mind, Beatrice decided to ignore the aforementioned possibilities and instead crept out of bed to grab sleep-inducing melatonin from her bag. In her frazzled state, she knocked the thing off an oversized bureau and almost collapsed in frustration. "For the love of God! What is with me?" she exclaimed aloud. She bent down to pick up various trashworthy objects, from defunct hotel room keys to gum wrappers, and tossed them back into her purse. Her Moleskine notebook lay open almost under the bed and, as she reached for it, she stopped short: There was blue lettering on two of the open pages.

This time, the message—in the same blue ink and handwriting—read:

PAY ATTENTION: Don't thumb your nose folks, take a tip from mine. Hear today, gone tomorrow. Your new eyes may deceive, so trust your old ears.

This was getting seriously strange. Who would have written that message? Ben? But he'd hardly known her when she received the first one. It just didn't add up. And what did it mean? And what was with the wonky musical theater lyrics? Those weren't from *Gigi*!

When her cell phone rang suddenly, she jumped as if the Marquis de Sade himself had appeared, and ran, Moleskine in hand, to take the call.

"Hello?" she answered, out of breath.

"Hey, Bea, you okay? You sound weird."

She exhaled. "Ben."

"Yeah, I wanted to check on you."

"Because you acted like a shit earlier?" Beatrice unconsciously rubbed her forehead. She was grateful for a familiar voice. One that didn't sound sinister.

"Well, at first, yeah, but then I saw that guy coming from your room a minute ago on my way into mine and I thought I'd really driven you to desperation. A bit beneath you, don't you think?" He sounded like he was joking, but his voice still held a bit of sharpness.

"Guy?"

"Yeah, that huge bald guy. I really had your type pegged wrong."

"Ben, I'm serious, what are you talking about?" Dread filled her voice. "What *guy*?"

He caught the jagged edge in her tone. "I just saw some guy leaving a gift in front of your room. Veruca probably had someone deliver one of her surprises. I figured he was going to ring your bell." He hesitated. "I mean the doorbell to your room. That wasn't an innuendo."

Beatrice figured that didn't merit a response. Phone tucked between her ear and shoulder, she padded across the carpet toward the massive ornately carved door to her room, probably an antique dating back to when the king's jester died of leprosy in this very suite, and opened it slowly. Sure enough, just outside sat a box. It looked like some kind of child's magic kit in the shape of a top hat with the word "Abracadabra!" embossed on black satin. She let go a sigh of relief.

"Yeah, there's a box right here."

"Like I said. Is it chocolate? 'Cause if it's chocolate, it's only fair to share."

"Let's see." She bent down and easily lifted the top off. Then she froze and gagged. Her garbled scream echoed through the hotel, pinging off the original moldings and gigantic brass doorknobs.

Ten enormous brown cockroaches squirmed in and around the box at her feet.

Ben jogged down the corridor from his room toward hers. He slowed to a stop in front of Beatrice, mouth agape when he spotted the tentacled insects. He bent down, shut the box, and tried to put a comforting arm around her shoulders. She shrugged him off. "Why would you do this to me? Do you think it's funny? Is this your version of a magic trick?"

"I don't think it's funny at all. I would never intentionally scare you."

Beatrice knew what he said was true, but she would have preferred to label this incident an innocent prank. Otherwise, it
had to be a threat. In truth, she'd had a sense of foreboding for
some time. "But you're the only one who knows about how I
feel about the bugs," she protested. She fought it hard, but a lone
anguished tear escaped from her left duct, sprinting down the
length of her cheek and cliff-diving off her small, pointy chin. She
could almost hear it bellow as it fell—one last cry for freedom.

The Cockroach Slayer was frazzled. He ventured both ways
down the hall, as if hunting the bald man, then ushered Beatrice
inside. He closed the door tight and sat beside her on the bed.
She tried to calm down, implementing whatever she remembered
of Dolly's yoga meditation—something about breathing? Ben
was shirtless and barefoot, dressed in only jeans once again.
They sat alone together on a bizarrely tall bed. Why was everything in this room oversized? Was Louis XIV a giant or something? Suddenly, Beatrice wasn't sure what was driving her
hyperventilation: the bugs or the boy.

She inched away from him. "Do you sleep in jeans? I've now
caught you twice in the middle of the night and you're never in
pajamas or even sweats."

"I sleep naked." Ben shrugged sheepishly.

Oh, for the love of God! Beatrice did everything in her power not
to follow that train of thought. She snapped herself out of her
reverie before it could go further. "Wait, did you say that guy *just*
left?"

"Literally, like three minutes ago."

"Where's Veruca?"

"Still back at the party. Look, I want to get rid of the bugs.
Are you going to be okay? I'm sure this was just some kind of
mean-spirited joke," he said doubtfully, running a hand through
his Apatow slacker hair until it stood up straight.

"I'm fine," Beatrice answered as she went to the window.

Ben started toward the door. "Lock it behind me." As he left, he peeked his head back in. "Bea, do you want me to come back? I can sleep in here. I mean, on that chair thing or whatever?"

Beatrice shook her head and attempted a wan smile. As much as she would have appreciated the security, she wasn't confident that she could handle any more emotional confusion. She felt it in her gut. Or maybe it was some other part of her intestinal tract. Whatever part made a person want to throw up.

Ben said good night and shut the door with a click.

Now perched on the windowsill, she scanned the sidewalk for movement. Out on the dark rain-dampened street, a lone man dressed in black walked to the corner and turned out of view. From where, she wondered, did she recognize that gleaming head?

Suddenly, the golden ropes hanging beside her looked more like noose material than window dressing. A chill ran up Beatrice's arms, reminding her of a childhood game she used to play. She and her friends would drag their nails lightly down one another's head and neck and chant, "Crack an egg on your head, let the yolk drip down." In those days, the resulting goose bumps were a rush. Right now, they weren't so novel.

Was she being threatened? If so, why and by whom? Maybe this was an Axis indoctrination or hazing. You didn't need to know about a person's phobia of cockroaches to realize that a box of them would be disturbing. Beatrice wouldn't give Kendra, Imelda, or Dreyfus the satisfaction of mentioning the incident, just in case.

She thought about the goddess Sakhmet. The bugs were certainly unexpected, but no real disaster had struck. At least not yet. Beatrice picked her notebook up off the floor, where she'd dropped it earlier. And she felt surprisingly little shock when she saw that the words in blue ink had vanished once again.

A sharp knock at the door startled her. Why hadn't she bolted it per Ben's suggestion? Beatrice clasped one hand over her mouth and grabbed an antique silver letter opener in the other for protection. She saw the knob turn and heard the hinges creak, as it slowly swung open.

Ben! She exhaled. The Cockroach Slayer closed the door behind him, eyeing her cautiously. Because that's how people eye women who are armed and unhinged.

"Okay, Lizzie Borden. You gonna put that thing down?"

Beatrice lay the mail opener on the eighteenth-century giltwood desk, thinking, apropos of nothing, that the pretty object was the most unnecessary office supply. When she looked up from examining its engraved handle, Ben was inside her closet, pulling an extra comforter down from a top shelf.

"What are you doing?" she asked. "I thought you were going to bed?"

"I am. I'm sleeping here."

Beatrice glanced at her bed and then unconsciously back at Ben. "Here?"

He carried the blanket and a pillow over to the chaise longue (or "chair thing" as he'd so eloquently called it) and dropped them at the foot. "Here, actually. Unless you want me *there*."

She wasn't in a joking mood. "I told you I'm okay."

"Beatrice, you had a weapon poised for attack when I got here."

He called her Beatrice. That meant serious business. "I didn't know who you were! I thought you had gone back to your room."

"I knocked. Do you think a murderer would announce himself?"

He had a point. Beatrice slumped down on the bed and crossed her arms. Her hands were still shaking. She clasped them together so Ben wouldn't notice. "You think someone wants to murder me?"

The corner of his mouth twitched, restraining a smile. "I'm more worried about that hotel lobby clerk. I'm afraid you'll sleep-walk down those red velvet stairs and stab him with your mail opener."

Beatrice was intent on staying angry with Ben so she didn't have to face the real source of her fear, but the image of her as a letter opener–wielding assassin was sort of funny. Or maybe she was overtired. Either way, to stop a laugh from surfacing, she thought about death, destruction, and really bad *Saturday Night Live* sketches.

"Fine, sleep here," she snapped, once under control. "But quit furrowing your brow at me. You look like a shar-pei." With that, Beatrice crawled from the foot to the head of the bed and slipped under the covers. She turned around and caught Ben watching her. "And stay over there."

"No problem." He grinned. "Just don't flash me those sexy heart undies again."

She groaned and turned onto her stomach, burying her face deep into one of six squishy hypoallergenic pillows she'd chosen from the pillow menu. Snickering, Ben crossed the palatial room to the curtains, closed them by dragging a discreet brass rod, and then flipped the switch to the main lights.

Thirty minutes later, Beatrice was wide awake and wishing she hadn't bluffed about sleepiness. Adrenaline from dissipating fear was coursing from her toes to her split ends and Ben's proximity just feet away in the dark wasn't helping. Her mind wandered aim-lessly, random thoughts pinging around in her brain.

Finally, she couldn't take it anymore. Still staring up at the swirly patterns on the ceiling, which by now she'd memorized through the blackness, she whispered, "Hey, Ben? Are you awake?"

"I am now."

"Sorry. Go back to sleep," she apologized. It sounded just as insincere as it was.

Ben's blanket rustled as he flipped onto his back. Was he sleeping in his jeans? "What's up?"

"Do you have a favorite horror movie?"

"Seriously? That's what you want to talk about? It's the middle of the night. I was hoping for a more salacious question like, 'Want to play Truth or Dare?' Or 'Do you want to get in bed with me because that chair must be really fucking uncomfortable?' Something like that."

She was silent for a beat and then continued rambling. "Did you know that more women than men see horror movies?"

"She's finally lost it, folks."

"Hey, I was thinking. Maybe I should have been an FBI agent. Then I would know how to protect myself."

"Okay. I guess that's our next topic?" Ben said. "First of all, I'm pretty sure that twenty-one is not too old to switch careers. You can't 'should have been' anything yet. Second of all, seriously?"

"I like TV cop shows."

"Well, that *would* qualify you."

"Whatever. What do you know? I'd totally kick your ass if I was an FBI agent."

"I'm sure." Ben sighed, tucking his hands behind his head as if he was lying on a beach. "Maybe instead you should create a TV show about an undercover FBI agent who disguises herself as a postal worker and then stabs people with mail openers."

"*Zip Code Red*!" Beatrice exclaimed.

"What's that?"

"The name of the show."

"What? No! That's terrible."

From their opposite ends of the room, Ben and Beatrice started laughing a little and, pretty soon, neither could stop. As the day's tension lifted, exhaustion had been replaced by slaphappiness. Tears streamed down Beatrice's face as she struggled to regain control. Finally, she managed, "Whatever. I'd kick your ass, if I was a TV writer too."

They were contentedly quiet for a minute.

"Hey, Ben?"

"Yup?"

She paused. "Why did you snap at me today?"

Beatrice wasn't sure what gave her the guts to ask and she bit her lip as she waited for his response. Ben took so long to consider the question that she started to imagine that he wouldn't answer. He'd gone still. "I'm not sure. I think . . . I don't know what to say. I don't want to say the wrong thing." Well, that was an unsatisfactory answer.

"Okay," she said. It really wasn't.

An extended silence fell, hanging more like a semicolon than a period. He broke it. "Can I tell you something?"

"Sure."

"Yesterday was my mother's birthday."

It was matter-of-fact. His voice didn't waver. She hadn't been expecting this.

Beatrice was swallowed whole by guilt. She had given Ben a terrible time that evening. She'd yelled at him, *twice*. Now she wanted to sit up in bed and apologize face-to-face, but she knew she'd be breaking some unspoken rule. Talking to a shared ceiling was like being in a confessional: no eye contact, no shame. There was a reason he had told her about his mother in the dark. Beatrice hoped her voice wouldn't convey too much pity. He'd hate that. "Ben. I'm so sorry. Why didn't you say anything?"

"There wasn't really anything to say."

"Do you miss her a lot?" It was a dumb question.

"Every single day."

"That sounds hard."

"It is."

She closed her eyes tightly against her own stupidity. Ben was the Cockroach Slayer, which made it easy to forget that—at any given time—he had his own personal drama playing out. He had snapped at Beatrice that evening, she realized now, because he was upset and sad. Despite his sometimes innocent flirting, he wasn't sending her mixed messages. That night, he had just been being moody with a *friend* with whom he felt he could be himself.

"I'm sorry I woke you up," she said. This time she meant it.

"I'm not. Anyway, I wasn't sleeping."

"Sometimes it can be hard to sleep with someone else in the room."

"That's true. It also can be hard if your legs are hanging off the side of a chair." The lightness had already returned to his tone, though he sounded tired. "Unless?"

Beatrice smiled. "Get comfortable, buddy, 'cause you're not sharing this bed."

"You don't trust me?" asked Ben, his voice fading, as he dropped heavily toward sleep.

"I do," she answered honestly.

"You don't trust yourself?" he mumbled.

But before Beatrice could concoct an acceptable response, Ben's breathing deepened and she knew he was asleep.

28

WHEN BEATRICE WOKE UP, Ben was gone and only the crumpled extra comforter remained.

Two weeks and three new cities after leaving New York, her most vivid memories were of airport tarmacs, hors d'oeuvres, açaí martinis, and, unfortunately, cockroaches. Still, she wasn't sad to leave Paris and the bug box behind, and she was looking forward to the last stop on this whirlwind itinerary: Rio de Janeiro. Gary and Madeline Bernstein's Brazilian phase had lasted longer than most of their other preoccupations. At one point, Beatrice wondered if, given the option, her father might have actually adopted musician Gilberto Gil and set up permanent camp in his vast art studio, discussing blues, rock, samba, and politics.

As a child, Beatrice had played an educational computer game called Where in the World Is Carmen Sandiego? The elusive spy, in her wide-brimmed hat and red trench coat, was almost always hiding in Rio. The place held a certain mystique.

Beatrice knew that she'd not be scouring dark alleys for double agents or even markets for local crafts, but at least she'd get a glimpse of this complicated city, a snapshot to unravel and recall. She'd accepted hobnobbing with the same jet-setting group of high-flying, hard-trying scenesters. At least they all read *The Chronicles* avidly and, these days, they all knew Beatrice.

She felt like Norm from *Cheers*. But without the beer gut. At parties and on the street, the occasional stranger even recognized her, sometimes confusing her with Veruca.

On the extended plane ride to Brazil, Beatrice was pondering the heavens from above through a section of transparent floor. She picked distractedly at her nail polish though the gels were like sealed plastic and wouldn't budge. Once transfixed by the experience of flying, Beatrice was now an old hand and bored. An angel dies and a cynic is born every minute. Reversing that trend is the true test of character. She was over tabloid rags and Anne Hathaway movies, too lethargic to budge, too tired for sleep, and too brain-dead to read another oh-so-sensual sentence of her latest Latin American Literature book. And one could watch Imelda—with her wiry fingers and pencil-thin arms—apply and reapply liquid eyeliner only so many times. The fact that she could do it without a mirror was impressive, but that party trick had grown old months before.

As if sensing her silent desperation and wanting to capitalize on it, Kendra approached Beatrice from up the aisle. The youngest Bernstein could hardly look at Kendra now without trying to superimpose a billowing ribbon trailing from her hand. But her stilted *Terminator* movements, large hands with short nails, swollen knuckles, and mixed martial arts–appropriate muscular thighs made it challenging to imagine grace.

To her surprise, Kendra kneeled at her side. "Do you want to see the blog's stats and metrics or what?"

A wary Beatrice leaned her elbow on her right armrest and her chin in her right hand, squinting to decipher the numbers and graphs on Kendra's screen. The publicist was the only person among them to use a PC, which she claimed worked just as well as anything Apple, even if it didn't look like "a toy." She pulled up *The Pfeffernoose Chronicles'* online analytics, Excel spread-sheets and charts, offering information on unique users, page views, and market research statistics on readership.

She pointed a knobby finger accusingly at one particular graph. It wasn't her fault. She didn't know how else to point. "Apparently, fans are mostly women and gay men from ages twelve to fifty-five, plus individuals from very low- or very high-income households." It was official: From RV parks to gated communities, the blog was a huge success. Beatrice went from feeling punchy to pumped up in a matter of seconds. She unbuckled her seat belt and leaned in to study the information. Kendra, irritated at finding her nemesis's hair in her face and tickling her nose, grunted and shoved the whole computer onto Beatrice's lap.

Readership had grown exponentially, topping out at twenty-three thousand daily unique users thus far. That number continued to climb as other successfully viral blogs like *New York* magazine's *Vulture, The Huffington Post, Style.com, Elle.com, The Daily,* and *Gawker* started posting regular links to her stories and retweeting. Veruca's blog was on every "must-read" list and her newest fan page boasted over 100,000 of her nearest and dearest friends. *Make new friends, but keep the old,* the song said.

The collecting of all these so-called friends made Beatrice miss her true best friend terribly. Nothing is lonelier than a room full of virtual contacts, who are neither close nor personal. Why hadn't the Muppet responded to Beatrice's litany of e-mails? Though the messages grew necessarily shorter and shorter, Beatrice typed and sent a note to Dolly every other night until finally she simply wrote: "Are you out there, Rocket Man, or am I just sending these into an abyss?" Radio silence.

Was Dolly really so angry about Beatrice canceling plans that final night in New York that she wouldn't even write back? Despite the chaos, Beatrice had remembered to send a message from the plane with Kendra's help. "That was something!" she argued. But no one was listening, besides the voices in her head. And even they screamed, "You're full of shit." Maybe the server was down at school. For two weeks.

"The numbers are really good, Beatrice, and they keep climbing," Kendra was explaining. "They adore Veruca. Or you as her." The feedback was positive. Beatrice smiled at her, mostly as an experiment. Kendra stood up abruptly, snatched the laptop from Beatrice's lap, and snarled, "Just don't screw it up."

Kendra swayed with the turbulence all the way back to her seat at the front of the private jet, which made the ribbon dancing slightly easier to envision.

Dreyfus, still half asleep, was staring at Beatrice. "Why do you keep checking out Kendra's ass?"

"I'm not, Dreyfus, please. Get your mind out of the gutter. It's just in my eye line."

Beatrice had kept Kendra's secret to herself, but it wasn't easy: She was aching to tell Ben. Eyeing Dreyfus, passed out again with his glasses lopsided on the bridge of his nose, she wondered if he knew about Kendra's Olympic hopeful past. She figured maybe not, as she'd not heard word one about it, not a reference to floor exercises, *Dancing with the Stars,* Nadia Comaneci, or even a disparaging ribbon-related nickname. Finding herself sans distraction again, she reached into her purse to check her notebook for more blue ink messages. It was blank.

Instead of retiring to the dining area when dinnertime came around, they were served by stewardesses who marched ceremoniously down the aisle with huge cuts of skewered meats, their very own Brazilian *churrascaria* in the sky. But Beatrice wasn't hungry. She performed a silent puppet show with her knife and fork, which ended savagely in an inevitable stabbing.

———

In Rio, the air smelled like diesel gasoline. The Maybach met the motley crew on the tarmac, then wove right and left past largely dilapidated but beautiful old buildings either decorated with or destroyed by graffiti, depending on how one looked at them. "Signs are defined by how we read them," Beatrice's father always said. "And so is the riot act." As usual, Beatrice was like a terrier, panting at the surroundings. Only this time, her cheek was pressed up against the glass, leaving a mineral powder streak, as their armed guard ordered her to keep the windows closed. *The man with the gun gets his way.*

In no time, the group was settled in pretty apartment-style seaside rooms at Ocean Suites Resort, overlooking Leblon's less populated beach. The boutique hotel's bleached-out modern décor with light leathers, white woods, and canary yellow bedding had been deemed—by Veruca or Kendra, as no one ever really knew—more appropriate than the more formal Copacabana Palace. On the downside, American elevator music belted by Barry Manilow and some lounge lizard calling himself Prank Sinatra pumped through speakers at the hotel. Even non-English-speaking guests found themselves singing "New York City Rhythm" or "New York, New York," as they descended to the lobby and walked out the automatic glass doors onto the streets of Rio.

Not that Beatrice was to *ever* walk *anywhere*. Humidity had serious ramifications for the girls' hair. Their stylist, Paul, would not have them destroy his masterpieces with fresh air! To hear him tell it, each strand's shaft would expand from the heat, allowing in all manner of dulling and drooping toxins. He nearly passed out from distress during the explanation alone. Thus, Veruca and her cohorts only took cars, that same car actually, though it hardly seemed possible. Beatrice had noted with some surprise that a cigarette burn on the left-hand passenger door, perpetrated by Imelda back in New York during a particularly drunken ash-ing attempt, was omnipresent in every car they rode in, in every city. Flying that same driver to each location was one thing, but how could Veruca possibly be shipping the car around in such a timely fashion?

Beatrice had only an instant to sit down on the bed, running a hand over the brand-new duvet. (Veruca insisted that the cov-ers all be previously unused, after a revolting *20/20* special she watched about what guests actually do with their bedspreads.) The room had a sweet little dining table that Beatrice knew she'd never use, a minibar with Pringles and Brazil nuts, and a cheerful view through sheer white curtains.

Thankfully, this first event was not a pool party, though it was poolside. Beatrice had dropped more unnecessary weight on this trip, as Veruca seemed to subsist primarily on tomato juice and she was always at the socialite's side being educated about the newest wacky anti-aging "stem-cell" serum, Swarovski eye-lash accessory, or canine charity. Still, there was no way she'd wander around in a tiny Brazilian bikini, no matter how much Dreyfus insisted the suits were "fabulous" or Ben dared her. Beatrice generally liked to keep her butt to herself. Plus, as soon as they drove up to the beach she noted that Brazil boasted by far the most striking beauties per capita. All the women had miracu-lously juicy bubble butts without any cellulite at all. Some had to be genetic; others were the result of openly embraced plastic surgery.

At this point, Beatrice drafted her blog posts before she even hit the festivities. Tonight, for example, she planned to post: *"Oi! That's hello in Portuguese to all you wretched folks stuck in the US, while we explore Rio's sexy samba parties. No! Just kidding, Munchkins. You know I wish you were all here too, sipping cachaça (that's Brazilian rum) and fresh watermelon juice with the Cariocas (Rio locals). It's just beyond!*

Carnival wasn't for months, but this party announced the beginning of rehearsals for the world's greatest celebration (*no offense to Mardi Gras,* wrote Beatrice). The girls were dressed in vintage one-piece Norma Kamali skirted bathing suits in bright fluorescent colors from traffic cop yellow to bubblegum pink, paired with ultra-high wooden and straw wedges. Maria Oiticica jewelry made from local pods and seeds—passing as upscale beads—added an urban tribal vibe. Beatrice's hair—now honey colored thanks to Paul's handiwork—was parted to the side and swept back in a loose chignon with a retro runway bump toward the back. Her green eyes popped under ultrathin dark liner and meticulously attached eyelash extensions, another beauty treatment she'd posted about on their international journey. "Creepy doll eyes," Ben teased. He may have poked fun, but he also couldn't seem to keep his corneas off her irises.

To the unknowing onlooker, Beatrice might easily have been the crew's queen bee. She was now a fully indoctrinated member of Veruca's gang. In observing the media princess so closely, she had unconsciously picked up some habits, including the socialite's coy crinkling of the nose whenever she was digging in her heels. She'd also perfected the blank stare, which Veruca—and now Beatrice—used to avoid communicating an actual opinion, perhaps about a given reality TV star or gossip columnist.

Beatrice had become one of Veruca's greatest confidantes, though they mostly interacted in public. Apparently, the socialite could more comfortably admit weakness to her alter ego. After all, it was like talking to herself. Between energy drinks and air kisses at parties, press conferences, ribbon cuttings, gallery shows, and bar openings, she often clutched Beatrice's hand and through plastered smiles whispered, "I'm tired like I've pulled an all-nighter every effing night of my twenty-one years. You're the only one who understands."

Occasionally she'd ask Beatrice a personal question about her upbringing, but as soon as her blogger began to answer, Veruca's eyes would glaze over. She would peer distractedly over Beatrice's shoulder and interrupt, "How's my hair? Is there lipstick on my teeth?" (Tabloids speculated that her lips were naturally the color of summer peaches and vibrant sea coral—in the vein of Gertie—and Veruca preferred to keep that speculation alive.) Beatrice considered confiding about the bald man and the cockroach package but quickly decided that Veruca had enough on her plate. Tonight, as they sat together in the car, the socialite glanced over at Beatrice and sleepily asked, "What's that purplish eye shadow you're wearing? It's to die for, Beany. Just beyond."

The eye shadow had been featured on the blog the night before. Veruca never read the damn thing, yet she seemed perfectly content to demand Beatrice's undying devotion to it.

"It's the mineral one by that Russian makeup artist."

Veruca scrunched up her nose.

"It's called Borscht."

Veruca nodded absently, as if she'd already forgotten the question. Despite her irritation, Beatrice suddenly realized en route to the party that, since this wild ride began, she hadn't spent an instant worrying about her future as a substitute schoolmarm or Mabel building Nicaraguan houses with Javier Bardem.

As they exited the car at the Copacabana Palace, Veruca yawned inaudibly and shot Beatrice a knowing wink. She took a deep breath, opened her eyes wide, and, with that, she was awake and ready for her evening's activity, which—as she made it seem with every party—must be the most extraordinary fête she'd ever had the distinct pleasure of attending. Every new rock star, politician, royal family member, or contestant on *Dancing with the Stars* was led to believe that Veruca's interaction with him or her was the highlight of her life.

Ben tagged along as always, shaking hands with Veruca's new acquaintances for the first few minutes and then doing his own thing: reading in a corner, chatting with local musicians, poking fun at Beatrice. But since the Parisian cockroach debacle, their spat, and then talk about his mother the night before, his mind seemed elsewhere. He was so distracted that when Beatrice baited him, admitting a deep love of Green Day, he didn't even bother to argue with her. Instead, he gazed blankly at her and then returned to his book. They were all pretty tired, she supposed.

Guests mingled around the pool, under tents trimmed with twinkling white lights and ornate flower arrangements. Capoeira dance fighters swayed and sparred majestically at one end of the courtyard, though jaded partygoers could hardly be bothered to notice. Tropical fruit seemed to just hang suspended from the stars above and pineapples glowed like illuminated lanterns. The turquoise saltwater pool was filled with sea creatures like mini-octopi, sea turtles, and parrot fish. A sushi chef dove down every so often to grab a sea urchin for the next plate of uni. Trays of *cachaça* cocktails floated at the top without spilling. And it was night, but everyone wore sunglasses (aviators, Ray-Bans, over-sized Veruca-style Phyllis Diller frames, mistakenly referred to as Jackie O) and stood around pretending not to care about the promising straw tote gift bags waiting behind the bar in regimented rows.

After a particularly scintillating conversation with an eight-foot-tall Brazilian model about the pros and cons of beach versus jungle photo shoots, Veruca leaned over to Beatrice and whispered, "I don't know where Kendra went and I can't see Imelda because everyone here is so tall, thin, and beautiful. I expect Dreyfus is off servicing some adorable cabana boy, so would you mind finding that impossible boyfriend of mine and making sure he's all right?"

Beatrice nodded and scurried off to find Ben, *finally*. She thought she'd never escape. At the bar, she ordered two extraordinary-looking caipirinhas made with fresh chunks of sour yellow passion fruit and crispy mint so green it glowed like phosphorescence. She overtipped the bartender by some unknown amount—foreign currency being so like Monopoly money—and scanned the crowd for the Cockroach Slayer, discovering him on the periphery in conversation with a musician. The band was clearly on a break. She snickered to herself, bobbing and weaving around other party guests until she reached him. "Ahem. Sorry to interrupt, but your drink—oh, *next* drink—has arrived."

Ben jiggled the empty glass in his hand, then set it down in a terra-cotta planter, almost teetering over in the process. He stood up with a flourish, as if he'd been bowing. He was obviously *muito* intoxicated. (Beatrice had learned a Portuguese word or two from the friendly bartender.) "Thanks, Beano. This is my friend Gabriel. He's playing tonight, but he also has a rock samba punk band that he'll jam with as soon as he blows this pop stand. Gabriel is a *real* musician. Right, Gabriel?"

"Jam at the pop stand?" She wasn't sure she'd ever seen him this drunk.

Gabriel—a supremely short, rather rotund young man with a shaved head and a mole on his cheek—looked pleased with himself as he nodded and shook her hand. He was forced to excuse himself, as the band was starting up again. "That's my friend," explained Ben. Then he smiled at her, as if seeing her for the first time that evening. "Why, you look lovely tonight, Beano. Beano. That's funny. Lovely, loverly Beano."

"Thanks, Drunky." She giggled. Usually Beatrice could hardly distinguish Ben's intoxication from his normal state of superior snark. Right now, she detected a definite slur. "Go big or go home tonight, huh?"

"You know how I do." He grinned, swaying just slightly. "Go big and go home. You hit the boredom wall, yet? 'Cause I'm 'bout ready to climb it."

"Before we walked in." Beatrice sighed, but she smiled.

"You feeling better? Last night was kind of insane."

"Less *bugged*? I am."

He cringed at the bad pun.

"How 'bout you?"

"I'm perfect." He grinned. "Or I was before you made that awful joke."

Truly, she was trying to push the roaches out of her mind. And she was feeling a bit cheered by the drinks and attention from pretty Brazilian men, who smiled at her wherever she went. She made eye contact with a passing male swimsuit model.

"Oh, I see how it is." Ben smirked. He flashed that magical smile, then grabbed her hip lightly. "Hey, the trip's almost over and we haven't seen anything. Really, *you* haven't seen anything. Let's sneak outside. Just for a couple minutes. Gabriel told me the club where he plays after this is just around the corner. Let's go see what it's really like in Rio. What do you say, *newbie*?"

Beatrice glanced nervously over to where Veruca stood talking to a young male surf trunk designer. "No, Ben, we shouldn't. She may need me for something."

"She's not your mom, Bea. And if I know Veruca, she sent you over here to placate me anyway." Beatrice couldn't deny that. She self-consciously pulled down her dress at the hem, sending it far too low at the bust. She pulled it back up quickly.

"You're funny," said Ben, bemused and drunk.

Maybe it was her own sizable intake of Brazilian rum or Ben's goofy smile, but Beatrice felt suddenly emboldened. "Okay, we can go. But just for a couple minutes and only because I feel bad for you."

He grabbed her hand. They slipped past the event's bouncer into extravagant marble halls with vaulted ceilings—yet another maze without directions—and eventually down red carpet-covered steps out into Rio's balmy night. They stood outside for a moment holding hands, inhaling the beach breeze carrying scents of smoky street food and briny ocean water but also urban grit. Sounds of chatting, tinkling laughs, broken glasses, and bossa nova emanated from bars in and around the Zona Sul beaches (Leblon, Ipanema, Copacabana), as if traces of the partygoers themselves streaked the festive air. People spilled out onto the streets. Beatrice was dizzy with liberation. Or was she dehydrated?

That was when she realized that she and Ben were still holding hands. She let go so fast that she gave herself the first documented case of wrist whiplash. Ben studied his own hand intently, as if it held a cryptic message, and raised a single eyebrow as his gaze shifted to her face.

"What?" she snapped. She was uncomfortable with the way he was looking at her. Like he'd just discovered the map to her mind.

"Just when I think you're all well-groomed and girly, you're all clammy." He feigned wiping his palms on his shirt.

"If anyone's clammy, it's you. You look like you've been chanting with shamans in a sweat lodge," she protested but then secretly tested her hand against the side of her bare thigh. Dry as the desert. "So, where is this place?"

The duo walked silently on the patterned sidewalk toward Ipanema. Sugarloaf rose like two conjoined Hershey's Kisses in the distance above the strip of shore. Water lapped against the sand like a gentle chiding, and jewelry sellers displayed blue-, green-, and mango-colored beaded necklaces to passersby. Beatrice couldn't help but think about how much her parents would love being here.

Beatrice and Ben turned down a small side street and discovered the steps leading to Gabriel's club. It was unlike any venue Beatrice had ever seen. Inside was a gigantic multileveled courtyard, where scantily clad people of every age danced as if possessed. The levels rose so high that the top tiers disappeared into haze. The people looked like extras from *Dirty Dancing,* only multiplied exponentially and in all shades of color. Everyone spoke Portuguese, when they bothered to speak at all, and no one seemed to notice their presence. Beatrice felt instantly that this—for the first time—was what it was like to be a foreigner, transported out of any familiar element.

Ben shouted above the music, "Gabriel said that this is one of the places where they actually rehearse for Carnival. Apparently it goes on all night long and into tomorrow."

"It's amazing."

And in an instant, Beatrice was spinning. Someone grabbed her hand and twirled her around. She recovered, saw no one in front of her and, looking down, realized that the culprit was a tiny older man, at least seventy-five years old, in a sweat-soaked yellow shirt. He shot her a warm grin, which seemed like the perpetual state of his face. "I have no idea what to do," she tried to tell him, bending at the waist so he could hear her from high up on her heels. He just shook his head, leading her through some steps. Fortunately, as she was remarkably uncoordinated, the details barely seemed to matter.

Ben, in the midst of ridiculing her, was swept up by a woman Beatrice could only imagine was her partner's wife; she was at least the correct diminutive size and advanced age. The club's energy was almost savage, and the more Beatrice spun and dipped, the more liberated she felt. She had been to a lot of bar mitzvahs. The hora never felt like this.

The string of songs bled into each other and ended with a

decisive bang. She and her partner bowed to each other, his head almost hitting the floor as he swung enthusiastically down. He then wandered off, probably in search of a better dancer. Beatrice hadn't ever felt this exhilarated. A hand rested on her waist and she looked up at Ben, standing behind her. He called into her ear, "Hey, let's get one of those coconuts with the straws from that main street and cool off."

They ducked out, laughing about how elderly Brazilians had out-energized them both. And a few moments later, they were leaning against a building, passing a coconut back and forth. A soft breeze cooled the back of Beatrice's damp neck. "I can't believe you didn't have enough money for two coconuts."

"Big talk from a woman with no wallet at all."

"*You* lug that heavy bag around all the time! Besides"—she spun around and posed with a hand on one hip and her head tilted to the side—"I couldn't exactly fit a wallet under this."

He nodded his approval while sipping from the coconut. "I see your point. Not much left to the imagination. Not that *I'm* imagining anything, of course. I'm way too much of a gentleman for that. But where's your trusty recorder? How will you possibly remember all the essential facts about Brazilian bikinis and granite-colored eye shadow for your insightful blog?"

She pointed to her head. "Not just a hat rack, my friend." Then she peered up at him more seriously. "You really hate my blog, huh?"

"You mean Veruca's blog."

"Well, yeah, Veruca's blog."

"Honestly? I think you could be doing something more . . . more. There are probably better uses for that hat rack of yours."

"Whatever that means. You sound like my parents."

"Always the way to a woman's heart."

They leaned against the building silently for a moment. He

offered her the coconut. She shook her head, so he set it down on the pavement by their feet. It was practically empty anyway.

Sharing tropical fruit juice in a foreign land is a very intimate thing. A true confession was the inevitable next step.

"I started writing again," Ben mumbled, unconsciously scratching his stubble.

He shushed her before she could respond. She clapped a hand over her own mouth. "Don't get too excited, but I've been talking to bands, composers, and club owners wherever we've traveled. I pitched a few ideas to a friend with a pretty well-respected blog. He likes the idea of using me as a correspondent."

With her hand still covering her mouth, Beatrice managed a muffled, "That's fantastic. What finally inspired it?"

He took hold of her wrist, pulling her hand off her mouth. "I figured if people were reading your drivel, why wouldn't they read mine?" She hit him in the arm. He feigned pain.

"I know you're an amazing writer," she said.

"You haven't even read my writing."

"But I've heard you talk about music and I know how smart you are. Or at least how smart you think you are."

"You think I'm smart?"

Beatrice didn't answer. Instead, she shoved him again in the arm. He shoved her lightly back, his hand lingering on the outer recesses of her collarbone. "Your hair looks ridiculous." He smiled, tugging a renegade strand.

"Does it? I'm sure I look ridiculous." Her hand flew up to her face.

"You look pretty good to me."

They were close now, their noses almost in Eskimo kiss territory. Ben was Veruca's boyfriend. Beatrice knew she should go back to the Copacabana to Veruca, Kendra, Dreyfus, and the eight-foot-tall models who all looked like Imelda, but she couldn't will herself to move. Thick air filled the space between them. Letters formed in his pupils, but she couldn't quite read the words. Maybe if she leaned in closer. He rested his forehead against her own.

"Beatrice! BEATRICE!" They were jolted out of their hypnotic state by the sound of Kendra yelling. Only then did Kendra spot them, leaning so companionably against the building. She stopped short and shook her head angrily, marching over like a snorting rhinoceros. Was she foaming at the mouth?

"You have a job, Beatrice. A job. I don't know why you think you're here, but it's not to gallivant around Brazil drinking coconut milk while you should be interviewing people. Who do you think you *are*? You're just pretend, an illusion that could be wiped away like chalk and instantly replaced. Your hair is a total disaster. Get yourself together and get your ass back to the party. Now! Or I'll make sure Veruca fires you."

"Jesus, Kendra. Relax. We were just—"

But Kendra was done with Beatrice. She moved on to Ben. "And you. You! I can't even bother."

"Shame," he retorted, unfazed. "Your opinion is always so valuable."

She stormed back toward the Copacabana and the epicenter of Beatrice's emerging mess. Beatrice could feel dread rising from her gut as she saw the potential fallout as a catastrophic slide show. She pushed up off the wall. "I better go."

He stood straight up too, his face registering disbelief. "Seriously? I think we should talk."

"I should never have left."

"You shouldn't have taken twenty minutes and had your first authentic experience of this entire trip? They pay you to write the blog, Beatrice. They don't actually own you."

"I know, Ben, and Kendra is horrendous, but I do have responsibilities!"

"To who? The feisty girl I met in the basement, the one who practically tried to kill me even after I'd helped her out, would never have let someone treat her like trash. That old Beatrice wouldn't have cared about crap like spray tans and eyelash extensions. She wouldn't have given up her old brown bag. And she definitely wouldn't have been invested in being liked by these sycophants."

"That girl would also have never owned this dress or gone on this trip!" Beatrice was getting angry, her voice rising over chaotic samba beats and competing drunken conversations. This was just like Paris: He was flipping the switch on her. One minute they were a team and the next she was being judged. "Sycophants like who, Ben? You're so convinced that the old me was too good for all this. I guess you imagine that naïve Beatrice Bernstein has been corrupted. But I'm an adult. And here's the truth, *man:* I would never have even gotten to know you unless I got sucked into this universe. This is your scene, not mine. And that is your *girlfriend* hosting that party."

Ben flinched. He bit the inside of his lip and kneaded his fists against his thighs. "You're right. I got seduced by her whole world just like you did, sucked into the Veruca Pfeffernoose orbit. She just has this way, you know, of . . . but I'm not going to use that as an excuse."

"If you've realized the error of your ways, then why are you still here?"

"I guess because there's no other way to spend time with you."

Beatrice froze and then narrowed her eyes, her head spinning. First he insulted her and now he was confessing to having feelings for her, while dating Veruca? She felt confused and exposed. She deserved better than this. "That's so twisted," she heard herself scoff. "Does that even sound valid to your own ears? You're still with Veruca, staying in her room and doing who knows what with her at night—because you like *me*. Do I look stupid to you?"

"Sometimes. Like right now your hair is kind of—"

"Don't try to be cute! Just forget it. I'm going back to the party, where I'm paid to be. You have no idea what you want and I'm sick of being toyed with by Veruca, the Axis, by all of you!" She started away, but he caught her midstride.

"Beatrice, wait. You know Veruca and I don't spend time together anymore. We've had separate rooms since London. I don't even think she likes me really. I know everything is screwed up, but—"

Beatrice spun around to face him, her cheeks flushed again, but this was no dance. "She doesn't *like* you anymore? You're not getting any action, so you've decided to rebound with her pathetic little alter ego?" She allowed herself to wonder for just a millisecond if he was being sincere, but her own guilty conscience only fueled her anger. "You know what kind of girl I'm not, Ben? The kind who steals her friend's boyfriend. Who's trying to corrupt me now?"

"Oh, give me a break. You're being absurd."

Anger at her infantilizing parents, at Ben's condescending tone, and at her own poor choices pulsed through Beatrice's veins all the way to her shaking fingertips. The Moleskine message had said, *Trust your old ears.* She would go with her instincts: She was being played for sloppy seconds. Her allegiance needed to be to Veruca. "You know what? Maybe I'll go find myself that fling after all. At least some random dude wouldn't put me in this crappy position."

Finally, Ben's face reflected a parallel rage. "You know what, Beatrice? I don't even care. If you have so little faith in me, do whatever the hell you want. Maybe it'll finally shake your head loose from your ass."

Hurt and fired up, Beatrice glared at her onetime friend. It's amazing how different a man looks once he's pissed you off. "Screw you, Ben. Seriously. I'd rather sleep with the cockroaches."

And with that, Beatrice stormed back to the Copacabana. It was, after all, the hottest spot north of Havana.

29

BEATRICE STOMPED BACK INTO THE PARTY, adrenaline coursing venomously through her body. She caught sight of her reflection; her hair was indeed askew, frizzy tendrils spazzed around her face. Her mother might have called the curls Pre-Raphaelite. Beatrice called them a pain in the ass.

On a mission, she stalked over to the bar, cut in front of several thirsty partygoers, and interrupted one midorder. "This is an emergency. I need a glass of any liquor you've got, straight up."

"Excuse me, there's a line!" yelped a waifish strawberry blonde. Beatrice shot her a look so withering that she clammed up and grabbed her boyfriend's arm for safety.

"You just want *cachaça*? No passion fruit or simple syrup?" the bartender prodded.

"Yeah, just the liquor. And make it snappy, okay? I'm in need," she commanded. This same nice man had coached Beatrice on Portuguese words an hour earlier, but now she had no time for sentiment. Normally, he might have gotten angry, but he could tell she was unhinged. Plus, she'd given him an astronomical tip earlier. God bless Americans with no concept of foreign currency. He grabbed a bottle of clear astringent alcohol and poured it into a shot glass.

"I said *glass*, not shot," she demanded. "I'm not a miniature person and I don't want a miniature glass."

"Okay, but this stuff is strong."

"I'm counting on that."

He handed her a tumbler of *cachaça* and tried to offer her some limes and a cocktail napkin, but she was already storming away, chugging. How dare Ben insinuate that she had changed when he was just as guilty of using the people he disdained! Especially after she'd agreed to sneak away. Especially after they'd almost kissed! And how dare Kendra talk to her like a servant. And screw Veruca for dragging Beatrice to amazing countries and never letting her experience them! She was like a caged animal. What did Veruca expect? Beatrice was sick of others profiting from her hard work. She was even angry at Dreyfus for getting to disappear at will and Imelda for being conveniently mute. Beatrice was furious and rapidly getting drunker.

"Excuse me?" A guy who looked about her age, in a New Order T-shirt, vest, fedora, and ripped jeans pegged above saddle shoes, tapped her on the shoulder. He was obviously American.

"What?"

Taken aback by her tone, he let his mouth hang ajar for a beat.

"Cat got your tongue? Talk, kid."

He quickly recovered, as he was accustomed to dealing with divas. "If this is a bad time, I can come back, but I just . . . well, I was flown here to cover this party for my blog. I write about celebrities and that kind of thing and I've always been fascinated by Veruca Pfeffernoose."

"What an inspiring story. I'm teary-eyed. Really."

The guy actually looked hurt. Beatrice took a deep breath. This man-boy didn't deserve abuse, even if he was dressed like the poster child for hipster youth. It was as if an H&M vomited all over him. He was also all blurry. Maybe that bucket of *cachaça* was a bad call. In the distance, Beatrice spotted Veruca whispering to a woman who looked exactly like Carmen Miranda. The weirdness never ceased.

She sighed. "Veruca is over there, if you want to interview her about her new Brazilian bikini cover-up and tote bag line."

"No, see, the thing is, this party is cool and all, but I'm more interested in her art obsession. You know, like what she writes about on the blog, along with all that style stuff? I heard you're also into art and I know you're a *Bernstein,* of the art world Bernsteins."

A fresh surge of anger rose within Beatrice. She laughed maniacally. "Right, Ace. What *she* writes about."

"Did you just call me Ace? My name is Brian."

"Whatever. I'm sure Veruca would just love to answer all your questions because, well, obviously she knows so much about art and culture, right? She's so damn insightful."

"Are you saying that Veruca doesn't write the blog? I mean, I guess that's not so surprising, but I mean she's part of the process, right?"

"I don't know. To be part of the process, do you have to actually *read* the blog? Like do you have to ever have actually visited the bloody site?" Beatrice felt her knees begin to buckle. Her face was hot and pulsating, white spots were dotting her vision, her eye twitch returned.

"So, *you* write the blog?"

"I dunno, Ace. Why don't you do some digging and figure it out?"

Beatrice strutted away, unsure she could stand up much longer. But just as she spotted a prime stretch of wall against which she could prop herself upright, an ugly face appeared too close to her own.

"Decided to finally grace us with your presence, Princess?" Kendra spat. "I always knew you were bad news. It's one thing to try to replace me in Veruca's life, but now you're hitting on her boyfriend? Why would he ever like *you*? She's an icon and you're just a poser—and shabby like that ugly brown bag you carried. Well, we broke you of that habit. Good doggy. Now come with me to find Veruca. She needs you." She patted Beatrice on the head and turned on her high heel to walk away. Beatrice grabbed her by the Diane von Furstenberg shirt and yanked her back around. Kendra gurgled as her collar pulled against her throat.

"No, *you* listen, Kendra. I'm sick of everything about you. I'm sick of your nasty scowl, your ugly attitude, and your stupid Black-Berry BBMing and texting all the damn time. I'm sick of your pathetic attempts to seem important, when no one actually cares. I'm sure there's some Psych 101 bullshit reason why you're like this: Maybe Daddy never paid attention or Mommy made you anorexic when she rode you about the size of your ass or your dog died of cholera or your sister beat you with a stick or your thera-pist couldn't get you to ingest the boatloads of mood-stabilizing medication you so obviously need. Or maybe this is all because some guy, who doesn't love you, ruined your ribbon ballet career. But the truth is, I don't care why you're mean and horrible. You're the poser. Not me. Everyone hates you because you're a deeply hateful person. And I'm sure, whether I disappear from her world or not, one day Veruca will wake up and realize that keeping you around as 'bad cop' isn't worth the pain of looking at your disgusting face."

Kendra's face contorted into an emoticon gape. "And you think *I'm* mean?"

Beatrice exhaled a deep breath, let go of Kendra's shirt, and threw her own pointy chin in the air. "I'm not coming to see what Veruca wants right now. I'm also not fetching or sitting or rolling over, no matter how tasty the biscuit. This well-behaved little pup needs a day off the leash. Oops. Guess my doggy train-ing got derailed."

Kendra growled and stalked off, as Beatrice rushed toward

the closest exit, knocking her head on a hanging pineapple, and outside to their waiting car. Like it or not, a cab was out of the question because she had no cash. She climbed inside the Maybach and asked the driver to drop her at the hotel. He would return for the rest of the group.

The car's air-conditioning shocked her back into reality. As her thigh stuck and unstuck to the black leather seat, she wondered if she'd made a mistake. Maybe she should have talked to Veruca before storming out, at least to tell her side of the story. But what could she say? Just minutes before she'd almost allowed Ben to kiss her. And she'd almost kissed him back. If Kendra hadn't arrived, she wouldn't have stopped it. The realization was like a smack in the face. "No. I would never have let that actually happen," she said aloud. "It was the mango-scented breeze and that sweet old man at the Carnival rehearsal. I lost myself for a second, but I would never have *actually* let anything happen." She groaned, tearing at her ponytail with manicured nails. "That's right. Blame the sweet old man, Beatrice."

"Did you say something, miss?" asked the driver.

"Oh, sorry, no. Nothing important . . . or even true."

Beatrice knew she shared blame for this predicament, which darkened her mood even more. Ben thought she was naïve, but she knew exactly to what devils she'd sold her soul. As the car coasted past, she glanced out the tinted window at the corner where she'd left the Cockroach Slayer minutes before. He and the coconut were gone. He probably threw the fruit out. Even in his anger, he couldn't bring himself to litter. The pulsing in Beatrice's head waned as spinning commenced and the first inklings of nausea arrived on the scene. That trough of rum was a bad choice, since she hadn't eaten a bite of food since . . . who could remember when?

An image of the Brazilian beef skewers on the plane ride over

passed before her closed eyelids. As she groaned, so did her stomach. Fortunately, they were nearing Ocean Suites. Beatrice stumbled out of the car, through the lobby's glass doors, and into the
elevator, where she endured a Barry Manilow lullaby the entire
way to the fifth floor.

30

WHEN BEATRICE HOBBLED OUT OF BED in the morning, the
view in the mirror was not pretty. Apparently, there *was* something uglier than a drunk publicist. Her hair stuck out in every
direction. She had raccoon eyes from smeared black mascara and
eyeliner, which she'd clearly forgotten to remove. Her skin, even
obscured by the previous night's makeup, was a deathly shade of
puce. But it wasn't her appearance that prompted her to dash to
the toilet bowl and toss whatever cookies remained: Her head
pounded like a bass-heavy car stereo set to max volume. "If
you're going to take me, Lord, do it now," she whimpered against
the cold porcelain.

When she was a child, Beatrice and her father once had the
stomach flu at the same time. They lay on either side of her
parents' king-sized bed, watching *The Price Is Right* and cursing
any mention of food from the estimated cost of peas to frozen
chicken. Now, lying on the tiled hotel bathroom floor, praying
that it was recently and thoroughly cleaned, Beatrice recalled
that day and desperately wished that she could be teleported
home. Not "home" to Veruca's place with the frothy cocktails—
ew, cocktails—and matching pillows. For the first time since this
journey began, she pined for her parents' home on West End
Avenue, even for their uncomfortable couch.

The thought of Daddy's Soup Surprise still made her want to
hurl. But at least her family demanded only basic, fundamental

respect. She hadn't even been mature enough to tolerate them in return. In that moment, so far from New York with its familiar bodegas, sidewalks, and stoops, Beatrice realized that, for all her claustrophobic complaints, no one had actually been suffocating her. Sure, her parents were overprotective, but she alone had assumed a defeatist attitude. What stopped her from building an interesting life was fear. After all, she'd been carrying around a blank notebook for almost a year. Nobody else had stopped her from writing in it.

Sometimes the most profound realizations are also the most obvious. Like Dorothy from *The Wizard of Oz*, Beatrice considered tapping the Moleskine notebook against the toilet three times and whispering, "There's no place like home."

Though the carpet felt rough against her bare knees, Beatrice crawled into the bedroom to find her cell phone. She would call the Bernsteins, confess, and apologize. Feeling blindly inside her cluttered bag for that *damn* BlackBerry, she got poked by an unfamiliar object with sharp edges, about the size of a playing card. She pulled it out and discovered a small laminated map that she'd never seen before, hand-drawn with directions around some square maze. There was a clear beginning and end, marked with a gold letter "D," but there was no indication of where to use it.

Beatrice could not at present guess at the corresponding location, let alone who had slipped it into her bag. She thought of Ben, the only person with whom she might have shared the find, and felt a sharp pang. Concentrating on the map was making her dizzy. She inched back to the toilet and stuck her throbbing head deep inside.

A few hours of porcelain god–worshipping later, the waves of nausea subsided and she felt somewhat restored. Flat Coke and

Brazilian saltines had magically appeared while she slept (thank you, psychic butler service). No one had called, so she jumped into the shower and threw on jeans, her own comfy old pair that didn't constrict her sensitive stomach. She was surprised Penny had bothered packing them. What would she do without that woman?

Outside, the sunlight was harsh on Beatrice's hungover eyes. But soon she uncovered old Forever 21 sunglasses from her clown car of a purse, and bliss was restored. (That's "bliss" relative to the last eighteen hours.) The particular happiness associated with wearing one's favorite cozy jeans is always magnified on leisurely Sunday afternoons.

Aimless wandering wasn't safe in Rio, but Beatrice, in re-searching for the blog, had targeted clusters of nearby boutiques and galleries. First she examined that mysterious laminated map. What did "D" stand for? Dolly? Dorchester? Detention center? Maybe the map was intended for someone else's Balenciaga. She hadn't worn a bag the night before. For now, one thing was cer-tain: This was not a guide to Rio's Zona Sul beach area, which was a grid, not a maze. Maybe it was a map back to sanity.

Beatrice walked along a side street, stopping at a gas station store to peruse the refrigerated shelves. She opted for salty Bra-zilian banana chips and a Guaraná soda (made with *this crazy jolt of natural caffeine from a local plant,* she planned to write). She was hungry but not yet ready for unprocessed food. For now, she was all about the cans and bags, the freeze-dried and fried.

During the kind of mute transaction rooted in a language barrier, Beatrice handed the store owner what she thought was the correct amount of money and he handed her back most of it with a smile. Afterward, she strolled happily along, chomping away and ogling pretty buildings and pedestrians. At the next major thoroughfare, she turned right toward Ipanema, where most of the shops were based. En route, she stopped into a pharmacy and bought several of her father's favorite Brazilian soaps.

Beatrice practiced her *"Oi!"* greeting on as many people as possible, while wandering through swimwear boutiques in one surprisingly modern mall, all sky-high escalators and glass. The notoriously friendly Brazilians appreciated the attempt, but when she shouted an enthusiastic hello at one paranoid old Argentine man, he thought he was being cursed. He had to be talked down by his wife. "I am not a Nazi just because I moved from Germany to Buenos Aires in 1945!" he kept yelling in Portuguese. Nobody actually suspected him, least of all Beatrice, who couldn't understand a word he said.

Most stores sold bathing suits, surf gear, Havaiana flip-flops, or bright geometric-patterned sundresses with spaghetti straps designed by Brazilian locals. But when Beatrice happened upon the weekly Feira Hippie market, she reached the pinnacle of her traveler's high. (Like it or not, patchouli speaks a universal language.) Sellers of varied heights and girths spread local arts, crafts, jewelry, clothes, oils, and trinkets on blankets and tables in a town square.

Fearing "vacation goggles" that move people to purchase folksy knickknacks, only to discover upon returning home that the items make no sense outside their native locations, Beatrice sidestepped "Christo" carving and postcard displays but paused at one booth showcasing more contemporary art. Collages with thick textured paint and images riffing on traditional portraits combined folk themes and religious imagery with drawings of modern gangsters, street performers, and government workers. Shocks of fluorescent yellow and pink showed through cracks here and there. A young, skinny Brazilian twenty-something with brilliant green eyes was manning the booth and, though Beatrice couldn't speak Portuguese and he didn't know a word of English, he managed to communicate that he was the artist.

He introduced himself as João and, with pride, directed her to his Web site on a glossy graffiti flyer. Beatrice bent down to scan the works scattered on cardboard and chose two pieces: one for herself and one for Veruca. Without the socialite, she would never have ended up at the market on this bright Sunday afternoon. And maybe she felt a bit wrong about the evening before. Guilt can be a powerful impetus in purchase, especially when buying art, through which one experiences a wave of virtuosity propelled by a sense of cultural superiority.

Also, it never hurts to kiss a little ass.

Beatrice said good-bye to João, who—mistaking her wave for jazz hands—responded with directions to the nearest samba school. Beatrice retraced her steps back to the hotel, never noticing the Argentine man and his frazzled wife still claiming innocence at her back.

31

BEATRICE RETURNED TO OCEAN SUITES cradling her brown-paper-bagged collages. From around the corner, she peered through the window and saw Dreyfus and Veruca splayed across a floral lobby couch. Kendra was busy obliterating the front desk staff, so loudly that Beatrice could hear sporadic words through the glass. Something about not bringing the beach closer to the hotel entrance? Young Miss Bernstein wasn't at all sure of her impending reception, but—flight reflex notwithstanding—it was too late to run. They'd clearly spotted her.

Veruca and Dreyfus waved, while Kendra scowled and abused her BlackBerry. That was per usual. Beatrice, feeling every bit the prodigal friend, smiled back and strolled in through the automatic doors, relieved that the mood appeared light.

"Looks like someone had a successful day," noted Dreyfus, gesturing with his chin toward her packages.

"I checked out the neighborhood and I think I found some potentially good stuff for the blog."

"Some of us are better by night, others by day," he quipped.

"Oh, that's right!" Beatrice plopped down by him and Veruca on the sofa. "Something about a tryst with an adorable pool boy?"

"I don't kiss and tell," Dreyfus said, turning up his nose. "Okay, that's not true." The three coach potatoes laughed.

"What are you guys doing down here?"

Veruca's red hair was particularly vibrant against the drab

upholstery. She wore a wide-necked electric blue top that slid off one perfectly tanned bony shoulder. "Well, Kendra is abusing the hotel staff, though I've told her it's really unnecessary."

"She is so very good at that," said Dreyfus. They nodded to each other.

"And we're waiting for our bags 'cause we're leaving," she cooed. "Don't try to stop me, Beany. I'm just beyond exhausted and homesick. I need a New York fix, but fast. You know how that is, right, BB? Needing a change? I need to fly north for the winter."

Panic was now wreaking havoc in Beatrice's belly. Nausea crashed over her like a tsunami. The group was going home three days early and not pit-stopping in Mexico? That had to be her fault. She swallowed hard. "But . . . but, Veruca . . . you talked about tequila y sangrita near the Camino Real in Mexico City and smoking Cuban cigars. Are you sure you want to go home? I mean, why now?"

"Oh, I'm sorry, Beany. I hope you're not disappointed. I know you want to visit as many places as possible, but I just have to get back. We have lives, right? And I suppose you have classes. Remember those?"

"I'm trying to forget," said Dreyfus, tucking his arms behind his head, as though sunning himself beneath the lobby's fluorescent lights. "What a buzz kill."

"No, V," Beatrice protested softly, "I'd never be disappointed. I just . . . I hope my leaving early last night didn't affect anything."

"Did you leave early last night, Beany? I swear, I couldn't have even found you anyway amid all those models. Really, those giraffes must have a totally different worldview from up there. I'll have to ask Imelda. Besides, I was blotto. What was in those caipirinhas?"

Veruca seemed chipper, but then she always put on a happy

face. Beatrice tried to read those blank but twinkling different-colored eyes, the crinkled nose, pursed lips. "Really, Beany, I'm just fine. Though I'd prefer that you stopped examining me like that. I don't have a temperature. I'm just feeling tugged home. You're sweet to be concerned." She reached out a hand and patted her friend's knee. "And your suitcases are already down here. Now, show us what you've got in those packages. Is it tomato juice? I'm famished."

"Let's hope it's a different pair of jeans," grunted Kendra, who had come over to check out Beatrice's finds despite herself.

The packages! Beatrice had almost forgotten. "Oh, I found this incredible artist at the Hippie Fair!" She told them all about João and his poignant, innovative work. "I thought maybe you would want to partner with him like you sometimes do, throw him an event and fly him to New York. Discover him, you know? You could help his career and introduce some fresh blood."

"Like that kid could play ball in New York's art world," Kendra muttered. But Dreyfus shushed her.

"Anyway, I bought you one. I hope you like it."

The socialite opened the package with zeal. The image was of a young Brazilian socialite with Louis Vuitton luggage but posed like ancient royalty with bits of Brazilian political comics as background. "It's beautiful, Beany. Really. He's so gifted. Thank you. This is so thoughtful. I'd love to get him some exposure."

Kendra reached for Veruca's hand. "Come on, V, let's get these incompetents to pack it somewhere where it won't get destroyed." Kendra pulled the socialite up to standing and they walked over to the front desk, leaving Dreyfus and Beatrice on the couch.

Once they were out of earshot, Beatrice feigned nonchalance. "So, where are the others?"

Dreyfus burst into laughter so loud that Veruca and Kendra turned to look. Thankfully, they were too far away to ask questions. "Oh, Sweet Bea. You make me laugh." He sighed. "You really are so obvious. Imelda, as if you care, is upstairs looking for that absurd amulet she wears. She's lost it under the bed, I'm sure. We barely slept last night. I was feeling a bit frisky."

"You and the pool boy were with Imelda?"

"Oh, no, but my room is next door to her suite, you know." He winked. "And Ben, since that's who you're actually wondering about, was sent home this morning."

"Sent home? I don't understand."

"Do you ever, Sweet? Well, it's very simple." Dreyfus cracked his neck to the left and then right. It sounded like breaking bones. "Veruca sent him home. Apparently, she wanted to break it off."

"Because of something he did?" Beatrice figured Kendra might spread salacious lies (in other words, report the truth), but then wouldn't Veruca be angry? Sometimes it's less settling to be off the hook than on it.

"No, goofy, because of something he did *not* do, which is do it for her anymore." Beatrice twisted the gold stud in her ear and tried to appear nonchalant as she listened. "To save face, Veruca concocted some excuse about his mother needing him for some family event, but it wasn't true, of course. Oh, Sweet Sweet Bea, you're so naïve. Stop looking at me with those big doe eyes. She's just over him. She met this gorgeous Brazilian surf trunk designer last night at the party. That's why she's so tired! She spent the whole night examining his trunks. And by that I mean doing the nasty in his studio. So she sent Ben home ahead of us. He flew *commercial* this morning." Dreyfus shuddered.

Beatrice heaved a sigh of relief. But how strange for Veruca to use Ben's mother as an excuse. It seemed sort of crass, unless she didn't know that his mother had passed away?

Dreyfus raised a single eyebrow at Beatrice. "I did hear about what almost happened last night before you left, Sweet Bea.

You're lucky Kendra doesn't like to upset Miss V. She told me, but she won't tell our fearless leader. Personally, I'm glad he's gone. He was too good-looking for a straight man. Plus, I don't like him taking advantage of you because he needed a rebound." Dreyfus pinched her cheeks with mock adoration.

Beatrice forced a weak smile. "Yeah, I mean, he would obviously have never liked me, when Veruca was an option."

"Obviously, Beany. I mean, I love you and all, but . . . you know. She's Veruca Pfeffernoose and you're, well, adorably clueless, as they say. But you knew that, right? I'm not hurting your feelings? I heard he hit on three Brazilian models at the party before he finally left last night."

"Of course," she managed. And then more robustly, "I mean, Ben was clearly grasping at straws. But those caipirinhas sure were strong."

"Especially"—Dreyfus raised his eyebrow again and threw an arm around Beatrice's shoulders—"when you drink them without the passion fruit."

How did he know? But then they always did.

32

ONCE KENDRA FINISHED YELLING at the poor hotel staff and a mortified Beatrice feigned a bathroom emergency to sneak back in and apologize, the motley group was transported to the airport via their chariot with phantom driver. As usual, when they piled out onto the tarmac, the driver angled his face toward the ground. Beatrice felt her knees and lips crack as she stepped out. She couldn't do much for her aching body, having napped all morning on the bathroom floor, but she felt around in her bag for her lip gloss. Discovering it missing, along with her grasp on reality, she climbed back into the car to search.

Standing by the door, the driver mumbled something Beatrice couldn't quite hear. She poked her head out and peered upward, but the sun in her eyes was glaring. All she saw was light. "I'm sorry. I couldn't quite make out what you just said. Have you seen my lip gloss? It's this pinky peach color like a watermelon Jolly Rancher. Not quite as tasty, of course."

"I've seen a lot of lost lip gloss in my day," the driver said. "But a lost lip gloss is kind of like a lost sock or even lost jewelry. It may signify a need for change."

Beatrice had half expected some wise Yoda-appropriate words from this strange person who followed them around the world. But this seemed like nonsense. "Okay," she said. "Does that mean you aren't going to help me find it?"

"No," the driver responded. "It means that sometimes the

head rooster does not rule the roost. Sometimes things happen that we can't explain. And sometimes, although we may at first feel disappointed, a lost lip gloss, which seems to vanish magically into thin air, can signal the beginning of a new chapter."

Beatrice was getting impatient. It was hot. Sweat pooled behind her knees. "Are you saying you stole my lip gloss? Because you can have it. It's not so important to me. And it looks good on everyone 'cause it changes color based on your skin—"

"No, I don't have your lip gloss. Only you can possess that." The driver smiled. Beatrice could just make out a round chin, as the clouds moved, slowly revealing the bottom half of the driver's face. She climbed back out of the car, not quite getting her head around lip gloss as metaphor. Lip gloss, after all, was effing lip gloss. "All I'm saying is that you conjured this. So give yourself a fighting chance to find the right color. Maybe you've used the changing kind enough for now. Share it with someone who needs it more. And don't be so damning to those who have mistakenly chosen the wrong shades," the driver continued. "Take care, Beatrice. Maybe I'll see you again."

"I'm sure," she murmured, spellbound at the sound of her name coming from that mouth. "In New York."

The driver walked around the car and ducked inside with a peculiar gait, reminding Beatrice of something elusive from her past. Did the driver send her the cockroaches in Paris? The car glided away.

"Hurry up!" screamed drill sergeant Kendra from the base of the plane's retractable staircase.

"Keep your pants on!" Beatrice hurried over to her waiting companions and mounted the steps behind Dreyfus.

"Yes, do," he seconded to Kendra, turning to Beatrice on his way inside. "'Cause you know those kankles don't look good in skirts. Am I right? So did you finally really meet our mysterious

driver? Was our friend deformed? Missing a nose, as we suspected?"

"I didn't see the driver's face." Beatrice felt oddly protective.
She knew Dreyfus would just poke fun at the lip gloss advice. It
may have been confusing, but it was well-intentioned and maybe
had merit. Perhaps her time for transformation was coming to
an end. For Dreyfus's benefit, she mustered a fake grin. "I'm pretty
sure our driver is Elvis."

"Or Tupac!" he cried. "How hot was Tupac, BTW? Damn
shame."

He disappeared inside the plane. In a moment of habitual
traveler's anxiety, which should be less pronounced when flying
private with a staff of twenty, Beatrice reached into her purse to
confirm her passport's location. It was in the large zippered side
pocket, as usual. But as she pulled her hand back out of her bag,
she felt something cold and bulbous against her skin. She closed
her fist around the oval object and pulled it out. Here was the
lip gloss she thought she had lost. But when she peered at it, it
seemed to have dulled.

Beatrice studied the packaging and, for the first time, processed its name: Shape-Shifter.

33

ONCE IN THE AIR, Beatrice assessed her situation. Veruca's mood was not impacted by Ben's departure, just as she'd assured Beatrice. The socialite shifted her chair into a reclining position and bopped her designer collaboration Keds to whatever Lily Allen song projected through her earbuds. Lily Allen had, after all, recorded this version of the album for Veruca alone.

If anything, the Axis members seemed withdrawn. That was no change for Kendra, but Dreyfus, after glancing at his iPhone right before liftoff, was suddenly in no mood to joke or cajole. Imelda, who generally shot shy smiles across the plane seats at Beatrice, stared into space as if transfixed by floating particles of light, clutching her heart-shaped locket.

To hear Dreyfus tell it, Veruca encountered some hot Brazilian "bum bum" and Ben was "sent home." He had been ordered to the principal's office, to bed without supper, but was it for bad behavior or because he'd fallen out of favor? More details had been revealed en route to the airport, while Veruca wore earphones. Apparently, whispered Dreyfus, Ben was seen leaving the party with one of the Amazon-height women, a spokesmodel for a new perfume called Landing Strip as a play on Brazilian waxing.

"Trashy, if you ask me," sniffed Dreyfus.

"What else would you expect?" chimed Kendra, who had—as always—overheard. She shot a meaningful glare at Beatrice. Last night's battle royale was not forgotten. Though Beatrice wished it didn't, the thought of Ben's tryst stung. She wasn't surprised that he'd picked someone up so quickly. Even if you didn't know him, he was good to look at and funny and smart and . . . a total asshole.

That was important to remember. Beatrice might have imagined that Ben was cool and even special, but ultimately he was a judgmental hypocrite. And possibly a liar.

Somewhere between stumbling into her hotel room the night before and face planting onto the bed, Beatrice had wondered if she should have heard Ben out. He'd said he liked her. And, as bad as she felt about it, she had feelings for him too. But that was before he'd left without so much as an e-mail or text and before she learned how he'd spent the rest of his evening.

Now Beatrice sorted through the canvas tote of travel goodies that awaited her on her plane seat each flight. She pulled on fuzzy socks and rubbed shea butter lotion into her palms (*to combat dryness,* she'd blogged), but she left the earplugs and eye mask inside. She hated to feel deaf and blind, unable to get her bearings.

An amorphous foreboding twirled like a rickety Ferris wheel in her gut. Briefly, she wondered if she was having a premonition. Perhaps she should alert the other passengers, lest the plane go down. Veruca probably had Burberry parachutes waiting, complete with bartenders to pop out midair and offer themed Skyy Vodka cocktails. But, in her heart of hearts, Beatrice knew that her questionable behavior was to blame for the nasty sensation. Guilt and shame were hard to digest. And so was *cachaça.*

Though Beatrice slept for a while on the flight, she noticed they arrived home in a truly record amount of time. Since when did it take two hours to fly from Rio to New York City? It really felt *that* short. But that, she reasoned, simply wasn't possible.

34

THE GROUP LANDED AT JFK. Inexplicably, instead of taking the Maybach, they hopped into regular yellow cabs. The taxis were reserved, though, waiting stubbornly just outside baggage claim, despite protests from other angry homebound New Yorkers, whose rage rebounded upon return to their native city.

At the Dorchester, Beatrice's luggage was carted upstairs. Immediately, she jogged up the apartment halls to find Dolly, proving that—with enough drive—a person can actually run in Uggs. She didn't know why Dolly hadn't responded to her e-mails, but she hoped that nothing terrible had happened, that she hadn't been conspicuously absent for traumatic events in her dear friend's life from a sprained ankle to the cancellation of *Dancing with the Stars*.

Beatrice arrived at Dolly's loft and knocked. No one answered. Amid takeout menus, a note scrawled in blue ink was pushed halfway under the front door. Beatrice fished it out. It was from Dolly to her skittish apartment mate Marcy: "Dr. Bunsen called. Your session has been bumped to 4pm on 11/7 as you requested, when the waiting room is less crowded. XO, D."

"They're gone," croaked Goth Girl from behind Beatrice. The girl's inky black lipstick, nails, hair, and eye makeup was even heavier than usual. How absurd it suddenly seemed that this person groomed so arduously in order to achieve the filthiest possible look. Maybe Beatrice was just happy to be home, but she almost found Goth Girl cute. She could have hugged her, if it wasn't for her bared teeth and layer of grime.

"Oh, thanks. They're gone at classes?"

"No, prom queen." Goth Girl already seemed less adorable. She rolled her eyes and drew her face close, so Beatrice could smell the tang of cigarettes and cinnamon Big Red gum and see the infected pink ring around her nose piercing. "They're gone. Like *gone*. Didn't you hear?"

Adrenaline coursed through Beatrice's veins, sounds around her fading in and out like she was underwater. "What the hell do you mean?"

"They got murdered by mutant cockroaches!" Goth Girl lapsed into cackles, laughing and pointing.

"Are you kidding me? Is that supposed to be a joke?"

"I guess they don't have too many cockroaches in Pfeffernoose Land, huh? Just a whole bunch of zombie sheep. Are you even awake? Bah! Baaaaah!" Goth Girl snapped her fingers in front of Beatrice's eyes.

"What is wrong with you? I thought you meant that something horrible happened to them."

"Well, being friends with you seems pretty shitty."

Beatrice was over this whole scene. Now, more than ever, she wanted to find Dolly and make sure everything was okay. "All right. Move along, lunatic." She turned back to the door to write her own message on a menu and gestured dismissively with an almost royal flourish.

"Oh, you think you can just banish me from my own apartment building? I see how it is." Goth Girl stood back, peering up and down the corridor. Then she raised her voice as loud as possible: "THE PSYCHO STALKER IS BACK!" she shouted. "HELP!"

An ungodly shriek rose from the far end of the hall like a

Braveheart battle cry, causing ears to mysteriously ring from the Dorchester all the way down to Washington Square Park. Beatrice whipped around. At the end of the corridor stood the flannel nightgown–wearing blond girl who had freaked during the Marcy incident. *Here we go.* "Stalker! The stalker!" she yelped. "The V-Pfeff stalker!" The hallway broke out into bedlam, as Beatrice tried to convince a bunch of descending hockey players of her harmlessness. "I'm just looking for my friend!" she yelped, as they inched closer. Just her luck, Hormone Guy was among them.

"You know me, right? I'm not a stalker! Tell them!"

He nodded his head. "I know her, all right. If you know what I mean?" He nudged his nearest friend and made humping gestures with his hips, channeling *Grease*'s Danny Zuko. Was this guy for real?

"You hit that?" asked his equally brilliant buddy, distracted from his valiant mission to save the apartment building. "Stalkers must be crazy in bed, dude."

"You know it!" said Hormone Guy, handing out high fives and pounds to the rest of his pals. His 'roid acne seemed to be getting worse: A thick trail of pus-filled welts marched up his neck, disappearing into his hairline.

"I'm standing right here!" said Beatrice. "You can't lie to your friends about sleeping with a girl when she's standing directly in front of you. How dumb *are* you?"

The boys went silent, until Hormone Guy had a lightbulb-worthy idea. "You live in the basement, right? Or you used to? How would I know that unless I'd been down there with you?"

Goth Girl nodded. "The caveman has a point. She did live down there, doing lots of stalkerlike things like making voodoo dolls and sticking them with pins, and of course cooking crystal meth." Beatrice groaned, looking to the cracked ceiling for guidance. As if in answer to her prayers, a heaven-sent Dolly appeared in the stairwell's entryway.

"Oh, Doll, thank goodness!" She ran to her friend, who—to her surprise—shot quickly past as if in midtango. Beatrice followed like a lost puppy as Dolly marched toward her room. "These people don't believe we're friends. Tell them, okay? Save me?"

Dolly paused, key in hand, standing in third position at her door. She glanced at Beatrice and at the crowd, then used her sweatshirt sleeve to wipe some residual sweat from dance class off her forehead. "Friends? Oh, I don't think we're really friends," she said. "Friends don't invite you over and then leave you sitting outside their door for hours alone, when you're the only senior to get a *chorus* role in the school's professional dance exhibition for potential companies and you've just been dumped by a guy you never liked in the first place." And, with that, Dolly quietly turned her key in the lock and slipped inside, leaving Beatrice to fend off an angry mob.

35

AFTER AN HOUR-LONG CONVERSATION WITH FRANK, the
security person in the building, Beatrice cleared up the whole
"stalker" situation.

He seemed like a nice enough man and even handed Hormone
Guy a "beat down" in the form of a good chiding. His large belly
protruded above his uniform's cinched belt, indicating that he
might not be the speediest officer in pursuit. Still, he gave an
authoritative impression. If he'd needed to force her into cuffs or
stop her from running à la *Cops,* Beatrice imagined he could
probably have held her in place with one chunky hand tied behind his back. Plus, Frank watched a lot of *Law & Order: SVU*
reruns and knew a thing or two about interrogation, mostly of
child molesters. He dreamed of the day Benson and Stabler would
finally get together, never mind that the male detective had left
the show. But, in the meantime, he took copious notes on how to
approach "perps."

Hormone Guy turned instantly submissive as the truth
emerged about his claims of sexual conquest. Frank—whose
three sisters and single mother had instilled deep respect for
women—made one call and had the jock enrolled in date rape
counseling. As he confided in Beatrice, "That guy just seems like
the type. Did you know that sexual predators' behavior often
escalates? One minute they're flashing someone and the next
they're making some lady's skin into pot holders." Beatrice felt a

little sorry for Hormone Guy, but sensitivity training couldn't hurt.

Meanwhile, Frank was so surprised by her story that he asked her to repeat it twice. He scribbled in his notebook, more for his screenplay than for any police report. At regular intervals, he shook his head from side to side and repeated, "That's really insane. Now, tell me that part about the supersized roach again?"

He asked her to describe her basement studio so many times that Beatrice finally offered to show him the damn thing. Off she and Frank went on a two-person field trip—down memory lane for her—to her former rancid boudoir. As usual, the hinges creaked as the basement's stairwell door opened. They were welcomed by the overwhelming stench of mildew and that broken air conditioner plunking out SOS in Morse code. They made their way downstairs, guided by the first floor's light. Something scurried underfoot. Frank actually yelped and tried to cover it up with a cough. Beatrice realized with misguided pride that, by now, she was desensitized.

She flipped on the light, which flickered, revealing the same basement relics: dirty old cardboard boxes, broken appliances, dank cavernous corners filled with spiderwebs and who knew what else. Frank took a minute to absorb the scene and then swiveled with eyes wide. "You lived here? Really? You didn't live here." She nodded, and he shook his head again. "Your parents paid for this? Where did you sleep?"

She walked to the closet-cum-"apartment" and opened the door. But in place of decrepit bunk beds were janitorial supplies. Her mouth dropped open, likely catching asbestos particles like snowflakes on her tongue. She walked tentatively inside and circled several times. "There used to be bunk beds in here. These mops weren't in the corner. I've never seen this bucket!"

Frank peered inside too. "Well, it's not fit for someone to

sleep here, so maybe they turned it back into a closet. Maybe so your parents couldn't sue?" He shook his head in distaste.

"But I never told them that I moved out. How would the administration know?"

In the back of her mind, a tiny notion began to form. "How could they know?" was certainly a frequent question in her world lately. Beatrice silently thanked Frank for believing her story. Dolly threw her to the wolves, a reality she hadn't yet processed in the commotion. That confirmed Beatrice's lingering suspicion that Kendra never bothered to send a cancellation message the day of their departure from New York. Beatrice's eyes began to well up. Or maybe she was tearing from the fumes.

Always intuitive, Frank patted her on the back. "Let's get out of here. I don't even like us breathing this air." She was about to follow him out of the closet when something caught her eye. It was her favorite laminated map drawn by Gertie, still tacked to the wall. Veruca's moving people hadn't bothered to bring it up with the rest of her stuff. And Beatrice hadn't noticed.

With Frank's help, she removed the map and placed it gingerly into her bag, after wiping any dust and scum off on her jeans. When they closed the closet door behind them, she noticed that the room number had been removed. It was almost as if her time there had ceased to exist. If it weren't for Ben and Dolly, two people with whom she was not currently on speaking terms, she might believe that she'd imagined it all.

She and Frank marched up the stairs and out of the basement. When they reached the ground floor again, they said good-bye. He was off to the Campus Security lounge for a beer and cop show marathon. (They regularly drank from confiscated kegs while trying to guess whodunit.) "That was insane. Really insane," he mumbled.

"The housing office just wouldn't help me. Can you believe that?"

Temporarily taken aback, Frank lifted his pants by the belt loops like an Old West sheriff. "The housing office? Kid, I gotta break it to you: The housing office isn't gonna put a student in that apartment, even off campus. That there's an insurance liability. Nah, kid. Someone out there really doesn't like you."

Frank walked off, muttering, "Insane. Really insane."

Intellectually, Beatrice understood that Frank was a random security guy she'd just met, but she felt an irrational sadness at seeing him go. So this is what the bottom of the barrel looked like. Not so scenic. But enough wallowing: She had a sinister theory to investigate.

Beatrice charged with purpose toward Veruca's rambling quarters. Behind the socialite's front door the rules changed, sometimes for better and sometimes for worse.

36

IN THE LUNACY AFTER LANDING back in New York, Beatrice had neglected to check her backlogged voice mail. She pressed the 1 key until her phone automatically dialed and then punched in her security code: M.A.P.S.

The first few insistent messages were from Dolly, left just hours into the trip.

Bea, it's me. I'm running late to meet you because they're posting the casting for my dance recital a day early. I'm going to talk to Stephen, but then I'll be over. I told Veruca to tell you I'd be late, but just in case, save me an oxygen facial!

Bea, it's me again. I'm at your door, but no one's here and your phone is going straight to voice mail, so that's kind of weird. Maybe you're holding all calls because you're expecting me? Ha—just kidding. Look, I'm really bummed. I totally got passed over for that part as the Pillow Fairy in the modern interpretation of *Sleeping Beauty*. I thought it was basically definite, but they said I missed too many official prerehearsals while I was with Isadora. Then, even worse, I went to Stephen's house to break things off with him and instead walked in on him and Cynthia together.
Apparently, she dumped the poet and they're in *love*. It was

disgusting. I thought I didn't like him like that, but it still felt awful. I need some TLC.

Bea, it's Dolly. Are you kidding me? You're not standing me up. You can't be. I'll just wait here. I'm still outside Veruca's door. Are you okay?

Beatrice, it's Dolly. I told Stephen, Mina, and Cynthia that it wasn't true: You hadn't changed and forgotten us. But apparently you're disposing of me, just like you disposed of everyone else. After all these years, thanks for nothing.

As Dolly fiddled with the phone to end the call, Beatrice heard her protest, "No, officer. I'm not stalking Veruca Pfeffernoose. I don't even *like* her."

By now, Beatrice was pacing outside the door to apartment 333. As she listened to the messages, she looked for evidence of Dolly's presence in the same spot weeks before, an imprint of her silhouette, a chalk outline on the carpet, a piece of pink string lost while doctoring toe shoes.

But the next message was even more alarming, confirming what Officer Frank's comment had led her to suspect: "Beatrice, it's your mother. I've been trying to contact you for days. Listen, we just got a refund check from the housing office at school. They say your room reservation was canceled in time for the deadline. We're happy to save the money, of course, but that raises the somewhat curious question of where you're living. Your father is concerned. And that's a fact. Call me back."

Their money was refunded? Dolly told Veruca she'd be late? Stephen and Cynthia were sleeping together? Gross. Floating pieces of a fragmented puzzle fused together in Beatrice's brain. *Who were these people?* As the parts merged, the picture became clearer, like one of those optical illusion posters when the secondary image eventually comes into focus. Now it all seemed so obvious. Maybe Beatrice hadn't wanted to see.

She clicked off the phone, threw it in her bag, and swung Veruca's door open. Everything looked pretty much the same: central ottoman, daybed, DJ station. No one was around. In fact, the space felt eerily quiet. And it all looked so staged. Like that empty club the morning after, without the crowds or mood lighting, the loft lost its appealing artifice. The term "optical illusions" repeated in Beatrice's head like a skipping CD.

She placed her bag down and surveyed the room. So this is where she stood. During a few months packed tight like a lifetime, a centrifugal force had picked her up and taken her on a wild ride. Now it dumped her back where it all began.

And then it happened: Her eye caught something moving by the kitchen. She marched over to a stark white garbage can and looked inside. Around the perimeter scurried the gigantic brown cockroach of her nightmares, the largest water bug Beatrice had ever seen. She shrieked and backed up several feet, as it twitched its dark dirty tentacles, crept out, and sprinted across the room under Beatrice's beloved daybed—a bad omen if there ever was one. She shuddered, disturbed by dark forces alive in a space she'd once mistaken for a sanctuary. Oxygen facials be damned.

That was when Beatrice noticed a wooden frame sticking out of the can. As terrified as she was of that cockroach-infested bin, she needed to see what else was inside. Beatrice couldn't kowtow to demons any longer. She tiptoed over to the garbage, half expecting some evil being to jump out and attack. When nothing happened, she peeked inside. A crumpled paper towel was obstructing the view, but she knew instantly what lay beneath: João's collage that she'd bought for Veruca.

As Beatrice removed it delicately with the very tips of her fingers and nails, her heart began to pound, fury mounting. Veruca had feigned interest and then trashed the gift. Clearly, the socialite wasn't interested in helping this young Brazilian talent. She was interested only in helping herself.

Dolly had suspected—hell, *she* had even suspected—such a possibility from the outset, but Beatrice had allowed herself to be blinded for convenience sake. All of a sudden, she remembered Kendra's comment when she'd presented the gift to Veruca: "Like that kid could play ball in New York's art world."

Thoughts raced at warp speed, accelerating and gaining momentum, until they stopped short at an answer in the mental equivalent of a ten-car pileup. Given a moment to clear the wreckage, Beatrice realized the truth: Veruca wasn't interested in art. She wasn't even interested in being perceived as someone who "knows about art" for the sake of status. Instead, Veruca was using artists, partnering only with those who were willing to play ball and bringing them publicity in exchange for a cut. As the reality dawned on Beatrice, she clutched the mounted collage with white knuckles. Worst of all, Beatrice had inadvertently helped corrupt the Bernsteins' own universe. She'd tainted her home.

Home. Frank was on to something when he said, "Someone really doesn't like you." Beatrice felt dizzy. Veruca hadn't randomly taken an interest in her. Their "mutually beneficial" needs weren't coincidental. Veruca had known who Beatrice was—well, who her parents were—from the very beginning. She'd always planned to hire her to write the blog and use her insider knowledge to create an aura of credibility. She'd admitted that, hadn't she?

Beatrice ran to her bag, tucked the collage inside as best she could, and fumbled for her cell phone, dialing Dolly's landline. The phone rang several times and then an answering machine picked up: "Hi, you've reached Dolly and Marcy. Please leave a message at the sound of the tone. But don't make the message too long. We don't like the machine to get too crowded." *Beep.*

"Dolly, Doll. I know you're there. Pick up, okay? I know you're mad at me, but this is really important. Seriously." She waited. Beatrice was about to abandon ship when she heard the clatter of the phone being picked up.

"What? What's so important, Beatrice? Like you would even know what that meant."

"Doll, oh thank goodness. I'm so glad you answered."

"You're lucky I still have a conscience. I felt a tiny bit guilty leaving you out in the hallway with those maniacs. I'm pissed, but no one deserves to be accused of stalking. I know that because it happened to *me* while I was waiting for *you* that night."

Beatrice winced. "Doll, thank you. Look. I'm sorry. I'm *so* sorry. I've been a terrible friend and I think, although I know it's no excuse, that I'm not the only one who's been manipulated. I'll explain it all to you later, assuming you'll allow me, but right now I just need you to answer a question for me."

Dolly sighed. "What's up?"

Beatrice was amped up, lapping Veruca's main room so quickly that sparks flew from below her sneakers. "When you first got to the Dorchester, when I was home sick before I ever got here and this whole mess began, how did you meet Veruca?"

"Seriously? Jeez, you're so obsessed with her. It's kind of lame."

"Dolly, just trust me."

Beatrice could hear noises in the background. Dolly was doing her post–dance class cooldown exercises while talking to demonstrate disinterest. "I dunno, I told you. I sneezed. She said, 'Bless you' and invited me over."

"That was it—just a sneeze and you were in? She didn't say anything else?"

"Yeah. Well, actually, now that you mention it, she did ask me if I had a best friend—I mean, I just assumed that she was deciding if I was worth knowing or something like that. And she kept saying that I should invite any friends that arrived at school directly to her apartment that day for her housewarming party. She said I was interesting and bound to know cool people."

"It was her."

"What was her?"

Beatrice groaned. "She's the reason I ended up in the basement. Of course, I should have realized it. She knew details about the closet that I hadn't told her, but she said you mentioned the cockroaches and—"

"Me? I never talked to her about your room. I never really spoke to her at all, once you arrived. She seemed to take a much bigger interest in you." Dolly was still angry but also intrigued. The thumping in the background stopped. She'd paused her stretching. "But why would she make you live in that closet?"

"She canceled my room reservation, Doll. She made sure that I was as miserable as physically possible, so I'd live anywhere and do anything to get out of there. She created an untenable situation so she could rescue me with the blog. The dumbest part is that I continually accepted that she knew things about me that she shouldn't. I think I might have actually believed that she was magic somehow. How dumb is that? There are like four different entrances to three different basement areas in the Dorchester. How did she know where I was living when she moved all my stuff upstairs? No wonder she left Gertie's map in the basement. She wanted to make sure I couldn't find my way home."

Dolly gasped. "OMG, you seriously think she went to all that trouble to make you miserable? Why?"

"Because she does whatever serves her purposes. I'm just hoping those purposes aren't as dangerous as I think. I gotta go deal with this. But Doll, just so you know, no one told me you were running late the day I left. That doesn't excuse my behavior, but I just want you to know."

Dolly was quiet for a moment. "I figured Veruca might not have told you, after she started scheduling those dance sessions for me whenever we had plans to hang out. She obviously didn't want us spending time together. I mean, Veruca is the person who told me they were posting the cast list early, after I mentioned we were planning to spend quality time."

"Oh, Doll."

"You think she made me late on purpose?"

"I think it's possible."

"Do you think she made sure that I got that bad part?"

Beatrice smiled despite herself. "That I have no idea about, Doll. But I know you deserved a better role either way."

"I guess with Isadora and everything, I kind of thought that Veruca had some sort of otherworldly power too. It sounds silly now."

"She's powerful, for sure. But not in quite such a lovely magical way."

Beatrice hung up and sank to the floor, her back against the ottoman. In true cult leader form, the socialite had separated Beatrice from her old life. For all the perks that Veruca extended to the group, why hadn't she made sure Beatrice's BlackBerry worked internationally? She wanted Beatrice out of touch, Patty Hearst–style. All the better for Veruca Pfeffernoose brainwashing, my dear.

This was too much. The media princess wasn't going to get away with this.

37

FIRST, BEATRICE NEEDED SOME EVIDENCE. She suppressed the urge to run like a maniac into Veruca's quarters with no plan and some very intimidating—suddenly acquired—nunchaku skills. Instead, she grabbed her bag and slipped back out the door into the hallway. She scanned the area for a safe place to collect her thoughts and hopefully some information. An ominously stained women's restroom door stood about thirty feet to the left. Perfect: No Axis of Evil member would dare set foot in such an unsavory place.

And who could blame them? Apparently, this was one of the shared restrooms Beatrice had heard about. Stray strands of hair were flattened to the moldy wet tiles and, from inside separate showers, two girls chatted loudly above the din of hammering water about some guy's erectile dysfunction. Their Victoria's Secret peach bath gel did nothing to overpower the stench of urine in Beatrice's chosen stall. She gagged a little but then pulled out her Mac Helium, sat atop three carefully placed toilet seat covers, and stole WiFi from a router called CannabisLover. Apparently, the owner was too high to set up password protection.

First, for giggles, she typed "Veruca Pfeffernoose childhood" into the Google search window. As expected, a number of links came up with information based on conjecture and rumor. One Web site linked Veruca to JFK's, Kurt Cobain's, and Heath Ledger's deaths, offering up digitally aged images. The caption suggested that miracles of plastic surgery had kept her young but that the socialite was actually at least seventy years old. Beatrice shrugged. She hoped she looked that good at seventy.

There were no clear answers about Veruca's background. Her history remained an unsolved mystery. And in this crazy media age, it could only be intentionally so. Beatrice tapped her foot impatiently as she considered her next move. She had only once asked the group how they met and she racked her brain to remember their answer, working to get past that evening's haze of magic s'mores. What was it that Dreyfus said? *Trust your old ears,* she thought, recalling the notebook's advice.

Frustrated, she clicked around on her computer, noticing a new desktop screen saver she didn't recall uploading. The photo was taken from the window of her childhood bedroom. And Dreyfus's words came back to her in a flash: "I went to Saint Mary's, naturally. These girls went to Spence and Nightingale, although Mel almost had to finish at Dwight after an incident with a randy professor. . . . I have a better idea than manicures and rehashing the days of schoolgirl skirts and those damn Saint Mary's required navy jackets, khakis, and red neckties."

And suddenly Beatrice knew. In truth, she'd known in her gut all along. But she had to confirm her suspicions. She searched Saint Mary's Prep on her laptop and dialed the number on her phone. "Development," she croaked, when prompted by an automated voice.

Finally, a real live person answered. "Saint Mary's Admissions and Development Offices."

"Hi, I'm calling to verify information about a former student."

"Okay. For what purpose, may I ask? Depending on the pertinent information, those records are not open to the public. We may need you to fax us documentation."

Beatrice froze. Of course, she would need a believable excuse.

"Hello? Miss? Are you still there?" the woman asked.

There was no time for paperwork, not that Beatrice had legitimate cause anyway. And she hardly relished sneaking into and rifling through files at her college's registrar's office. It's not like that pink-haired housing office hag was going to . . . that was it!

"Sorry, dear." Beatrice cleared her throat, affecting an older voice. "This is Estelle Ogvlogovich from the student's university housing office. Between you and me, I'm just trying to avoid some unpleasantness. You know how *overbearing* these parents can be." The administrators in registrar's offices were always grumpy. Why should this one be any different?

After some hesitation: "Do I ever."

"I have this student who's trying to get into housing for next term. But in looking over his file, I realized that, while he claims to be a Saint Mary's alumnus, there's no record of his transcript. Very bizarre, of course. So I thought, before I contact him and his crazy parents, I'd go directly to the source. Do you think you could help me? I don't need any details, just confirmation of his attendance."

There was a pause while the admissions assistant considered the question. "I shouldn't."

"You'd really be helping me out. No one will ever know. One underpaid, underappreciated administrator to another?"

There was another silence and then, "Just this once. Because I know how those parents can be. What's the student's name?

"Dreyfus Donatello."

"Dreyfus Donatello. Doesn't ring a bell. Let me just search." Beatrice could hear the *clickity-clack* of computer keys as she braced herself for an answer. "No. No, there doesn't seem to be anyone listed here named Dreyfus at all and certainly not someone who would currently be college age. There's no one under the name Donatello either. Are you sure that's his name? Maybe I have the wrong spelling?"

Beatrice could make out mumbling in the background, as she used her shoe's toe to kick away a stray tampon wrapper. "Wait, hang on one second," said the nasal voice. "Oh, really? Well, that can't be. How odd! Ms. Ogvlogovich? According to Paula in my office, there used to be a janitor here with that last name and she thinks she remembers that his son—who was quite small at the time—may have been named Dreyfus. I'm not sure if that's your boy, but either way, he definitely never attended this school as a student. And even that would have been ages ago. Paula has been here forever." There was a pause. "No, Paula. I'm not calling you old."

Beatrice clicked off and sat for a moment in awe. Her whole body vibrated. The Axis of Evil was not at all what it seemed. And Veruca—well, who did that make her? If Dreyfus never actually attended, then it was no wonder he'd gotten the prep school's dress code wrong. Beatrice had been staring out her bedroom window and walking past those boys for too many years not to realize his mistake. They didn't wear red ties. They wore gray.

Beatrice felt like an idiot. He'd said Kendra went to Spence. But what Upper East Side Spence girl lived in a trailer park while training to be a ribbon gymnast?

So what was the H.O.S. crew? Now, that raised a different issue. She'd heard the term bandied about, especially by Dreyfus, but what did it mean?

Outside the stall, the two shower buddies had turned off their water streams. "How long has that girl been in that stall?" one of them whispered. "Um, like forever," the other girl responded. "Maybe she ate fish at a diner. Never order the fish. I only ever eat curly fries."

Beatrice heard the squishy padding of wet flip-flop-clad feet and the swing of the door. She was alone. She needed to work fast. She Googled "H.O.S. crew" and then "H.O.S." on its own. Some mentions came up about Veruca and her entourage, hinting at a secret society, but none guessed what the acronym stood for. Otherwise, all that came up was some band called Hearts of Space and Urban Dictionary definitions of the word "ho." Beatrice was pretty much up to speed on that, thank you very much.

Beatrice stuck her hand deep into her purse and pulled out her Moleskine notebook. She wished silently for a moment and opened it to the center page. As she hoped, a new message had appeared:

> PAY ATTENTION: Don't pass the plate, dear, don't pass the cup. It's all up to you to expose the truth. Even a roving apple doesn't fall far enough from the tree to forget its roots.

She'd moved *up* here to Veruca's home, trusted her ears *belatedly*, and now she needed to find her way to their rooms and search out some concrete evidence. No question that the Axis of Evil had been lying, cheating, and stealing, but Beatrice needed to discover their true identities and figure out how Veruca was orchestrating their scheme. Why had they needed to come home from Brazil so suddenly? She wanted to get to the bottom of that too.

But first, before leaving the bathroom stall, Beatrice really did have to pee.

38

INSIDE VERUCA'S APARTMENT, Beatrice bolted toward the interior labyrinth, only to find that a fresh paint job obscured her eyeliner breadcrumb trail. *Damn.* "On purpose?" she wondered out loud, paranoia spreading through her like dye before an MRI.

She jogged through the endless passageways under crown moldings. Stopping to catch her breath, Beatrice looked about frantically for any clue to her location. Light glinted off a shiny object around the bend and she turned the corner to discover one of the obscured white call boxes. She eyed it suspiciously. Were the intercom lines tapped? She couldn't risk it.

Panicking, she let her bag fall to the ground. Or had it practically jumped off her shoulder? *Damn!* She dropped to the floor, collecting her wallet, random receipts, and—of course—the map she'd found in her bag in Brazil! But where did it lead? The halogens in the hallway suddenly dimmed and a spotlight focused on a dark object in the corner. Too involved in her search to question the lighting shift, she tiptoed closer, discovering one of Dreyfus's bow ties lying limp on the ground.

In an instant, the message was clear: "D" was for Dreyfus! His room was where the evidence would be. Beatrice silently thanked her invisible guide, who had somehow anticipated this moment. She kissed the map, oriented herself, and followed it without much difficulty to his door. Taking a deep breath for bravery, Beatrice slowly nudged the door open and peered inside. Fortunately, the coast appeared clear. She was about to creep in and start looking, for what she wasn't sure, when she heard a footstep close behind her. She whipped around to find Penny standing there. The housekeeper stared at her unblinking. "What are you doing?"

"Penny!"

The housekeeper's stoic expression morphed into a warm smile, alleviating any fear on Beatrice's part. Penny didn't *seem* to be evil.

"Beatrice! I didn't realize it was you." The stout housekeeper looked her up and down. "You really need to put on some weight."

Beatrice laughed. "Is this Dreyfus's room?"

Penny didn't bat an eye. "Yes. This is Mr. Donatello's room and he's out right now. But I'm sure he wouldn't mind you taking a tour." She looked right and left and then led the way inside.

The two women tiptoed across Dreyfus's space, which looked a bit feminine even for a fabulous gay man. The bed was covered with fur throws and anchored by an oversized pink padded leather headboard, perfect for Barbie's Dream House. No time for design scrutiny. Beatrice ran over to a bureau, pulled out drawers, and started searching.

Penny shook her head. "Not there." She pointed toward the bed. "Here."

"Under the mattress?"

"No." The housekeeper stuck a hand behind the huge headboard and pulled out a Jimmy Choo shoe box. "Bingo!" She smiled, handing it to Beatrice, who dumped the contents onto the duvet.

Mostly, the box was filled with memorabilia, junk to anyone else. And it seemed to belong mostly to Imelda, not Dreyfus, including the picture of that unattractive boy, her first kiss. Seriously, was that eye of newt? Beatrice was about to abandon the search when she spotted an old photograph still tucked in the corner, under a fold in the cardboard box. It pictured the Axis of Evil in strange orange uniforms and red chefs' hats, holding up what looked to be pinkish slabs of meat on wooden prongs. The sign above their head read HAM ON A STICK: HAVE YOUR H.O.S. TODAY!

Imelda was much paler and had jagged teeth. Was she an exotic ethnicity or just tanorexic? Dreyfus had terrible acne, and Kendra's ratty perm was pulled back in a scrunchy. She wore a "Christian Rock Rocks!" pin, presumably without irony. Seriously? H.O.S. stood for Ham on a Stick? That's ridiculous, Beatrice thought. Her father, who loved ham almost as much as he did his children, probably would not have agreed.

Beatrice slipped the picture into her back pocket.

"Look in there," Penny commanded, pointing to a white wicker bedside table that looked a bit out of place. It was more like cheap outdoor furniture.

"On top?" Beatrice asked. Penny shook her head.

Beatrice crossed to the table and gave the surface a little shake. To her surprise, the top lifted to reveal a hidden cubby. Inside were papers, receipts, and some girl-on-girl porn DVDs. That was random. But before she could even consider that evidence, she found a stack of familiar-looking envelopes like the thank-you notes she'd seen Veruca receive on several occasions. Inside, she found pay stubs for multiple checks. Several were for over $100,000 for appearances at concerts, album release parties, fashion shows, and, yes, gallery openings.

Beatrice hit pay dirt: There were check stubs from several fine artists' bank accounts—like Maldrake Maldrake Capri and Guillard Croissant—for varying sums of money. There were also receipts for sales of artworks by these famous artists, famous thanks to Veruca. Just as Beatrice suspected, the socialite and the Axis of Evil had intentionally—and for a sum—raised the value of certain artists' work using their own notoriety, taken gifted work in exchange, and then sold it for massively inflated profits. She saw her own last name, "Bernstein," scribbled on a loose piece of paper too and something about video installation artwork with the words "stone cap" scribbled underneath. She couldn't figure out to what it referred.

The socialite was insider trading and, worse, it was working: Veruca Pfeffernoose was influencing the art market, ramping up buzz for her allies, and, by default, robbing talented true believers of focus. Not only did she not care about João, she needed people like him to remain obscure. His presence would only interrupt the flow of her payroll artists. Judging by the stubs marked "burying," there was some other sinister element to the plot too. *Burying.* That sounded bad.

But there was no time to cringe in revulsion or bask in self-congratulation for being belatedly correct. Suddenly, Beatrice heard a low mumble that soon morphed into voices: one grumbling, one shrill. She made eye contact with Penny, who nodded. Beatrice shot up, glancing around like a trapped animal. Penny gestured toward a closet door and pulled a duster from behind her back. As Beatrice dove into darkness, still clutching pay stubs, she saw Penny throw the junk back inside the box, stuff it behind the bed, and commence dusting as nonchalantly as possible. The last thing Beatrice wanted was to implicate Penny.

Crouching in the closet, she was reminded of the map game she played with Gertie. Only her parents' hall closet had smelled of lovely familiar things like damp raincoats and perfume. This closet reeked of mutant musk incense. The plastic bin next to her was filled with all manner of odd objects. She looked closer: Dreyfus's sex toy stash. She jumped back a couple inches and exclaimed, "Gross!" But she couldn't help eyeing it with curiosity.

Gradually, Beatrice distinguished the voices: Dreyfus and

Kendra arguing. She could make out occasional words: "accusations," "reformulate," "destroyed." As soundlessly as possible, she inched closer to the doorway's crack and peeked into Dreyfus's room.

Through a thin slit, she saw them enter. Discovering Penny, they paused their argument and dismissed the housekeeper, who hurried out with an apologetic glance toward the closet. Beatrice wouldn't have been surprised if they stripped off their human suits to reveal scales. She could only see Imelda, lying in a vintage slip across the enormous bed. She looked bored, absently toying with her necklace, and glancing up every so often at—though out of Beatrice's view—what must have been Dreyfus and Kendra standing in front of her.

"There must be a way to fix this," Kendra barked. "I refuse to believe that we're screwed. I didn't put time and energy into this project just to have it fall apart."

"Well, what do you suggest? The blogs are all aflutter about it and you know *she* is probably on to at least some of this by now." Dreyfus's voice held its usual droll tone, but an unfamiliar tension had crept in.

"I blame you, you know."

"Of course you do."

"Well, I told you she was a terrible choice. She's so moral and righteous. It's irritating."

"She's not *that* moral," he said. "She almost made out with Veruca's boyfriend. You should have let her. We could have used that as leverage against her now."

"Maybe. But I couldn't give her the satisfaction."

"Anyway, we couldn't stop *him* unless we had access to her e-mail. We were so close."

"Ben?"

"Not Ben. The other *him*."

Beatrice flinched at the mention of the Ben incident. The "she" to whom they referred was obviously her. But who was the "him" they wanted to stop? And how would her e-mail be helpful? They were clearly worried about her squashing their plans to hijack the art market. Veruca was like some culturally aware supervillain. Beatrice adjusted her stance. She needed to squat for a good view of the room, but her legs kept cramping. After this was all over, Beatrice resolved, she would sign up for Pilates classes.

"Yeah, well, that was just another incredible decision on your part," said Kendra.

"Me? You chose Ben. He was hot, indie, and accessible, and he comes from money. He was perfect. Anyway, if you hadn't gone all Tyra crazy on Beatrice, she might not have flipped in Brazil."

Beatrice was stunned. *They* chose Ben? Who was controlling the show here, the Axis or Veruca?

"Enough!" a voice boomed. Though the bed was in Beatrice's immediate eye line, it took her a moment to realize that the voice originated with Imelda. Not only had the mute model spoken, but she shouted with an accent as thick as if she'd been simultaneously raised in New Jersey, Long Island, Brooklyn, and Queens: "Enough with the two of youse. I'm ova your bullshit. I'm sittin' heya listenin' to this crappola and none of it is solvin' this problem."

Well, one element finally clicked into place: Imelda was silent because, when she spoke, she was appalling. Her gruff voice didn't match the ethereal, statuesque ice queen image she projected. And just when Beatrice thought she couldn't endure another surprise, Dreyfus appeared and settled onto the bed next to Imelda. He sidled up beside her from behind and threw an arm around her waist, kissing her neck. "Don't be upset, Mellie. We'll work this all out. Don't even worry your pretty little head about it. You just relax and Kendra and I will figure this mess out."

Imelda smiled up at him and gave him a long, lingering kiss on the lips with some tongue for good measure. "Shaw thing, hon." The girl-on-girl porn suddenly made sense.

Beatrice almost peed herself. Dreyfus wasn't gay? He was dating Imelda? Why would he pretend to be gay? Unless he really was having sex with men too and they had some kind of open relationship? She didn't think so. They looked pretty coupled off. Plus, Dreyfus had dropped all traces of overt flamboyance, which seemed absurdly over the top in retrospect: no flourishes, no sashays, no sassy pursing of the lips. Beatrice glanced over to the sex toy bin and felt tempted to look inside.

"Do you think we can get Ben back?" asked Kendra.

"Not a chance in hell. He was adamant about leaving Brazil."

"But not because he liked Beatrice, right? I mean, why would anyone like *her*?"

"I think he might have liked her. She's kind of a hot piece of ass." Imelda paused her open-mouthed gum chewing and smacked Dreyfus. He rubbed his cheek like her assault actually hurt and continued, "No, but seriously, she's got a nice rack, pretty face. Why not?"

"Because she's not our Veruca, that's why not! We created the perfect creature. No one should be beyond her . . . *our* powers of persuasion."

Beatrice understood that now, stuck perilously in the closet without an escape plan, was hardly the time to get caught up in extraneous details, but Ben may *actually* have liked her? Dreyfus thought she had a nice rack? She glanced down and checked "the girls" out.

Kendra came into view, pacing beside the bed. "What's our next step?"

"First, we need to convince Sweet Bea to refute the rumors. Do you think another Balenciaga would help?"

"All I know is I ain't givin' up my seat at the shows and shit. Dreyfie promised me the whole Chanel line for next season." Imelda pouted. Dreyfus comforted her with another peck on the neck. She smiled, grabbed a cup by the side of the bed, and spit into it. Beatrice gasped audibly and then threw a hand to her mouth. Imelda wasn't chewing gum. She was dipping with chewing tobacco. Who *were* these people? This was like watching Discovery Channel!

"Honey, you just keep Veruca where we need her and let us worry about the rest," Dreyfus cooed. Imelda's hand went to her amulet, as if to make sure it was intact.

Kendra's tone grew fiercer. "Well, no way are we losing out on the money and freebies now. If you think I'm ever going back to working at that Ham on a Stick stand at the Paramus Mall, you are sadly—"

"I've got it," interrupted Dreyfus, sitting up. "Playing on her guilt about the near hookup with Ben, we'll convince Beatrice to deny rumors about her writing the blog. With her legit art world connections, people will stop calling Veruca a phony with 'less cultural curiosity than Paris Hilton.'"

Beatrice's interest was piqued. She pulled out her BlackBerry and clicked on the Social Media icon: Sure enough, *The Chronicles'* Twitter and Facebook pages were alight with comments and questions about who truly wrote the blog. She scrolled up. The frenzy was spurred by that blogger she met at the Brazilian party, @LittleBoyBrian. He'd written about their conversation: *Who REALLY writes "The Pfeffernoose Chronicles"?* his post began. Oops.

Dreyfus unveiled his plan: "We'll get Beatrice to coach V on necessary talking points, so she sounds like she has a clue. Then we'll phase out that self-righteous pest slowly, so she'll fade away.

Bye-bye, Bernstein. In the meantime, we'll develop a new interest for Veruca. Maybe novelists. We'll find a new expert to blog as Veruca about literature."

"And make money off that *how*?"

"We'll get a kickback from publishers and writers who want their books to be the hottest new commodity. We'll maintain the Pfeffernoose stamp of approval, so to speak. We'll insist that they gift us signed first editions that we can resell for more money down the line and a percentage of movie rights. And we'll insist they fly us around the world to book readings and fairs. It's the same damn thing really."

"It's genius, actually," admitted Kendra. "The worlds are totally intermingled and Veruca will still have credibility. I mean, if Oprah hasn't monopolized the market with those stupid book club segments."

As luck, or perhaps fate, would have it, at that exact moment, Beatrice's cramping legs gave out and she fell backward with a bang, kicking open the closet door. In moments, Dreyfus, Imelda, and Kendra were standing over her, peering down accusingly.

Dreyfus, the quickest to recover, offered her his hand with a flourish. He was back in character, nervously pushing his glasses up on his nose. "Sweet Bea, whatever are you doing back here? Let me help you up, darling." He shot Imelda and Kendra a scolding look. They backed into the room. Imelda flashed Beatrice an anxious smile and Kendra retreated to scowl in the corner.

Beatrice accepted Dreyfus's hand for help but wiped her palm on her jeans once standing. Just being near these people felt dirty. She wanted to bathe in Purell. And she couldn't help but wonder what "burying" meant. What atrocities were these people capable of committing now? Hey! That was a haiku. Creativity strikes at the most unexpected times.

"I was looking for Veruca." *And writing poetry.*

"In the closet?" Kendra snapped.

"Well, no, but I thought this was her room and I wanted to borrow her yellow Calypso sweater. Then, when I heard you coming, I guess I got embarrassed that I was taking it without asking."

"Well, you found *us,* Sweet Bea. Veruca is out right now. Said she needed some air."

Beatrice walked from the closet into the room, which pretty much matched the hot-pink headboard in tone: Everything was meticulously mismatched and in different proportions (oversized mirrors, chairs, cupboards). The wild opulence made her beautiful suite seem understated.

"Philippe Starck." Dreyfus gestured, suggesting that the famous designer himself had conceived the room's decor. She didn't believe a word he said, although the bathroom's tub—which was the size of a wading pool—did boast a water-bound chair. It was probably a fake. "Can I get you a drink? You must be parched. I know I'm just insanely dehydrated from the plane ride. Coconut juice or perhaps some Vitaminwater? I know you like the berry flavor."

Before Beatrice could answer, Dreyfus turned his back to the group and poured the pink sugary liquid into an oversized martini glass. He handed the beverage to Beatrice, who accepted it distractedly, observing the group with new eyes. Once exposed, Dreyfus's and Imelda's carefully concocted personas seemed blatantly obvious.

"Whose room is this?" she asked. "It's amazing."

"It's ours," said Dreyfus carelessly.

"It's Imelda's," said Kendra.

Apparently, Dreyfus and Imelda shared a boudoir. They exchanged an exasperated look. Beatrice had caught them off guard and their game.

"So, what can we do for you?" Dreyfus asked, sitting down on the bed and patting the area beside him. "We were worried, Sweet Bea. You've acted so erratic for the last twenty-four hours. And I'm not sure if you heard, but some blogger in Brazil got wind that you've been writing *The Chronicles* for Veruca. Of course, your writing is far superior to her scribble scrabble, but we all know she lives and dies for art. I wish we could make them understand."

Beatrice couldn't believe the gall. After all she'd overheard, the runt was still trying to manipulate her. She lifted the drink to her lips to stop disdainful words from flowing outright. She would tread carefully.

"Right. The most curious thing, though: When I walked into the main room, I noticed that João's painting was in the garbage, of all places."

"Oh, you saw that?" Dreyfus began. "Well—"

"I threw it out," Kendra interrupted. "Why do you need to suck up all the time? Veruca already likes you for some twisted reason. Get over it."

"I see. So you're in charge of disposing of Veruca's artwork?"

"I've been around a lot longer than you, Beatrice," Kendra hissed through clenched teeth, spitting Beatrice's name like it was poison.

It was now or never. Beatrice plunged ahead. "So, Dreyfus, tell me again about the Brazilian pool boy you had sex with in Rio? But this time I want the nitty-gritty details: Who was the top? Did you go down on him? I want to hear all about your man-on-man action."

Dreyfus opened his mouth to respond and then closed it again.

"Okay," whined Imelda, "we get it. You heard from the claw-set."

Dreyfus shushed her, but she waved him off. The gig was up.

"I did," admitted Beatrice. "And the thing I'm wondering now is how quickly I can ruin Veruca. How much do you think she'll bribe me to stay quiet? From the looks of the pay stubs I found in that cubby, you guys can afford to give me quite a bit." She had to push the envelope. There was more to this scheme. She was sure of it.

The conspirators exchanged worried glances. "But, Sweet Bea," Dreyfus ventured. Beatrice shot him an incredulous glare. Really? How dare he co-opt her mother's nickname. He started again: "Beatrice. This isn't like you. You're a nice person. I'm sorry you got mixed up in this, but ruining Veruca is not the answer."

"The way I see it, she's been lying to me and screwing with my relationships since the day I met her. And she deserves to pay. So I think I'll expose her and destroy her whole scheme. I mean, you guys are part of it, but she's obviously the mastermind. So that seems fair, no?" Beatrice smiled sweetly. "Unless you want to tell me the truth about all this? 'Cause I'm dying to know. And maybe then you can cut me in."

Was there another option? Kendra lost patience. "Veruca has nothing to do with this, okay? Ruining Veruca is pointless. She doesn't control or even know anything. She's just a vessel, a 'droid. She might as well be an adorable little mannequin. We created her."

Dreyfus shook his head and rested his forehead in his palm. He took off his glasses and cleaned them on his sweater vest. "Here we go."

"What does that even mean?" asked Beatrice. "Veruca can make her own decisions. You might as well spill. Maybe if you do, I'll go easier on you."

Dreyfus took a deep breath. "I can't believe this. I suppose

we have no other option. Veruca doesn't know who she is, quite
literally," he explained. "The three of us met a few years ago,
working at Gucci at the Short Hills Mall—"

"I know about H.O.S. Try again. And don't waste my time
lying because I'll leave with these pay stubs and expose you all."

"Right." Dreyfus winced. "We were working at a Ham on a
Stick at the Paramus Park Mall. We recognized ambition in each
other, a desire for better lives and nicer things, but we weren't
sure how to up our social status, so to speak. None of us had the
appearance of breeding or "the glow" to rise in society. We saw
that being a leader required charisma. And a lot of it. We fanta-
sized about worming our way into celebrity gifting suites and
jet-setting to parties around the world. Most important, we needed
to make money without working for it. You were loving it too,
I might mention, before you get high and mighty."

"If you wanted acceptance into that cool-kid world, why not
just get a job at a gallery, learn to DJ, start a T-shirt company, or
go to Cooper Union or something?" Beatrice asked.

"Don't you think we tried, you idiot?" Kendra shouted
abruptly. "Oh, it's just so easy, right? You come from this haughty
Upper West Side leftist family, so you think you're in *Franny and
Zooey* or something! What a load of crap."

Kendra sank wretchedly into an oversized leather-back library
chair. She looked shrunken by comparison, reminding Beatrice
of an evil stepsister, vexed and angry because the prince chose
someone else. "One night we were closing up H.O.S. and in
walked this adorable girl. She was pretty and charming and had
that elusive vibe." Now that all was being revealed, Kendra told
the story dramatically like it was some rich family history, a romantic tale of pirates, deep blue seas, and stolen treasures. It
made Beatrice crave popcorn. Kendra continued, "It was like a
gift. She had no idea who she was. Some sort of amnesia, we sup-

posed. So you see, it's not her fault and you should leave her alone."

Beatrice couldn't believe what she was hearing. "So you never went to the police to help her find her family?" They seemed to believe the story they told, but she couldn't do the same. Veruca was hardly "lost." "You just believed that she was an amnesiac? That doesn't happen very often, you know."

"Well, if it was true, we figured she didn't have much before." Dreyfus sighed like he'd heard the boring story a million times. "She was wearing like a J. C. Penney housedress, for goodness sake." Apparently the gay act had been aided by an actual appreciation for fashion. "We probably saved her from a lowbrow existence. What a waste. And if it wasn't true, well, why would she make that up and keep it going all this time?"

"You were never afraid that she'd eventually remember and get upset?" Beatrice wasn't buying Veruca the amnesiac for a second.

"Well, first of all, who would get upset about all this?" Dreyfus gestured to the ostentatious décor. "Second of all, we had Imelda for that."

"I studied to be Wiccan with the librarian at my middle school. She was the only one who would tawk to me. She tawt me a few spells, ya know. Well, maybe they weren't exactly spells, but she taught me hypnosis, which is easy with people who aw awlready supersusceptible because of amnesia and stuff. Then she died in a freak Renaissance Faire accident. This is awl I have left." Imelda looked sadly down at her amulet.

What planet was Beatrice on? So she *had* spotted Imelda in the studio apartment downstairs, chanting in a circle with that Goth New Age crew. Still, those people were just playing around; otherwise Goth Girl would have turned her into a cockroach and eaten her by now. There was no way Imelda was staving off

Veruca's memory. And, yet, there was one unexplained phenomenon that remained unclear. Beatrice asked, "So what's with all
the dead people look-alikes? How did you make that happen?"

The entire Axis clan looked at her like she'd lost her mind.
"What the hell is she tawking about?" Imelda asked Dreyfus.

"It's just, how do you explain Isadora Duncan appearing out
of nowhere?"

"Who the hell is Isadora Duncan?"

"Or, okay, Jerry Garcia? I saw him DJing here once."

"You mean that random old guy with the beard?"

Dreyfus said, "Sweetie, I think you're over our heads now.
There may be a resemblance, but Jerry Garcia died years ago. We
certainly didn't raise anyone from the grave. Would that we could.
Just think of the money we could make." Dreyfus allowed that
possibility to marinate for a moment. "That Isadora lady is just
some loser Veruca picked up along the way. She has a bunch of
kooky older friends like that. I just try to ignore them." He
puckered his lips in distaste.

"And the cockroaches at my door? The messages in my Moleskine notebook?"

Dreyfus, Kendra, and Imelda looked legitimately perplexed.
"Now you've lost us completely," said Dreyfus. "Maybe you're
the one with psychological problems." Beatrice paused for a second to consider the situation. *If they didn't send the cockroaches, then
who did?*

She had other issues to sort out. "So you just pretended to be
a gay man?"

"People do find them so much more fabulous and me so much
more palatable that way. And women just spill everything. I
mean, my Lord, I think you would have confessed every relevant
carnal sin, if I'd been bored enough to ask."

Beatrice rolled her eyes. "And Kendra, you're like her PR, as it always seemed. Only you literally plan her every thought and move?"

Kendra nodded. "Finally. A little credit. And don't act like you didn't like it, Sweet Bea or whatever the hell your dumb beatnik hippie name is. The all-access perks, the products, the trips, the hotels. You lived that shit up, so don't pretend you're any better than the rest of us."

Beatrice put the back of her hand to her forehead, as if to check her own temperature. "I'm oddly, I dunno, dizzy. Does anyone else feel the room spinning? Maybe I caught something in Brazil?" Beatrice tried to get up but started to wobble.

"Probably dengue fever," said Dreyfus.

She fell backward onto the bed and slurred, "I'm just gonna lie down for a second. I hope you don't mind. I just can't keep my eyes open and—"

She was out cold. Kendra and Imelda looked mildly concerned. Dreyfus sighed. "I needed to stall her. I figured that nasty Vitaminwater would hide the flavor of the roofies. What? Don't look at me like that. I used to clean toilets at a frat house."

Kendra raised a single eyebrow. "Impressive."

"This gives us time to put our plan in motion. Let's leave her. She'll be out for hours. Forget saving face with the art community. We need to find someone from the literary world to replace her immediately, the new Jonathan Safran Foer, but without that bothersome integrity. Afterward, we'll come back here and take compromising photos of Beatrice, so if she tries to sell us out, she'll have zero credibility."

"But we just told her the story, like morons," Kendra snapped. "Why didn't you stop me? I thought we had no choice."

Dreyfus sighed. "It may be the truth, but it sure doesn't sound like it. No one is going to believe that crap. It will just get lost among other bogus theories online."

"Aw, Dreyfie. Yaw're a genius. I knew there was a reason I loved yew." Imelda sighed. She and Dreyfus started making out again.

"Okay, Pamela and Tommy, make the sex tape later. Let's get out of here. We only have so much time for damage control before people start thinking Veruca's just another Lohan. Then it's crotch shot central or no press at all."

"I'll find the Black Lipstick gawls too," said Imelda, temporarily separating from Dreyfus's face. "One chick has some cewl new tricks to teach me."

Dreyfus grabbed the pay stubs from his victim's now loose grip. Without a glance back at Beatrice, who was drooling on the Hooker Barbie bed, they slid on their sunglasses and left. That was one sorry Mod Squad.

39

AS THE DOOR SLAMMED BEHIND THE AXIS OF EVIL, Beatrice slowly opened one green eye, feeling a swell of pride at her dramatic ability. She hadn't acted since a tenth-grade performance of *Cat on a Hot Tin Roof,* in which—through some unforgivable costume department error—she ended up on stage after intermission in only a hat, a skirt, and a bra. After that, the theater was forced to live on without the youngest Bernstein.

She'd been around these maniacs long enough not to accept an unsolicited drink in the middle of a confrontation. Besides, no one actually drinks Vitaminwater. One just gets it for free at sponsored events and then uses it to take Tylenol at some inopportune time, when it's the only drink lying in the backseat of the car. Beatrice rose slowly, ears perked for footsteps in case Imelda forgot her magic wand and knuckles of toad. What a crew of crazies. She felt in her bag for the digital recorder they'd been so insistent about her using and clicked the Off button. She'd recorded the entire exchange, eavesdropping and all.

Now, how the hell would she get out to the main room without getting lost? She didn't have much time. Beatrice stuffed whatever pay stubs still remained into her pocket. She grabbed a Post-it and scribbled on it:

Thanks for the refreshment. I hope you don't mind, but, in your absence, I took a few mementos to remember you by. Feel free to

retaliate or try to publicly humiliate me, if you don't mind my
posting an unedited recording of our entire illuminating conversation
for the world to hear. It's been wonderful knowing you all. Just
beyond.   XO
                                              Beany Baby

She stuck the note on the Jimmy Choo box and placed it strategically on the bed. Satisfied, she turned to leave and discovered
Penny waiting in the doorway. Beatrice exclaimed, "You're my
lifesaver!"

"Not me. You conjured this all."

Someone else had said the same thing recently. "Now, how
do we get out of here?"

They made it safely back to the apartment's exit, but their
parting was bittersweet—like chocolate but not as fattening. "I
always liked you best." Penny winked, standing on tiptoe to kiss
Beatrice's cheek. Then she disappeared back into the maze. Beatrice was bummed. She would likely never see Penny again. But
she didn't have time to wallow. She dug in her bag for her cell
phone and dialed quickly.

"You rang?" answered a familiar voice.

"I did. Can I come over?"

After the usual exchange, Ozzy the elevator man opened the prewar elevator's metal gate. Oddly, he was humming *Gigi*'s "I'm Glad
That I'm Not Young Anymore." It was a strange coincidence, Beatrice had to admit. She walked down the wallpapered corridor, past
a framed photographic print of Robert Doisneau's *The Kiss by the Hôtel
de Ville*. It occurred to Beatrice that her parents had probably chosen
the romantic picture. Maybe their taste was more varied than she
had imagined. She rang the bell. It was time to pay the piper.

Gertie's hulking assistant, Oscar, opened the door to the

scholar's apartment. Instead of blocking Beatrice's entry, though, he nodded in greeting. From him, that was like a ticker tape parade. Beatrice ducked inside before her parents could emerge and spot her from their own apartment down the hall. She noted with comforting familiarity that Gertie's mauve door was badly in need of a paint job it would never receive. Old acrylic coats in green, beige, and wine peeked around the knob in layers, chipping off here and there.

Photographs lined the entryway: black-and-white pictures of Beatrice and Gertie as children in Central Park, in MoMA's old sculpture garden, and at the Harvard Club with their parents, aunts, uncles, and grandparents. Collectible nineteenth-century lithographs were mounted beside captioned newspaper clippings, featuring Gertie with significant intellectual figures: feminist Gloria Steinem, author Joan Didion, *New York Times* columnist Gail Collins.

Sitting with her legs tucked underneath her on the velvet couch, Gertie wore an oversized black knit turtleneck that billowed around her. On the old trunk in front of her—which probably belonged to a turn-of-the-century steam train traveler—sat a lopsided ceramic mug made by Beatrice in fourth grade. The scholar drank only green tea. Something had to separate her from her hazelnut coffee–loving fans, after all. A used tea bag was shriveled on a now tie-dyed sheet of paper towel. She peered with displeasure through her tortoiseshell reading glasses at a dense manuscript on which she was making edits. Her lips were, of course, bright red.

Beatrice cleared her throat and Gertie looked up. "Little Bea!" she cried. She sat up, reaching her arms out for an embrace. Beatrice's sister smelled the same as always: like rosewater, old books, and, yes, a little pipe tobacco. It felt like they hadn't seen each other in years.

The younger sister threw off her peacoat and sank into their great-grandfather's cracked leather chair. Thanks to Gary and Madeline Bernstein's disdain for all things old and Gertie's love of history, her apartment was entirely furnished in family heirlooms.

"So you're back?" The question was loaded, of course. Gertie rarely said anything light.

"I am."

"I'm glad, Bea. Mom and Dad have been worried sick and I didn't dare tell them what I knew. I had to stop Dad from going up to your apartment to make sure you weren't on drugs. He watched some PBS special on crystal meth. Or maybe it was an episode of *Breaking Bad*." In all likelihood, Gertie had been more concerned than their parents. "You know, that girl Kendra was an intern at *In the Dark Room* years ago."

Now it was Beatrice's turn to react. "No! I didn't know that. They weren't exactly straight with me. Do tell." She sat forward in her chair, as was only appropriate for sisterly gossip.

"We had to fire her. First, we caught her snooping in our company files, looking at contracts to determine our pay scale for contributors. Then she started contacting poets directly and making these bizarre negotiations with them, promising fame and fortune, endorsement deals, and cocktail parties in exchange for working with her. Really out of her element, if you ask me. Little did she realize that most poets thrive on grit, not lemon drop martinis. You don't exactly become a poet to make cash. Anyway, when that failed, she submitted a poem that we loved. Unfortunately, we loved it because it was written by Stanley Kunitz, an already famous poet."

"She plagiarized." In Gertie's universe, this was the most heinous offense. That and cutting funding for public television. Beatrice could not even feign surprise.

"She plagiarized this beautiful poem 'The Layers.' She probably thought it was about hair extensions."

Beatrice laughed.

"Anyway, you seem to have figured her out for yourself. For what it's worth, those strange Veruca stories I warned you about weren't damning to her. She sounded like an unwitting victim of that Kendra girl and some man named Dreyfus."

Beatrice sighed. "I'm not quite sure how she's involved, honestly. If only I had listened to you."

"You had to get there on your own, kiddo. Do you want some tea?" Gertie rose, slipped on a pair of embroidered Chinese slippers, and shuffled into the kitchen. As always, their great-great-aunt's Iris and Herringbone sugar dish sat on the coffee table–trunk, filled with red jelly beans. Beatrice popped one in her mouth and tried to place the flavor (sour cherry? cinnamon? raspberry?).

"The water is just boiling."

Beatrice could hear the rumble of the burner and pot jiggling above the gas flame. Gertie leaned against the kitchen's door frame and nonchalantly asked, "So did you find the map?"

"Map?" Beatrice stopped midchew. She raised her eyes slowly to her sister's. "*You* planted the map in my bag in *Brazil*?"

"Well, not me exactly. Oscar."

"Oscar, like Oscar Oscar? Like your assistant and bouncer Oscar? What? Why? How?"

Gertie crossed her arms. "Well, I was worried about you. But I'd also heard rumors about what those people were up to and I figured you were on the inside in a unique position to find out more. You wouldn't listen to a word I said when I tried to talk to you, so I sent Oscar to Paris—not Brazil—to leave the map in your bag. It must have taken you a few days to find it?"

"But how did you know your way around Veruca's apartment

to trace the route? Why didn't you make it clear what it was for?"

"Some woman named Penny helped us out. She used to work with Oscar as a museum security guard. And I didn't label it because I was afraid it would fall into the wrong hands."

Beatrice took a moment to digest this information. The enormous bald man—of course! It was Oscar's familiar dome she'd seen bobbing its way out of sight down the Parisian sidewalk that sparkled like onyx.

That was when she remembered the bugs. Beatrice sprang to standing. "But Gertie, I think Oscar might be bad or involved somehow. I don't want to alarm you, but he left this threatening magic box outside my door and—"

"Yeah, about that box," Gertie said with uncharacteristic reticence.

"You knew about the box? You *didn't* know about that box. I refuse to believe you knew about the box."

Gertie wore a guilty smile. "I'm sorry, Sis. I am! I know you're phobic about cockroaches. But I wanted to make sure you were alert to the fact that something sinister was going on. I wanted you to be aware."

"Aware? *Aware?* Gertie!"

"Sorry, Sis. Really. But it was out of love. I promise."

"You're insane." Beatrice sighed and flopped back into the chair. After this, there would be very little that could surprise her. She'd give her older sister grief later.

"So, next stop Mom and Dad's?"

"Yeah, yeah. I'm going to swing by and explain the whole thing. Well, most of it. But first I need your help with one other little thing, if you don't mind? I know I've been kind of a pain in the ass lately—"

"Kind of?"

"Look, I'm back from Planet Vapid and I need some sisterly advice. Plus you owe me after that cockroach stunt. I can't *believe* you did that."

Gertie's wide red lips were set in full smirk. "What do you need?" She sat down on the couch across from Beatrice.

"Well, it involves a little snooping, if you don't mind. I have a hunch about something and I need you to get information from a few of your friends. I'm your blood, Sis. So don't make me pull out the big guns."

"Which would be what?"

"Did Mom ever find out what happened to her beloved suede Robert Clergerie boots?"

Gertie whistled. "Wow, blackmail. You did learn a thing or two from that dilettante crew. What did you have in mind?"

40

GROWING UP, BEATRICE OFTEN TRUDGED HOME from school knowing she was already in deep trouble, ready to deny bad behavior, from missed homework assignments to indiscreet cigarette smoking in Riverside Park. This time, she was prepared to confess. Worse than breaking rules, she'd betrayed her parents' entire value system.

She'd barely depressed the bell with Gertie at her side than she was welcomed with bear hugs and the unique happy grunts that accompany a family's reunion. She exhaled. "I'm here to explain."

Beatrice, her parents, and her sister sat down at the kitchen table with Fairway cranberry muffins, baguettes, gouda, and olives. Any excuse for food seemed like a good one to the Bernsteins. Beatrice started at the end, explaining how the Axis of Evil had attempted to take control of a segment of the art world. And, worst of all, how she'd unintentionally helped them.

Her parents listened with rapt attention. Madeline shook her head repeatedly, muttering, "Is that a fact?" Gary, who often got lost in the chaotic minutiae, grunted and asked, "Which one was the socialite again? I can't keep track of them all. What's with all the idiotic names?"

Gertie said, "I'll tell Conroy you said sorry for running away at that party. Truth be told, he was a bit miffed. You know how he can be."

In the end, the Bernsteins seemed less shocked by the Axis's grim dealings and more interested in Beatrice's travel.

"Tell me about the shops in Paris," said her mother.

"Tell me about the ploughman's platters in London and the rum in Brazil," urged her father.

Beatrice changed into an old comfy T-shirt, then returned to the table to describe her journeys. She just wanted to wear her own stuff. Thankfully, she'd considered her family throughout the trip and brought back some appropriate souvenirs. She pulled out the Brazilian glycerin soaps for her father.

"You can get them here, I know, if you order them."

"But these you brought back yourself from Brazil," he said, examining them affectionately.

She gave her mother an asymmetrical black cashmere poncho, trimmed with different types of heavy lace, created by that tiny sewing collective from the Russian village.

"But you didn't go to Russia?" her mother asked.

"No." Beatrice smiled. "This is from Harvey Nichols—the Barneys of London—and they're just obscenely priced. Bought with art world blood money, I suppose, but why shouldn't we profit from their deceit?"

"Indeed!" Madeline draped the luxurious poncho around her shoulders. "Just beautiful."

Last, Beatrice gave Gertie the most special gift of all: a laminated scrap of paper. "It's a hand-drawn map," she explained, "to the street where Proust was born in Paris. I didn't get to go because I was being carted off to cocktail parties, probably with Oscar in hot pursuit. But I had the hotel concierge draw me directions."

Gertie was speechless, which was quite unusual. "Oh, and one last thing," said Beatrice. She grabbed her purse, stuck her hand deep inside, and came out with her last tube of Veruca's

Shape-Shifter lip gloss. She handed it to her sister. "It intuitively changes color based on your needs. Of course, it may very well come out red. But maybe it could be interesting to find out? And I'm sure no matter what, it will look awesome."

"How could such a positive transformation come out of such bizarre circumstances?" asked Madeline. The Bernsteins all shrugged.

Too much cheese later, Beatrice reluctantly pushed her diner chair out from the table. "I need to go do something on the computer," she explained. "Then I have to head out. But I'll see you guys in a few days. I promise."

"A few days?" her father exclaimed. "We'll see you tonight, young lady. It's my opening and I intend to show you this new series I've created. I think it's my best work yet." How could she have forgotten? Beatrice almost hadn't made it back in time. She would have felt awful had she missed the event. The return from Brazil was a lucky twist of fate.

As she readied to leave, she pulled Gertie aside. "There are still a few things I don't understand. I didn't want to freak Mom and Dad out, but one of the pay stubs said 'burying' on it. You don't think that means—?"

"That they killed someone?" Gertie giggled. "No, Beany."

Beatrice rolled her eyes. "Okay, I know. What a silly little sister you have. Just tell me what it means."

"'Burying' is what they call intentionally obscuring another artist's work: stealing slides from a gallery, spreading lies, severing their connections."

"Right. That makes more sense."

"I heard Veruca's crew might be up to such things. That's part of what I was hoping you'd find out. Supposedly they snuck into a gallery and burned some work by an up-and-coming female artist from Berlin and also spread lies about her having white

power ties. *Artforum* had compared her work to Maldrake Maldrake Capri's but said she 'far surpassed' him in talent. I'm sure
he hired them to bring her down. To 'bury' her. Do you think
you've stopped them?"

Beatrice considered that for a moment. "I'm not entirely sure.
I'm still missing pieces of the puzzle. Hey, you don't know any-
thing about messages in a Moleskine notebook, do you? Did
Oscar leave me anything else?"

Gertie shook her head. On that point, Beatrice would have to
remain confused.

"I'm so glad to be home," Beatrice admitted. "This house
never looked so good."

"As Proust said, 'I never realized how much beauty lay around
me in my parents' house, in the half-cleared table, in the corner
of a tablecloth left awry, in the knife beside the empty oyster
shell.'" Gertie headed back toward the kitchen table where Gary
was busy smelling his soap.

Madeline walked Beatrice to the door, where she squeezed
her younger daughter tightly. "You're a brave, independent young
woman and you're headed somewhere really great." She smiled.
"And that's a fact." Then she returned to the kitchen table to drink
espresso and debate a vacation destination outside of New York.

As Beatrice left to complete the most difficult part of her
transformation back—and forward, really—to a better version
of herself, she hoped that her mother was right.

41

AS THE MET ROSE GRANDLY IN THE DISTANCE, Beatrice realized she'd forgotten her wallet at her parents' house, having removed it from her bag to show them foreign currency. Other than a few coins in her pocket, she had no way into the museum. On her walk up the steps, though, a random man approached her and said, "This is a friendly city." With that, he handed her his metal "M" button. Feeling lucky (and a little immoral), she slipped his button onto her T-shirt collar and wandered inside. Some things are meant to be.

At the Temple of Dendur, Beatrice threw the international coins from her pocket into the wishing well: euros, pounds, reals. A little bit of luck couldn't hurt. She was counting on her loyalty to the temple for a bit of ancient good fortune as well. It was funny how the statues looked less ominous now and more like, well, regular old statues. She looked out the window onto Fifth Avenue and noticed kids swinging and hopping through a playground. Had that always been there? The scene was hardly sinister.

This time, when someone came up behind Beatrice and tapped her shoulder, she didn't jump. And it wasn't a security guard. Ben looked pretty much the same as the last time she'd seen him, though slight dark circles betrayed unrest. He had showed up on short notice at her pleading, but he didn't look remotely pleased to see her.

"Thanks for coming," she said formally.

He shrugged. "I like the Met."

Beatrice knew full well that he'd probably never been here before. She imagined how much easier the conversation might be with a PowerPoint presentation to illustrate her thoughts: "This graph indicates how bummed I am that we're not speaking. The pie chart's sizable orange section demonstrates the overwhelming percentage of people who currently think I'm a moron. The green sliver indicates the small chance that you're actually the fourth member of the Axis of Evil. This yellow section reminds me of mustard and kind of makes me want a soft pretzel."

Snippets of Dreyfus and Kendra's earlier conversation echoed in her head: "No, he was adamant about leaving. Adamant." Then Veruca hadn't sent Ben home. He'd left of his own accord.

"Beatrice. Are you gonna speak or what? I can't stay long." You know you're in trouble when they use your full name.

Beatrice motioned to the pool's stone ridge and they sat down. All around them, people wearing fall clothing—cashmere scarves, hoodies, tweeds—clustered in intimate groups. Outside, the weather had turned cooler since Beatrice's last visit. The air carried that tingly smell of impending snow. But it wasn't winter quite yet. Now the sky was gray and the first few drops of a cold rain had begun falling, hitting the angled glass windows and trailing languidly down.

Ben looked expectantly at her, fiddling with the silver zipper on his corduroy jacket and habitually rubbing his hand along the stubble on his cheek. "So why am I here?"

"I guess I don't know." He rolled his eyes. "What I mean is that I wouldn't have blamed you for ignoring my calls. I think the way that I behaved in Rio was . . . ghastly."

"*Ghastly.*" He suppressed a tiny smile. "That's dramatic."

"I feel like I owe you an explanation and probably an apology," she continued. "No matter what your intentions may have

been, the truth is that you and I are"—she cleared her throat—
"friends. You've been my closest confidant over the last months,
and I guess I was just hurt that you hated the blog so much. And
you called me out on some things that I wasn't ready to confront.
I'm sorry. I'm rambling."

"Luckily, you ramble more attractively than most people," he
said. "But that doesn't mean you're off the hook."

"No, I know." Beatrice unbuttoned her coat and shrugged it
off her shoulders, as a flash of heat shot up her back. *Was it hot
in here?*

"Nice shirt." After changing at her parents' house, Beatrice
had forgotten to switch back to her Veruca-sanctioned outfit. She
peered sheepishly down at her oversized Matt's Bar Mitzvah T,
featuring soccer balls and a tagline that read MATT HAS REACHED
HIS GOAL!

Of course, she had to look like an idiot. "The point is that they
told me that Veruca sent you away and I felt awful because—"

Ben flushed in anger. "They told you that she *sent* me away?
She's ridiculous. Who does she think she is?"

"So she didn't send you away?"

"No, I left. I left the instant you and I—" He paused, unsure
how to finish the sentence. "After our argument, I left right away.
I called her and let her know I was going. I basically had to have
the conversation through Kendra, but what else is new?"

"But not before hooking up with a Brazilian model?"

"Oh, is that what they said? Nice." He wasn't laughing. "I'm
afraid your sources are unreliable again. There were no Brazilian
models. Well, at least not in Rio. Maybe they would have cheered
me up." He hesitated. "Did you have your fling?"

"Yes. That night I had a torrid affair with my bathroom floor.
Projectile vomiting can be so sexy." He smirked. She continued,
"So you left because . . . ?"

"I left because there was nothing left there for me."

"Because you and Veruca were over."

"Because Veruca was the last thing on my mind," he confessed. "Look, I know I didn't handle this perfectly. And while I don't think that I deserved your battery of insults or the distrust, I probably could have done things differently."

"Things? Like maybe you could have broken up with Veruca before you tried to make out with me? That was a lot to digest at once."

"And here I thought you were the queen of digesting large quantities at once." He made a face. "Why does that sound dirty? I just meant that you like to eat."

Beatrice laughed. Then she cocked her head to one side and placed a hand on his arm. "So, do you forgive me?" She was hoping to appear irresistibly doe-eyed, going for the full Amélie.

"I forgive you." Ben sighed. "But I still think you're difficult. Let's make a deal: Next time I try to kiss you, I promise I won't have a sugar mama paying my way, if you promise to actually believe that I like you."

"The next time you kiss me?" She smiled. He nodded. "Which might be when?"

"Am I on a schedule?"

"It's just that I'd like to be prepared, you know? I have an event tonight at Argolian Gallery downtown and then a dinner at Ipocrita in the Meatpacking and then I need to take my pet cockroach to the groomer—"

If only to shut her up, the Cockroach Slayer leaned in and kissed Beatrice right then and there, in the middle of her favorite place on earth, on her favorite stone bench, with myriad tourists and New Yorkers—hopefully including Mabel Palmer—looking on. The youngest Bernstein was sublimely happy. Ben was like a personified amalgam of her favorite things: beach bonfires, honeysuckle, cedar closets, perfect buttery T-shirts, twinkling lanterns, baking bread and chocolate chip cookies, BBQs with friends, lazy Sunday afternoons, sparkly cement sidewalks, sixth-grade love letters, chenille blankets, and apple orchards. Plus, he was really hot.

If the situation had resolved differently, Beatrice might have tainted her favorite place forever. But as it happened, she left with Ben's arm slung around her shoulders. The rain had stopped. The clouds had parted. And always secretly optimistic, New Yorkers lounged on the museum steps watching a street performer's rendition of "The Dock of the Bay." Beatrice was so thrilled that she made Ben stop at only two of her favorite pretzel vendors en route home, though she did insist that they walk the whole way. When they'd almost reached the west side of the park, in a small, secluded inlet, Ben dropped Beatrice's hand momentarily to tie a loose shoelace. When he stood up, he tucked that ever renegade strand of hair behind her ear and pressed his lips against hers again. "I felt like maybe a proper kiss was in order, you know, without all of New York City as an audience."

Beatrice smiled blissfully back. Never could she remember feeling quite so happy. Just then, a familiar scent reached her nose. Was that . . . ? Orange blossoms! "What?" Ben asked. "Why are you sniffing like a Doberman?"

Just as Beatrice realized what surrounded them, he saw it too. In chilly late fall in the middle of Central Park, they had stumbled into an enclave bordered by what looked like thousands of orange blossoms in full bloom. It was an impossibility, and yet there it was.

42

TRIPPING CHEERFULLY ALONG UNEVEN SIDEWALKS and subway grates on the park side of Central Park West, Ben and Beatrice rehashed their shared romantic idiocy: Her crush commenced on day one. He nearly lost his mind sharing her Louis XIV hotel room. Of course, they'd almost kissed that night in Brazil. All such "revelations" would have been painfully obvious to any bystander. But when members of a burgeoning couple invest feelings without confirmed reciprocation, they naturally become irrational, insecure, and just a little bit dumb. So this was all news to Ben and Beatrice.

"Ben, I have to ask you something. Promise not to get mad?"

"Does anyone ever keep that promise?"

"How well did you know Veruca?"

He frowned. "I mean, she was my girlfriend. Are you asking if I knew her biblically?"

"No, but thank you for the reminder," Beatrice snapped. "I meant, do you know about her background or her family?"

"I guess it's kinda weird, but not really. I knew that she just moved here. When I asked about her family, she changed the subject. Since I don't like to talk about my mother, it didn't seem that strange to me."

"You talked to me about your family."

"You badgered me. I was powerless against your journalistic stratagem." He smiled. Both Ben and Beatrice would likely be wearing goofy grins for many honeymoon-filled months to come. "I assumed she came from LA and that she was an only child. It sounds strange now, when I say it. I know way more about you in only a month or two, but then you never shut up."

She punched him. This time sort of hard.

"No, but seriously, we just had a different kind of relationship. She did her thing and I did mine. I was just her hot piece of ass." He tilted his jaw sideways and posed.

"So you weren't involved in her art world stuff?"

Ben stopped walking, unknowingly in front of an ice cream cart that prompted Beatrice to yearn for a chocolate éclair pop. "I don't understand where you're going with this. You know I don't know anything about art. What's up?"

Beatrice shared the sordid details: the conversation overheard between Dreyfus and Kendra, their true identities, Veruca's supposed nonidentity, cash-filled envelopes from a small but now powerful handful of corrupt wannabe artists, the suppression of real artists who wouldn't "play ball," Ham on a Stick, acne, and Imelda's horrible accent.

They were well into the nineties on Broadway before she finished her story.

"First of all, I knew Dreyfus wasn't gay," said Ben, as they waited on and by the curb, respectively, for the light to turn. (That's how you know a real New Yorker from a transplant: Transplants wait *on* the curb. Natives wait *by* it and trust they won't die.)

"That's all you have to say? About this whole thing? Nothing about me hiding in a closet? Nothing about insider trading? Nothing about Ham on a Stick?"

"Veruca would change in front of the two of us sometimes and Dreyfus would be like drooling all over himself. It was disgusting. I've never seen a gay guy so interested in boobs."

Beatrice was incredulous. *That was it? That was his first reaction?*

"What? Ham on a Stick sounds disgusting and so do his sex toys in the closet. Happy?"

"And the relationship with you?"

"You mean, the fact that it was manufactured? That they chose the best-looking guy at the most underground music venue in the city, thinking that I lent guaranteed cool factor?"

"So modest."

"I'm an ideal specimen. What can I do?" He posed. "Although now that I know I was handpicked by a straight guy, that's kind of weird. I'm thinking Veruca had a say in it, though—and maybe more of this than you think."

"And the rest?"

"The rest. I wish it surprised me more. I guess we're both supremely guilty of looking the other way, but that doesn't mean that we sanctioned it, Bea. You would never have gone along with any of this had you known."

A "gong" echoed from Beatrice's BlackBerry. She searched for it in her bag.

"What the hell was that?"

"A text!"

"What volume is that thing on?"

"I didn't want to miss it." She paused, read it, and smiled. "It's from my sister, Gertie, who you'll love, BTW." He gestured impatiently for her to continue. "So, you know how all those *Rolling Stone* and *Village Voice* music editors hated your writing?"

"Thanks for being so blunt. 'Hated' is a perfectly fine word. Doesn't hurt my ego at all."

"Well, they didn't."

"What?"

"I had Gertie check out my hunch. Turns out the Axis never

sent anyone your samples. I'm thinking they didn't want to risk catapulting you into a different sphere, where you might lose interest or even eclipse Veruca. God forbid you had your own thing going on."

Ben ran a hand through his hair and was appropriately quiet for a moment, while he digested this new information. It seemed to agree with him. To be sure, he asked, "How does Gertie know?"

"Gertie is just Gertie. She knows all."

They walked in silence past a bodega. A green-and-clear-plastic curtain protecting bundles of flowers still dripped water from the earlier rain. "So you really tape-recorded Kendra and Dreyfus's whole conversation?"

Beatrice nodded.

"You're like my own little Nancy Drew." Ben pulled her toward him in a head lock and kissed her dome. "Tell the truth: Did you upload that whole recording, Beatrice Bernstein?"

She shook her head. "I didn't. I couldn't. It just seemed too awful for Veruca. I'm not sure she even knows half of what's going on. I couldn't humiliate her that way. But I did post a last message to her adoring fans."

"Saying what?"

"You'll just have to read it. The Web site is The Pfeffernoose Chronicles dot com, if you don't know."

He laughed. "I think I can remember that. And what about that receipt with your name on it. What's a 'stone cap,' you think?"

Beatrice shrugged. "Drug paraphernalia? A limit to how much pot I can smoke? A gray fedora? Who knows?"

They walked hand in hand, contemplating its meaning. "Who knew I'd eventually snag the Cockroach Slayer?" she said.

"I know. If Veruca hadn't sent me down for my bike that day, I might never have fallen for the girl in the towel cape."

Beatrice stopped walking. The mysteries, it seemed, still

abounded. Did anything happen by chance? "Veruca *sent* you down to the basement that day? Knowing I'd be there?"

"Yeah." He shrugged. "I never did figure out why she needed *my* bike."

43

WHEN BEN AND BEATRICE ARRIVED back at the Dorchester, they planned to part ways but got wrapped up instead like two knotted necklace chains in a make-out session against the building's stone façade. "This is getting indecent," he mumbled against her lips. "Wait, *can* this get indecent? Like tonight?"

Beatrice smirked and stepped a safe distance away, straightening her jacket and T-shirt. Her cheeks were flushed, her hair mussed to any Hollywood stylist's satisfaction. The bigger the hair, the bigger the love, experts believed, and her hair was country star large. "I'm going to assume by that you mean that you'd like to *finally* take me on a proper date?"

He nudged her in the calf lightly with his Nike-clad foot. "That depends on what you mean by 'date.'"

"Incorrigible," she chided, taking a step back toward him and futzing with the highest snap on his jacket's collar. "While I'd love to take you up on your gentlemanly offer, I have my father's opening tonight in Chelsea. In like an hour, actually."

"I guess your dad might notice if you missed that."

"I think so. You know artists: so temperamental. Especially when they raised you."

Ben shook his head with mock sympathy. "Poor Sweet Bea! What did they do? Send you to bed without Renoir?"

"Worse! They sent me to bed to read about Renoir!"

"Okay, okay. I'll let you go," said Ben, planting a last kiss on her lips, reddened like a child's post cherry popsicle.

She began to walk reluctantly away but then turned back. "Would it be weird . . . no, forget it," started Beatrice. She shoved her hands into her pockets.

"What's up?"

"Would you want to come?" Beatrice felt like an idiot asking him, when he'd be meeting her parents by default. It was all a little fast. "Is that weird?"

"Weirder than a top hat full of cockroaches, art saboteurs, and mute Jersey girls? No. I think you're okay." And there was that crooked smile again like a graph's upward trend. "I'm in. But you owe me a date. And by 'date' I mean wear your heart underwear."

She stuck her tongue out at him. "I'm going to go grab some of my stuff from Veruca's and change. I need to pack and get out of there ASAP! See you in thirty?" Beatrice graced his cheek with a quick peck and then hopped between sidewalk cracks toward the building's entrance.

She left Ben shaking his head. "Spazz."

Beatrice ran inside before he could change his mind.

Upstairs, the door swung open to reveal Dreyfus and Imelda squirming on the ottoman like a couple of maggots. At least they were fully clothed. Beatrice, who might have imagined she was numb to surprise after the day's occurrences, was almost impressed by their gall. First they dosed her, then they got their plot foiled, and finally they got it on unabashedly atop the ottoman? She didn't have time to watch the train wreck unfold in front of her, although the height difference was mildly fascinating. She needed to get her stuff and go. Beatrice cleared her throat loudly, like an old man on the bus.

Dreyfus's face remained buried in Imelda's chest. "Yeah, we know you're there, Sweet Bea. We just couldn't care less."

"Really? That's so surprising coming from a pair of sociopathic lunatics like yourselves. You're such class acts. Don't let anyone tell you different." She wanted to get out of there *tout de suite,* but walking out now would seem like giving up ground.

Imelda glared at Beatrice and then pushed Dreyfus off her. They both sat up. "Tawk about the pot callin' the kettle black," she spat. "I want my pictcha back."

"What the hell is a 'pictcha'?" Beatrice needed subtitles.

"Just give it back!" yelled Imelda, taking a step toward her. Beatrice figured in a brawl she could take the lanky toothpick.

The closer Imelda stepped, the more Beatrice stared. It wasn't the model's voice alone that detracted from her looks. As Beatrice peered all the way up that wet-noodle frame at Imelda's tiny head, she could have sworn her teeth had moved out of line into a jagged cluster. One violet contact had shifted out of place, revealing that her eyes were actually a putrid brown. Her complexion had gone sallow like in the H.O.S. picture. *Oh, that was what Imelda meant by "pictcha."*

"Now, now, pet," said Dreyfus without budging. Beatrice noticed that old acne scars had risen to the surface of his skin. She flinched. Dreyfus misinterpreted her disgust as fear. "Oh, naïve Sweet Bea, we're hardly going to hurt you. You won, don't you see? You've cost us the largest commission we'd ever been offered, stopped our operation in its tracks, and, if you haven't already, you'll destroy our reputations, I'm sure. What's left for us to do?"

"Apparently, roll around in your own filth," she retorted. Imelda bent her knees, ready to lunge. Beatrice rolled her eyes. She needed to get out of there. After everything that had gone on, she wasn't going to be late to her father's opening. "I'm going to get my stuff," she said, stalking toward the hallway to her room.

"Good luck," replied Dreyfus, toying with a loose thread on his sweater vest. "Kendra put the whole place on lockdown and only she has the keys. You know Kenny G. She never gives up."

Beatrice stopped in her tracks with her back to Dreyfus. She thought she'd felt the last chill creep slowly up her spine, but she was wrong. Goose bumps as large as, well, Dreyfus's acne scars rose from her fingers to her toes. Something was supremely wrong. Just when she'd let down her guard, the Goddess Sakhmet and her "unexpected disaster" had finally come to call. "Where is Kendra?"

"Who knows?" Dreyfus shrugged. Beatrice turned to face him. He and Imelda wore satisfied smiles.

She spoke softly, but with a deadly seriousness, channeling her middle school principal: "You listen clearly, you leeches. I have yet to actually post your disgusting plot on Veruca's blog. You tell me where she is now or I will upload every last detail. You'll be lucky if they even let you back into the Paramus Mall, let alone anywhere you'd actually want to go."

"How can we know for sure we can trust you?"

"You can't. But what choice do you have? I'm not sure of everything you guys did, but I'm assuming it wasn't all above-board. You could be looking at jail time."

Dreyfus and Imelda exchanged nervous glances. They'd played their final card and it wasn't a trump. Imelda shrugged and folded onto the ottoman with a sigh.

"Stone called."

"Stone?"

Dreyfus looked at her in disbelief. "Did you learn nothing from our trip? Jesus. I thought writers were supposed to be observant. Mr. Stone. Maldrake's art dealer from Paris." Beatrice nodded tersely, trying to recall the conversation she'd overheard outside the bathroom at that French château. "Apparently, Maldrake needed Kendra downtown to try to finish an already dead plot. I swear she'll do anything for that moron. God knows why!"

Beatrice's eyes opened wide literally and metaphorically. God wasn't the only one who knew why. There was no such thing as a "stone cap." There was only "Stone" the art dealer and Maldrake Maldrake "Capri" the artist. And with the name "Bernstein" scribbled on that "burying" receipt she found, there was only one place Kendra could be.

44

BEATRICE HAD NEVER RUN AS FAST as she did out of Veruca's apartment and down the bedraggled staircases of the Dorchester. Outside on the sidewalk, she channeled her no-nonsense mother, screaming "Taxi!" repeatedly before she even made it to the curb. Miraculously, one stopped. Running to jump inside, she almost knocked over a homeless man dragging a rolling Louis Vuitton suitcase in place of a shopping cart. He leaped out of her way, wanting to keep a safe distance from the crazy girl in the cheesy bar mitzvah T-shirt. "So grunge era," he lamented, taking a swig off his bottle of trendy elderflower liqueur. Someone had been going through Veruca's garbage bin.

Inside the cab, which smelled like sweaty gym socks instead of the Maybach's perpetual new car scent, Beatrice gave the driver the Chelsea address, adding a filmic, "And hurry!" She began searching Maldrake's name on her BlackBerry. Was this nightmare ever going to end? Would she ever exorcise the Axis from her life? When would she get to change out of this damn dorky T-shirt? The Wikipedia results popped up and, at the very bottom of his profile with an asterisk, it read: "Maldrake Maldrake Capri (né Melbert Melbert Capcock) was rumored to have spent years as a bus ad–renting, cheap suit–wearing real estate agent in Paramus, New Jersey."

Melbert was Kendra's unrequited love. Beatrice imagined him selling her mother a trailer in a park near the ribbon ballet gym.

Her mother probably never realized until it was too late that he'd set his eyes on a bigger prize than some RV commission: her athlete daughter. It was all so Lifetime Original Movie! Where was Delta Burke when you needed her?

No wonder Kendra had gotten so drunk at London's dungeon party. Maldrake showed up canoodling with that model. So cruel!

But there was no time to feel bad. Beatrice needed to stop them both from destroying everything!

She considered calling Ben, Dolly, Gertie, and even her parents for help, but there was no time. She didn't really have a plan, as she hardly knew what to expect, but she would have to take care of this alone. Beatrice searched her bag for her Moleskine notebook. She felt sure a note would be waiting inside, though she was unsure what that meant about her grasp on reality. She was not disappointed. In that familiar blue ink, a message read:

PAY ATTENTION: One more time for old time's sake.

For once, the message made sense: This was the last stop on her journey. And this one was for the old-timers.

Either traffic was mercifully light or the driver had followed her instructions to speed because they were already pulling up in the alley behind the gallery, the setting—shortly—for Beatrice's father's big show.

That was when Beatrice realized she had no money. Right. She'd left her wallet at her parents' house. She searched frantically in her purse, but there was nothing there. "Wait here!" she instructed the driver. He was happy to oblige. Extra money would mean more visits to his intuitive acupuncturist.

When she stepped out into the lumpy tar alley, daylight was

fading. Beatrice was not surprised to find the back fire door resting open on its thick hinges. She reached for the handle and
cranked it slowly, hoping to avoid making a notifying sound. All
at once, a million horror movie fans throughout the world
screamed, "Don't go in there!" They had no idea why.

Inside, it was almost pitch-dark, but Beatrice could hear angry whispers somewhere nearby. The art was stacked in crates
and on metal shelving above, almost to the ceiling. She crept in
and followed the voices, skulking from behind one enormous
canvas to a gigantic sculpture and thanking the art world silently
for its recent bigger-is-better trend.

As her eyes adjusted to the light, she peeked from behind a
painting (of either fruit or internal organs) and saw Kendra and
Maldrake glowering at each other. He shifted from foot to foot.
The hand she could see shook. Why was he so jittery? Sweat collecting between folds in his forehead aged him. Just how old was
this guy when he'd seduced a young girl?

"You're just bitter about London!" he sniped. "You fouled
this up on purpose, you whore."

"I'm bitter about so many things that it's actually hard to
choose one, but for some insane reason that's not why I'm here,"
Kendra answered. "This is a mistake. Do not do this."

"What do you know? I have nothing left. My last show tanked.
I need this!"

"You're talented," gushed Kendra, still enamored of this horrible man. She placed a loving hand on his arm. "You can do
anything. But you need more time. Just give it to me."

That was when Beatrice noticed a glint of something small
and metallic in Maldrake's other hand. A lighter! He was about to
set fire to the gallery and all the work inside! The rumor Gertie
repeated about the Axis burning other artists' work had actually

been true! There was no time to call the police. Beatrice needed to get that thing from Maldrake, as Kendra's "reasoning" was ineffectual.

"No!" he protested. He clutched the lighter tightly in his gnarled paw. "It's too late."

"I know what that feels like," said Kendra. "It was too late for me too. But you'll move on. You'll be okay."

Maldrake laughed, a serrated guttural sound. "What? Your 'ribbon-dancing' career again?" As his fingers formed air quotes, Maldrake almost lost his hold on the lighter. "Here's some news for you about your supposed dream, Kendra: You sucked."

Maldrake had taken it one step too far. Kendra's jaw dropped open. She inhaled sharply, clenched her hand into a fist, and pulled back a bizarrely muscular arm to punch him. The situation was getting out of control. This was Beatrice's moment: She stomped as hard as she could on a loose sheet of plastic bubble wrap. The sound erupted like a barrage of tiny firecrackers, startling both Kendra and Maldrake, as the youngest Bernstein took a running leap at the artist. As she landed on him, she smelled his sour, acrid breath on her face, his rank pomade-greased hair. Taking advantage of his surprise, she fought to tear the lighter from his hand. He struggled to stay standing.

Then, suddenly, with the strength of a thousand strong men (okay, maybe one very fit and angry PR woman), Kendra shoved them both. Maldrake teetered like an axed tree before they fell against the wall. It turned out to be of the temporary variety, this being a gallery and thus constantly changing shape. The entwined enemies crashed painfully through the plaster and landed on top of each other on the gallery's stark white floor.

Apparently, the opening had already begun. Once she wiped the residue from her eyes, Beatrice looked up and saw her parents, Gertie, Dolly, and Ben staring down at her in shock. The lighter—which under halogens didn't look like any arson device she'd ever seen—was lying inches from Maldrake's hand. She grabbed it and climbed up off him, patting the dust from her jeans. That was when she realized she held a small portable flash drive.

"Well, Sweet Bea," said her mother, who looked—and evidently felt—divine wrapped up in her new lace poncho. "That was quite an entrance. And that's a fact."

45

"YOU'RE AN IDIOT," PRONOUNCED KENDRA. "I was about to get it from him."

The mess had been cleaned up and the hole obscured by the oversized painting Beatrice had hidden behind. After a bit of explanation and a big Muppet hug from Dolly, Beatrice returned to the storage room, with the nervous gallery owner close behind, to collect her bag. Kendra followed her to the back.

Beatrice bent over to grab her purse off the dirty floor. The mostly popped sheet of bubble wrap was lying innocently beside it. That plastic was the real hero. Beatrice almost wanted to keep it as a memento.

Kendra stomped a foot, getting the youngest Bernstein's attention and unintentionally drawing focus from the gallery owner, who was now badly in need of a Xanax. Though she'd been planning to ignore the PR monster, Beatrice relented. "It didn't look like you were getting anywhere. Besides, I wasn't convinced you would have the fortitude to stop him, if push came to shove. No pun intended."

Still clutching her BlackBerry, of course, Kendra gestured erratically. "Stop him from what? You just told your family that you thought he was going to burn down the gallery!"

Beatrice tugged on her T-shirt to straighten it and stood up tall. "At first I did. I knew something was off and I wasn't going to let him hurt my father and his friends. I figured you guys planned to have Maldrake copy my dad's work. And I know all about your moral flexibility when it comes to plagiarism, since Gertie told me about *In the Dark Room*. I just didn't know to what lengths you all would go to make your precious commission."

"We're not psychotic."

"That's debatable."

"Well, we weren't going to burn anything down."

Beatrice had unraveled the plan rather quickly, once faced with the flash drive. "I know what you were going to do, Kendra. Maldrake was obviously going to erase my father's video and then quickly upload and release it as his own tonight online, claiming plagiarism if my father ever showed it. Right? The man has no ideas of his own, apparently."

"You don't know the first thing about his talents."

"You were counting on my father to e-mail me a sneak peek that you could steal from my computer. I'm sure you transferred my files to that new Mac Helium yourself in hopes of finding it. But my father wanted to show me the material in person, so you couldn't get your hands on an early copy. And Maldrake was no help."

"He could have helped. He's *someone*, Beatrice." As usual, Kendra pronounced Beatrice's name like it was a synonym for anal warts.

"But if you still love Maldrake—I'm sorry, *Melbert*—so much, then why try to stop him from implementing the plan? Judging by this thing in my hand, he'd already downloaded and erased my father's work from the computer. My father was trying to fix the problem when we fell through the wall. That's why Maldrake was here, right?"

Kendra snorted, though Beatrice clearly spoke the truth. It takes a bad liar to know one. The answer was all over Kendra's twisted face, as she ground her teeth, jaw flexing. "Oh, I see. You thought no one would believe he created it. You thought it wouldn't help his career. It would just hurt it because everyone would see that it couldn't possibly be Maldrake's work."

"He just needs more time to develop as an artist!" defended Kendra.

"So you're protecting Maldrake again," continued Beatrice. "How's that worked out for you so far?"

"Are you almost finished back there, Beatrice?" called the worried gallery owner, cat-eye glasses slipping down her nose. This young woman was a *Bernstein,* so she'd be patient. But they'd already broken down a wall. The gallery was experimental, but she wasn't interested in pushing *structural* boundaries.

As the PR machine swiveled on her high heel to exit out the back, Beatrice called after her, "Hey, Kendra."

"What?"

"A wise woman in a London chip shop once told me, 'Don't ever give up anything for a man. He won't do the same for you.'"

Without bothering to glance back, Kendra shook her head. "Maybe that woman wasn't so wise. If I recall, she was fall-down drunk."

Gary walked his daughter through the concept of his new video installation project. Still images of the Temple of Dendur were superimposed over time-lapsed video footage of the Bernsteins' living room. What he was exploring, Beatrice's father explained, was the notion of experience: Could you transport an ancient relic out of its original context or look at an artwork online in the comfort of your own home and still have an authentic experience? As the beloved older artist expected, Beatrice connected to the piece, especially the sequence when Waldo the cat unknowingly wandered past statues of the goddess Sakhmet and flopped down for a quick nap. The critics loved the work, calling it stimulating, touching, and funny. For Beatrice, the piece demonstrated that her father had given serious consideration to her argument about the importance of leaving New York.

Gary moved on to debating tequila versus mezcal with a Mexican sculptor (who secretly preferred Bud Light), and Beatrice made her way over to Ben, who was leaning against the lone unadorned white wall.

He smiled. "Yet another good outfit. Once again, totally appropriate to the event."

Beatrice looked down at her cruddy bar mitzvah T-shirt and jeans. "Yeah, I never really got to change."

"Don't go changing."

"So where did Maldrake go, anyway?"

"Your mother wanted to call the police, but I assured her that it would be fine. He'd be the architect of his own undoing." Beatrice tilted her head quizzically. Ben gestured toward the gallery's entrance. There was a crowd gathered outside. "Maldrake is currently out front throwing an impromptu press conference, announcing his new career as a rapper."

Beatrice's mouth dropped open. "No! You're lying!"

"I couldn't make it up if I wanted to. I almost feel sorry for the lunatic."

"Well, don't. In no time he'll be heading to some self-consciously no-name bar down the street to drown his sorrows in an underage model."

"I can understand what Kendra sees in him."

"So you met my family." Beatrice took a step toward Ben and flirtatiously tugged at his corduroy blazer.

"I did. Not in the world's most traditional way, but that seems in keeping."

"Not the world's most traditional family."

"Whose is?"

"So how'd you even end up down here?" asked Beatrice. "I thought for sure you'd be uptown, wondering why I'd dangled meeting my family like a carrot and then left you starving."

"Not just a hat rack." Ben pointed to his head.

"That's my line!"

"I went to pick you up for our 'date' from Veruca's apartment. Imelda and Dreyfus told me you left to meet an ex-boyfriend. I figured you actually came here, so I followed suit. By the way, is it me or did those two get uglier like overnight?" He contorted his face and clenched his fingers into a monster claw. Then he attacked her neck with it. Beatrice giggled. "I was a little worried when I got here and didn't see you, but that was about thirty seconds before you fell through the wall, so."

"The real question," said Gertie, who strolled up beside them in signature head-to-toe black and handed Beatrice her wallet, "is how did *you* get here with no money?"

"Oh, crap! The cab!" Beatrice turned to run out the back. She probably owed the driver about $300 and her firstborn by now. Maybe she could sell her Mac Helium.

"Wait, Sis!" called Gertie. Beatrice stopped midstride and glanced back at the Proust scholar. "I'm wearing the new changing lipstick color you got me. Do I look different?"

She did not. Her lips were the exact same shade of red.

Beatrice ran out into the alley, where, in place of the taxi, Veruca and the town car waited. The socialite looked lonely and small among the boarded-up back doors and overflowing garbage bins. She waved, her shock of red hair wild above a Burberry trench, well suited to the earlier rain. The uneven tar glistened where the water pooled.

Beatrice slowed. When at last they met, the socialite took both her hands, weaving her cool fingers through Beatrice's own.

"How are you, Beany? I know it's only been a matter of hours, but it feels like forever since we last talked."

"I know what you mean," said Beatrice. That morning, she'd woken up in another country, mixed up and cloudy. "V, I don't know if Kendra told you, but I can't write your blog anymore." She plumbed the depths of Veruca's gaze for recognition. Did she know what led her to this spot on a ripped-up stretch of pavement in Chelsea? But neither her yellow nor her gray eye conveyed a message.

"Oh, don't worry about that. It was all a bit absurd anyway. But it was fun while it lasted, wasn't it, Beany?"

The youngest Bernstein nodded. "It was just beyond." At that, the socialite had to smile. Darkness was beginning to descend around them. "You're all alone out here?" asked Beatrice.

"I'm never alone, Beany." She grinned at her driver, who stood quietly by, face obscured as always below a cap.

"Where are you going? Do you want to come inside?"

"Oh, thank you. That's sweet. But I have places to go, people to see. Well, don't look at me like that, Beatrice. I'm not dying!"

It was now or never. Beatrice asked, "Veruca, who are you *really*?"

She giggled. "You know me, Beany! I'm Veruca Pfeffernoose. I'm an apparition. I'm concrete. Or to put it into the most relatable terms, I'm a soft pretzel and a Creamsicle in one. Good, bad, but never ugly. Don't you see? I come and go fluidly like liquid mercury."

Wasn't mercury poisonous? "But are you safe?"

"Safe? Well, of course. I *am* a grown woman, after all. I learned to cross the street by myself ages ago. And friends are everywhere. I answer to a higher power, you know." Veruca leaned in as if she might reveal the secrets of the universe. "The media." She giggled, dropping Beatrice's hands and covering her mouth with her own dainty palm.

Beatrice stuck her tongue out at the socialite, who laughed even harder. "Anyway, Miss Bernstein, this is all actually about *you*. Now you have everything you need."

"Everything I need?"

"The confidence, the wardrobe, the dude." Veruca squeezed Beatrice's left shoulder with affection and then slipped her hands into her Burberry pockets. It was getting chilly; a quickening damp wind cut through clothes to fragile bones.

So Veruca knew about Ben. Beatrice felt awful. "V, I mean, I hope you don't mind. I just—"

"Mind? Oh, Beany! It took you guys long enough. I've known you were perfect for each other since before that ridiculous cockroach incident. Now *that* was a scream in more ways than one. Anyway . . ." Veruca trailed off, smiling brightly.

Beatrice was speechless. Did Veruca actually orchestrate that first run-in with Ben? Beatrice knew she'd never get finite answers. Evasiveness was the socialite's specialty and this was clearly good-bye. She would run into Veruca in the Dorchester's elevator (if either chose to risk her life in that deathtrap) or in classrooms, if the socialite ever bothered to attend. But their attached-at-the-hip moment was over.

Might as well resolve what she could. "V, I have to ask you one last strange question." The socialite nodded. "*You* know who *you* are, right?"

Veruca laughed so loudly that, all over Manhattan, miserable old misanthropes in dark apartments finally saw the light. "Of course, Beany. Do you? PAY ATTENTION!" She smiled wickedly.

Beatrice's mouth flew open. "It was you! Of course, it was you.

You sent me those messages in the Moleskine notebook! You helped me."

Veruca crinkled her nose. "I haven't a clue what you mean."

"But why the song lyrics?"

She shrugged. "I have a soft spot for musical theater. It gets a bad rap, wouldn't you agree?"

"But the last note was Eminem."

"Who doesn't love Slim Shady?" Some things are simply universal.

"But I still don't understand how this all happened."

"I like to think of it as synchronicity, Beany. The universe works in mystical ways and I, for one, do what I can to push it along. You and I needed to meet, and the rest, as your sister Gertie might say, is history. And that's a fact."

"But why me, V?"

"If not you, then who? Your father's work was at stake." Veruca shrugged, suppressing a grin. "Plus, everyone deserves to fly south for the winter once—or at least across the pond in fall—don't you think?"

Beatrice was stunned. So much for her newfound unflappable self. Maybe Veruca knowingly got her home in time to stop Maldrake's scheme, but she couldn't possibly have known what Beatrice confided before they ever met to a disrespectful pigeon! Was there such thing as a guardian angel? And if so, would she really wear corset tops?

The socialite—or whatever she was—gave Beatrice a last hug like a warm electric blanket on a cold day. The instant she backed away, the evening's chill settled back in. "Be good, Beany Baby. But not too good, 'kay?"

Pausing in front of the car, Veruca added, "Oh, and tell your friend the Muppet to chat with the university's Dance Department chair. I'm pretty sure she'll sort out a better role for Dolly in the showcase." She winked and ducked into the waiting limo, as the driver shut the door behind her and turned toward Beatrice. At that moment, the clouds parted and the moonlight shifted, illuminating a shockingly familiar face under that cap.

"Penny?"

Far from being the burn victim or phantom Beatrice and Dreyfus had imagined, the chauffeur was a dear friend. The "housekeeper" offered a sheepish smile.

"It was you?" Beatrice whispered.

Beatrice felt lucky to have been swept up in this whirlwind, but she also felt injured. No one likes to be fooled. That's why practical jokes never make anyone but the doer laugh. In Rio, Beatrice cried alone in the car's cool backseat and her friend—in the driver's seat—didn't say a word.

Penny had expected that reaction. This wasn't her first rodeo and there was always plenty of bull. She reached out and patted Beatrice's arm. "I'm so sorry, Beatrice. But it's not my job to impact the flow of events. Also, as the saying goes, no pain, no gain."

"It's not your *job*?"

"In a manner of speaking."

"Penny, I just don't understand. Guiding people, foiling strange plots—this is your work?"

Penny shifted uncomfortably. "Well, helping people is always good business, right?"

Could someone—*anyone!*—speak English for once? Beatrice shot the housekeeper an impatient look, accompanied by a smirk, perhaps borrowed from Ben. Penny shrugged sheepishly. "Can you at least tell me if Veruca realizes that the Axis is bad?"

The housekeeper nodded. "There's very little about which our girl is unaware. As you know, those three miscreants think

they found her, but she discovered them. If believing she's mal-
leable prompted them to help her find a public voice so she could
more easily help others, then maybe there's such thing as a
necessary evil." Penny frowned. "Personally, I think their thirst
and ambition are stomach-turning, but she makes sure there are
repercussions."

"And Veruca doesn't mind all the crazy parties, that whole
nonstop lifestyle?"

"Even the angelic want to have fun." Penny glanced at her
watch. "Honey, we have to go."

A tiny wave of panic tumbled over Beatrice. "I'll never see
you again?"

"Oh, you know Veruca. She *loves* to make appearances." The
answer was cryptic, as usual. Ever short and stout, Penny strained
upward and gave Beatrice a kiss on the cheek. "Don't worry.
You've got it under control. Besides, you're not the only person
in your world who may need a bit of prodding down the line."

"How do you know?"

"Let's just say a little birdie told us so."

Suddenly, a shiny black pigeon with oil spill–colored feathers
and a yellow faux-hawk flew from behind the car and landed on
Penny's shoulder. And the housekeeper—who was nothing of
the sort—climbed into the driver's seat. Veruca lowered her window and waved good-bye. Through the crack, Beatrice thought
she spotted Isadora with a multicolored scarf wrapped around
her neck, the tips curling in the evening wind. The car's glowing
lights evoked four halos. And the vehicle seemed almost to levitate
before pulling away, leaving a trail of orange blossom–scented
exhaust in its wake and kicking up a cloud of dirt that sparkled
like fairy dust.

Her tears safely huddled inside their ducts this time, Beatrice
stood on the pavement staring after her elusive friends. Was her

life just a fleeting instant in the sands of time for them? Perhaps Veruca and her crew of ghostly friends manifested this entire world of socialites, artists, pop stars, designers, skateboarders, and authors. Maybe the whole universe was populated by their inventions of people. The socialite had definitely conjured a new version of Beatrice.

If she couldn't quite say with a straight face that she believed in magic, Beatrice certainly believed in the mystical otherworldly powers of Veruca Pfeffernoose. Maybe Eternity, Miracle, and L'Instant Magic weren't just fragrance names, after all.

46

THE NEXT DAY, BEATRICE SKIPPED up the industrial stairs of the Dorchester, sliding her hand along the smooth painted railings. She walked that dull apartment building hallway with tattered puke-colored carpet to 333. As usual, the door stood slightly ajar. She took a deep breath, unsure of who she'd find waiting inside. Dreyfus and Imelda, whom she'd silently dubbed the Terrible Twosome, could be up to almost anything. She readied herself to search those blinding white corridors for her former room, no matter who tried to block the way.

But what she saw when she opened the door surprised her more than any scenario she'd imagined: The palatial abode was empty. And without the ottoman, daybed, DJ station, and Italian garbage can, the space had turned back into a pumpkin. She was faced with a regular old "loft" apartment with two stripped cots, one small window, and two-sided tape remnants from former residents' tapestries and Beyoncé posters.

"Optical illusions," Beatrice murmured. But, for a moment, she wasn't sure what constituted reality. The only objects in the room to suggest habitation were her old boxes—sealed carefully with packing tape—and suitcases, including her new Louis Vuitton duffels from Veruca. At least that indicated she hadn't dreamed up the entire experience.

Atop the pile sat Beatrice's trusty brown leather bag, perfectly worn as always. Beatrice grabbed it and transferred the contents of her bag from new back to old. She slung it over her shoulder and ventured out to find Ben and Oscar.

In a flash of genius inspiration, Beatrice decided to give Gertie João's previously discarded artwork to give to Oscar as a gift; he did love collages and he had helped deliver the map. Bald artists are notoriously loyal, so now she had a big strong friend for life, who was more than happy to help her move heavy boxes. And that was the best kind of friend to have.

She put her hand on the doorknob, poised to leave, but then she stopped. Beatrice swung around and returned to the pile of boxes. She grabbed the now empty gray Balenciaga and stuffed it a little guiltily into one of her suitcases. It was, after all, a beautiful bag.

Epilogue

BEATRICE LUCKED OUT: A STUDIO OPENED UP on Dolly and Ben's floor. Apparently, after the date rape seminar, Hormone Guy—who always got his own room because his feet smelled so bad—realized that he wanted to be a therapist and left school to pursue a more focused program elsewhere. In time, other tenants stopped "mistaking" Beatrice for "that meth-head stalker who pulled a Robert Downey." Sometimes, when she passed that basement door, she considered flinging it open and tiptoeing down the steps to visit her creepy-crawly newspaper creature friend or the cockroach's family. She did owe them an apology, assuming he never made it home. She felt a little bad about that, but maybe he had his own adventure.

An irrational fear always stopped her. She felt that perhaps once she went down those steps, the sound of the air-conditioning vent's dripping would overwhelm, the room would spin, and suddenly she'd find herself back in the predicament of a few months ago, before Veruca, before Rio, before Ben. She'd be the girl who never left home, dreading graduation.

In a world where everything was upside down and the most unexplained phenomena were possible, there was always a risk that what seemed to occur never happened at all. Call it *The Wizard of Oz* effect. (That story was quite resonant lately.) If she descended those stairs, maybe everything would suddenly undo itself: Her parents wouldn't be in Holland on vacation and visiting with the red-light district artist from Madeline's upcoming show. Dolly wouldn't have told Stephen to screw himself and convinced the Dance Department chair to give her a prime showcase role. And Gertie . . . would probably be exactly the same. But Beatrice wouldn't have postgraduation plans to travel with Ben, among other places probably to Costa Rica, where she'd surely find herself lounging in a hammock on the beach as in her spa vision. Upon return, she resolved to find work that actually interested her and, in the meantime, she wouldn't stress it. More important, if none of this had happened, Beatrice would not currently be outlining an article—in her Moleskine notebook, thank goodness—on the definition of "fame" in this media-saturated era for publication in a fledgling online magazine. Notebooks existed to be written in, not toted around like so many albatrosses. And it took Beatrice only twenty-one years and a few countries to figure that out.

Despite still rocking their sparkly diamond tennis bracelets, which were most certainly "gifts" from Veruca, professors went back to treating Beatrice like a regular student. No one—least of all "Beany Baby"—could blame them for accepting presents in exchange for leniency, considering their low adjunct salaries. Life returned to an elevated version of normal.

Over the next few weeks, Beatrice caught herself scanning streets for Veruca's car. For all she knew, the socialite's next "mission" was just across town. In the Dorchester's lobby, at parties, and even passing Goth Girl séances that smelled of potent clove and patchouli, she had phantom sightings of Imelda, Dreyfus, and Kendra. They'd clearly moved out of apartment 333, but there was a small part of Beatrice—in the very back stark white passageways of her mind—that expected the Axis to reappear.

But, as is always the case, just when Beatrice gave up looking for Imelda's head bopping miles above a crowd or Kendra's arm flailing, they reappeared: On a snowy December afternoon, she was wasting time at a corner newsstand waiting for Dolly, when she flipped through an *Us Weekly* and came across a picture of Veruca at some MTV awards show in LA. She almost missed the image, as the wet pages were stuck together. The ethereal socialite posed—in black leather leggings with zippers at the bottom, a black sequined top, and signature Louboutins—with her back to the camera. She tossed her red hair and pursed her ever-coral lips with humor, looking over her shoulder like an updated Sandy from the final scene in *Grease*. As usual, she looked amazing.

The caption underneath her picture read:

THE READER!
Longtime elusive socialite and consummate party girl Veruca
Pfeffernoose makes an appearance at the MTV Video Music
Awards to announce the launch of her new blog, "Veruca's
World." Like in her former blog, Pfeffernoose will apparently
share tidbits about her hard-partying, jet-setting ways,
but—instead of focusing on the art world (so last season)—
she'll be letting the world in on the latest cool literary
endeavors. V-Pfeff will also be working in conjunction with
Libraries for America, a charity that builds and renovates
libraries across the globe in hopes of boosting literacy rates.
Read on, V! You know we love you, girl.

A second image, below, pictured Veruca walking down Robertson Boulevard in Los Angeles—making the ten-foot stroll down "paparazzi boulevard" from Kitson boutique to the Ivy restaurant—in distressed jeans and a T-shirt that commanded READ BETWEEN THE LINES.

Underneath was a final image of the Axis, dressed in bright orange community service construction vests. Dreyfus was bent

NORA ZELEVANSKY

over, picking up what looked like a dirty diaper, while Kendra swatted at flies with her BlackBerry. Imelda fiddled dumbly with her amulet. The caption read: *Commissioned by V-Pfeff, the H.O.S. posse will spend the next couple months picking up garbage from the biggest dump in Nigeria. Once cleaned up, this will be the site of a new library and literacy center. Now that's the kind of trashy pickup line we can get behind!*

Beatrice beamed. So Veruca had found a way to punish the threesome! She'd sent them far away from parties and fashion shows to do gritty charity work for a few months, probably in hopes that it might inspire do-gooder impulses. Judging by Kendra's grimace, they wouldn't be learning valuable lessons anytime soon. For many, this type of experience would hardly be punishment, but for the shallow Axis, cleaning up garbage in a foreign land in honor of literacy was as appealing as a root canal. And it afforded less fun medication.

Beatrice couldn't help herself. She bought the magazine and, when Dolly came arabesque-ing down the street, she had the pages dog-eared and ready. The Muppet shook her head with appropriate fascination and maybe the tiniest drop of disdain. Of course, as was her habit, she had already mostly forgiven any slight.

Later, back at the dorm, Beatrice knocked and waited outside Ben's studio. He hustled her inside and kissed her hard against the closed door. When they came up for air, she whipped the magazine from her trusty brown leather bag.

"Doing some heavy reading?"

"Yeah, at Veruca's prodding. Apparently, she's really concerned about literacy rates."

"Oh, I'm sure." Beatrice pointed out the article as Ben flopped on the bed to read it. "She's out of her gourd," he said. "They'll pull this off too, I guess. At least for a while. Did you look at the new blog yet?"

She shook her head. "I think I'll avoid it."

"You know, I never read your last *Pfeffernoose Chronicles* post. You think they took it down?"

Beatrice shrugged and sat down at his desk in front of his laptop. "May I?"

She typed in the web address one last time and waited while the pixilated colors came into focus; the loading bar read 40, 85, and then finally 100 percent. Her post remained untouched. "It's still up. You know, I actually never looked at it either. I just posted it from my parents' house and then went to meet you at the Met that day."

Ben rose from the bed and stood behind her, reading over her shoulder.

The post was a single picture: that old image of Dreyfus, Imelda, and Kendra from the mall job days. They looked even worse than Beatrice remembered. Ben laughed heartily, then took a closer look. "Wow. That's just disturbing."

Underneath, Beatrice—as Veruca—had written:

November 12
Dear Readers,
No one knows better than you do what my life can be like: I may at any given moment sip Chiapas espresso martinis with a princess from Dubai or soar just inches above perfect turquoise water on a traditional French Polynesian boat—helmed by a man in a loincloth—in Bora Bora. And, though I know I play coy, I am aware that those scenarios can sound pretty fabulous compared with doing homework in a poorly lit apartment with a roommate who doesn't wear deodorant or sitting in a beige cubicle under fluorescent lights playing solitaire at that first painful assistant job.

That said, even I sometimes feel lost in the chaos and

get nostalgic for simpler times. Yes, it's true. Every once in a while, I have a melancholy day or two, whether I deserve to indulge or not.

So today's post is a tribute to the people we all used to be, even the less proud versions. The above picture is, of course, of my inner circle (Dreyfus, Imelda, and Kendra) before, well, before they knew about much besides Ham on a Stick, apparently, which I suppose does beg the question: Who are they actually? My authenticity has been called into question lately too. Who am I? That question is so convoluted that I could hardly wade through the sea of bullshit (pardon me), if I wanted to retrieve an answer. As far as I'm concerned, we are all amalgamations of old versions of ourselves (just ask Joan Didion) and imprints of our experiences and people—borrowed mannerisms, habits, expressions, lipsticks—with whom we are lucky or unlucky enough to collide along the way.

Who knows? Maybe we all invent the worlds that we inhabit in a way. All I know is that whoever my three best buds really may be, I'm grateful that they changed into whoever they are now, in part because I would probably never have known them otherwise and in part because, well, they all looked so heinous before, right?

XO

—V

Beatrice scanned the comments below. Excluding myriad responses based on the photograph comparing the Axis members with various onscreen monsters, the messages were gracious despite the socialite's bad press at the time. By exposing the Axis and purging herself, Beatrice had made Veruca somehow more accessible to her followers.

One reader, JenWhy402, summarized: *You may not know who you are, V (or whoever really writes this blog), but we do. You're the girl we all want you to be: our best friend, our sister, that perfect girl we hated in high school, that train wreck celebrity who makes us grateful we're just regular folks, the vapid socialite, the misunderstood loner, the girl we love, the girl we hate, the girl with two different colored eyes. We'll miss you and this blog.*

Beatrice was about to close the window when she noticed a note from VGirl333: *PAY ATTENTION: I think Veruca is most lucky to have met the insider not pictured here: Beany Baby Bernstein. She is just a stellar, beautiful individual, who manages to move through every possible scenario with class and grace (even while caught off guard, rocking a bamboo bathrobe and a samurai hair knot). Bea, a little birdie told me that looking out your childhood window in September while sick as a dog, you wished for a more exciting life and freedom. You think I found you, but you actually conjured me in that moment. I arrived on the scene to help you change and, okay, I stirred the pot a bit in the process. (Every girl deserves a bit of fun, right?) You were rightly put off by my motley crew of misfits, but that was why I needed you. It was an honor to know you. It was just beyond. XOXO*

A comment just below from Tzvee8431 read: *Who the hell is this VGirl333 crackpot? You're probably the kind of crazy who stalks celebrities, thinking you're "psychically linked" or something. Are you the psycho who pulled a Robert Downey in the dorm and climbed into someone's bed? Stay away from Veruca and get a life!*

For once, the socialite had read the blog. And somehow she'd also read Beatrice's innermost thoughts so many months before, as Beatrice wished for change, all alone and flu addled on her childhood windowsill. Veruca Pfeffernoose was an unconventional kind of fairy godmother. Maybe she really was seventy years old. Maybe she was 1,070 in some alternate time and space.

"You didn't skewer her at all," said Ben after reading Beatrice's post.

"I figured the picture was humiliating enough for that group. Plus I was culpable too. And I have them to thank for a few new good things in my life." She smiled, oh so coy.

"A few things like what?" he fished.

"Like my new Balenciaga bag, for one."

"Right, right." Ben peered at her, scrunching his nose, mocking Veruca's adorable expression. "And that's all?"

"No." She paused, gazing up at him from under seductive lids and running a hand up his chest. "I also got to keep the bathrobe."

Ben groaned. Beatrice laughed and stretched her arms up high. "I'll be right back. I need to go grab my Latin American Lit book from my apartment."

"Great. Then, when you come back, you can tell me the story."

"What story?"

"The one about you and Veruca in bathrobes together."

She rolled her eyes. "Okay, Hormone Guy."

"Wait! Now that you're settled into your new apartment, I have a housewarming gift for you, *newbie*." Beatrice smiled at the nickname. Ben rummaged through the mess on his desk and came up with a pizza delivery menu. A neat freak, he was not. He handed it to her. She looked at it doubtfully. "Thank you, but I prefer John's."

"No, turn it over."

On the other side of the menu was a scribbled drawing in green ballpoint pen—a map, she realized belatedly. An artist, he was not either.

"I drew it so you'll always know how to get from your apartment to mine—the whole forty feet." If she hadn't already adored him so much, she would have fallen for him then and there.

Beatrice place a hand on either side of his face. "Thank you."

"You're a weird girl, Beany Baby Bernstein. But I like you."

A moment later, Beatrice wandered out of Ben's apartment in a sort of dream state, not even unnerved by the chants emanating from Goth Girl's place.

Suddenly, she felt a tickle in her nose, just the tiniest inkling at first, which tiptoed up her nasal passage and eventually erupted in an enormous sneeze. Was she getting sick again? She really couldn't afford to have a cold during finals, considering the disastrous past semester. She sneezed again.

Two women, who appeared to be Veruca devotees by the look of their "literacy" charm bracelets, passed within feet of her.

"Bless you," the blonde said, shooting Beatrice a forced smile.

"Thanks."

But then, loudly enough so that Beatrice could hear, she confided to her friend, "That flu is *so* last season."

Beatrice smirked. The Dorchester's hallway, which was not at all windowed, lit up from no apparent source with a warm golden glow. A witness—had there been one—might have described the light as a reflection of Beatrice's bliss.

Acknowledgments

Since this is my first novel, I'm tempted to thank everyone from my elementary school English teachers to the nice checkout man at my corner bodega for the many Cherry Coke Zeros that kept me alert enough to write.

In lieu of gratuitous gushing, though, I'll offer an overarching thank-you to my supportive friends, family members, teachers, editors, and neighborhood grocery clerks throughout the years. You know who you are. Mostly.

I am endlessly appreciative of my agent and now friend Anne Bohner of Pen & Ink Literary, who has been enthusiastic, honest, direct, and, most important, full of humor from the outset. You had me at "popovers." (Thank you, Cayli Cavaco Reck, for choosing fantastic neighbors.)

At St. Martin's Press, I am forever grateful to Dan Weiss for taking a chance on a new novelist and a quirky book and for valuing "funny."

I am very lucky to be matched with my editor Vicki Lame, who is impossibly upbeat, lovely, responsive, clear, and kind. Thank you for reading and re-reading the manuscript countless times and never lodging the smallest complaint. Also, thank you, Sarah "JJ" Jae-Jones, for your ideas, delivered with disarming dry wit.

To my husband, Andrew, who encouraged me even at my grouchiest, thank you for giving me the good seat. Without our brainstorming walks, which I love and value more than you realize, who knows where the Axis might have wound up?

To my sister Claudia, who actually *did* write the included poem "In the Dark Room" at eight years old during an ERB test and was generous enough to lend me her words: You sure were a weird kid. And brilliant too. Thank you for enduring my hourly calls about takeout options.

From start to finish, many people were generous enough to read this book and offer notes. I'd especially like to recognize three: Rachel Leonard, who helped me repeatedly despite contending with a newborn; Laura Tremaine, who offered invaluable notes and unchecked enthusiasm; and Peter Soldinger, who probably read more drafts than my editor and I combined.

Thank you all for your encouragement and positivity. I consider myself fully charmed.